WAR FOR HUMANITY
THE WRATH OF BLACK SCAR

A.R. LERWILL

War for Humanity: The Wrath of Black Scar Copyright © 2020 by A.R. Lerwill. All rights reserved.

Cover designed by Birch and Birch

ISBN: 978-1-5272-5609-5

Dedicated to Mum & Dad

The fight for survival is not our only destiny

'Imagination is more important than knowledge. Knowledge is limited. Imagination encircles the world.' - Albert Einstein

Narrator's Note -

I have been bestowed the great honour of compiling this tale and have spent many sun-cycles travelling far and wide across the lands, researching and translating in my endeavour. The following events have been sourced by various means, including surviving documents I have acquired, and stories handed down through word-of-mouth. What you are about to read is an unfinished version, as there are a few documents I have yet to write into the narrative. I have attempted to give the most accurate historical account; however, some of what you will read may seem contradictory or exaggerated. I cannot be held accountable for the reliability of the sources provided to me, but I have tried to keep consistent detail throughout. I have made manipulations to the chronology for dramatic effect, although, I believe this to be of no great significance, and will not jeopardise the overall responsible and authentic depiction. All names and places are real.

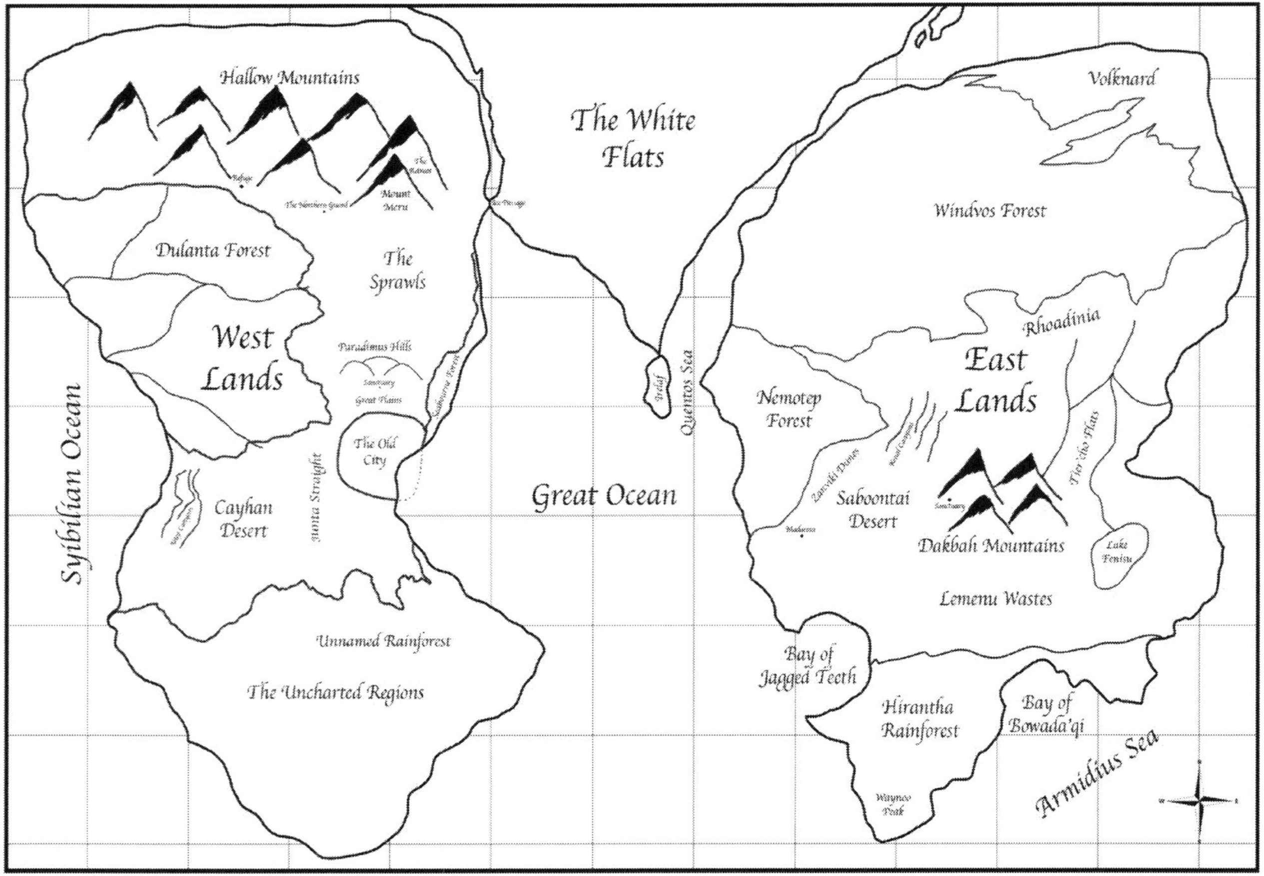

(Not drawn to scale)

Languages

Common Tongue - What this story is written in

Ramasha - Mainly spoken in the northern region of the West Lands

Latigo - Mainly spoken in the Mid to South region of the West Lands

Gerhami - Mainly spoken in the northern region of the East Lands

Masuaai - Mainly spoken in the Midwest to South regions of the East Lands

Khan'ulad- Mainly spoken in the eastern regions of the East Lands

'Black Tongue'/Bezurak - centauri language

Old Tongue - The dialect from the ancient times

Chapter One
The Lone Survivor

It was once said that there are more stars in the universe than grains of sand on any beach. To imagine such abundance was so clear to him, for it was as if he had awoken upon an infinite bed of gleaming suns.

Overwhelmed by the gold vastness before him, he could make out the blurred outline of the horizon as he regained his vision. It was apparent that he had been washed up on an endless beach. As he became fully conscious, he acknowledged that, miraculously, he was still alive. His immediate confusion subsided as he took a deep breath and coughed out the remaining water from his lungs. Around him, he could hear the muffled sound of waves dancing back and forth against the shoreline, whilst the water flowed against his feet. He took a few deep breaths. His fists clenched the wet sand, and he moved his partially submerged face. His nostrils were aflame, and his lips were dry and bleeding. His clothes were saturated and heavy upon his weak frame. Finding enough strength in his arms to push himself up, he spluttered and rolled around into a sitting position. This movement made him aware of an injury to his head.

He felt perplexed, looking out at the sprawling ocean that lay endlessly before his eyes. For a while he sat there staring listlessly, not moving. The disorientation gradually subsided, and he began to digest the circumstances. Sudden flashes of vague memory eclipsed his mind's eye as he began to recollect how he had become stranded on this lonely beach.

Several moon-cycles beforehand he had set forth on his travels. It was a custom for trainees to venture out across the known territories of the dangerous world, to gain experience and gather more understanding, away from the isolation and safety of home. This task would prove his independence and resourcefulness out in the wilderness. All of the sun-cycles of training were coming to an end, and soon he, Aldber, would face the final test, and would hopefully be initiated into the formidable Galardros (the name means 'guardian' in the Ramasha language). The order had been established many generations ago to protect the vulnerable tribes against the humans' sworn enemies, the centauri. Now the dominant species of the world, the centauri were more commonly referred to as the Enemy, and they had been at war with humanity for countless sun-cycles.

Aldber had been specifically given the objective to travel all the way across to the other side of the world to the Dakbah Mountains, with the intention of gathering important information for the escalating war effort.

At first, he set forth over the vastness of the West Lands, and then took a direction eastward towards the coastline. He intended to seek passage upon a ship bound across the Great Ocean for the East Lands. Voyages between the two continents were scarce, but he had been fortunate enough to meet tribesmen who had found and mended a vessel. He was sceptical as to whether it would last the perilous journey but decided not to waste this rare opportunity. He persuaded the crew to let him join them in exchange for an extra hand on deck. They were agreeable, although somewhat suspicious about his motives for joining them. Even in these times of hardship there was still hostility between the struggling humans.

It was the first time that Aldber had ventured out this far away from home, let alone ever been on the ocean's waves. The first night aboard was particularly unpleasant, as he became accustomed to the rhythm of the boat clashing against the ferocious tide. He involuntarily emptied the contents of his stomach on several occasions. Clean water was strictly rationed, so he spent the first few days dehydrated whilst keeping quiet. He had been allocated a space as a resting area, amongst cargo in the storage room, below deck; this was where he fashioned a makeshift bed, using his cloak for a cover and rucksack for a headrest, and would spend the first few nights alone after finishing his duties. The sound of creaking wood and the fowl stench permeating through the ship became familiar to him. It was uncomfortable, but better than facing the relentless cold winds on deck.

'So, has sickness taken your voice, or do you speak, boy?' one of the shipmates directed at him on the third day as they were pulling in the mornings' catch of fish.

'I do,' he replied gingerly as he tugged on the netting.

'What is your name then? Come on, we thought we had a mute amongst us,' the shipmate continued.

'My name is Aldber,' he uttered and diverted his gaze.

'Well, Aldber, it is a pleasure to meet you!' The tribesman chuckled and gave the young man a firm pat on his back, before helping to pull the catch on board. They then started to unravel the netting to pick out the helpless fish. 'What brings you on board this ship? It is funny for someone like you to be wandering around the wilderness on his lonesome.'

Aldber started gathering the flapping fish into a basket and then told the shipmate the rehearsed alibi he had run through in his mind: his tribe of origin had been massacred, and, like these people, he wanted to start a new life in the East Lands. Aldber hoped that the sensitivity of the subject matter would dissuade them from asking any more questions. Whilst he had no business that was untoward, he felt it necessary not to disclose his true identity as a Galardros trainee, in case it attracted attention of the unsavoury kind. Although the order was respected by many, there were some who were cautious towards it as well.

'I can understand,' the shipmate replied, his voice lacking either surprise or sympathy, as though hearing about such brutal events was the normal case. 'That is the reason why we felt compelled to abandon what little we had. For too long we have faced disease and scavenged to survive. We have been promised better fortunes in the East Lands, hopefully, safely away from the Enemy.' He then picked up his basket of fish and they took them below deck to prepare for eating.

At that evening's meal Aldber was introduced to the rest of the crew. They were friendly enough and offered for the lone traveller to join them for a drink of their ghastly tasting mead. Aldber declined and decided to go to bed in an attempt to get as much rest as he could, as he was still battling the unpredictable movements of his stomach.

Over the course of the next few weeks, he adjusted to the motion of the boat and started to enjoy the life at sea. There was simplicity to living out in the sprawling ocean, away from the dangers on land. It was the first time in his life that he had lived with strangers, away from home, and, gradually, he became more relaxed and less guarded with his new company. Every morning he would help to bring in the catch and would spend time below deck gutting fish, whilst becoming acquainted with different members of the crew. They were always willing to tell tales about their lives. As he heard more about these people's harrowing struggles, Aldber's understanding about tribal life broadened, and he felt great empathy for what they had been subjected to. They became his friends, although he still maintained the same alibi, however much he hated lying.

One morning during their voyage, a shipmate lost his balance and accidentally fell overboard into the water. Relying upon his minimal experience of swimming, without hesitation, Aldber tied a rope around his ankle, haphazardly jumped in to rescue his shipmate, managed to fight against the tide, and grabbed the man. The rest on board took the other end of the rope and pulled them to safety, before they could drown and descend into the merciless depths. For nights to come, all would joyously retell the gallant story of Aldber's brave and reckless heroism, each time adding more elaborative and fantastical detail, influenced by the heavy ingestion of mead. One evening they described how he dived elegantly into the water; the next, grappling with the rope that had wrapped around his neck; the next, fighting off sea creatures, as they were pulled to safety. In his own unique way, Aldber had proven his worth as a shipmate and gained respect amongst the men.

By the time the ship arrived on the shores of the East Lands, Aldber was saddened to leave his new friends. As the vessel neared the coastline, they cautiously looked for signs of the Enemy, before finding a suitable cove and mooring. Once they disembarked, the young traveller, much to the crews' bafflement, politely declined their offer to join them on their journey northwards, having been specifically instructed to head towards the Dakbah Mountains. They gave him a headscarf and goggles as a departing gift, humoured by his impractical choice of clothing for the harsh conditions he was soon to encounter.

Aldber walked into the Nemotep Forest and found shade away from the midday sun. Here, he checked his belongings. He was wearing a long dark jacket, a beige shirt with stringed V-neck collar tucked into dark trousers, and comfortable knee-high travel boots. He had worn these ragged clothes for many moons, and they smelt putrid. Around his waist was a utility belt with a thigh strap to holster his pistol. He checked how much ammunition he had, emptied his rucksack to calculate how many days he could ration his supplies, and used the sun's trajectory through the sky as guidance, before setting forth on his way towards his destination.

The prospect of travelling in these foreign lands was equally daunting and exciting for Aldber. Whilst many humans would seldom take the life-threatening risk to travel across this inhospitable terrain alone, he would rely only upon his knowledge and instinct. To avoid contact with the Enemy in these unfamiliar surroundings, he had been taught to stay under cover and preferably to travel at night. There had only been a few occasions when he had been in contact with the Enemy, and each experience had been a tormenting ordeal.

Aldber would spend the following few weeks hiking through the dense woodland and hills, staying away from open areas, where he would be exposed and vulnerable. He bathed in cool streams, hunted prey, and every so often would risk making a fire to cook his meal. He observed that the climate was not too dissimilar to what he was accustomed to in the West Lands. He had short rests in the undergrowth, often disturbed by distant alien noises. Because of his unease at the prospect of being found by the Enemy, he became severely sleep deprived and deliriously lost his bearings but was driven by the hope that beyond the woodlands, and into the open desert, he would find safety.

As the woodlands disappeared and grasses steadily gave way to sand, the scenery became exotic. Because of the intensity of the heat, he removed his long overcoat, covered his head with the scarf, and put on the goggles to shield his eyes from the sand particles.

Aldber scaled the large Zanviki Dunes for a day or so, until the landscape evened off and opened onto a plateau that stretching for as far as the eye could behold. Bewildered by what he saw, he took a break and sat there for a while, digesting the breath-taking and equally haunting view of the Saboontai Desert. In these desolate lands ancient city ruins were scattered everywhere, debris from aircrafts peppered the dunes, and small abandoned settlements could be seen, which were the only remains, and a saddening reminder, of the countless attempts to restart human civilisation that the Enemy had come along and destroyed. The heat rippled like a translucent wave upon the sand. He squinted to make out the distant cluster of vast stone buttes that silhouetted the horizon.

He continued onwards, seeing barely any sign of life apart from the odd small creature that scuttled off when it noticed his presence. He had to bear the burning heat and swirling winds in the daytime and torturous coldness in the night.

By the time he came across the encampment of a small tribe, Aldber had lost track of the days and had become thoroughly disorientated. He was spotted stumbling obliviously past by one of their patrol who approached, clasping a spear defensively. Aldber had a very poor understanding of the Masuaai language, and the tribesman questioned in this dialect. He was dragged into the campsite past bewildered onlookers and into a darkened tent where he was shunted onto a chair to await the tribal leader. Once it was understood that he could not speak or understand their language, an interpreter was brought forward who had a competent understanding of the Common Tongue.

'I am *very* pleased that you understand what I am saying,' Aldber said with a forced smile whilst cautiously eyeing those who surrounded him. By now, in the shade and away from the exhaustive heat, and having regained full focus, he understood the severity of his present circumstances. He rested his hand vigilantly upon the grip of his pistol, hidden under his jacket.

'What brings you here?' the interpreter questioned in a hard tone and unfamiliar accent.

'I am heading towards the Dakbah Mountains. I apologise for entering your territory without permission,' Aldber said in a calm manner, with a neutral facial expression, whilst sweat dripped down his cheek. The interpreter looked at him sceptically, before turning to translate this to his superiors. Thankfully, they accepted this, and the atmosphere suddenly changed once the destination of the traveller's intentions had been shared.

'*Dakbah Mountains*,' many of them spoke in broken Common Tongue as they all stared wide-eyed at Aldber with a new sense of admiration, knowing full well the importance of that place and who was associated with it. Meanwhile, he nodded encouragingly, trying to appear friendly, and slowly loosened his grip off the pistol.

The tribal leader entered. He was a tall dark man, scantily clad, his head shaved, with fangs adorning his neck. He gazed at the captive suspiciously, but once everything had been explained, and a mutual understanding established, the leader's demeanour changed, and he welcomed Aldber with a firm handshake and a broad smile.

They offered him food and water, before giving him a bed in

another cool and darkened tent, away from the sweltering heat. The following day, once adequately rested and hydrated, Aldber was shown around the camp by the leader. Like the tribes of the West Lands, those who resided here were insular, evidently hostile to outsiders, and everyone shared the same second name to identify with their tribe. As they were fortunate to seldom have any disturbances from the Enemy, the tribe were able to enjoy the luxury of lighting powered by a salvaged rickety generator. All wore minimal clothing, covering their skin with light leather garments and chains. All of these new sights and smells were fascinating for the curious young traveller.

That evening, the tribe welcomed their guest by hosting a feast of foods that were unfamiliar to Aldber's taste palate. This was followed by a ritual dance performed by many of the young women, before there was singing around a large fire at the centre of the campsite. The whole tribe enraptured in unison, sending praise to their sun god. It was the first time that Aldber had met a tribe that had their own deities and did not believe in the Supreme One, the god whom he had been raised to believe in. At first, he was indifferent, but was curious and respected their way of life. He found the whole experience to be both insightful and captivating. They treated him like one of their own, sharing great tales of their heritage, which were explained in parts by the translator, who by now was exhausted with his translation barriers.

Aldber even attracted the attention of a few of the older girls he had seen dancing, who were mystified by this exotic and handsome young man. The entertainment finished as the desert became cold in the moonlight. The guest's final hazy memory of the evening was walking back to the tent and having to refuse the advances of some of them. They were not easily swayed and proceeded to enter his tent to try and seduce him. He had never been with a woman before, and as tempting as the offer may have been, it would have been disrespectful to his hosts to fool around with one of their daughters, so he declined the offer, shepherded them out of the tent, and went to sleep.

The following morning, after saying his farewells to the tribe, Aldber set forth from the camp with fresh supplies and a feeling of enrichment from his visit. Within a few days he passed under the shadow of the great stone buttes that pierced the blue sky, whilst making his way closer to the Dakbah Mountains.

He was finally nearing the objective of his travels.

As the terrain began to incline into barren mountains, he knew he was getting closer to his destination. There was no vegetation, birds skulked high above, and the searing heat was hard to withstand. As the sun ascended to its highest point in the sky, Aldber took refuge in a small cave entrance in the valley. He pulled off his boots and doused his blistered feet with water before lying back to rest.

Our young traveller knew from his training that it was advisable to ensure your surroundings were secure before taking an afternoon rest; however, this precaution had slipped his mind as he lay there. Had he walked further into the cool depths of the cave he would have changed his mind. The rustling of boots and the sound of his snoring were amplified by the acoustics of the cave's walls, and this was only bound to disturb the four-legged scaled creature, which people of this part of the world call a lizados. It had been inconveniently woken by the commotion, but all the same intrigued by this new scent. Upon inspection, it saw this large prey lying motionless. It edged closer, licking its lips. This could have been an abrupt end to the young man's travels, had not a small clump of rock broken off and tumbled down, disrupting his slumber.

Aldber was at first startled by the echoing sound, but nothing could have woken him more than the sight of a large beast running towards him with its tongue frantically extended. The traveller managed to roll out of the way just as the creature dived towards him; he then got to his feet and ran straight out of the entrance into the open. His feet burned on the sand as he put distance between himself and the beast, all the while cursing under his breath at his stupidity for not checking the cave. The ravenous creature lunged after him, carrying its weight upon its muscular legs. Aldber pulled the gun from his holster, turned in one swift movement and fired a shot, hitting the beast in the chest. It barely made a difference, only enraging the creature more so and equally exasperating its prey.

Aldber jumped for a small rock ledge and pulled himself up in time to avoid the creature biting off his exposed feet. From this vantage point he looked further up to see if he could climb out of the valley; however, the jagged surface was not forthcoming. He found grip and began to scale the rock face, whilst hearing the sneering disapproval of the beast below. But his attempt was short-lived; as the rock gave way, he lost his handling and scrambled desperately, before descending toward the hard valley floor.

Aldber hit the ground on his back and was winded by the collision. The beast advanced and he managed to kick its face before drawing the gun to shoot it again. This time the lizados let out a sheering cry of pain that echoed through the valley. The creature took a few moments to regain its focus before pouncing at him again, and this time it locked its fangs onto the weapon. Aldber lost his grip and the creature spat the pistol aside, before jumping at him. It bit into the hand that was shielding his face and crunched down savagely. Aldber despaired, overwhelmed with searing pain, and smacked the creature hard in the side of the head with his free hand. He dislodged his wounded one and was able to roll out of the way. He regained his footing with blood pouring everywhere. They looked each other in the eye, circling around as Aldber tried to draw nearer to the weapon. But the beast was smart enough to know his intentions; it stopped and prepared to run for the final kill. Aldber stood firm, and in that moment accepted that, due to his own absent-minded mistake, there in the valley he would meet his fate. Suddenly, the lizados started scuttling towards him and pounced.

A gun shot.

The beasts' corpse flew through the air, knocked Aldber from his feet, and landed on him, impaling him to the ground. He lay there for a moment, suffocated, expecting the creature to reawaken and rip his face off, but it was lifeless, incredibly heavy, and omitted a gut-wrenching odour. The young traveller remained still, looking up at the blue sky, whilst the skulking birds waited patiently overhead. Out his peripheral vision, he saw two sets of human hands appear either side of him, pulling the large carcass off him. He took a deep breath, looked around, and to his astonishment saw a dozen or so cloaked figures surrounding him. One of the new arrivals extended a hand, and he accepted the gesture, getting to his feet. The faces of these strangers were concealed. One stepped forward and removed its hood, revealing a tanned and bearded young man, with shoulder-length hair and tribal markings trailing down the side of his face.

'Next time, I would suggest you wear something suitable before picking a fight with a lizados,' he said in perfectly enunciated Common Tongue with a thick eastern accent, nodding towards Aldber's bare feet. The young traveller looked down with embarrassment, as the other cloaked figures all started to laugh at his expense. Adrenaline was still flowing through his body, and even though they had saved his life, he felt humiliated that they were laughing at him. He felt the impulse to strike out at the tattooed one for this, but instead rationalised, restrained himself, and took a deep breath. 'It was just as well we were nearby, could hear the noise you and your friend here were making, and arrived just in time.'

'Thank you. I...'

'It is quite all right; these parts are known for being a breeding ground for ghastly beasts like this. Besides, you saved us the task of finding our next meal.' The newcomer smiled. His facial expression then changed, and he questioned sternly: 'what brings you here?'

Uncertain who these new people were, Aldber then relayed the rehearsed story of being a lone travelling tribesman, like he had told the shipmates and the desert tribe. He tried to speak convincingly whilst looking confidently at all who surrounded him.

'I do not believe that for one moment. You do not look like a tribesman,' the tattooed man interjected. The hooded figures raised their guns cautiously. Aldber swallowed hard and estimated the likelihood of escaping from this situation: it was evidently not in his favour. 'We were under the impression that someone fitting your description from the West Lands would be visiting these parts. We may have a problem if you have trespassed.'

It was in that moment that Aldber realised who these masked people were. He had finally found his brethren and would not retain his true identity any longer. He stepped forward and cleared his throat to project his voice.

'I am Aldber, Galardros in training, sent here by request of Grand Master Vivid and the elders of the western Sanctuary,' he revealed. There were audible gasps amongst those gathered. The un-hooded man smirked and stepped forward to shake Aldber's hand.

'It is a pleasure to finally be acquainted. Master Ahura has been expecting you.'

The surrounding men then proceeded to lower their guns and hoods. Everyone raised one hand, placing it sideways against their foreheads and then reached into the air, this being the order's special salute. They then proclaimed in unison (although some were feeble attempts of the Common Tongue) the oath of the Galardros: 'In the name of.'

'I am Le'Dada, one of Master Ahura's most highly acclaimed

warriors and a member of the council,' the tattooed man explained, as a dressing was brought forward for Aldber's gaping wound that was still bleeding profusely. 'My men and I were conducting a routine patrol of the parameter when we heard all of the commotion.'

'Impeccable timing,' Aldber sighed and smirked as he looked across at the dead beast. Others gathered broken tree branches and tied these with ropes around the carcass to lift and carry it. Meanwhile, a warrior gathered Aldber's belongings from the cave, returned them to him. Aldber slowly pulled on the boots over his scorched feet. He was then escorted through the valley by the soldiers and walked alongside Le'Dada, telling him about his journey so far.

'As this is the first time you have been out to these parts of the world your body will be adjusting. Out here the heat can be tiring. It is very rare that we have any trouble from the Enemy, which is why the Sanctuary was established up here in the mountains.' Le'Dada pointed to the barren scenery.

Aldber had been told stories of the Galardros' operations here in the East Lands, of the complex cave systems within the mountain region. Until now he had felt uneasy but was finally in the company of like-minded people and knew that he had overcome the worst part of the journey.

Or so he thought.

The group walked further into the valley past dried riverbeds and dead vegetation. The sun passed over the sky, casting shadows against the mountainside. Aldber was offered water, and conversation was limited, as few spoke fluently in the Common Tongue.

They came to an abrupt stop and Le'Dada signalled for him to look up to his left, where way up high there was a large opening. A soldier whistled and a moment later several ropes were thrown down for the arrivals. Aldber was invited to ascend, so he took a rope and pulled himself up to the large cave entrance where armed guards flanked two large artillery guns. One proceeded to search the visitor, and was thorough in looking through the rucksack, before tapping him down.

Le'Dada then ushered him down a passageway illuminated by a stream of electric lights that winded into the caves. The ceiling was just high enough for Aldber, although he had to duck a few times. The smell was stale, and the air warm and thick. As he was guided through, he looked to either side at other passageways leading off to rooms full of large containers and sleeping quarters.

The passageway opened up and Aldber was shown into a large room where a crack in the ceiling revealed one ray of sunlight that streamed down through the dimness, hitting the centre of the floor. There were many Galardros standing around computer terminals whilst deep in discussion. At the far end, he saw suspended in mid-air a large green three-dimensional holographic projection of what appeared to be a map of the Dakbah Mountains. Stood by its side was a tall, tanned, bearded, and elderly man, in combat uniform and wearing a cloak of superiority. He was looking at the floating image whilst others around him were providing updates. When he heard the commotion, he turned and saw the new arrivals. He was informed of the visitor and his expression changed from serious to delighted. He walked forward and welcomed Aldber with open arms and hugged the young man.

'Aldber, it is an honour to finally meet you! We were not sure when to expect your company.' Master Ahura leaned back and held the new arrival's arms with a warm smile. 'I hope you were able to find a safe passage through the dunes and desert?'

'Master, it is an honour to be in your presence. It was quite an exhausting journey and I had a brief encounter with a scaled beast. However, your men came to my rescue. Thank you for inviting me here.' Aldber bowed respectfully.

'That is my pleasure. We have not had a visitor of such distinction for a while now. I hope that Grand Master Vivid is in good health? How is Hecta, the old devil?' Master Ahura laughed.

'Both are very well,' Aldber said with a shy smile.

'Excellent, excellent. Come! You must be tired?' Ahura then gestured. 'You shall be taken to private quarters to rest.'

Le'Dada guided Aldber down a passageway to a small room where a bed had been prepared, with a bowl and jug of steaming water left beside it. A medic arrived, who asked the patient to sit orderly, and proceeded to meticulously remove the saturated temporary dressing under the light provide by a small lamp. She poured warm water into the bowl, and used a cloth to clean away excess blood, before applying an anaesthetic ointment, and then sewed up the large holes in his hand. Aldber sat silently with gritted teeth as the procedure took place, flinching when the sharp needle pierced through his skin, whilst remembering the teachings.

'*Accept the pain, do not resist it,*' he thought. '*Surrender.*'

After a new dressing had been applied, he was left alone to unclothe, before collapsing onto the bed. His whole body felt weakened from the fall during the fight. He then fell into a light slumber, with thoughts of the desert creature circulating in his mind, only to abruptly awaken a few moments later in panic, and then felt assured that he had finally reached safety.

Once rested, he went back into the control room to meet Master Ahura and the other council members. He marvelled at the holographic projector.

'It is a fine piece of technology, predating the dark times, that we salvaged recently. We have just managed to make a connection with a surviving and functional satellite that is in orbit. We use data to get a reading of the local area, helpful for understanding the terrain and movements of the Enemy,' Ahura explained as the green glow of the hologram reflected against his face. He then turned to Aldber. 'Now, I will show you around the complex.'

The master then proceeded to give his distinguished guest a tour of the caves that stretched for miles into the mountains. Aldber was astounded by their ingenuity to have constructed this base; there was an air ventilation system, water irrigation feed, several plantations exposed to sunlight. He was shown the forgery where guns and swords were produced using designs and manufacturing techniques predating the ancient times. He was shown where materials were mined, where clothes were made, the main medical facility. The most unexpected and staggering place of all was the glittering caves. Deep down below surface level, Master Ahura guided him with torchlight to a cave that opened up into a large expanse. There, the air was cooler, and he could hear the echoing sound of a stream running through its centre. The sight amazed Aldber. Before him, adorning the stalagmites and stalactites, were millions of gleaming minerals, illuminating the whole expanse with a radiant and eerie white light.

'Isn't it magnificent, Aldber?' Ahura's voice echoed. 'Whilst the Sanctuary was being built, these minerals were discovered when an explosive charge activated accidentally, revealing this cave that stretches much further than the naked eye can see. No one is allowed to touch or extract any of them. We believe this is how nature intended for them to be and we do not disturb the order. Many have spoken of mining them for jewellery, but this is not necessity, for there is no need to wear tokens of status here, for such a mentality is not our priority.'

The master led Aldber back from the depths of the mountain to the control room to show him the holographic image of the local region once more.

'We have made progress against the Enemy in recent moons, pushing them away from the Dakbah Mountains, with the intention of providing a habitable space for the tribes to thrive.' He pointed to a river that slithered through the mountains and onto the Tier'cho Flats to the northeast. 'Upon these banks we hope to one day create a new settlement where life can resume, where shelter can be provided, and children can be brought into a free new world.' Aldber saw hope and an element of doubt cover Master Ahura's battle-hardened and weathered face. 'Our most immediate concern is of Madarosa (it means 'metal fort' in the Gerhami language), it is the Enemy fortress further southeast from here.' Master Ahura then pressed a few buttons on the computer console. An image appeared of a grotesque metal structure situated upon a plateau. The sight of it horrified Aldber. 'This is the Enemy's largest stronghold and footing in the East Lands. For many sun-cycles we have fought the forces based there. In time we will launch an offensive to take it.'

It was then that Aldber finally had the opportunity to bring up the subject, which had been the objective of his visit to the Eastern Sanctuary. 'Master Ahura, do you have any new information about Irelaf?'

But before the leader was able to respond, they could hear large screams coming from afar and heading in their direction. They both turned to see a group of Galardros running into the cave, bearing in their arms a wounded warrior. Aldber helped to clear a table and the severely injured man was placed onto it. He was screaming in pain; blood poured everywhere, and his throbbing guts were on display. As medics were called, and several soldiers gathered water and medical equipment, some of the men surrounded the hysterical warrior and held his flapping limbs down. Master Ahura then stood by his head, rested his hands gently upon the dying warrior's shoulders, and bowed his head in prayer.

'What happened?' Aldber asked one of the soldiers who stood watching helplessly.

'We were ambushed by a small pack of the Enemy in sector five,' the warrior stuttered in broken Common Tongue. Blood, sand and sweat covered his face. 'We were returning from a patrol and they suddenly came out of nowhere... *Out of nowhere!*'

The wounded man looked up to Master Ahura with cold fear drenched across his drained and pale face, whilst the last breaths of life expelled from his body. It was the same horrifying look of despair Aldber had seen in the eyes of many men in the West Lands.

The helplessness. The realisation. Darkness.

Aldber would spend the next few weeks at the Sanctuary, often leaving the caves to accompany Le'Dada and his men on surveillance missions to the borders of the Dakbah Mountains. He learnt more about the customs of Galardros life out here in these inhospitable lands. During this time, they rarely saw the Enemy. Everyone remained vigilant and had the same corrosive paranoia he felt back at home.

It was soon time for the young traveller to leave for the West Lands. Master Ahura gave him a parting gift, which was a blade with a beautifully embroidered sheath, which Aldber was thankful for. Arrangements had been made for Aldber to join a voyage of Galardros who wanted to visit the West Lands and his home, so they set forth back through the mountains, rode across the desert upon fur-covered camen beasts, trekked on foot through the woodlands, and eventually came to the coastline. There, other Galardros were waiting with a new vessel that was larger than the previous boat and was in much finer condition.

A few weeks later, Aldber awoke in his hammock below deck. It swung with the tide as light pierced through cracks in the ship's framework. Unbeknownst to him, during the night water had leaked into the ship, so when he jumped down to stretch and put on his boots, he was welcomed by a small pool of seawater. Not the most ideal morning greeting. He cursed to himself and picked up his soaked boots to take on deck to dry out.

As he wrung out his wet socks, one of the shipmates informed Aldber that they only had a day left before they would arrive upon the shores of the West Lands, moor the vessel, and then plot a route further north. This was an exciting prospect because he was looking forward to returning to the western Sanctuary. He spent a long while looking out across the ocean, thinking about his journey so far and the expectations associated with the ending of his training. But all of this seemed overshadowed by what he had learnt from further conversations with Master Ahura, which was utterly unnerving. Now, more than ever before, he had a restless urge to return home. He walked around to the starboard, clasped the railing tightly, and gazed northwards across the ceaseless horizon towards the source of so much of his concern.

A short while afterwards, storm clouds were approaching, so he joined the crew and turned in early. He tried his best to sleep, but the gradually building force and sound of waves smashing against the ship only made it possible for him to have an uneasy and light slumber.

He was awoken late into the night by the full force of the deafening storm. He turned in his hammock to try and find a comfortable position as it swung erratically, but bolted upright a few moments later, when another large smash ricocheted through the vessel. He pulled on his boots that he had sensibly left inside his hammock and jumped down. He could see that the rest of the crew had vacated, and the cabin was empty. There was distant shouting coming from above deck, which was muffled by the sound of the storm and creaking of the strained wood.

A large wave hit the ship. Aldber lost his balance and was thrown hard against the hull, landing face-down in the shallow water. Momentarily, he got to his feet, spat and snorted out the salty liquid that had entered his mouth and nose, and vigorously shook off the water drenching his face. His whole body started to tremble with agitation. His head felt numbed by the coldness. Disorientated, he waded through, moving towards the doorway, finding balance against the empty hammocks that were swinging wildly, as the ship gyrated under the colossal force of the storm. He was close to the doorway, when suddenly the whole ship violently rocked from side to side, throwing him off balance. Large cracks started to appear in the hull and water started gushing into the cabin. For a moment he stood there frozen, transfixed by the large volume of liquid. By now the water had risen rapidly to above his knees. On the opposite side of the cabin another large crack appeared, and an explosive torrent flooded in, destroying everything in its path. Aldber turned around and frantically waded forward towards the stairs. Sharp debris started floating towards him, cutting into his sides and splintering his hands. By now the water was at his waist, as he desperately pulled himself up the stairway. He lifted his soaked leg forward and kicked the door open, before stumbling out on deck, and falling onto his hands and knees. As he caught his breath and brushed his wet hair aside, he looked up and could not believe what was before him.

Brief flashes of lighting illuminated the view as a cacophony of thunder resounded. Freezing rain poured down heavily as gigantic waves danced viciously around the vessel, surrounding it like moving walls that surged high into the blackened skies. Shipmates were running around, frantically trying to throw off equipment weighing the ship down, as others pulled on ropes to control the sail in an attempt to steer the vessel out of the monstrous storm.

Aldber stumbled forward, trying to maintain balance as the vessel rocked violently, whilst narrowly missed flying debris as he helplessly witnessed several men fall overboard and perish. He saw an unconscious warrior sliding along the deck nearby, so quickly ran over and pulled him to cover. But unbeknownst to the young warrior, the mast had succumbed to the winds and was beginning to snap at the base as the sails fluttered violently. The large piece of wood started leaning sideward and, with an almighty crack, came plummeting down towards him. Instinctively, he partially jumped out of the way, but his body was tangled by flaying ropes from the sail that curled around his body and slung him against the mast. Aldber's arms and legs wrapped around the wood. His head collided with the mast and was split by the impact and began to bleed. The mast crunched against the port-side of the vessel, pivoted momentarily, flipped, and then tumbled off the side of the boat. Aldber managed to retain his grip, facing downwards, but was catapulted from a great height into the air, before smashing down onto the surface and descended into the ocean.

Winded by the force of the collision, Aldber was consumed by the cold water and helplessly started to sink upside down, narrowly avoiding the broken mast that surged downward past him. He opened his eyes and watched as another crackle of lightning illuminated the scene. The large hull shook from side to side before another wave pressed against the vessel and it abruptly overturned, spilling the remaining shipmates to their watery demise, and he looked on in despair.

With what strength he could muster, Aldber manoeuvred his body around, pushed his arms upwards, kicked, and desperately waded to the surface, as dead bodies sank around him. Blood poured from the wound in his head, further obstructing his view, and precious oxygen escaped his lungs, as he relentlessly scrambled against the current. When he eventually resurfaced, he drew a deep breath, before the strong current pulled him under once more. He desperately pushed against the water and resurfaced, before manically swimming towards a large floating piece of the ship's wreckage to grip onto. He was disorientated, and could barely breathe, as freezing cold rainwater pelted him from above. Another crackle of lighting blinded his sight and the thunder pulsated through his body. He looked at the vessel as most of the framework started to break apart and sink into the ocean. His splintered hands shivered and were covered in blood as he hoisted himself onto the debris, and then held on with what energy he had left, whilst expecting an imminent wave to come along to devour and cast him into the merciless depths of the ocean.

Aldber awoke with a jolt and gasped for air. Looking around with puzzlement, it took a few moments for him to regain his breath and register his surroundings. He was sat in a small cave nestled next to a raging fire, sheltered away from the howling storm that was now surging outside and bombarding the coastline. After having washed up upon the shore, he had stumbled into this refuge and had slept for hours curled up next to the flames.

He had the discomforting realisation. For a moment he was struck with grief, thinking about the other shipmates who had lost their lives drowning at sea. Unable to fathom how he had managed to survive, Aldber took a few deep breaths to try and calm himself, before touching the wound on his head, which was now healing but still throbbing painfully.

He had the suspicion that the injury might have caused some minor memory loss, but his gaze returned to the elusive flames and his mind wandered, remembering what happened on his trek to the East Lands, and all the information he had acquired during his stay at the Sanctuary. He suddenly felt compelled to get up and leave, knowing full well the severity of what he had learnt, and the implications it had for his people, that urgently needed to be reported to the council. But he would have to wait until the storm had passed and the coming of daybreak, so instead he pulled the ripped jacket tightly around his weak frame, sat back, and settled once more. The flickering fire offered warmth and comfort as he looked out of the cave entrance into the bleak night beyond.

Chapter Two
The Old City

The following morning, once the storm had subsided, Aldber walked out from the cave. Trying to get his bearings, he looked along the coastline and could see that during the night fragments of the ship had washed up on shore and were lying amongst the other remnants of the storm's destruction. He rummaged around the wreckage and broken trees for any provisions he could salvage, as apart from his weapons, all of his other belongings had been lost. Amongst the remains was a small bottle with droplets of precious fresh water inside, which he vigorously fed into his dry throat, causing him to splutter. He had not eaten since before the boat's destruction, so anything of sustenance that could be found would be worthy. He managed to find a small box containing soggy bread, forced the salty food down his throat. His stomach protested, but he ignored the gag reflex. Afterwards, he dusted off his clothing, cleaned any excess sand out of his pistol, and counted the small amount of ammunition he had left.

The lone traveller started to make his journey inland, however he was still unclear as to where along the long coastline he had been stranded. He knew that for a day's trek he would go through the Seabourne Forest until reaching the outskirts of the Old City. He pressed on through as the terrain inclined and it seemed that he was not able to escape the remnants of this storm, for it was progressively making its way inland as dark clouds formed overhead.

In the late afternoon, he came to the ruins of a large bridge that had once stretched over a river, which was now dried up, and the bed further below now thrived with vegetation. He took cover to inspect the surrounding area. Once he was convinced that it was uninhabited, he ran across its first segment, manoeuvring around large holes and scaling large cables that had once sustained the structure. It was possible that this bridge led to the great metropolis, so following the road would take him in the right direction. However, these areas were common supply routes for the Enemy, so he was wary to follow the road directly. Overhead, he could hear birds singing as he ran across to the other side of the bridge and found cover.

As the sun passed along the horizon it was gradually covered by cloud. Aldber found shelter as rain started to fall heavily, so he would have to wait until the storm had passed, until making any further progress. He found a comfortable position at the base of a tree, shielded under the canopy of the branches, and sat down. He closed his eyes and waited calmly. The temperature changed, and far away there was the crackle of lightning and the close drumming of rain, like the firing of a thousand guns. His focus was drawn to his breathing against the harsh rainfall as he became fully immersed with the environment around him.

'*Clear your mind. Be at one in the present. You are a simple respiring entity, one droplet in the ocean, a leaf in the forest, part of the greater reality,*' he thought. '*Surrender.*'

He felt connected with everything that formed and flowed around him, in perfect stillness. He could feel his heart beating softly as he breathed in deeply. Embracement. Accepting the exterior world. In this quiet meditation he sat there contently until the storm would subside. It gave him perspective, knowing that all these struggles his people were facing were somewhat insignificant in context against the magnitude of nature, all of the Supreme One's will.

Once the storm had passed, he pressed on through the woods in the dead of night, using fragmented moonlight through the tree line as his guide. When tired, and needing to rest, he climbed up a tree and chose a suitable branch on which he precariously lay.

The following morning, Aldber was awoken by the dripping of water and the harsh racket being made by a pesky and curious bird that was perched on an opposing branch. Feeling displeased by this abrupt wakening, the lone traveller made a grunt of disapproval and flicked his hand repeatedly to usher away the bird, which reluctantly took off.

The young warrior rubbed his eyes and took a moment to compose. He was a high enough distance above the woodland floor to avoid being seen, and from his estimations, close enough to the top of the canopy to climb up and get a vantage point and view of the surrounding region.

He stretched and scaled a few more branches, pushed through the wet leaves, and cold winds hit his face when he emerged. The sun was rising behind him, casting radiant golden sunlight over the vast majestic woodlands that sprawled ahead. It was a world very different to that of his ancestors; much had been reformed and overgrown, though there were stark reminders of the past, for there in the far distance he could see the unmistakable outline of the enormous stone and metal structures of the city ruins.

It took the whole morning of trekking until he emerged from the woodlands to the outskirts of the Old City. Before him was a gargantuan wall, or what remained of it, as large segments had been destroyed or fallen away. What still existed reached high into the sky. For anyone who had never set eyes upon a structure of this scale before, it would be a foreboding sight, but to Aldber this was all too familiar. This great wall circled around what was once a great feat of human engineering, a pinnacle of civilisation before the dark times. It stretched for hundreds of miles to the north and south. He had heard that certain parts had not been so well preserved; some were fully submerged below water, as the landscape had changed dramatically.

This metropolis was built in a time very different to what Aldber knew and he was astounded by how much had survived, considering the countless sun-cycles that had passed by. It was a true testament to the architects of times long gone, who had used complex materials that had withstood the onslaught from the extreme changes in weather conditions.

The city once spanned far across the continent, its different sectors made up of smaller cities that had been swallowed within this grand structure. Large parts of the inner city still remained; however, it was now a desolate and dangerous place.

Aldber found a point along the wall that had given way, the rubble piled in such a fashion that it would be feasible for him to negotiate over. He climbed up the large pieces of stone on his hands and knees, looking back occasionally to the woodlands to makes sure that he was not being followed.

He reached over the verge and before him stood the great buildings of old. The immediate structures on the outskirts were somewhat picturesque and overgrown with thick foliage. This subsided as one progressed further into the dark murkier depths, into the belly of the fallen city.

Aldber could not determine where in the metropolis he had entered. He decided that he would find a recognisable landmark to get his bearings, so that he could navigate the next stage of his journey. Making his way through the outskirts, the buildings here were relatively modest in size, compared to the imposing giants that loomed further ahead.

During his younger sun-cycles, when he used to come down to the Old City to explore, Aldber used to imagine what these places looked like in their prime. Destruction and further degradation had replaced the elegance. He passed under a building that had fallen on its side, balanced against its neighbour; both covered in vines and exquisite plants. Below him, grasses had broken through the fractured concrete. There was an abundance of plant life in what seemed like an eerie place. The whispering winds were the only sound.

The ruined metropolis sprawled far and wide, high into the sky, and also far down below. Huge underground networks burrowed deep into the foundations far below the surface. The variety of places meant that many tribes co-habited, either risking living exposed in the tall skyscrapers, or down below in the sewers and catacombs. Conditions were harsh. Disease and famine were common. On the few occasions he had met tribes residing here, he had seen horrific sights, people pushed to the limits of desperation. Over the countless generations, they had adapted to their environment, and had required less sustenance and light in order to cope. Unclean water, malnutrition, and being deprived of sunlight had had lasting effects, with gruesome consequences. When food was scarce some had resorted to cannibalism. Incest was rife. Like the tribe he had met in the desert, here, all tribes remained defensive and private, and showed hostility to each other. Many had agreed to have Galardros appointed to protect them against the Enemy. These specially selected warriors were of the mowoni caste; they devoted themselves to protecting and teaching the tribes and worked alongside the leaders to ensure the survival of the people. The mowoni accompanied them wherever they migrated and often married into the families.

Living in the Old City offered shelter, and animals thrived there, enough for the tribes to hunt, operating undercover in the dead of night in order to avoid being hunted by the Enemy. However, this vast metropolis was also the habitat for those savage beasts that roamed around in hordes with ease, never deterred by the humans, attacking the scavengers for sport. The bitter hatred and fear amongst the tribes was utterly suffocating.

Aldber felt incredibly fortunate, considering the upbringing he had been given at the Sanctuary. Far to the north, outside of the city walls and in the hills, had been established the base of the Galardros of the West Lands - his home.

As he progressed, the magnificent structures around him dominated the skyline. There were clear blue skies overhead, and yet down here on the street level everything was shrouded in cool shadow.

He started to bare north and would spend the next few days negotiating through the rubble, whilst being vigilant. He would cross over old highways, climb down the vast interior of buildings, and wander down the hauntingly empty streets.

One late afternoon, he came to a large lake. Its weight had penetrated the street, the body of water descended far down into the earth. It stretched far across the horizon, flowing into a large hole at the bottom of a skyscraper on the opposite side. He could have chosen to either walk around its perimeter, which would cost him valuable time, or instead swim directly over the lake and in through the building on to the other side.

He surveyed the surrounding areas to make sure he was alone, before exposing himself and gradually wading into the water. He gritted his teeth as he accepted the cold temperature, trying to resist shivering as he submerged his whole torso and started swimming slowly across. Above him, he could hear the crumbling of stone as large fragments of ruin started cascading down, making a startling noise as they hit the ground, the sound vibrations magnified between the walls of the buildings. As he swam further into the lake, he looked below the surface at foliage that was growing on segments of the cracked street. When he got near to the building, he took a few dives under water to calculate how far down into the building he would have to go. He took a deep breath and swam into the building's interior, eventually resurfaced, hoisted himself up into the new space, and started to make his way through until he finally saw light on the other side.

The sight before him was quite amazing; the body of water flowed further to a point where it suddenly dropped. The lake descended into a waterfall and the city in the distance was visible through a mist projected at the water's edge. He climbed out of a shattered window, and precariously climbed across the outside of the building, until he found ground on the side of the lake. From here, he held on tightly to the nearest building and shimmied along. Below him was a sheer drop where two colossal shards of land had risen and collided. To attempt to jump down the waterfall would be certain death. He started climbing down, finding grip in the moist earth, as the large body of water cascaded by his side. He breathed in deeply, cleared his mind, focused, and descended, and whispered to himself: 'surrender.'

Once he had reached the bottom, he quickly ran to find cover, making sure he was safe in this open area. The sun was falling behind the silhouette of buildings to the west. As he passed along a boulevard, he noticed on a wall an assuming red marking. To any unknowing onlooker, it may not have appeared out of the ordinary; however, Aldber knew this to be the marking of Galardros. He was close to an underground base. Hopefully they could provide help.

Making sure that he had not been followed, Aldber entered the ruins of a building next to the marking. Inside was a stairway; he was barely able to make his footing because of the decreasing amount of sunlight. At the bottom he rummaged underneath the stairwell and found a small torch that had been appropriately concealed. There was a large circular grate on the wall leading into the sewer system. He undid the latch and had to use both hands to pull open the heavy rusted grate. Once he was inside and had closed the grate carefully behind him, he used the faulting torch to inspect the sewer that passed before him. Thankfully, waste no longer flowed there, so he would not have to negotiate through the revolting stench. Adjacent was a passageway; his instincts told him to follow this path, and so he scaled the sewer to the other side. Cautiously, he took out his pistol as he walked down the passageway. It led out into an open area of catwalks and large pipe networks flowing off in various directions. High above, fading sunlight pierced through a grate in the surface, casting a large stretched symmetrical pattern upon the scene. His footsteps echoed against the steel as he moved along, and the distant dripping of water thudded like a heartbeat. He walked down a stairway and saw at the far side of the room a large door with another red marking painted across it. When he approached it, he looked around to make sure no one was lurking in the shadows. Using the butt of his pistol, he started to give a series of knocks and scratches in code that would make out the letters 'A.T.M', the first letters of the syllables for the name 'Altamos' — the great founder of the order.

A few moments later a small viewfinder slid across. It revealed a pair of eyes that checked him meticulously, before the person pulled back the finder and unlocked the large reinforced door. There, stood before him, was a man holding up a rifle cautiously, adorned in the weathered combat clothing of the silo, the soldier caste. Without hesitation, Aldber raised his hand and gave the salute and said the oath. The man then lowered his weapon, stood firm and returned the gesture, his demeanour now less hostile. Aldber walked through the entrance, and the silo checked they did not have unwelcome guests, before swiftly closing the door behind him.

'It is not very often that we have unannounced guests here at the operation,' the silo explained in a hard and uninviting tone. 'Follow me.'

The soldier led Aldber down a passageway that was illuminated by orange electrical lighting, until they walked out onto a catwalk overlooking a large open room where fan systems lined the opposing walls. In here was a gathering of soldiers. The room was full of equipment and supplies, and at its centre was a large table with maps strewn across it. They proceeded down a stairway and the silo introduced Aldber to his superior. The squad leader was gaunt, her short, dark hair greying prematurely, a subtle twitch in her eye.

'What brings you here and who are you?' the captain questioned as she finished returning documents to one of her comrades.

'My name is Aldber,' he announced in a formal manner. 'I am a trainee. I have just returned from the East Lands, and by chance came across your base.'

'Aldber?' the captain said with intrigue and exchanged looks with the door guard. 'I have heard of that name before.'

'Oh, really?' the visitor asked awkwardly.

'You probably didn't receive the warmest of welcomes, but we try to maintain secrecy about this base, even away from tribesmen, as they often unwillingly bring along unwanted attention.' The captain gestured for Aldber to join her at the war table. 'Unfortunately, you have joined us at a bad moment; earlier today a horde of the Enemy attacked the Fabado tribe in sector twelve. Several of my men perished attempting to protect them.'

Around the table were stood tired silo, all with mournful grimaces upon their faces. Some had bandaged wounds, and there was the unmistakable smell of aggravation. The harsh realities of the struggles against the Enemy were all too apparent. Aldber often felt detached from the ongoing hardships of survival, this fight for life. Each of these men and women had sacrificed themselves for the cause. They had left behind their loved ones and sworn allegiance to the order. It was not like they had much of a choice. Often, in times like this, when their efforts seemed in vain, the struggle seemed impossible.

The Enemy had become too strong, resourceful and cunning.

'Have there been any positive developments?' Aldber asked wishfully.

'We have observed several supply routes that lead out of the city.' The captain pointed on a map to their present location, which was in the north-east of the grand metropolis. From here, Aldber could determine where they were in relation to the hills. The silo then pointed at several markings she had made that showed where the Enemy had noted activity leading towards the main frontline further inland into the heart of the city's ruins. There was a distant rumble from an explosion, causing the room to rock. It startled some of the dejected warriors, and a small crumble of concrete from the ceiling tumbled onto the map, which the captain brushed away. Unfazed, she continued: 'Our strategy is to attack these supply routes in order to weaken their efforts. We do not attempt full assaults, unless in extreme circumstances, like this morning, where we are often outnumbered.'

Being around these warriors only highlighted the harsh realities. This had been the same tactic for many sun-cycles: to protect the tribes and maintain a level of presence that would deter the Enemy. It was a cycle that had maintained a discomforting balance where the humans were no longer dominant. These soldiers were all part of what was left in the effort for their species to survive. How long this would go on for was anyone's guess, especially now that Aldber knew something so important that could change everything.

'Captain, the reason I came down here was to request extraction from high command. I need to return to the Sanctuary, immediately,' Aldber explained with an intense look.

'Unfortunately, I doubt such a request can be granted so easily. Resources are stretched so thinly that we are not even able to have regular ammunition and supply drops. We are even limited to getting the sick lifted out of here.' She then pointed to the far corner where several medical beds were positioned, and the wounded were being attended to.

'I understand.' Aldber nodded firmly, masking his disappointment. 'And I am sorry that you have been stationed here in such dire conditions.'

'*Left here*,' he thought, biting his inner lip.

'There is no other choice.' The captain gave a half-hearted smile and subtly shook her head. 'You are welcome to use our facilities and I am sure we can give you something to eat.'

'That would be appreciated,' he said warmly, and gulped, for inside he felt a deep sense of despair, knowing full well he would have no other option than to risk his life further by hiking the rest of the distance through the labyrinth of these treacherous city ruins back to the Galardros' stronghold.

'I can help you!' a voice called from behind. Aldber looked towards the source and saw a man only a few sun-cycles older than him and of a similar build. His clothes were marked with oil.

'Not this again.' The squad leader frowned.

'You can help me?' Aldber asked.

'Well, sort of.' The man then walked forward and outstretched his hand. Aldber accepted the gesture and shook it. 'I couldn't help but overhear your conversation with the squad leader. My name is Kip, I am one of the Sky People, and the captain of the Aeupheur.'

The Sky People had abandoned life upon the surface and taken to the clouds to live on aircrafts they had salvaged. They had little contact with the tribes or the Galardros.

'It is a pleasure to meet you, Captain. How can you help me?'

'If I can find my crew, we can help you.'

'Don't listen to him, Aldber,' the squad leader interjected from behind. Aldber turned to face her. 'When we went to help the Fabado tribe, he was with them, but they claimed he wasn't one of their people. We felt obliged to bring him here, but don't know quite what to do with him.'

'It is like I explained earlier: I lost my crew and need to return to them and my ship,' Kip spoke in an assertive manner and shook his head at the squad leader's lack of trust.

Aldber read the man's facial expressions and mannerisms. His intuition told him that the man was being honest.

'Captain, as much as I appreciate your consideration, I am unable to assist with locating your crew,' Aldber said warmly. 'If I was not pressed for time, I would have helped you.'

'Aldber, that is very kind of you.' Kip smiled. 'It is nice to see that not all the Galardros are so suspicious!' He exchanged cautious glances with the squad leader.

'I wish you the best of luck with being reunited with your crew.' Aldber then started to turn to face the squad leader but stopped when he felt Kip's hand on his arm.

'Wait,' Kip whispered. Aldber faced him once more. 'You seem like a decent guy. Look, any time you need help in the future,' — he then handed the trainee a slip of parchment — 'just contact me.'

Aldber unravelled the parchment. Written on it was a series of numbers.

'What is this?'

'It is a transmission code. It can be used with a transmitter device to contact the cockpit of my aircraft.'

'Why haven't you used this to contact your crew?'

'Because none of these soldiers have a device. How do you Galardros cope with only using messaging birds? How primitive!'

'Thank you.' Aldber folded the parchment and then stuffed it into the inner pocket of his jacket.

'Come on, you.' A silo came forward to escort Kip away and put a hand on his shoulder.

'*Get your hand off of me!*' Kip objected and smirked at Aldber, before he reluctantly obliged to follow. 'Nice meeting you, Aldber. Remember what I said.'

'I sure will do, Captain.' Aldber nodded and watched as the man was taken off in the direction of the entrance.

'I wouldn't believe a word that comes out of that man's mouth. He reeks of trouble,' the squad leader said.

'Where is he being taken?'

'To find his supposed crew.'

A short while later, the guest sat with some of the silo as a serving of rations was provided. Aldber gladly ate the sustenance as those surrounding him told stories about their horrifying encounters. He could see fear stricken across their tired faces, hope dwindling with every word they uttered.

Afterwards, the young warrior was offered a bed to rest, but declined the offer, as he had to continue on his journey and hoped to cover a good distance before nightfall. Saying farewell to the captain and her men, he then left and took a large sigh of relief as the large door closed behind him. The depressive atmosphere in the base was contagious.

He did not want to feel powerless anymore.

Many hours later, after changing direction northward and having trekked relentlessly until the last trickles of sunlight slipped over the horizon, Aldber used an oil lamp gifted by the silo to guide his path. He found shelter in a room at the top of an industrial block, reachable only by a staircase, and surrounded by panoramic views through empty windows.

It was here, in the darkness, that he decided to settle himself before sleeping, by meditating. He placed the extinguished lamp to one side and stood in the middle of the room.

With both eyes shut, and still fully aware of his surroundings, he could imagine he was anywhere. Feeling the warm breeze wafting through the room, whilst smelling the dankness and fumes from the lamp, he followed his breathing and emptied his mind of thoughts. He could feel energy pulsating throughout his body as each breath oxidised every nerve-ending in his limbs.

Throughout the many sun-cycles of training, Aldber had been educated about the dormant powers that he harnessed, and so readily wanted to unleash, in order to reach his full potential. Beforehand, he had been frustrated with his shortcomings, but knew that achieving this would require consistent hard effort and patience. He imagined his arms flaying freely, as his body was suspended in the air and his feet no longer touched the ground. The weightlessness was unfamiliar, yet welcome.

A distant sound. The diversion of attention.

Aldber opened his eyes, looking around to find the source of the disruption. The room was illuminated by moonlight. Another sound, this time closer.

It took a few moments for Aldber's eyes to adjust and fixedly digest the room. He immediately reached for his holstered pistol and knife, looked around with agitation, breathing in deeply as his heartrate increased, and a warm sensation enraptured his body, whilst making sure he was stood with a stable posture.

He was not alone.

The young warrior cocked his pistol and tightened the grip on the blade, looking around as the dusty floorboards creaked below his feet. There was a small gust of cold wind, which drew his attention to a window adjacent that looked out over the grim view of the buildings beyond. His heart started pounding relentlessly in his chest, his stomach felt like it was collapsing in on itself, his mouth had gone dry, and his palms were sweating. And then, much to his horror, from the murky depths emerged a dark hand, its fingers as thick as a man's wrist and covered in fur. The hand grasped onto the window frame and, without a moment's hesitation, Aldber fired, but missed. The sound ricocheted throughout the room and out into the night. A drop of sweat flowed down his cheek and dropped onto the dusty floor with what felt like an almighty thud. Another hand appeared and the metal bent under the weight of the colossal figure.

Above him, Aldber could hear the sound of movements, as the frame of the building strained, baring the weight of three other beings that were climbing onto the roof. In front of him, the two hands held tightly onto the window frame for support and suddenly a large black shadow launched upwards and burst through, landing on the floor, as rubble crashed onto the ground far down below.

Aldber stood his ground, trying to stop his body from shaking from the adrenaline pumping through his veins. The beast had its head bowed and was breathing heavily through its nostrils, its features concealed under a thick mane of fur that covered its head and upper-back. Its body was clothed in leathers and plated armour. Suddenly, two large fists slammed down onto the floor, cracking the wood and creating large indentations, and the whole room seemed to shake. The beast slowly raised its head to reveal a snarling face, its eyes possessed with fury, and saliva dripping from its large fangs. It then then rose onto its hind legs, drawing to a height bigger than any man. It puffed out its chest and clenched its fists by its sides as its gaze pierced through the darkness at its prey.

One of the centauri stood before Aldber.

In a split moment, it lunged for Aldber and he rolled out of the way, turning to fire as it crashed against the wall. It launched for him, roaring with malice, its large hands extended towards him. It ran at the human with a velocity that, to the untrained, would have meant immediate death. The young warrior ran around, jumped and kicking the enraged beast, as it chased him around the room. Aldber made his way towards the stairwell, but the centauri sliced forward, catching his leg and causing him to trip and fall, and the beast dived over him and smashed through the banisters. Aldber quickly found his feet as the undeterred beast reappeared and snarled, before climbing up and throwing itself towards the human. Aldber then thrust his blade upwards, slashing through the beast's lower jaw and penetrating its brains as its large frame engulfed him. Aldber fell in time for the beast's lifeless body to fly past him, as the mass crumpled to the ground. He spat out blood that had covered his face and got to his feet before looking up at the high ceiling. Above him, large fragments of the metal structure started to fall to the ground. The metal had been ripped away, exposing the moonlight that streamed down, casting an eerie white glow upon the scene. He could see three large figures silhouetted by the night sky, so stood defiantly. They jumped down, and the wooden floorboards cracked under the immense force.

He was surrounded.

They all screamed with disgust that he had killed their accomplice, and stood for a moment, two balancing on the knuckles of their front fists, one on its hind legs brandishing a blade, and all spitting with outrage. At once all three centauri launched at him. The warrior ran for the one closest to the stairwell, dodged its advance, jumped, flew towards the stairwell, and landed hard. He rolled down the flight of steps and recovered in time to manoeuvre around, then fired several shots at one of the beasts as it emerged, killing it instantly. He got to his feet and ran into the room. Behind him, the two remaining beasts came hurtling down, destroying the stairs and ignoring the body of their deceased ally. The pursuers got onto their hind legs and started running relentlessly for Aldber. The human had no other choice but to jump out of the window on the opposite side of the room. They burst through the wall after him as he fell helplessly downward, his fall partially broken by a large skylight further below. Glass shards cut his face as he descended and entered the new building. Below were several thick electric cables hanging loosely across the room. He gripped onto them and swung forward, lost grip of his pistol, and crumbled onto a ledge. The two centauri soon followed, their fall partially broken by the cables that could not hold under the sheer weight. The cables snapped as the pair fell to the ground, smashed against the hard floor, and the blade fell to one side.

Aldber knelt down for a moment to regain his breath, and grasped his chest, which was in excruciating agony from the fall. Below, he could hear the two disorientated centauri getting to their feet and exchanging remarks in the Black Tongue. Aldber looked around, surveying possible escape routes, but knew he had no option other than to climb back out of the skylight. He did not have much time, so ran and jumped from the platform, grabbing onto one of flaying cables and swung across the room. Below, the two centauri started jumping, trying to grab at him, their roars shaking the room. Aldber then found grip onto another cable, curled his arms and legs around it, and started to climb up to the skylight, but suddenly, one of the centauri appeared from out of sight, jumped at Aldber, and they both fell towards the ground, the beast below cushioning their fall and they all dispersed across the floor. Disorientated, Aldber shook his head and spotted the centauri's blade. He quickly scrambled towards it, grasped onto it just in time, spun over, and with both hands pushed the blade deep into the chest of one of the beasts, as it loomed over him. It screamed with pain and tumbled over him, pinning him to the ground. The other soon pounced, moving its deceased accomplice aside with one swift movement, but Aldber was able to roll out of the way as the centauri stood at full height above him, a wicked look of victory covering its vile face. But this was a premature notion, because Aldber then swung the blade upward screaming, slicing at the centauri's head, which burst open. Blood and bone exploded everywhere as its large corpse crumpled to the ground.

Half of Aldber's body was trapped under the remains of his opponents. He mustered the strength to pull himself out, before stabbing both of the beasts repeatedly to make sure they were definitely dead, as their lifeless corpses lay in a sea of red. He discarded the blade and fell back to the ground panting desperately for air, and let out a small shriek of exhaustion, astonished that he was still alive. He pulled himself away, rubbed off as much blood as he could, grasped his aching chest, and started to stumble away in a state of shock. To the side was a door that would take him away from this horrific scene.

Aldber entered the main foyer of a skyscraper. He checked that the surrounding area was clear, then stumbled through until he found a stairwell. He held onto the guiderail tightly and staggered upwards until his body could take no more. He kicked through a door into a corridor and found shelter in a small room hidden away with a tattered mattress at its centre. He fell onto it and pulled his jacket around him. His whole body felt weak and he shivered from the cold. He curled up, rocked as he breathed in deeply, hugged his torso, and burrowed his head below the fabric, trying desperately to remain calm. He tried to muffle the sound of his uncontrollable coughing as a searing pain sliced through his chest.

Outside, he could hear the roars of the Enemy, others who had been attracted by all of the commotion. Aldber was exposed, being so close to where the bodies of the deceased centauri lay. He did not have the strength to leave this place, and could go no further, so would risk lying here to recover.

The warrior tried to empty his mind, even though he was consumed by fear and the echoing snarls surrounded him. It was overwhelming. He lost track of time as the endless night continued, expecting the Enemy to find him and awaiting imminent death.

Aldber passed into a reluctant sleep as the roars became distant upon the breeze. His dreams were filled with horrors of his escape, and he awoke repeatedly in cold sweats, his heart burning feverishly inside his chest.

At daybreak, he was awoken by a discomforting coughing fit and coiled as his stomach muscles contracted. Dust scattered around him as he emptied the contents of his sore throat.

For a moment he lay there staring at the floor, recollecting a vivid nightmare he had once again experienced whilst asleep. The harrowing imagery was as nauseating as the confrontation he had been in the previous night.

He looked out of the window at the peaceful street below. Above him the skies were blue and thin clouds glided causally on by. He sat up, checking that he was still intact and had not left behind any limbs at the fight. His chest was still aching, and he suspected he had broken a few ribs from the fall. Tapping his utility belt, he had the disconcerting reminder that he had lost both of his weapons, but he didn't want to risk returning to the dead bodies to find them, in case there were other centauri waiting for him.

Once he had mustered enough strength, he descended the skyscraper, having lost count the night before of how many levels he had scaled. When he entered the street, he checked that the coast was clear and followed the sun's trajectory to make his way further north.

As he negotiated through the ruins of the city, he managed to reach the outskirts by late morning. The distance between the buildings and the northern wall was always a dangerous passage because it was an open and barren stretch. The young warrior knew he was in the right area because the part of the wall closest to the Sanctuary had been well preserved.

He found cover inside a small building and surveyed the surrounding area. He was still cursed with memories from the previous night's ordeal, and the nightmare, so he gave himself a few words of encouragement under his breath, before running out into the open towards the gigantic wall before him.

Once he was at its base, he followed the smooth rock-face until he found a security door that would take him inside. The door was severely rusted and barely hanging from its hinges. He carefully opened it, as the loud creaks echoed out, and then carefully stepped inside.

The hollow inside of the wall comprised of stairways that led off in several directions, some leading to the very top where there were catwalks and viewing platforms. Aldber was less concerned about the scenic views and started to manoeuvre through, with no light to guide him. As he reached the other side, he pressed up against the surface and shimmied along, until finding a crack of light where there was another doorway. How much danger he was still in was not certain, but he decided against keeping a low profile, so kicked the door wide open, creating a racket, and emerged out onto the grassy wilderness beyond.

Before him stretched the luscious Great Plains. It was a far more welcoming sight compared to the bleak grey monstrosity behind him. In the far distance were the silhouettes of the Paradimus Hills (the name means 'paradise' in the Ramasha language) stretching far along the horizon. With haste, he made off from the Old City, at first vigilant not to be seen so close to the ruins, before becoming more relaxed in his pace. Out here, there was plenty of animal life and vegetation for the centauri to feast upon, but thankfully, they seldom bothered venturing out into the hills.

As the morning went by, he felt reassured about his trajectory, when the two distinguishable hills appeared. They met so closely, the winding spurs a natural passageway more than wide enough to pass through, but still unassuming, as it snaked along until emerging into an open valley. It was an ideal entrance for a secret base.

Aldber entered, checking behind him once more to make sure he was not being tailed, and followed the pathway. Both hills dominated the skyline above. The unassuming track was lined by dense foliage, and higher up he could see patrolmen watching him with their guns trained. He eventually emerged out into the open valley with anticipation.

He was finally home.

Before him was an impressive valley with a flat, open expanse and hills circling above to either side. Far off in the distance, at the very peak of the hills to his left, he could see a grand waterfall cascading down, sunlight glistening against its sparkling waters, the remnants a series of small streams trickling down by his feet. To the right of the waterfall he could see wooden and stone buildings, hidden away amongst the dense foliage of the tree line and surrounded by a defensive wall. At the far side of the field was a docking bay, where several salvaged aircrafts were receiving maintenance.

It was here, so many generations ago, that Altamos, the great founder of the order, had led his followers, and together they had constructed this great base for their operations. Hidden away in the valley, thousands of Galardros before him had gathered to fight the cause, honour the code, train and serve. In this sacred place, Aldber had spent his sun-cycles growing up and learning the ways of his people.

As he walked along the grassy open, he could see a patrolman approaching on horseback. He galloped up to Aldber with his rifle held high and stopped momentarily. Our fearless young traveller gave the salute and they both said the oath in unison. 'It has been many moons since we last saw you, young Aldber,' the patrolman remarked, tugging on the reins of his horse to control it and then sniggered. 'I have to admit that the Sanctuary has been somewhat quiet without you around.'

'I thought it was about time I came back.' Aldber smirked at the irony of his statement. The patrolman nodded and wished the young warrior on his way before galloping off.

Aldber walked on towards the stronghold at the foot of the hill. Above him, the facilities burrowed deep into the rock-face, all connected by walkways, and stone and rope bridges, all ascending higher up and touching the side of the waterfall.

As at present he was not in the most desirable physical or mental condition to engage anyone, he wanted to avoid small talk and the embarrassment of being welcomed upon return. He moved swiftly up through the settlement, trying to maintain a low profile whilst longing for the comfort of his bed, if only for a short time, before addressing the pressing issues. He passed several Galardros and gave brief polite acknowledgment but kept his head down to avoid being spotted by one of the elders.

He walked onto a stone passageway where unlit torches adorned the walls. Facing towards the valley were small living quarters, and his abode was halfway down. Once he entered, we carefully closed the door behind him, and let out a sigh of relief.

His room was small, with minimal decorations and furnishings, but was adequate. Adjacent was a window looking out over the idyllic valley below. There was a table with a bowl and jug upon it, a chair that he usually dumped his clothes and equipment on, and a small bed in the corner. He undid the buckle on his utility belt and threw it onto the chair, before carefully collapsing onto the bed, cupping his hands behind his head, and stretching out his legs.

Bliss.

Moments later, there was a firm knock at the door, and before permission was granted, it opened, and an assistant appeared.

'Aldber, the council requests your presence,' the man said in a formal manner. The resting new arrival opened one eye, at first jaded and unresponsive, before sitting up attentively.

'Right away?' Aldber retorted, winching as his chest hurt.

'Yes.' The door slammed shut and Aldber slumped back down. He was convinced he had made it to his room without being spotted by any of the elders.

'I guess that rest can wait!' He laughed, looking up at the ceiling, and cursed at his exhaustion and pain, before getting to his feet to make his way out.

Chapter Three
The Sanctuary

The assistant was waiting outside and, once Aldber appeared, he asked the arrival to look presentable before being summoned in front of the council. Not only had the young warrior been given inadequate time to rest, but he thought to question this request. Although, admittedly, he had not taken care of his appearance over these past few weeks, and probably looked undesirable by standards of the order, where appearance was always important. So, refraining from answering back, he took a detour on his way towards the council tower, and stopped by a small pond that fed from by a stream leading from the waterfall way up higher on the hillside.

This semi-circular pond had a large weeping-willow tree hanging over it, casting a shadow over the water in the afternoon light. There was the calm rustling of branches and detached leaves glided across the water's surface. This was a meeting place and there were a few Galardros sitting on the raised rim of the pond, fully engrossed in discussion. Aldber was interested in the fountain to the side that was against a wall adorned with a mirror. When he saw his reflection, he looked predictably dishevelled; his shoulder-length brown hair was greased and covered in blood and other excrement. His skin was tanned from the visit to the desert, his eyes darkened, and his stubble was thick. He proceeded to bathe his face in the cold water, drinking some to quench his thirst, and the bowl soon filled with blood and dirt. He then attempted to make his matted hair look tidy and dusted off his clothes before leaving the pond, still looking noticeably scruffy.

He took a direction southward, walking through the vast complex of the Sanctuary, and headed uphill towards the waterfall and at its base walked around the perimeter of the pool. Here, the hillside was a vertical rock face, and the pathway followed alongside it before veering off left onto a small outcrop, where stood the council tower that overlooked the sheer drop to the valley floor far down below. It was a circular domed structure made from sandstone held up by large pillars. Inside were eight stone seats circling the building, facing inward. It was here that Grand Master Vivid and his seven councillors had their daily sessions.

The order's leader was of the third and most prestigious caste that was called the bura, the reconnaissance warriors. The council was made up of elders from all three castes that were elected for their exceptional bravery, skill and wisdom.

As the young warrior approached, two armoured guards, who bore large spears, stopped him. He was informed that another meeting was coming to an end and so would have to wait a few moments.

Aldber looked out over the deep descent into the tranquil valley below. It was early summer so was humid, and everything was in full blossom. Insects danced through the air and the hills were covered in vibrant greenery.

The changing of the seasons had not always been this way.

Countless generations ago, after the dark times, there had been the seemingly never-ending winter, when the last remnants of humanity had survived in the bitter cold. It was believed that during that time the centauri had arisen from the ice and had evolved at such a fast rate that the tribes were not prepared. The two species fought desperately for resources and soon the humans were the ones being hunted and their superiority over the world had been taken away. Many generations later, when the snows receded, Altamos brought his followers here. It was a story Aldber had been told many times during his childhood.

Altamos had been a tribesman like any other, living in destitution, trying helplessly to survive, whilst fending off continual attacks from this new species they referred to simply as the Enemy. It was said that one day, the all-powerful Supreme One, the divine creator and ruler of the universe, visited him. It was proclaimed to Altamos that one day a prophet would come who would bring salvation to his desperate people. He was told that the humans must have faith and believe that their hardships and pain would not last forever.

Altamos had been bestowed a gift and responsibility, so he'd made it his life mission to go forth and speak the prophecy to all of the people. Word spread throughout the tribes like wildfire and many spoke of the gallant preacher. With this newly found strength, he would bring together the best warriors he could find and established the Galardros. It was a resistance against the Enemy that would fight for humanity and await the chosen one.

They built their secret base, mining stone from the local hills and collecting resources from the abundant surrounding woodlands. Having excavated technologies and designs from the ancient times, they were able to develop weapons and armour. The foundations of practice were laid by installing a code to which every member of the order would swear an oath. Throughout his lifetime, Altamos would galvanise the people together. Tribes were allocated warriors to protect them, and many from far and wide praised him. Delegates from the West Lands travelled across the Great Ocean to the east and spread the word, preaching the message of the Supreme One. They showed the ways of the Galardros and established a foothold on both continents. It is believed that during this time the Common Tongue was first acknowledged over both lands.

In his twilight sun-cycles, Altamos would build fortifications further north, and way up in the Hallow Mountains built the Retreat, his final resting place. He would elect a successor, named Daoman, who would carry on his good work and continue the struggle for many sun-cycles to follow.

Before now, the humans had been petty prey to the Enemy, but Altamos had been instrumental in bringing about the uprising of his people and, consequently, a conflict had since ravaged the world. The Enemy had grown in size and had become resourceful in combating the resilience of the weaker species.

Various traditions had been created throughout the world praising the Supreme One, but the simple act of faith and prayer for salvation was the most important ritual. Other religious beliefs had risen but nothing could surpass the almighty word and influence of Altamos.

There were other sects, including the Votaries of the Source, but most of the practices were taught to the tribes directly by the warriors of the Galardros. However, as the conflict intensified, people became impatient and started to question when the prophecy would be fulfilled, as there was no end to their hardships and suffering. Many started to cast doubt upon the prophecy and tribes started to relinquish their bonds with the order, criticising it for its fanaticism and shortcomings.

Over many sun-cycles, the prophecy had become a story of old that many did not speak of, or just passed down as legend. However, all of the grand masters since Altamos had faith and made it their duty to carry on by the sacred word. Grand Master Vivid was the fifth successor to the great founder and had been in the position for many sun-cycles. He was now a battle-hardened and wise old man, now in the twilight sun-cycles of his life.

Several people passed Aldber as the previous meeting ended. The two guards stood aside, and he was invited to walk up onto the outcrop. The young warrior straightened his posture, cleared his throat, and tried to be as official as possible, even though he was sleep deprived and his ribs were aching severely. As he neared the tower, an assistant gave him a welcoming smile and ushered him inside.

'Grand Master Vivid, Councillors, Aldber has returned from his travels,' the assistant announced.

All heads turned and looked as the new arrival walked into the centre of the tower with his hands clasped behind his back. He bowed consecutively to every member of the council. There was silence and a mixed reaction in return. Aldber faced Grand Master Vivid, an opposite image, dressed in a ceremonial long, dark robe with clean, short white hair and beard. He was delighted to see the young man. To his right side was Bura Hecta, whose face was stern as usual as he gave an acknowledging firm nod. To Grand Master Vivid's left was Councillor Thortatel, a tall and slim bearded man, not too much younger than the leader, who could not have looked more disinterested even if he had tried.

'Aldber, dear boy, it has been a long time since you have set forth on your travels. We were beginning to wonder if you would ever return,' Grand Master Vivid said with a calm and gentle serenity. His hands were clasped below his bearded chin, looking up at Aldber.

'Yes, thank you for gracing us with your presence,' Thortatel remarked under his breath. To his left side was Councillor Gilliad, who tried to conceal his sniggering.

Repulsive individuals, Aldber always thought.

'Master, Councillors, it has been an eventful experience, to say the least.' Aldber projected his voice in a confident tone. He took a deep breath, smiled, and loosened up his posture. He was glad to see these familiar faces. Well, some more than others.

Aldber then started to describe what happened on his perilous travels around the West Lands, passage over the Great Ocean, and journey to the Dakbah Mountains, and being warmly welcomed by Master Ahura, before the tragic return journey.

'I joined several of Ahura's men and we set voyage from the East

Lands a moon cycle ago.' Aldber then paused and swallowed hard. 'A day away from reaching these shores, the ship was hit by a storm.' He then stopped to think of the horrific night as the elders looked at him with bafflement. 'As far as I am aware, I was the only survivor.'

The young warrior bowed his head as the memories of the horrifying event saddened him. A slight gust of wind swept through the tower and the sun cast light over the distant hills as afternoon passed by. The council exchanged concerned looks and hushed remarks, whilst Grand Master Vivid remained motionless.

'Aldber, the main objective of your travels to the Eastern Sanctuary was to gather intelligence regarding developments on Irelaf,' Hecta said with his thick North-eastern-Lands accent, looking at the trainee with grave intensity. 'Were you successful?'

The memories passed and were replaced by something much more unsettling and sinister. Despite it being a warm summer's day, Aldber was suddenly enveloped by a cold shiver at the mention of that name (which was Gerhami for 'lone isle'). He looked up and around at all the faces who waited eagerly for his response. Now, after having longed greatly to be in this position to deliver his findings, he was riddled with hesitation, knowing the consequences of what he was about to reveal.

'Master Ahura informed me that all of our suspicions have been confirmed.' He paused to see the reaction on everyone's faces. 'His bura stationed further to the north have confirmed that Irelaf has been adopted by the Enemy as a home and is now fully occupied. The grand fortifications they have been building across the entire island are near completion.'

The tower erupted as councillors started conversing feverishly. This was the inconvenient truth they had been expecting to hear. They were eventually silenced by Grand Master Vivid's calming hand gesture.

'This is something that must be discussed constructively, Councillors, without talking over each other.' Vivid looked around at the elders before returning his gaze to Aldber. 'What else were you told?'

'Master Ahura's men have not dared to go too close to the island and do not know what it is the centauri are doing behind the large walls that have been built along the coastline.'

'They have constructed a wall around *the entire island*?' Fukuro, a dark man with receding hair and a beard, interjected.

'Correct. Reinforced metal as high as the hills that surround us,' Aldber responded as many elders vocalised their concern.

'And I suspect they are being secretive for a reason,' Thortatel said gravely and looked at the other elders intensely. 'This is the turning point in the war.' He then glared at the leader and said, 'We are running out of time.' An uncomfortable silence then fell upon the council tower as they all digested the enormity of what had been discussed.

'In light of this news, I think it best to end today's session in order to digest and reflect. This evening I shall meditate on the matter. We will reconvene again tomorrow.' Grand Master Vivid stood up and walked towards Aldber. 'Dear boy, thank you for completing the objective and gathering the information. I imagine that you must be exhausted from your journey. You must rest now.'

Grand Master Vivid and the young warrior then walked out of the council tower and down the pathway. The two guards stepped aside and saluted, as the leader and his protégé walked towards the waterfall.

'I had no doubt that you would be capable of going out into the wilderness and would be able to navigate your way across the inhospitable lands,' Grand Master Vivid said softly. 'Was it what you expected?'

'It was, and more so, Master. It showed me the reality of our people's struggle and suffering. I saw some incredible sights and met some interesting people. With these new developments, all I feel now is the urge to face the initiation. I know that I am ready to take the next step.' They stopped, and Aldber turned to face Grand Master Vivid, who placed a hand gently onto his shoulder.

'And I am very sure that you are. Aldber, in two days' time you shall take the final test, so I suggest you rest well and prepare yourself,' Grand Master Vivid said eagerly. Aldber smiled and gave a small bow before turning to leave.

Behind him, Grand Master Vivid stood there for a moment, watching Aldber walk down the hillside.

The boy had done as expected.

From behind, the other council members were making their way from the tower. Thortatel passed with Gilliad at his side, who was jabbering as usual. Thortatel thrust Vivid a look of disapproval before walking off, as the leader looked on in his wake, knowing full well that many elders on the council had started to question his leadership.

Vivid would have a lot to contemplate in his meditations in the evening.

Aldber descended back towards the main complex and headed for the prayer room. There, he would give thanks to the Supreme One for returning him safely from his travels. Hidden within the hillside was a small man-made cave, one of the first installations carved out when the Sanctuary was built. Inside there was a low ceiling; it was illuminated by candlelight and incense enraptured the nostrils. Small mats were arranged in rows leading to the front where there was a simple altar of large candles. There were no depictions of either the Supreme One or even Altamos, just these places of worship where Galardros would come to find peace and attempt to connect with the divine, the source of everything.

Aldber knelt down on one of the mats and cupped his hands on his lap, keeping his back straight for a comfortable posture. The aroma around him was soothing. Under his breath he spoke out to the Supreme One, sending his gratitude for returning him home. Like all the Galardros and tribes who had faith, he had attempted make dialogue with the divine. It was something very few had mastered whilst alive, usually only when they had met their mortality were most able to return to the Source and fully reconnect. Aldber had always hoped that one day he would be one of the very few, to be able to find direct connection with the source of existence and could realise his full potential whilst still alive. He could feel energy flowing through his body and was utterly calm.

He would get there in time and was sure of it.

After a short while, once respects were paid, he made his way quietly out of the room, passing others who were deep in prayer. Leaving the coolness inside the cave, he walked out into the late-afternoon sun.

'Well, well, well, if it isn't wonder boy back from his travels!' Aldber turned when he heard the familiar voice.

Suddenly, two sets of arms appeared, engulfing and hugging him excitably. It was his best friends, Tala and Dev. The three of them laughed, happy to see each other once again.

'Thanks, Dev, I was beginning to get suspicious about when you two would try and surprise me!' Aldber replied.

Dev, tall and muscular, with short black hair, was a typical trickster, and looked amused that they had managed to catch their friend off guard.

'We were going to do a more elaborate welcoming, but thought that after a hounding from the council, you might not be in the best of minds for it,' Tala said and shook her hair playfully. She was dark skinned with bushy corkscrew hair. 'Word of your arrival travelled like wildfire.'

'Yeah, it seems like there is no way of getting any peace and quiet for long in this place. I thought I would be able to get some rest before making my grand entrance,' Aldber said sarcastically. Dev rolled his eyes and smirked, giving Aldber a light punch to the shoulder.

'Come on then, you can tell us all about where you have been in the secret cave,' Dev said. Pleased to be together once more, the friends chuckled and Aldber threw an arm around each of their shoulders as they walked off.

The troublesome three had been reunited.

They collected towels and walked into the large main building that housed training rooms, the food hall, and medical facilities, and then took a stairway off one of the many stone corridors that led into the hillside. Down there, mining had halted, and various trails led off to dead ends. There was one hidden pathway that many did not know existed, which delved deeper into the side of hill. It was down here that the three friends ventured, aided by torchlight. They were heading for a cave that they had discovered many sun-cycles ago on their curious adventures, a hidden place the majority of the Galardros ignored.

Having negotiated through a small gap, they walked out into a large cave that had been created by water erosion. On the far-left side was a small waterfall, water that had seeped through cracks at the top of the hill now creating a pool that dominated the cave. From where they were stood circling around to the right was a beach of sediment. In the roof of the cave was a large crack through which sunlight shone down onto the beach. The ripples of water cast white reflections on the black stone wall and the sound of water echoed around them.

The three friends took off their boots and left them by the entrance before walking around the outside of the beach until reaching the water's front. Brilliant sunshine radiated down upon them. They laid down their towels and started stripping down to their underwear. Aldber found it discomforting removing his top and Tala winced when she looked at him.

'Aldber, what happened to you?' She looked concerned, pointing at his torso that was heavily bruised.

'I had an encounter with the Enemy when I was taking passage through the Old City. I was attacked by four of them and barely managed to get out in one piece,' he said as he threw the shirt down, before removing his trousers and sitting down on the towel. 'I have seen them before now, but never this close. They were vile.'

His two friends nodded, relieved to see him alive.

'When I was shadowing Silo Kai, we went far south into the depths of the city ruins. It was an unmerciful place,' Dev explained as he started wading into the cool water, splashing it with his underturned hands. Tala followed behind him. 'How tribes still manage to survive there is beyond me. I joined a squad of silo for three mooncycles. Thankfully, we had assault rifles to defend ourselves… from a distance.'

'How about you, Tala? What did you do on your travels?' Aldber sat up, hugged his knees and watched his friends.

'I travelled far north to the mountains and accompanied the Maluna tribe. Mowoni Goba showed me how he collaborated with the people. They were so welcoming. It feels like so long since the beginning of our training that I have forgotten what tribal life was like,' she replied.

Their friendship had started seven sun-cycles prior. Tala and Dev had come from their respective tribes for selection and instantly the three had struck up a bond. Aldber's friends had not returned to their native tribes since, as it was custom for trainees to cut ties and to swear allegiance only to the order.

'I travelled across the ocean and made my way to the Dakbah Mountains, on my way inviting unwanted attention.' He raised his left hand that was now scarred from the bite marks.

'You would have to, Aldber!' Tala shook her head in mock-disapproval.

'And what was the Eastern Sanctuary like?' Dev asked as he sneaked behind Tala, reached underwater and picked her up. To her surprise, he cradled her, and she threw her arms around his neck for support.

'Dev, *don't you dare!*' she said looking into his eyes with a warning expression. They had been lovers for many sun-cycles now and he still liked to play games with her. He then smiled mischievously, which she knew was a bad sign. '*Dev!*'

He then jumped backwards, and Tala let out a little scream as they submerged under the water. Aldber laughed, stopping momentarily because it hurt his chest. When they resurfaced, Tala took a deep breath and swept back her hair, before slapping Dev lightly on the chest. He found it all very amusing and waded backwards into the water.

Aldber then told them about the Galardros in the East Lands and his not-so-straightforward return journey. He then joined them in the water and gave himself a much-needed wash.

'When I was summoned before, I found that the atmosphere in the council was awkward. I know that a few of the councillors do not like me, but I could tell I had walked into something,' he explained. He splashed water against his face and rubbed the dirt from around his neck. 'And once I told them about Irelaf it suddenly got their attention.'

'Is everything we heard true?' Dev asked. The couple looked at their friend with dread.

'Unfortunately so, it seems like the island fortress has finished completion. There has not been much activity, otherwise. It is as though they are waiting for something to happen,' Aldber said sceptically, 'but, time will tell.'

'Well, I am sure it is something we can handle!' Dev said with his usual over-confidence. His friends rolled their eyes, shook their heads at his self-assurance, and laughed at his expense, before all three of them proceeded to swim towards the waterfall. Underneath was a ledge for them to gain footing as they bathed, and the water cascaded over them.

'In two days' time, we will be facing the final test. I am not sure how many other trainees have returned and will be taking it with us,' Dev said above the sound of the loud rush of water.

'I have heard rumours from various people about what it entails;

apparently we have to go deep inside the hills to face challenges. There are a lot of secrets hidden within this hill that people do not know about,' Tala replied whilst stretching her fingers under the flowing water.

'What like?' Aldber asked.

'I have heard that there is another exit out of this cave that goes somewhere out to the other side of the hills,' Tala said as she waded out and swam back towards the beach.

The two men joined her as the sunlight began to fade. Aldber looked up as he dried himself. It was colder as the late afternoon gave way to dusk, the translucent moon rested in the sky and stars were appearing beyond the pink clouds.

'Aldber, I would recommend you go and have that injury to your ribs looked at,' Tala said with concern.

'You're right,' he replied, pulling the shirt slowly over his head and feeling pain surge through his torso.

'Once that is done, let's go and get something to eat,' Dev suggested, as they all put on their clothes and started making their way out of the cave.

That evening, the three friends went to the food hall and had a meal together. The room had a high ceiling, so the acoustics accentuated the loud discussions and clattering of plates amongst the various warriors, assistants and medics. The same basic meal was served every evening from the produce farmed in the valley. It was the first thing Aldber had eaten since being in the silo base, so he received the large portion eagerly and soon finished it.

'Meet me by the pond when you have both finished eating,' Dev announced, much to their curiosity. He had a mischievous grin on his face as he stood to leave.

'How has it been for you two, having been separated for so long?' Aldber dusted off the last crumbs from his hands onto the plate.

'It was fine. We were given special permission to use a message bird to correspond with each other.' Tala pushed her plate aside and turned on the bench to face him. Trained birds were used to pass on messages between Galardros; this was a privilege usually withheld for those fully inducted into the order. 'Mowoni Goba let me use his.'

'Have the council said anything about your relationship recently?'

'We have been given several words of caution about letting feelings get in the way of our duties, but both Dev and I know what our priorities are. So, tell me, did you meet *anyone* whilst you were travelling?' She looked at him with an inquisitive smirk.

'If you are referring to *that*, I did attract attention from some girls in a tribe out in the Saboontai Desert.' He suddenly felt self-conscious and straightened up as to appear more formal. 'But I thought it was not appropriate and would be disrespectful to the elders to get involved.'

'Yeah, whatever.' She rolled her eyes, placed a hand on his shoulder, and gave a mocking headshake. She was like the sister he never had. 'You will get there someday, I am sure of it.'

'I know. Besides, I have bigger concerns right now, anyway,' he said looking around at the other people gathered, before whispering to her, 'I am starting to get nervous about the final test.'

'I am nervous too, but I am sure we will manage, as long as we work together as a team through it. But for now, let us forget about that all for tonight and relax!' she suggested.

Aldber nodded enthusiastically, and they proceeded to clear away their plates, before making their way out towards the pond.

It was a cool summer's evening and they sat by the water's edge. Small insects flew by as they waited patiently in anticipation. Soon, Dev arrived with one hand concealed behind his back.

'What have you got there?' Tala questioned and playfully pounced for him. He swerved as she attempted to grab what he had concealed. She stopped and they looked each other in the eyes lustfully.

'It is a little homecoming treat,' Dev said with a smirk as he revealed a bottle of mead. Both Aldber and Tala gasped in amazement. 'This is a little something I have kept hidden away for a special occasion.'

The three friends then took a path up to a small ledge overlooking the valley, out of sight, where they would not be disturbed or questioned. There, they sat and spent the evening drinking the contents of the bottle and exchanging stories. Their laughter echoed out into the night as the landscape darkened, and before them, the clear night sky was scattered with countless stars.

Chapter Four
Childhood Musings

The following day, Aldber awoke feeling puzzled and thoroughly dehydrated. Having collapsed onto his bed at some forgotten hour during the dead of night, he was still fully dressed. He gradually mustered the motivation to get up and could see that maids had let themselves in whilst he had been sleeping, as they had left a fresh towel and filled the jug on the table. Thankfully, he had not slept naked again this time, so had avoided an embarrassing encounter. He poured the contents into the bowl and started splashing cold water against his face, before drinking some to alleviate his throbbing head. The trainee peered out of the window, squinting as the sun shone down harmoniously over the valley. He presumed it must have been early afternoon, judging by the immense heat. Down below he could hear the distant sound of crowds chanting, distinctly coming from the direction of the training yards. Aldber staggered from his quarters, and made his way down the hillside, through the complex, until reaching a set of stone steps that led onto a large yard, which was paved with cracked slabs with grasses growing through. The yard was surrounded by a wall lined with trees, upon which were sat spectators watching avidly. Before him were lines of tribal children who had travelled from afar and had been escorted into the valley blindfolded so that the secret location of the stronghold could be maintained. They were here to take part in trials. They were separated into groups and each had to wait their turn in order to face a small series of challenges before having a duel against one of the established warriors. Aldber gazed along the perimeter and could see Dev and Tala perched on the wall further down to the right, so he walked around the outside of the crowds toward them.

'Feeling a bit tender today, Aldber?' Dev cackled, seeing the look on his friend's face.

'Dev, I am *never* touching that poison *ever* again!' Aldber sulked as he hoisted himself up onto the wall to join them.

'We have been watching this group who are doing the platform task,' Tala said as she bit down on a piece of fruit and nodded towards the small group in front of them.

The young hopefuls had to take it in turns to make their way across a course of small tree stumps. These were not particularly tall or far apart, and balancing upon them was relatively straightforward, however, the main challenge was negotiating over them to the other side whilst a Galardros advanced from the opposite direction trying to throw them off.

The next hopeful to take the challenge was a squeamish boy. The others behind gave words of encouragement as he stepped onto the first stump. Once given the signal to begin, he started to jump across the course, taking a trajectory with no clear plan. The Galardros launched forward, jumping across the stumps like wind passing through woodland. The look of dread was all too apparent across the boy's face as he landed onto a stump near to the edge of the course and froze. The warrior neared and jumped, but the boy managed to avoid the advance and landed on a neighbouring stump. The small crowd of hopefuls cheered, although their efforts were soon diminished, as the warrior quickly swung around and kicked the boy in his side, sending him falling hard into the ground below. The whole crowd winced as the boy starting crying in pain. The warrior jumped down to pull him up and gave the boy a few words before ushering him to leave the trials.

'I will never forget the day we went through this. It was brutal. I actually considered turning around to leave when I saw what I was letting myself in for,' Tala said as she watched the boy drag his feet; he looked humiliated and brushed away tears as he left the yard. She looked at Dev who was finding it all very amusing and gave him a punch on the arm. 'It is not funny, Dev! Some of these hopefuls might face being outcast from their tribes if they fail.'

'You are right. I should not laugh. I guess we could be in a much worse situation tomorrow after the test. Look, Councillor Hecta has arrived!' He pointed far off to the right at the adjacent end of the yard where the councillor was descending a set of steps.

The crowds parted way respectfully and became silent as the experienced warrior proceeded through. He was tall, broad-shouldered, wearing a weathered tunic and boots, gauntlets adorning his wrists, a broad sword attached to his belt. He had short brown hair with a small upturned quiff and a beard with patches of grey around the chin. Undeniably, his most striking feature was a scar beginning at the top right of his forehead trailing all the way down past his eye to his top lip, where a chunk of skin had been gauged out shaped like the estuary of a river. He paced forward, looking straight ahead with his usual frown and grimace.

The hopefuls he was inspecting had made it through all of the challenges so far and a duel with him would be their final trial. They were not expected to win, by any means, but at least had to show a level of competence. The first to step forward was a girl that confidently took the sword handed to her by one of the assistants. She gripped the blade and positioned herself, not shying away from gaining eye contact with the warrior. He unsheathed his sword and advanced towards her with a downward slice, which she avoided, and they began fighting. After a few minutes of duelling, Hecta stopped and put away his weapon before congratulating the young girl, and asked her to climb the steps behind him, where she would be given further instructions about training. The crowd behind her cheered and she punched the air with satisfaction. Aldber and his friends applauded her, as another hopeful stepped forward.

'W-w-w-well, if it isn't, Little Aldber!' a voice said. The three friends looked down and there in front of them were stood two peculiar individuals, both short and disproportionately shaped. The one who had spoken was hunched and had a gleaming toothless smile, whilst the other to his side was equally odd and had a look of surprise upon his face.

'Oh, hello there, Grombl and Maloyk, how are you both?' Aldber was pleased to see them.

'V-v-v-v-v-v-v a-a-a-a s-s-o-o-o-o g-g-good, thank you,' Grombl managed to say. Maloyk, to his side, shrugged and smiled. He was a mute. 'When did you c-c-c-come back from your travels, Little Aldber?'

'Little Aldber?' Dev interjected, and both he and Tala laughed. Aldber rolled his eyes.

'Grombl, please don't call me that anymore, you can see I am too big for that now,' Aldber said blushing. 'Anyway, I arrived yesterday afternoon.'

'The Sanctuary has been q-q-q-quiet without you, hasn't it, Maloyk?' Grombl said turning to his mute friend who nodded in response. 'We have been given the jobs of looking after the weapons in the trials today. Will you be t-t-t-t-taking part in the trials today, Aldber?'

'No, I am just spectating today,' Aldber replied.

'W-w-w-well it is good to have you back! Bye for now, Little Aldber,' Grombl waved, Maloyk smiled and they both waddled off. Aldber had to ignore the repeated laughter of his two friends.

'Those two... I don't know,' Aldber said as he looked on. The two oddities moved through the crowd, demonstrating their authority, as young hopefuls looked at them with bafflement.

Grombl and Maloyk had once attended these trials; they had failed but had begged to be given a role at the Sanctuary as their tribe had abandoned them. Grand Master Vivid had taken pity on them and given them roles as assistants. They were always working various jobs around the base, inseparable without fail. Despite how much they embarrassed him, Aldber had grown very fond of them over the sun-cycles.

His attention was drawn once again to Hecta who was now fighting against a boy who was quick in moving, confident in his mannerisms, with a degree of cockiness, and the weathered warrior was not impressed. The elder paced around swinging his sword, attempting to catch the young boy off guard. He seized a moment of distraction and kicked the boy to the ground, before raising his sword to the boy's chin and demanded that he yield. However, the boy did not comply, and raised his sword upward, which Hecta quickly kicked from his hand. As the warrior turned away and called for the next hopeful to come forward, the boy started reaching again for the sword and got onto his hands and knees. Hecta turned and saw this and paced towards the boy, and to the shock of the surrounding audience, kicked him hard in the face. The boy crashed to the ground unconscious, blood streaming from his nose. Hecta stood over him, breathing heavily through his nostrils as he tried to control his temper. Aldber had seen that anger many times throughout his younger sun-cycles, shared the pain of the boy, and witnessing the warrior's brutality suddenly conjured uncomfortable feelings and distant memories of his past.

He had known the Sanctuary for as long as he could remember, and as far as he knew, had been abandoned there, an orphaned child. As a baby, he had been looked after by the maidens in the medical rooms, who nurtured him, whilst Grand Master Vivid kept a watchful eye from afar.

One of his earliest memories was when he began to walk, and the maidens used to take him for strolls around the pond area. He remembered leaning over the edge, watching his own reflection, able to acknowledge himself, but more fascinated by splashing the water with his hand and warping the image. All of the Galardros who passed through the stronghold became accustomed to the young boy and he soon started to gain fond admirers, who adored his radiant smile, purity, curiosity and spritely nature. Once he was fully mobile, it was known that the child would run around the facilities screaming joyfully at the top of his lungs, playing games with his imaginary friends and causing mayhem. He liked to play pranks on Grombl and Maloyk, who were ever susceptible to the child's wicked ways.

Grand Master Vivid was adamant that the young child would be kept within the safety and isolation of the valley, until he was ready to see the horrific realties beyond the Paradimus Hills. Within this seclusion, Aldber had outlived the clasp of disease that so commonly claimed so many young. Grand Master Vivid took it upon himself to teach the child to read and write in both the Common Tongue and Ramasha, a privilege usually reserved for training Galardros. During this time, the wise old master started to teach him many values, principles, practices of worship and rules, one especially being that he was forbidden to go beyond the perimeter of the Sanctuary valley. But as is the case, young Aldber had a restless heart and curiosity that outweighed his self-restraint.

He would have been six sun-cycles old at the time. It was a cold spring morning when he ran from the main complex out into the fields at the foot of the valley. Over the past few weeks he had observed the patrol patterns of the guards, and once he'd found a window of opportunity, ran through the open area, between the spurs of the hills, and out into the grassy open beyond. He would never forget his excitement when he saw the Old City for the first time. Once he had climbed through the gigantic wall structure, he descended into the treacherous outskirts and spent the next few hours exploring the magnificent ruins. He was completely engrossed and oblivious to the dangers he was subjecting himself to. As the day went by, the sun went down over the horizon and he started to question where he was, and panicked, realising that he was lost. He could hear the distant howls of something monstrous and took cover. Weeping in his despair, he knew that he had made a terrible mistake disobeying Grand Master Vivid. A search party had been sent and at nightfall Bura Hecta arrived on a hover-bike and managed to find the child, who was shivering and distraught. The elder calmly collected the boy, wrapped him in a cloth, and returned him to the Sanctuary. But once they returned, he erupted and started screaming at the small child for his disrespect and stupidity. Aldber remembered seeing Grand Master Vivid, who looked disappointed that he had gone against his word. They had to sit for a while afterwards, as Aldber wiped away tears streaming down his face and had to explain what he had done wrong, whilst repeatedly apologising. Once he had been forgiven, he was brimming with many questions about the Old City, which Grand Master Vivid had to answer. Aldber's first encounter with the dangerous wilderness had nearly cost him his life and he had learnt a valuable lesson because of this. He would not leave the valley again unless authorised. And since that occasion, the boy had regular nightmares about the city ruins that made him worry about sleeping and cemented his anxieties.

The child grew up seeing Grand Master Vivid as a father figure. In his teachings, the wise and gentle leader showed Aldber many marvellous things a tribesman could only dream of. When the time was right, one day they sat down to learn a new skill that thoroughly shocked the boy. Aldber would never forget when Grand Master Vivid asked him, with a mischievous wink, to keep a secret, before revealing a tattered old book. In it he showed Aldber page upon page of translations, all from an unfamiliar and peculiar scripture.

'Aldber, this is no ordinary speech. What is written here is the dialect of the Black Tongue, translated as Bezurak, the language of the Enemy,' Vivid said, turning through the delicate pages as the captivated child watched. Until now, the boy had heard rumours whilst eavesdropping on conversations, he had seen Galardros returning from missions covered in blood, but he had never seen these beasts that he had heard so much about. 'And you are going to be one of the very few who will learn to speak their language,' Grand Master Vivid said, looking at the young child who was overcome with excitement.

To this day, Aldber was dumbfounded that the Enemy had such an advanced language and he could not fathom how the humans had managed to learn it, seeing as the only contact the two species usually had involved bloodshed. As he was to understand, this was one of the only things the humans knew about the other species and the rest was guesswork based on observations. What equally puzzled him was why Grand Master Vivid would go to such great effort to teach him this; it was something that was never explained to him, although he suspected that the master saw great potential in him. He would learn how to make howls and roars to replicate the beasts, and its authenticity would improve as his voice matured with adolescence. They would convene their studies in privacy, and he was under the strict instruction by Grand Master Vivid to keep these lessons a secret, which he adhered to.

As Aldber grew older, and started asking more questions about the world, Grand Master Vivid educated him about ancient civilisation, the dark times, the struggles of their people, troubles with the Enemy, and the great tale of Altamos. Becoming aware of these horrors made the boy thankful for the life he had been given, knowing full well that the Galardros had his best interests at heart, so he accepted their way of life without question.

When the boy became more physically able, Grand Master Vivid thought it would be time for Aldber to begin training, as he suspected that the boy could be the chosen one that had been prophesied many generations earlier by Altamos. The leader was adamant, having witnessed so much intelligence and spirit in the child, that he gave Bura Hecta the responsibility of instructing him.

The memory of being saved from the Old City reminded the orphan of Hecta's temperament and he had feared him ever since. Hecta was a reclusive and difficult man who many claimed was one of the finest warriors the order had ever produced. On the day Grand Master Vivid introduced them formally to begin the training, Aldber felt slightly awkward and Hecta had been somewhat reluctant, believing the boy was not worthy of such hopes, but out of respect for Grand Master Vivid, had followed orders. Aldber knew that he was not going to expect an easy time ahead.

On that first day, Hecta, in his harsh mumble, told the enthusiastic boy to follow him uphill to a stream that seeped down from the waterfall and meandered through a set of private quarters. There, Hecta choose a tree, which he then hacked at with his sword, before using his brute strength to pull down the stubborn trunk. He handed the boy a blade and they started removing branches until the trunk was bare. He then instructed Aldber to help him pick up the trunk, which was substantially heavy for him, and Hecta waded into the stream that rose to his waist. He hoisted his end of the trunk onto the opposite side before placing a few twigs onto the trunk, which balanced precariously across the wood. The elder then waded over to the bank and pushed himself up.

'Aldber, if you are to become a fearsome warrior, able to take on the forces of the Enemy and be victorious, then you must conquer yourself. The biggest challenge you will face in life is not those who oppose you, but to overcome the inner enemies. You must surrender to what is, accept and improve, before conquering whatever stands in your way,' Hecta said and then pointed to the trunk as the stream flowed rapidly below it. 'I want you to stand on this log for as long as I instruct you to.'

Aldber thought this sounded relatively simple, so walked forward and stepped onto the log, placing one foot in front of the other, his arms pivoting to balance. He walked out to the centre of the stream and then turned to face Hecta. The warrior then placed several sticks on his end of the trunk.

'You will stay on this log until I say so. If you attempt to cheat, and walk off until I return, these sticks will become displaced,' Hecta said sternly. Aldber nodded, looking down at the stream below him. He had not been taught how to swim and the water did not look particularly inviting. 'Mind your surroundings, concentrate and *do not* become distracted.'

Hecta then walked away and Aldber watched as he descended the hill. The boy did not know how long he would have to stand there for. He took a long slow breath and straightened up, finding a point of balance that was comfortable. In this position he would stand for several hours, looking straightforward, trying to ignore the rumble of the stream below and the cackle of birds overhead echoing into the valley below. The sun started to descend below the tree line and Aldber could hear his empty stomach making noises. The temperature began to drop, and he had to resist the urge to shiver. His fingertips wobbling as he maintained his balance. As pastel-coloured clouds painted the evening sky he started to feel weakness in his legs. Thoughts of resting and giving up began circulating through his mind. He started to resent Hecta.

Aldber's legs were aching so he went to reposition his foot, and, in that moment, made a miscalculation. He slipped from the trunk and scrambled for balance, before falling into the stream with a yelp of dismay. As he emerged above surface in a panicked frenzy, he attempted to scramble for anything to grapple onto, whilst fighting against the freezing current. Spluttering, he managed to find grip on grasses on the water's edge and pulled himself out onto the bank. For a moment he lay there shivering and looking up at the evening sky.

The boy cursed under his breath, thoroughly annoyed that he had failed, before getting to his feet to survey the circumstances. The trunk was still positioned as Hecta had left it, but all of the twigs had fallen away. He figured that he could place more twigs on either side and could get back on, making it appear as though nothing suspicious had occurred. He did so and repositioned himself on the trunk, feeling smug that he had fooled Hecta and would be able to get away with this minor mistake.

The boy would stand there motionlessly as evening turned into night. He had to control his shivering, his clothes saturated, and his breath turning to steam. It was completely dark around him; the stream was the only sound, above him the blackness penetrated by starlight.

When morning came, he was relieved when Hecta finally returned. He was invited to walk off onto dry land, looking noticeably sleep deprived and pale in complexion. Hecta walked over to look at the trunk before turning towards Aldber. He reached out and grabbed the boy's top, which was damp.

'Nice try, Aldber. Back onto the trunk for you,' Hecta said, not looking amused.

'But, Bura Hecta, I tried! It was too hard for me,' Aldber pleaded.

'You will try continuously until you have succeeded. You will find your true strength by yielding and not resisting,' Hecta said. 'When you lose at something, you must never lose the lesson. You either win or learn in life.'

'I don't know if I have the strength to do this.' The boy hugged his cold, shivering body.

'Do you think I have always been this way? You must fail before you can succeed. I am strong because I have been weak. I am fearless because I have been afraid. I am wise because I have been foolish.' The weathered warrior placed a hand onto the boy's shoulder and looked into his eyes. 'Do not let your past performance predict your future result. If you do not make mistakes, Aldber, you are not working hard enough. In order to overcome our fears, we have to challenge them. Clear your mind and attempt it once more.'

Aldber hesitated. Hecta gave him a nod of reassurance and then the boy returned to the trunk. He was thirsty, hungry, and his body felt weak, but he had no other choice than to avoid these sensations and would have to overcome this challenge. Hecta did not seem like the type who would let him finish a task half-heartedly. The bura replaced the sticks on the trunk and this time walked over to a large stone nearby underneath a tree, where he sat with his back turned.

Aldber took a deep breath and closed his eyes. He concentrated on the motion of his limbs, clearing his mind of any thoughts, was reminded of Grand Master Vivid's teaching of drawing from the Source, and became one with the moment.

Hours later, Hecta would invite him down off the trunk and told him he had passed this challenge, before telling him to rest. Not once did the elder smile at the boy or congratulate him.

A few sun-cycles passed. When Bura Hecta was not away on missions he would spend time teaching Aldber. It was on one spring morning, when Aldber arrived at a lesson, that Hecta presented him with a gift: it was a baby goat. These were usually farmed for their meat and wool, but this one had been chosen for a special task.

'Aldber, I am entrusting you with this animal. It is time you learnt about responsibility. You will rear this baby, feed it, and it shall sleep with you in your quarters.' He gave Aldber the lead. The boy knelt down and attempted to stroke the animal that timidly avoided his hand.

'Can I name it?' Aldber said excitably, looking up at the warrior.

'You may,' Hecta replied before turning to leave them.

Over the course of the next few weeks Aldber would look after the goat and they would become comfortable in each other's company. He decided to call it Bleat, a name derived from the sound it would make when Aldber presented it with milk. He became accustomed to the smell and it was common practice for him to clean the animal's faeces off his quarter's floor.

It was on one sunny afternoon that Hecta took Aldber and Bleat for a walk through the hills behind the Sanctuary. For miles these grass lands stretched. Once they had found a suitable spot, they took rest under the shade of a tree.

'Do you notice how your mind is often cluttered, that thoughts come and go?' Hecta asked, folding his legs as he sat down.

'Yes, often I can be doing a task, and something comes to mind that can distract me and can even change my mood,' Aldber said, joining him as Bleat grazed contentedly behind them.

'It is the unpredictable way our minds work. The key is to become concise with the way you think, to fully focus. With a little training, we can find inner calmness in whatever situation we may encounter. You must learn to observe and interpret your thoughts. The mind can play tricks on us,' Hecta said and then pointed upwards. 'Imagine that the sky is your mind's eye, and that the clouds are like your thoughts coming and drifting on by. These clouds can collect and block out the sun and cause a change in temperature, just like dark thoughts can cloud our judgments and change our emotions and outlook. With training, you can clear those clouds and create blue skies and warmth of perception indefinitely.'

'Is that something you have achieved, Bura Hecta?' Aldber said, ripping shreds of grass to feed the goat.

'I am getting better at it, but it takes dedication. You will reach a stage when you will be able to manage your thoughts without giving in to impulses. You must learn the ability to moralise and criticise your desires. We all have conflicted thoughts and competing needs. Just like having physical pain that can cause suffering, mental distress can be caused by the wrong beliefs and judgments.'

'Bura Hecta, what about nightmares?'

'Why do you ask?'

'Ever since I first went down to the Old City, when you rescued me, I have had a recurring nightmare about going back there, but in it I imagine that I see a crowd of people, whose faces I cannot see, and they are surrounding someone, taunting them.'

'It could be a reflection of your own emotions, Aldber. Keeping your irrational emotions controlled is not easy to develop. Our minds have been conditioned, so you have to unlearn certain things. It is our thoughts that manifest into everything we do, they are powerful enough to bring things into existence, for we manipulate our surroundings.'

'Does that give us the power to make anything possible?' Aldber asked. 'I feel like I could take on the Enemy all by myself!'

Hecta smiled at the boy's naivety.

'When I was a young idealistic boy like you, I lived with my tribe in the perpetual coldness and long nights at Volknard to the far north of the East Lands. I heard many stories about Altamos and the legendary Galardros. I wanted to change the world, so left my family and travelled here to join. But, as time went on, as I went through my training and was made a bura, I saw the bleak realities out there. The Enemy has a power you cannot imagine. I realised that I could not single-handedly take them on. What I came to see is that if I make a change to myself, I can then make an impact on those around me, and then they can make a difference to those around them. The repercussions of my actions would be like ripples in a pond. What I enacted then could help to change the world. But, just remember, Aldber - you can only expect the best of yourself. In my experience I have learnt that you cannot form too many expectations of other people,' Hecta became sullen for a moment, as if the memory of something long forgotten had resurfaced. Aldber was confused by the elder's abrupt contradiction and cynicism. 'There are many things in this world that can become true, but it all must start with oneself. Each morning we are born again and what we do today is what matters most. A tree does not simply grow in one day.' Hecta grasped a handful of soil and started letting the fragments seep through his hand onto the floor. 'You cannot judge each day by what you reap, but by the seeds you have planted. The Enemy thinks that they can destroy us, bury us, yet little do they know, Aldber, that we are seeds, burrowed in the earth, finding nutrients to grow, to blossom into something extraordinary.'

After their conversation, they started walking back towards the valley by the stream that sourced the waterfall. As they made their way back through the woodlands towards the Sanctuary, Hecta turned and abruptly took the lead from Aldber's grasp.

'You have proven that you are capable of being responsible for this animal.' He tied the lead around a tree, pulled a blade from his belt, and then said in a very forceful tone: 'Now, I want you to kill it.'

Aldber looked at Hecta, mortified as the blade was placed into his hand. He looked down at the goat that was oblivious to what was happening. The boy had become so fond of the animal and now could not bear to see it die.

'Bura Hecta, I, I, I cannot do it!' Aldber thrust the weapon back. Hecta shook his head with disgust before leaning forward, and without hesitation, stabbed the goat repeatedly. The helpless creature cried in agony as it collapsed onto the floor, before falling silent. Aldber launched forward and grabbed the bloody lifeless corpse, devastated by what Hecta had done. The weathered warrior wiped the blade with a remorseless expression upon his face, placed it back into his belt and frowned at Aldber.

'Boy,' the elder said sternly, 'if you are to become a true warrior, you must not create attachments. Death is a fact of life and everyone will meet his or her inevitable time. Clinging to those around you will only cause suffering, which is a weakness you must overcome.' Hecta watched as the boy hugged the corpse. 'Aldber, I can see it in your eyes — you have great fear within you. I know where it comes from.'

'Why did you kill him?' Aldber spluttered looking up at the elder, his eyes welling with tears and his bloodstained hands quivering.

'You must accept what cannot be changed,' Hecta said with a dry tone.

Possessed with a seething rage, Aldber screamed and suddenly threw himself at Hecta. The elder expected this response, grabbed the boy by the throat and slammed him down hard onto the ground, winding him, before kneeling down to look into the boy's glazed eyes.

'The greatest fear you have, Aldber, is that of being alone, of losing those around you, because of the deep insecurities you have about your parents and being abandoned,' Hecta whispered, then stood up and turned to walk down towards the main complex.

Behind him, Aldber rubbed his neck, regained his breath, and brushed off his tears. For a while he sat there gazing at the dead goat, digesting what Hecta had just said, and accepting the truth, however much he hated the elder.

With time Aldber tried to avoid fostering resentment and forgave Hecta for killing Bleat. As the personal training intensified, Hecta started to teach him sword-fighting skills, and put him through a rigorous routine. They would meet for many hours in the training yard and, over time, word spread of young Aldber's precocious abilities.

Many in the Sanctuary started to talk about the boy's undeniable potential. Once known as the little nuisance who would run around the grounds causing mischief, he was now being celebrated as something much more. There was mixed reception amongst the council, especially Thortatel, who considered Aldber to be a tool Grand Master Vivid had groomed to his undoing. There was some legitimacy to his opinion, however; Grand Master Vivid had always known something about the boy and was thoroughly pleased with the exceptional skills that he demonstrated and wanted to nurture the raw talent. Many started to speak once again of the prophecy. Aldber would soon be ready to take the trial to begin the formal training to become a Galardros. His relationship with Hecta had grown, and even though he still found the man to be intolerable and awkward at times, he was gaining his respect.

'Tomorrow you face the trials, Aldber. You have an upper hand compared to the other hopefuls, but you must never presume that you will pass through so easily. We must all practice misfortune. You must know your limits and where you stand. And, if you do not succeed, do not become affected and jealous. Always follow your intuition, be smart and be brave,' Hecta launched at him with his sword. The two danced across the yard, the shimmering sound of steel piercing their ears. 'Avoid your negative habits. You will not reach perfection, but practice will bring you close.'

Aldber somersaulted in the air as Hecta took a stroke for his feet. They clashed swords and then Hecta took a step back to acknowledge that the fight was over. Both of them bowed before walking to take a break by the side.

'Bura Hecta, I have always wanted to know: how did you get that scar?' Aldber asked, sitting down as Hecta rubbed the sweat from his brow with a rag. 'That is one mean claw mark you have there!'

Hecta was quiet for a moment; it was clear being asked about his scar aroused discomforting memories.

'This scar was not from a centauri, it came from the blade of a man,' he admitted. Aldber was dumbfounded. 'You have to realise that nothing in this world is plain black and white. We are driven to fight the Enemy, but do not be mistaken by the folly of man. It was many sun-cycles ago, when I was out in the deserts close to the Kraal Canyons; I had unfortunately stumbled upon the encampment of a group of bloodthirsty people called the Accursed Few. In Volknard we call them 'Strangelings'. These are mysterious and barbaric people with poisoned blood and mutations, who have no contact with the order. I was held hostage by them, and tortured, but managed to escape. I was tailed by one of their most prized warriors, their champion who they call the Skull. He was a formidable fighter, I have never seen anything like it, and it was like he was possessed by some kind of dark enchantment. I managed to escape but he gave me this scar as a memento.'

This was the first time that Aldber had ever seen Hecta look vulnerable. He was still evidently shaken by the ordeal. It was a reminder to the boy that however much he regarded the man in high esteem, the weathered warrior was not indestructible.

'Remember – you are not defined by what you think, or how you may feel, but by what you do and the will to act. You still have great fears within you, Aldber, which you shall overcome with time; it is something you can only achieve by yourself. Fear drives us all; it is what helps us to survive. You must manipulate that fear, harness the rage, but do not let it consume you. Anger gives you power, but it can also destroy you.' Hecta placed a hand on Aldber's shoulder and smiled, which was a rare occurrence. 'Good luck tomorrow, Aldber. I have great belief in you.'

Bura Hecta then stood up and Aldber watched as he walked away.

'Aldber, err, Aldber, will you snap out of that daydream!' Tala shouted.

Aldber flinched and looked away from the spot he had been transfixed on for a while. In front of him, Tala and Dev were stood looking up at him.

'Sorry to disturb, you looked so peaceful,' she said and started laughing.

'I was just thinking about my training,' he replied. He eased himself off the wall because of his chest injury and joined them. By now the crowds had decreased as the trials were coming to an end.

'Let's have a sword fight, Aldber. It has been a while!' Dev said and then threw his friend a sword. Aldber returned him a menacing smile. Dev then shouted to the crowds, 'Everyone, if you want to know how to fight, then watch two masters in action!'

Tala shook her head disapprovingly as Dev threw her a smirk. The two friends started to duel, moving swiftly, counteracting each other's advances, all to the pleasure of the surrounding audience. They laughed at each other as they moved across the yard. Several onlooking Galardros shook their heads with disapproval. Dev swung for Aldber and he ducked, the sword slicing a branch from a tree. They moved into the centre of the yard and by now everyone was watching. Dev lost his positioning, and in that moment of opportunity, Aldber kicked his friend's feet from underneath him. His opponent crumpled to the ground and they both raised their swords to each other's necks, whilst panting heavily. They looked at each other for a moment with caution, staring into other's eyes intensely, before they both erupted with laughter. Around them, the small crowd of hopefuls started to clap, which Dev was not pleased with. Aldber offered him a hand, which was reluctantly accepted, and pulled his friend to his feet.

'You know, I am always going to beat you, Dev,' Aldber said with a cocky smile, patting his friend on the shoulder condescendingly.

'Next time, I will win. You will see who gets the last laugh,' Dev retorted before throwing an arm around his friend's head into a lock, ruffled his hair playfully, and they both started to laugh. Tala approached and threw her lover a displeased glare.

The three friends then made their way through the crowd and walked away from the yard to enjoy the rest of their free afternoon together. They did not pay attention to several heckles coming from behind, as Grombl and Maloyk came barging through the crowd, thoroughly displeased by the shenanigans.

Chapter Five
The Final Test

The following morning Aldber awoke just after dawn, having resisted any late-night socialising to instead be sensible and rest well. As he was stirring, and his eyes remained closed, he listened to the soft flow of air passing back and forth through his nostrils. It sounded like the sound of waves lapping up against the shore, and in a moment of panic he opened his eyes. He was comforted to find himself in his quarters and not stranded on a beach once again.

A light rain fell outside, as fractured sunlight shone down across the valley. He sat there for a few moments in silence as the rain subsided, whilst listening to the fading patter of rain on the trees outside.

He decided to leave the quarters to stretch his legs. On the rare occasions that he did ever wake so early, he would go for a stroll around the grounds. It gave him time to gather his thoughts for the day ahead, and on this day especially he had a lot to prepare himself for.

The stronghold was quiet apart from a few warriors who were in the process of changing shift on patrol. Aldber walked down to the pond and stopped before entering the area. There, he spotted Councillor Kolayta. She was the only female on the council, was of mature age, wrinkled, though still beautiful, her greying hair tied in a ponytail, dressed elegantly in brown robes that were the ritual attire for a council member. She was sitting against the pond's side splashing water gently against her face.

Every time Aldber had taken this walk, without fail he had seen her performing this act. He was always inquisitive about this ritual she made, cleaning as if to purify herself for the day ahead. He watched her meticulously cup the water in her hands and rub it against the soft contours of her face, and droplets cascaded back towards the water's surface.

'Aldber, you know it is not custom to stare at people,' the elder suddenly said in a raised yet gentle manner and looked up towards him. He was astounded that she had noticed his presence. 'Come and sit with me.'

Aldber sheepishly walked down towards the pond and sat on the ledge next to her.

'Forgive me, Councillor, I was only taking a morning stroll and saw you sat here,' he said feeling embarrassed.

'That is perfectly all right, Aldber. I come here every morning to bathe myself before commencing my daily duties,' she said just above a whisper as she dried her hands on a small towel to her side.

'Why do you come here to do this?' Aldber asked, as he trailed a finger along the water's surface.

'I like to have a morning ritual. It is a way for me to prepare for whatever may arise in the day ahead.' She looked over the pond, watching as droplets of rain cascaded from the tree above and splashed onto the water's surface. 'Each of these water droplets form in equal weight, they cast ripples across the pond's surface in the same uniform pattern of circles. Just like them, we humans thrive off having patterns to associate with. We behave in loops, synchronise, establish connections, and bring a sense of order to the chaos. I find it so peaceful here, it gives me perspective.'

'It is far too early in the morning to be having an intense conversation,' he thought, looking over the water as he contemplated her words.

'It would seem that you must have a little morning ritual as well?' She smiled at him. 'To spy on people!'

'Say what you will, Councillor!' He smiled. 'Do you not find that these patterns can also exist in a negative way?'

'Yes, most definitely. We can often have negative habits that can manifest over time into regular toxic behaviour. That is part of our condition, to have these patterns of negativity that we need to break away from in order to grow. We do this through an effort of will. The first step is to acknowledge this behaviour and attempt to break away from the pattern. This comes with time and dedication. Self-awareness is important,' she said, looking at the young warrior. 'Do you know what one of the greatest lessons I have ever had may be, Aldber?'

'Tell me, Councillor,' Aldber replied enthusiastically. 'It is that you can have some form of power over changing what happens in the future by changing your attitude,' she revealed. 'But remember, there are many unpredictable things that can happen in the world, so you have to learn to adapt to them. This will only make you a stronger person.'

Aldber nodded, listening intently.

'Do you think this same rule could apply to humanity in our fight against the centauri?'

'How do you mean?'

'Perhaps our approach to the situation might be our undoing.'

'Most certainly, but it often takes a strong example in order to inspire others to do so. And a lot more than just attitude in order for us to overcome our enemies!'

'Yes, that is very true,' he said with concern and then looked across the pond as another droplet created a ripple.

'I am very pleased that you made it back from your travels safely.' She placed a hand on his wrist. Her expression changed and she looked into his eyes with sadness.

'What is it, Councillor?'

'Yesterday evening, we received news that the trainees Ral and Alejan will not be returning for the test today. So, it will only be you, Dev, and Tala, taking part.' She paused for a moment to compose herself. 'Ral was killed yesterday, attacked by the Enemy whilst returning across the Sprawls to the north.'

Aldber felt a discomforting shiver pass through his body. He had never been particularly close to Ral but had known him throughout their sun-cycles of training together. Councillor Kolayta had been very supportive, almost maternal towards all the young who she instructed. Losing Ral was like losing one of her own.

'Aldber, I want you to be very careful today. This test is not going to be easy and I know you have great potential. You have been one of the finest pupils I have ever taught,' she looked at him intensely.

'Just *be careful*. And once you have been fully initiated into the order, it will then be time for you to do what is expected of you: to fulfil your destiny.'

Aldber decided to reply with a formulaic response. 'Thank you, Councillor Kolayta, I will take your advice and do whatever is required of me.' He gave her a reassuring smile before politely excusing himself.

As he proceeded to walk around the grounds, he would think about Ral, about Kolayta's grief, about patterns, and most importantly about the impending task he was to face.

'No pressure,' he muttered to himself.

In the late morning he met Tala and Dev in the courtyard near to the entrance of the Grand Hall. They were deep in discussion when he arrived and stopped abruptly when they saw their friend approaching.

'Have I come at the wrong moment?' he said, pacing towards them, trying to restrain himself from sniggering at their apparent lover's feud.

'Hey, Aldber. No, it is fine,' Tala said quickly and gave him a hug, whilst throwing Dev a stern look.

'Are you ready for the test, wonder boy?' Dev punched him playfully on the shoulder.

'I am as ready as I'll ever be,' Aldber said confidently, whilst itching his neck. It was an unconscious habit he displayed when secretly fostering nerves. 'Did you hear about Ral?'

'Yeah, it is a shame. He was a good fighter,' Dev replied in his usual blunt fashion. 'As Alejan will be late, it leaves just the three of us to take the test together.' He then said in a dry tone whilst rolling his eyes, 'Lucky me.'

'Don't worry, boys, with my brains we will get through it with no difficulty at all.' Tala gave them both a condescending pat on the arm.

'Yeah, says she who is afraid of the dark!' Dev mocked and the two men started laughing, much to her disapproval.

'Judging by my recent experiences, I will probably land us in something stupidly, no doubt,' Aldber said self-deprecatingly. They all laughed.

'You know, I had a really restlessness night.' Dev became solemn. 'I did not sleep well and this morning I thought about my tribe, and my mother, of how proud she will hopefully be, and I thought about the ridicule I would be subjected to if I fail today.'

'Wow, Dev, that is actually quite profound for you,' Tala teased, before rubbing his arm to gesture she was joking, which he accepted, inhaling a deep breath to calm his nerves.

Aldber thought about his friend's poignant words as their attention was diverted to the far end of the courtyard.

From the Grand Hall appeared a small group of people; it was Grand Master Vivid and the other council members. All were dressed in their ceremonial robes, walking towards the three friends with grace and poise. The three hopefuls lined up in a row and made the salute. Once the elders stopped in front of them for inspection,

Grand Master Vivid made the salute, and everyone proclaimed the oath. He then gazed at the three trainees with admiration.

'Young prospective warriors, your training has come to an end and now you must face the final initiation test.' Grand Master Vivid stepped forward and went to each of them, individually cupping their hands in his own and giving a bow of his head. 'Tala, Dev, and Aldber. Please follow me.'

Grand Master Vivid led everyone from the courtyard and up into the woodlands away from the main stronghold. Aldber followed silently behind, trying to maintain calm even though his heart was racing, and his palms were moist. To his side, Tala and Dev were talking something amongst themselves, continuing their previous argument.

They walked onto a small open platform where stone slabs adorned the ground. In front of them was a ridge, on top of which was stood a large tree resting on the edge, its huge exposed roots slithered off in various directions. Below the tree was a large aged wooden door, standing either side were two armoured guards and one was holding a lit wooden torch. Here, the group stopped, and all the councillors stood to the side as Grand Master Vivid walked forward and welcomed the three trainees to join him. The two guards then pulled open the door and stood aside, as a large gust of dank-smelling warm air escaped from the dark depths within. The guards then approached the friends and searched them to make sure they were not armed or carrying tools. Grand Master Vivid walked back to join the other council members. Bura Hecta gave Aldber a nod of encouragement and to his side was Bura Thortatel, whose face remained motionless; his arms crossed over his chest.

The three friends looked at each other awkwardly before looking into the doorway. Aldber stepped forward and was handed the torch. He led them inside and immediately the door slammed shut behind them, they were immersed in darkness, and the torch gradually illuminated the new space. For a few moments they stood there breathing heavily as their eyes adjusted.

In front of them was a small room, roots from the tree spiralled down the ceiling burrowing into the earth. To the side were the remains of another trainee, all that was left were decomposing garments on a skeleton. This made the three friends gasp in fright. Aldber turned and looked at the door; there were scratch-marks and fragments of fingernails all over it.

'Hello there. You didn't get very far, did you?' Dev walked over and knelt down to inspect the corpse.

'I suspect he didn't like whatever was in there, retraced his steps, but was unable to get back through the entrance,' Aldber explained as they all examined the skeleton. 'He was trapped in here.'

'Great! So, if we don't make it through to the other side, we are done for!' Dev shook his head in disgust. He then stood, and looked upwards, as though addressing someone, and exclaimed: 'Thanks, oh, *wise elders*!'

'Our only choice is to go in and try to survive whatever the council has planned for us,' Tala replied. Aldber then inspected the room further and saw amongst the roots a small black circular glass bulb with a red light inside.

'Look up there, they have cameras watching us.' He pointed, and his friends followed his finger.

'They are keeping track of us,' Dev said as he went closer and tapped the device. Aldber then looked at the skeleton and rubbed his chin, deep in thought.

'On second thoughts, I don't believe they would have simply left the remains of a trainee here to decompose.'

'So, why is it here?' Dev asked, turning to question his friend.

'I presume as a way to deter us. It is part of the test.'

Tala, meanwhile, was looking at the roots above, touched one of them, and peeled off a waxy substance that was oozing down the wood.

'I have an idea,' she said, as she walked over to the corpse and knelt down to look into its empty face. 'Sorry, my friend, but I need to borrow this.'

Tala then pulled a femur bone out of the hip socket of the skeleton, to the puzzlement of her two male counterparts, before proceeding to rip her vest at the bottom and pulling off a large amount of material, which she then tied around the end of the bone. She then walked up to a root and doused the material in the waxy residue. Once all the material was fully covered in the black substance, she then dipped it into Aldber's torch, in doing so creating her own.

'You are always so resourceful, that is what I love about you,' Dev said, kissing her on the forehead, before leaning down to take another bone to make his own torch.

'I know.' She looked at Aldber with a smug impression, before rolling her eyes and shaking her head at Dev. 'I suppose I have to be, if I am *afraid of the dark*!'

'You two are just adorable,' Aldber muttered dryly, looking off into the unknown before them.

Once all three trainees had their own torches, they started to walk into a passageway that led into the hillside. They walked at a slow pace whilst exchanging anxious glances, watching the stone floor for any cracks, as insects and small furry creatures ran by their feet. The passageway led into a new room and they could tell from the change in temperature that it was a larger space. Dev then accidentally kicked a stone and it made a noise they could hear echoing out into the open before them. This caused all three of them to shriek. Aldber put up a hand to warn his friends not to move any further. He looked along the wall to the right-hand side and found a small carved trench in the rock. Inside was black liquid, which he assumed was a substance similar to what had fuelled the torches. He could see that the trench stretched off far into the darkness, so then put the torch to the oil and watched as it ignited, and the flame suddenly spurted off into the distance. It sped along the wall as it curved to their right, gradually illuminating the vast space ahead. Before them they could see a bottomless chasm, and on the other side they could see a large set of stone stairs leading up to five wooden doors. The flaming trail continued to spread, circling up the opposing wall, before coming down to the bottom of the steps where the flame met a brittle rope.

This soon burnt and snapped, unleashing a drawbridge that fell forward, giving them access across the chasm. The three stood there in amazement looking at the large room illuminated by the roaring flames.

They proceeded to walk slowly across the bridge and the wood creaked under their footsteps, whilst gazing into the abyss on either side, until they reached the opposite end, jumped onto ground with relief, and scaled the large set of steps. Once at the top they looked at the five doorways, all were open, although the friends could not see what was beyond. Tala walked forward to inspect them and decided to take the entrance furthest to the left. Suddenly, the door slammed shut behind her. Both Aldber and Dev vocalised their despair and launched for the door. They tried to force it open with their brute strength, grasping the seam of the door, but their efforts were in vain, and after a few moments they realised it would not budge.

'I can always count on her to do something like that. I think this is where we must all go our separate ways, Aldber.' Dev gave his friend a reassuring squeeze on the shoulder before walking forward to choose his entrance, before turning to face him. 'If you get into trouble, just remember to scream in that high-pitch sound like you always do and I will come running to save you.'

'See you on the other side.' Aldber's smirk was visible in the torchlight.

Dev proceeded to take the door on the far right, the entrance sliding shut immediately after him. Aldber stood there for a moment and gulped. As there was no indication of what was behind these doors, he picked the central one at random.

'Why do I get the feeling this isn't going to be pleasant,' he said dryly under his breath.

As he entered, the door predictably shut behind him and a gust of hot air followed, making the torch's flame flicker. He ducked and walked into a tight passageway that snaked off further and started to ascend on an incline into the hillside. Using the torchlight to guide him, he proceeded deeper.

Aldber eventually entered a large chamber with a high ceiling, the dark stonewalls were lined with burning torches and there was a damp musty smell lingering in the air. In front of him was a large stone maze, it circled around to either side and was too high to climb. His only option would be to enter it. He made his way inside as the walls loomed forebodingly over him. Below his feet were sand and small fragments of bone that cracked as he walked through, whilst the smell of burning oil emitted from his torch. As he made his way through, he used only his instinct to determine the direction he was heading in, looking back to see where the entrance had been.

Aldber neared the centre of the maze and stopped abruptly before entering, for ahead, and much to his horror, he could hear the sound of harsh heavy breathing. He stood for a moment and leant his back against the cold stone wall, before taking a fleeting glance further ahead.

There, at the centre of the maze, he saw the silhouette of a centauri. It was hunched over with its head bowed, its body shackled by large reinforced chains that were attached to the surrounding walls. Aldber put his hand to his mouth to prevent the sound of his cursing becoming audible. He looked once more. The beast looked like it had been tortured and starved, for its hairy body was severely cut and gaunt. In any other circumstance, if this was a human, he would have felt empathy and wanted to engage the captive, and he could have spoken to it, but all he felt was fear and indifference. The only way he would be able to make it through to the other side would be to pass the dormant beast.

The young warrior walked into the open, making subtle steps forward and holding his breath. He kept his eyes trained on the beast, which he assumed was sleeping. The trainee's heart raced in his chest and he could feel his body becoming warmer with the circulation of adrenaline entering his blood.

Aldber moved closer to the beast and reached the chains. In the foreground were three that were shackled to the beast's right limbs and torso. Further around, and near to the exit, were three more chains, which were attached to other parts of the beast. This system of shackling was the same on the opposite side. It was like a metal web. The first set of chains were suspended at different heights. He would have to push up the middle one in order to kneel down and step through. Holding the torch precariously in one hand, he anxiously looked over at the beast, before proceeding to lift the rusted heavy metal chain links with the other hand and pushed it up so that he could duck and pass through. As he moved forwards and lowered the chain back down, the chain wobbled, and the shackle creaked. Thankfully, it was not enough to disrupt the centauri.

Sweat was now dripping down Aldber's face and he had to take a few deep breaths to remain calm. All that he could hear was the beast's heavy breathing and the flickering flame of his torch. He walked towards the next three chains. As the beast was positioned leaning forward, it put more tension on these chains, which were strained under the weight.

Aldber walked forward, looked back at the dormant beast once more, and then started to push the middle chain upwards. He looked along the links to the bracket upon the wall, which looked rusted and brittle. As he applied more pressure it started to creak, and pieces of stone crumbled onto the floor. He slowly placed his first foot through, leaned under, being careful not to push too hard on the chain, and then swung around as the rest of his body went through. But as he performed this manoeuvre, the beast suddenly leant further forward. Just as Aldber stood upright facing the way he had entered, the bracket upon the wall gave way, snapped, and the strained chain went flying through Aldber's hand and collided with the beast's back, before clattering onto the floor. Suddenly, the dormant centauri stirred and looked around. In a split moment, it eyed Aldber and started spitting violently. Saliva flew everywhere, and its gigantic muscles tensed as it rose onto all fours. Its body was scantily clad in a tattered leather tunic.

The young trainee looked on in dread as the beast pulled with its almighty strength and the other eleven chains broke from the walls. Without hesitation, Aldber started sprinting for his life. The beast let out a ferocious roar, which echoed around the chamber, and started pacing after the human, whilst the chains swung violently in the air, cracking against the walls of the maze.

Aldber swiftly manoeuvred through the maze and could feel the breath of his foe on the back of his neck. The whole chamber erupted with the noise of the enraged centauri as it drew closer to him. The trainee knew he was very close to the end, making sure not to take the wrong turn that would lead to a dead end and almost certain death. But then he stopped when the roars ceased, and it seemed that the beast had stopped tailing him.

The young warrior looked around frantically, trying to see where it had disappeared to. The light around him dimmed and he looked up. High upon the maze wall was knelt the centauri, which let out a triumphant roar and was about to pounce. Aldber stood his ground, defiantly wielding his torch. They then both jumped for each other, as the chains flew around them in different direction, and in the mid-air collision, Aldber thrust the torch into the beast's overwhelming jaws, as he was engulfed, and they both crumpled onto the hard-stone floor.

Disorientated, Aldber felt his chest hurting and could hear the muffled screams. The torch was protruding from the centauri's mouth, the flames burning its throat, and the beast was tussling around on the floor in agony as the chains slashed against the surrounding walls. Without a moment's hesitation, Aldber got to his feet, jumped over the beast, narrowly missing one of the chains as it sliced past his head, and ran for the exit of the maze.

When he reached it, there was a reinforced metal door; despite being uncertain as to what troubles lay ahead, Aldber pushed it open, ran inside, and slammed the door shut. He could no longer hear the haunting screams of the suffering centauri.

Aldber was now stood inside a smaller room with a low ceiling lit by candlelight. Ahead was a wooden door and in the top right of the room was a surveillance camera; to his side he could see a small computer terminal screen. Suddenly, sand started pouring through cracks from the top of the walls onto the stone floor around him.

The terminal screen came to life and text appeared, which read:

'The door opposite is open. You are able to leave at any moment. The other trainees are in similar rooms. If you leave now you jeopardise their safety, as opening the door will unleash more sand into their rooms. You must make a choice as to when you think is best to leave.'

The text disappeared and Aldber understood it clearly. If he left now, he would sacrifice Tala and Dev, but if he waited for as long as possible, he risked drowning in this room. He could imagine that they would have received the same instructions as well. This was a simple game of cooperation and how long it would have to go on for was not certain. As all three had no communication with each other, he would have no way of determining their intentions other than if the amount of sand pouring into his room increased, which would signify someone had given in. All that he could do was wait. This was a test of endurance that could lead to death.

He knew that as more sand poured into the room, the harder it would be to open the door, so he stood by the opposite door and started pushing aside the mounds that were gathering. The sand cascaded down harder and was soon up to Aldber's knees and his attempts to partition the door had failed as he had nothing substantial to create a barrier. He looked at the screen repeatedly to see if any new instructions appeared, but it remained blank. He started coughing as sand particles filled the air and entered his lungs.

Suddenly, the flow of sand started to intensify rapidly. Someone had given in.

Aldber cursed under his breath, then composed himself as the sound of the sand gushing into the room became louder. As the space between him and the ceiling decreased, he attempted to climb onto the growing mound and balance himself. By now, the sand had reached halfway up the door, so if he did not make an attempt to leave, he would have no chance of escaping. He tried pulling the door, but it was jammed shut. Despairing that he might suffocate, he began smashing the door with his fists, cutting his knuckles repeatedly as the wood started to crack. His hands started bleeding and he let out a cry of frustration when a large splinter cut deep into a ligament. Without hesitation, he pulled the fragment of wood out of his skin and then returned to beating the door frantically with his damaged fists. Meanwhile, the flow of sand started to cascade at a faster rate.

Once a hole large enough had been created, he started to pull at the woodwork. Behind him, the sound of pouring sand was deafening. He started ripping segments off desperately as his fingertips bled. Soon there was a space for him to hoist through, so he mustered all his strength to pull his body upward, which was being dragged back by the consuming large body of sand. He grunted heavily as sweat and blood dripped from his hands and pushed his arms out of the hole.

'Help me!' he screamed.

Moments later two sets of hands appeared and started tugging desperately onto his forearms, but he was being dragged back by the weight of the sand and gasped in terror.

'*Come on*!' Aldber shrieked.

His two friends pulled with all their might, both groaning loudly. Aldber eventually burst through, and they cushioned his fall as they all fell to the ground. The sand started pouring through the hole and cascaded furiously onto the floor around them. Aldber got to his feet coughing erratically, which made his chest pain worsen.

'Thank you,' he managed to utter, gasping for breath. Tala and Dev quickly got to their feet, and they all took a few moments to compose themselves, hugged each other, and then started staggering away. There was only one passageway trailing off, lit by flickering torches, which led into the distance.

'I am sorry. I could not last in there any longer.' Dev looked at the other two who were both coughing profusely, whilst pulling shards of wood from their bleeding hands. 'I had to swim through a cave system in complete darkness. I nearly drowned and was disorientated.

When I entered that room, the sand stuck to me and I panicked. What happened to you?'

'I entered a maze where I had to fight a centauri,' Aldber replied. He looked over at Tala who was emitting a foul stench; she was covered from head to foot in dried brown excrement.

'I will not ask what you got up to, but it looks like you had an enjoyable time!' Aldber said, biting his lip to stop himself from sniggering. Tala threw him a very displeased look.

The three friends proceeded down the passageway and no one spoke, as they were all thoroughly exhausted. Much to their relief, they finally saw light further ahead, as the passage inclined towards the exit.

Once they emerged out into the open it was early evening, and a cool breeze and the racketing sound of insects met them. To their astonishment, they had arrived in a small grove to the side of the courtyard by the grand hall. Their attention was drawn to something that made them cautious once more.

Before them were several rows of cloaked figures standing in perfect formation, their identities hidden by hoods, each holding an upward-facing sword close to their chest. The three friends looked at each other, assuming this would be the final part of the test. They composed themselves and stood firm, expecting to engage in a fight. As they precariously walked forward, the hooded figures at the centre started to part ways and gradually the whole formation drew into two. Aldber, Tala, and Dev walked through cautiously, keeping their eyes trained on the cloaked figures. As the last of the formation parted, Aldber looked up ahead; at the top of the stairs looking down upon the scene was Grand Master Vivid flanked by the other of the council. As the three drew nearer, the formation of cloaked figures turned their way and resumed their position in rows. The three friends stopped at the foot of the stairs and looked up at Grand Master Vivid, who was pleased to see the three trainees had made it out of the test alive.

"Tala, Aldber, and Dev, you have completed the final test. It is with great joy that I can induct you into the order as Galardros,' Grand Master Vivid said loudly with pride, his voice filling the whole courtyard effortlessly. Behind him the councillors had mixed reactions. The three friends smiled at each other. 'A Galardros is a truly fearless warrior, and secure on every side, for his soul is protected by the armour of faith, just as his body is protected by the armour of steel. He is thus doubly armed and need fear neither beast nor men. To die in combat is considered a great honour that assures a place with the Supreme One. It is a rule that warriors of the order should never surrender. This principle, along with our reputation for courage, makes us greatly feared by the Enemy. You are now swearing a profound commitment to the cause.' The leader then stretched out his one hand. 'Now, Tala, please step forward.'

Aldber and Dev gave her a few words of encouragement as she straightened her posture and walked up the staircase, before being prompted to kneel before Grand Master Vivid as he produced his sword to perform the ceremonial gesture.

'I hope he knows what he is doing with that thing,' Dev

whispered. Aldber rolled his eyes and frowned at the remark.

'Tala, I proclaim you as one of the bura caste,' Grand Master Vivid announced, touching each of her shoulders with the cool blade. Having been given the highest rank, she smiled with satisfaction. The new bura stood up, bowed enthusiastically, and walking over to stand by Councillor Kolayta, who, inspecting the new bura's appearance and smell, refrained from giving her a hug of congratulation.

'Dev, please,' Grand Master Vivid continued, ushering him forward. Aldber gave his friend an encouraging pat on the back, as he ascended the steps and knelt before the leader. 'Dev, you have shown promising potential during your training. I have no doubt that you will be a fierce warrior. Taking into consideration your skill set, and how you performed during one of the most vital parts of the final test, I give you the honour of fighting on the front line. I proclaim you one of the silo caste.'

Vivid smiled at the initiated warrior, but the gesture was not returned. Dev could not hide the disappointment on his face at the announcement. He got to his feet with a sullen expression, remaining silent as he joined Tala, who rubbed his arm reassuringly.

'And now, Aldber.'

The young warrior took a deep breath and felt nausea manifesting in his gut. He could sense everyone's eyes were upon him. There was an unnerving silence. Tala, Dev, and the councillors all looked down at him with anticipation. All those sun-cycles of living and training here at the Sanctuary, and the big expectations thrust upon him, had led to this one pivotal moment.

Aldber painstakingly walked forward, each step feeling heavy to take, whilst looking down at the steps as he ascended. He glanced up at Bura Hecta at the corner of his eye, who looked at him with what the trainee noticed was a vague smile, the best that the weathered warrior could muster.

When reaching the top of the stairs, Aldber knelt and looked up into Grand Master Vivid's wrinkled and pale blue eyes. He felt like a little boy once again about to face a punishment.

'Aldber, you have done well.' Grand Master Vivid tried to maintain a neutral tone. 'You have exhibited great potential, and, although you have a reckless nature, and much to learn, it is with great honour that I proclaim you one of the bura caste.'

Aldber had been holding his breath and finally expelled with a long sigh of relief. To the side, Councillor Thortatel shook his head in disgust and said something unflattering under his breath. The new bura got to his feet, bowed to Grand Master Vivid, and then went to join his friends.

Below on the courtyard, all of the cloaked figures sheathed their swords and pulled back their hoods. Aldber noticed familiar faces in the crowd and knew this event would attract a lot of attention. Grand Master Vivid gave his sword to an awaiting assistant, and walked forward, as the assembled warriors looked up to him with admiration. The leader then raised the sacred salute, and everyone followed, proclaiming the oath, before the courtyard erupted with rapturous applause.

The councillors came forth to give the three new Galardros words of congratulation. Aldber could see that Dev was trying to hide his conflicting thoughts.

'Dev, you have been given a very crucial role. You will be on the front line fighting against the Enemy. You should be very proud of yourself,' Aldber said, trying to reassure his disgruntled friend.

'I am *ashamed* of myself! I promised to my tribe that I would get into a higher caste. I do not agree with Grand Master Vivid's decision in the *slightest*!' Dev said through gritted teeth. Tala threw him a concerned look.

'Dev, you have come so far and achieved so much,' she said rubbing his arm. This reassurance was not enough, for Dev turned away, pushed through the crowd, and stormed off from the courtyard. Tala and Aldber congratulated each other once more before she left to follow her upset lover.

'Aldber, or, should I should say - Bura Aldber?' said a sceptical voice from behind. He turned around to find standing behind him was Councillor Thortatel and the pesky Councillor Gilliad, who was tailing the other elder as usual. Thortatel looked down his nose at the new bura with a blatant look of contempt brandished across his face. 'Now, do not abuse this responsibility.' He then leaned forward, close to the young warrior's face. 'I shall be keeping a close eye upon your future performance.'

'Thank you, Councillor, I am very honoured,' Aldber said, bowing his head respectfully although frowning out of sight.

'Yes, yes,' Thortatel said with a suspicious look, before swiftly turning to leave. Aldber watched him and Gilliad move through the crowd. He could not fathom the reasoning of the man. Hecta soon approached, rubbing his hands together and nodding.

'I am proud of you, Aldber, but now you must show what you are truly meant to be,' Hecta said enthusiastically. 'After this ceremony all eyes will be upon you.'

'I know. I have much to do now.' Aldber smiled. 'Thank you for your training, Councillor, I am truly indebted.'

'I would not have thought that little brat I once knew could have turned out to be a fine warrior like you. I have even surpassed my own expectations. But I must say, do not thank me. It is my duty and it has been a pleasure.' Hecta bowed and turned to leave. Aldber stood there flabbergasted by the weathered warrior's generosity.

Aldber awoke in the middle of the night feeling disorientated. The moon cast a brilliant blue light over the valley and illuminated his quarters, where he was lying in bed. He could not understand why but he had an urge to go down to the Old City. Without another thought, he got up, put on his shirt and tucked it into his trousers, before pulling on his boots and jacket.

Outside, all was eerily calm. The dark sky above was clear. He walked down the passageway and headed for the docking bay, where hover-bikes were stationed. He found himself one, which was fully charged, disengaged the lead, and pushed the vehicle out into the open. He jumped onto it and the bike pressed down slightly under his weight, hovering just off the ground. He then fired up the engine, which made a low humming sound, before pulling on the throttle and sped off, down the hillside, and onto the valley floor.

Speeding away from the Sanctuary, the bitter wind clashed against his face. He meandered through the spurs of the hill pathway and out into the grass plains beyond. Before him stretched miles of flat land and in the distance, he could see the gigantic monstrosity that was the Old City.

Aldber relied on his intuition to guide him as he approached the ruined walls. He found a break to go through and descended into the city, which looked twisted and ghastly in the moonlight. He was drawn towards an old industrial complex. Upon arrival, he parked the hover-bike under suitable cover, proceeded to enter one of the old structures, climbed up the inside framework, and onto a catwalk.

In the distance he could hear the sounds of a crowd, synchronised like a chant. He walked out onto a gangway over an open area. It took a few moments for his eyes to adjust to process what he was seeing. Below him there was a large crowd of people circled around someone in the middle. The sound he had heard was these people heckling the person. He found an exit stairway and walked down to the surface and approached the crowd. They were all shouting in a strange indecipherable dialect.

Aldber started moving into the gathering and no one acknowledged that he was present, for their gaze was transfixed on whoever was in the middle of the circle. As he walked closer, he could see that ahead in the centre was a lone person. It was a cloaked young woman. She was crumpled on the floor, her face partly concealed by a hood, crying in despair, and trying to ignore the malicious taunts.

As Aldber walked up to her he could see that she was holding something closely in her arms below the gown. He approached her calmly, knelt down, and used his finger to gently lift up her chin. The moonlight illuminated her features as she looked into his eyes with dread. She was young, beautiful and vulnerable.

The crowds started drawing nearer and their chants grew fiercer. Aldber gave her a reassuring smile as tears flowed down her face and her lower lip trembled trying to enunciate something. She then looked down and revealed what she had been hiding. Aldber followed her gaze and shuddered. In her arms she was bearing a newly born baby. He recognised those distinct green eyes.

It was him.

Chapter Six
From Amongst the Shadows

Aldber awoke abruptly and bolted upright in his bed. It took a few moments for him to gather himself mentally. He was panting heavily, and his bed sheets were saturated with cold sweat. He got up, leant over the windowsill overlooking the valley, and attempted to decrypt what he had seen. This nightmare had reoccurred over the sun-cycles, but only this time had he finally proceeded further and approached the young mother and seen the infant. He had never dreamt of something that was so vivid, it seemed to hold something within it he could not presently explain and simply could not ignore.

His first day as a fully initiated Galardros had started awkwardly.

He poured water into the bowl, washed the perspiration from his body, put on his clothes, sat on the chair, and contemplated the nightmare for a while. The chants of the crowd were still fresh in his mind as though he could hear them out loud. The young woman seemed to have a familiarity although she was a stranger. The infant looked only days old, but he recognised the unmistakable resemblance to himself. He needed guidance in this matter, so set off from his quarters towards Grand Master Vivid's chambers.

Outside, it was a cool summer's morning, and birds were singing higher up on the hillside in the trees. Aldber passed several warriors who were preoccupied with their duties as he walked through the stronghold. As he headed towards the corridor, which led to the chambers, from an adjoining corridor Dev appeared. His friend instantly saw the look of urgency and concern upon his face.

'Aldber!' Dev exclaimed and was confused that his friend half-heartedly stopped to talk. 'Are you okay?'

'Hi, Dev.' Aldber read the look of concern upon his friends' face. 'Sorry, my mind is all over the place this morning. I am in a bit of a hurry.'

'Whatever is the matter?'

'I, err, had a nightmare again.'

'Like the ones you used to tell us about?'

'Yeah. I know this sounds absurd, but I need to talk to Grand Master Vivid about it.'

'Why?' Dev asked as he shepherded his friend to the side of the corridor to allow others past. He could see that Aldber looked reluctant and embarrassed to explain.

'This time I saw a woman. It could have been my mother.' Aldber rubbed the back of his neck sheepishly.

'Your mother? But I thought you don't know anything about your family?'

'I don't. That is why I feel compelled right now to speak to Grand Master Vivid about my past.'

'That is understandable.' Dev smiled warmly.

'How are you this morning?' Aldber asked, remembering Dev's reaction at the initiation ceremony.

'I am still angry, if I will be honest.' Dev frowned. 'I was just on my way to receive a debriefing.'

'Okay, well let's speak further later today?'

'Sure. I hope the grand master gives you the answers you were hoping for.' Dev patted him on the arm.

'That is what I am afraid of most.' Aldber smiled to conceal his nerves.

They parted company and he then walked further down the corridor towards the leader's chambers. It had large open archways and a steep bank to his right; from here he could look down the vast drop towards the valley floor. Ahead of him, two armoured guards dressed in ceremonial gowns flanked the large wooden door. Once Aldber had requested permission and the guards had made their enquiry within, he was let inside.

Grand Master Vivid's chambers had once been Altamos's living quarters when he had been the original leader. Nowadays, the structure was aged, but had withstood the test of time, considering the limited resources and skills they had to construct the premises. It was spacious yet minimally furnished: to Aldber's right was a seating area by a balcony that looked out over the beautiful valley below. Straight in front of him was a desk adorned with various contraptions, behind which stood a lavish chair, surrounded by bookshelves, where the leader would orchestrate his private meetings from, and adjacent were two smaller chairs for guests. To the right of the desk was a doorway that led into the master's bedchamber. It was from here that the leader appeared when he heard the main door shut. He smiled as soon as he saw who it was.

'Aldber, for what can I do the pleasure with such an early visit?'

He ushered for the young man to join him as they both took their respective positions on either side of the desk. The old man gathered his robes together and eased himself gently into his chair. He read the confused expression upon the young man's face.

'Master, I apologise if I have disturbed your morning meditations?'

'No, it is quite alright,' Vivid reassured him in a gentle tone.

'I had to come to you. I have had another irritable night of sleep again.' Aldber leaned forward and looked to the floor whilst rubbing his throbbing temples.

'You are still having those nightmares?' Vivid spoke with concern whilst twiddling the hair on his chin. Aldber nodded and slumped back casually in his chair, whilst looking listlessly into space.

'It was that recurring nightmare I have had for many sun-cycles. But this time it went further, this time I saw who they were chanting at: it was a young mother, she was clasping onto a small infant.' Aldber looked out onto the balcony, as he felt somewhat embarrassed. He then returned his gaze to look at Grand Master Vivid. 'I was the baby.'

'Very interesting,' Grand Master Vivid said, his eyebrow rising with curiosity and hands resting under his chin. He could sense that Aldber had many thoughts he wanted to externalise. There was a moment of silence.

'It got me thinking about things. Master, what happened to me when I was a child? Why is it I was left here as an orphan?' Aldber asked, before sighing deeply; this question had been troubling him greatly for many sun-cycles, like a heavy weight upon his shoulders, but he had avoided asking it until now because he simply did not want to face the discomforting revelation.

'I knew this moment would come eventually. You have always been an inquisitive boy and the greatest mystery in your life might be this.' Grand Master Vivid then proceeded to open a drawer and rummage inside the desk, out of sight, and pulled something out. All the while, Aldber watched him with bafflement. The leader stood up and walked around to join the young warrior in the second guest chair. 'Aldber, you must understand that I have never spoken about this to you before now because I wanted to protect you. I had to wait until the time was right.'

'I understand, Master, you have always wanted the best for me.'

'It seems coincidental that you should suddenly have this yearning for answers on the morning of your first day of duties as a Galardros. It could be a sign.' Grand Master Vivid brushed his white beard as he habitually did.

Aldber looked at Grand Master Vivid with puzzlement. He had tolerated the leader's vague and cryptic way of speech for many sun-cycles, but this was something bothering him greatly, for which he needed straight answers. Vivid could see the impatience in the young warrior's expression.

'I will never forget that fateful night when you first arrived in the valley. I had been taking my evening stroll, walking along the woodland, lost in thought and reflecting...' Grand Master Vivid suddenly stopped; he could see that Aldber was hanging on to his every word intently. He took a moment to compose himself before recommencing: 'I had been walking through the woodlands, when I had a chance encounter. You were delivered to me, an infant of only a few days old, wrapped delicately in a cloth, sleeping so peacefully. A stranger gave me the responsibility of looking after you. It was something, at first, I could not comprehend.'

'Why is that, Master?' Aldber asked anxiously, whilst sitting on the edge of his seat. He could see that the leader was finding it difficult to maintain eye contact and took a further pause to find the right words to say.

'You were given to me by a centauri,' Vivid uttered, evidently still baffled by the memory as he heard his own voice. A cold shiver swept down Aldber's body. He shook his head to make sure he had processed the words properly.

'Sorry, Master, I thought for a moment there that you said a *centauri*?' Aldber said, smiling nervously.

'That is correct,' Grand Master Vivid replied. He sat there silently for a moment, watching as Aldber digested the revelation. He could see the confusion manifest and eat away at the young man. 'The centauri delivered you to me, unharmed, and only said one thing; it pronounced, in its attempt to speak the Common Tongue, your name. And it gave me this.'

The leader revealed from beneath his sleeve a necklace; it was a smoothed grey circular stone that had been partially cracked. The remaining segment had a swirl engraving upon it, attached to leather. He passed it to Aldber, who studied the necklace meticulously, whilst looking utterly mystified.

'That marking you can see there on the stone is the symbol of the Genuba tribe. One that had relinquished its ties with the order many sun-cycles ago. It was only through my own investigations that I learnt of their existence. I did attempt to make contact with them, but they refused to acknowledge me.' He looked at Aldber who was studying every contour of the stone.

'Master, this does not make any sense! Why would one of the Enemy deliver me to you?' Aldber said with a sceptical frown.

'That, I have never been able to answer. I do not know the context behind how this came about, but for whatever reason, that centauri felt compelled to show compassion towards you, it put its own life in jeopardy and thought it was important to bring you to our safety.'

'So, the Enemy *knows* the location of our base?' Aldber said in panic.

'Quite possibly, although if the whole species knew of the hidden valley there would have been attacks since then. I sense this individual would not use that information against us. They went to great lengths, risking their own life in order for you to be kept alive, Aldber.'

Suddenly, all those sun-cycles of protection, the language training, the expectations, and the ridicule he had received from a few members of the council for, he presumed, compromising the secret location of the base and also challenging their views about the centauri, all made sense, because of this one profound event, which resulted in him being raised at the Sanctuary.

'What does that make of me? What does it *prove*?' Aldber looked up to Grand Master Vivid in despair.

'That is not clear right now, dear boy. Now is the time for you to discover why you were saved. I strongly believe that the roots of your past may help to unlock whatever it is we need to win this war.' Grand Master Vivid looked at him intently. Aldber was astounded. 'I have looked after you all this time because I knew there was something incredibly special about you, Aldber.'

'The prophecy?' Aldber uttered looking into the leader's eyes. Grand Master Vivid nodded. 'Do you think the Enemy knows of it?'

'It seems quite possible. For an extraordinary act like this to happen, they must have learnt of something.' Vivid rubbed his beard once more. Aldber looked down at the stone again.

'It does not make any sense why with that knowledge they did not decide to murder me.' Aldber sat back, rolling the stone through his fingers, and looked off into the distance pensively. 'I would have never expected one of them to act in this way.'

'There are many mysterious things about the world, Aldber. Let us, for a moment, consider the teachings of our order: all of the energy in the universe originates from the Source. It flows through us and we harness it for our own purposes. It is that one point from which anything can blossom, whether an object, or a thought, and the outcomes can be unexpected. We humans are not the only beings with the gift to make calculated decisions.'

'Wait.' Aldber returned his gaze to the master. 'Are you saying that the centauri can draw from the Source *as well*?'

'Yes, they can, as they too are a creation of the cosmos. They do not act solely on primal instincts.'

'What does that mean about them compared to us?'

'All living organisms have different levels of consciousness, which can be drawn from the Source, but the Supreme One has granted us divine right so we have a higher priority and state of being. All life forms are sacred, but some are more sacred than others. It is our right to fight for our survival and supremacy of this world.'

'How do you know that to be certain?'

'Because of the prophecy.'

'But how do we know that they don't have a similar prophecy? They are currently winning against us in this war.'

'It is highly unlikely that they have the ability for spiritual awakening or true connection to the Source. They are only rivalling us because of their sheer numbers and savage brutality. However, all of that will change and they are aware of it. If it is the case that they know about the prophecy, then how they responded to it is crucial. The centauri fear us more than may seem evident. If they have been made aware of the prophecy, they reacted equally by seeing its significance, and also in the opposite, by seeing it as a threat to their existence.'

'This centauri gave you this necklace as a clue. As though when the time was right, I would seek the answers to my heritage?' Aldber questioned, and looked at Grand Master Vivid, who maintained a neutral expression. 'Maybe, if I can find the tribe, I can also be reunited with my parents. Perhaps they know something, which could explain all of this?'

'That might possibly be the case,' Grand Master Vivid said as he placed his hands on the rests of the chair for support and pushed up his old body. He then asked the young bura to join him on the balcony. They then stood overlooking the deep valley. 'Aldber, we know very little of the operations of the Enemy. What we once thought were savage beasts are actually highly intelligent beings. It might be coincidental, but the council has calculated that your birth coincided with the beginning of the construction of the fortress on Irelaf.'

'Irelaf?' Aldber spluttered, looking off into the distance.

'It seems too coincidental to simply ignore. The countdown to the ultimate turning point of this war between our two species began around the same time when you were delivered here to the Sanctuary. You can now understand why I was adamant to teach you the Black Tongue in preparation, in case you were to be reunited with the centauri that saved you.'

'Then I must understand what happened, I must discover my origins in order to possibly unravel this conflict.' Aldber placed his hands on the stone balcony wall, grasping the necklace. 'I must set forth to find my parents.'

'Many in the council do not agree with my favouritism towards you, which I can understand, however, you have something within you, Aldber, something that is divine and good. I suspect greatly that the centauri know this as well. I made you a bura especially so that you would have the freedom to explore at your own convenience.'

'I thank you for everything, Master. I think it is now the time that I found resolution to these thoughts that have troubled me so greatly since I was a child.'

'Good luck, dear boy,' Grand Master Vivid said with a reassuring smile.

The leader watched as the young bura bowed and turned to leave. He then returned to look out of the balcony over the valley, and there he remained alone for a while, as a feeling of great unease surfaced.

Once Aldber had left Grand Master Vivid's quarters, he put on the necklace and concealed it underneath his shirt. He walked away from the leader's chambers and out into the gardens in order to evaluate the conversation. He sat down on the grass bank and pondered. His mind was congested; he had so many questions that needed answering. His heart was racing with excitement, knowing that he might have a chance to be reunited with his family.

He got up and raced off towards the grand hall, knowing that Bura Hecta would be the best person to speak to about locating his lost tribe. After asking several people about the elder's whereabouts, he was directed towards the training rooms.

Once he had found the one Bura Hecta was teaching in, he knocked, stood for a moment jittering with anticipation, and then entered, once granted permission. There in the room stood Bura Hecta with a small group of trainees who were doing combat training. The elder turned and saw the excitable expression upon Aldber's face. He asked his group to take a small break and ushered Aldber over to the corner to speak in private.

'Bura Hecta, apologies for disrupting your session.' Aldber tried to whisper, although found it hard to contain himself.

'What it is I can help you with?' Hecta asked.

'I have yet to be allocated a personalised code and need to gain access to the location files of all tribes in the West Lands. I have one in particular I am searching for. It is very important,' Aldber explained, looking around cautiously. Hecta saw the intensity in the new bura's eyes; he admired the young warrior's motivation but had reason to question his impatience.

'Wait until this session has finished and I shall show you,' Hecta replied. Aldber nodded and waited outside the room as the elder continued his instructing.

Afterwards, Aldber followed Hecta through the stronghold and into one of the resource rooms where several computer terminals had been installed. These were machines that pre-dated the apocalypse and had survived fully functioning. The operating systems had been reconfigured to suit the needs of the Galardros. The elder then provided the newly initiated warrior his own access code, which Aldber typed into the console.

'If a tribe is being guarded by a mowoni, we can keep track of their movements on a regular basis; however, if the tribe travels alone, only silo can give us updates that are not as frequent.' Hecta tapped a few symbols on the screen and brought up a large list of tribes, detailing estimated population, status with the order, and whereabouts. 'Which tribe are you looking for?'

'The Genuba,' Aldber said, looking down the list.

Hecta typed the name into the console and the large list whittled down until one result remained. Hecta clicked on it and a green map of the Old City appeared, segmented by a grid system, with a multitude of dots scattered across it, one of which was flashing.

'Their last whereabouts was three moon-cycles ago in sector nine. They have an estimated population of two hundred and fourteen and don't have any mowoni stationed.' On the top right of the screen Aldber could see the swirl symbol of the tribe, which was etched onto the stone on his necklace.

'Thank you, Bura Hecta.' Aldber abruptly turned to leave.

'May I ask why you are looking for this tribe?' Hecta asked over his shoulder. Aldber turned and had a broad smile upon his face. 'This is my family's tribe!' Aldber announced. Hecta looked astounded as the young bura turned to leave the resource room.

'In that case - you might be needing these.' Aldber turned around and saw the elder holding a pistol and blade. 'A warrior always needs to carry protection.'

'That is good point,' Aldber said and took the gifts. 'Thank you.'

'It is quite alright,' Hecta replied and patted him on the shoulder. There was a short silence. They both acknowledged how important this search was for the young warrior. 'And good luck!'

*

The young warrior grabbed his weapons belt from his quarters, before heading down to the hover-bike station where he signed a register to use one of the crafts. He chose his vehicle, withdrew the charging lead, and got onto it. As the bike had no navigational systems, he would have to use his instinct in order to find sector nine, but he was convinced from his past orienteering efforts that it shouldn't be too difficult to achieve.

Aldber launched from the station, meandered through the stronghold, down the hillside, raced off into the valley. The fusion engines quietly throbbed beneath him, whilst he ignored heckles from onlookers who were not impressed with his inappropriate speeding. The young bura dismissed their shouts and pulled down on the throttle. Way up high the surrounding hills were lush with green vegetation, the skies were blue and streaked with thin clouds, and the sun shone down harmoniously, painting the landscape.

He hurtled through the spurs of the hills and out onto the Great Plains, whilst recollecting his memory of the nightmare, accelerated, and neared the great stone and metal carcass of the Old City. As he entered and manoeuvred through the ruins, grazing pineer ran for safety as he drove past them. He gradually made his way into the heart of the old metropolis, and once he had found sector nine, he decided to go by foot, so stopped and parked the hover-bike under cover.

Aldber then started walking around the ruins, looking for any sign of recent human activity that could lead him to the tribe. He came to what was once a large industrial facility. The majority of the building had been blown away from an explosion; a chasm descended deep into the earth, up high there remained levels of the building that had been exposed. Most tribes this far into the city would stay below ground away from the Enemy, so Aldber found a loose cable that was suspended over the chasm, tested it to make sure it could support his weight, before sliding down it. He reached the bottom of the hole and landed on the dusty floor and then looked back up at the blue sky that was framed by metal rubble.

He took out his pistol and sheathed blade and proceeded into the dark depths. It was not far into his investigations that he could sense he was not alone.

His instincts had served him correctly.

Suddenly, a lone human appeared from a platform overhead. The figure jumped down baring a long pole. Aldber rolled out of the way to miss being impaled by the collision, as the metal smashed against the ground. The bura got to his feet in time as the being, whose face was shrouded by a scarf, started advancing towards him, swinging the pole violently. Aldber ducked, flipped to one side as the unknown person surged towards him, used his blade to deflect some of the swings, and then pointed his pistol at the face of the stranger, who stopped, panting heavily, knowing that one false move would cost their life. The stranger stood down and removed their scarf to reveal a man of middle age, his skin greased, hair dark, and stubble greying.

'What are you doing trespassing in our territory?' he questioned harshly and looked at Aldber with distain. 'We don't like any scum trying to get near us to steal our supplies.'

'I would not jump to any conclusions straight away, my friend,' Aldber said calmly. He then sheathed the blade and revealed the necklace. The man saw the recognisable swirl symbol. 'I am looking for the Genuba Tribe.'

'Where did you get that from? Why are you looking for us?' the tribesman questioned further.

'I have some enquires to make with your leader,' Aldber replied.

'Tough. We don't allow outsiders into our hidden dwelling.' The tribesman was evidently not one for straightforward diplomacy.

'Either you show me to your leader…' Aldber said and cocked the pistol, 'or I shall introduce myself. I mean no harm. I am a bura of the Galardros.'

'The Galardros?' For a moment they remained silent as the tribesman stared into the barrel of the gun. He then grunted and begrudgingly submitted: 'Follow me.'

'Thank you,' Aldber said calmly, and then holstered the pistol to show he was not hostile, but would keep a hand close by, in case the guard tried to lead him into a trap.

Aided by torchlight, they descended into the underbelly of the city, until passing through a corridor towards a guard-post where another tribesman was stood holding three dogs on a lead. The canines started barking furiously at the newcomer, and when he approached, they tried to launch forward to bite him, but were restrained. The young warrior remained calm as they were given admittance through a door into the dwelling.

They entered a large room and walked down a flight of metal stairs to the ground floor. There was the immediate smell of decay, dampness, and unease in the air. Around them were groups of people crowded around cylinder containers that were being used to contain fires. All the onlookers looked scared when they saw the new arrival walking past. They were all wearing filthy rags, and most were gaunt and dirty. He was taken to where large cloths had been draped to make a private area, where an elderly couple was sat on chairs upon a raised platform. Tribespeople were sitting nearby, preparing meals and ripping flesh off bones. Aldber proceeded to the two people, stopped before them, and bowed respectfully. They looked at him with caution whilst exchanging a few inaudible words with the reluctant patrolman, who then walked aside and stood glaring at him.

'I am Bura Aldber of the Galardros.' Aldber looked at the man who had a grimace upon his face.

'I am Manula Genuba and this is my wife, Layma Genuba.' The leader was old, his hair was short and grey, and his face was wrinkled. His wife was of similar age; her long hair held in a big arrangement. Both wore tattered old clothes. 'You should be aware that we do not ask for help from the Galardros.'

'That I respect, however, I have not been sent here for such purposes.' Aldber then took off the cracked necklace from around his neck and walked over to the leader for him and his wife to inspect. Manula looked at the stone meticulously for a moment with squinted eyes. To his side Aldber noticed that Layma recognised it immediately and looked at the visitor, surprised.

'This necklace once belonged to a tribeswoman of the Genuba. How did you get this?' Layma asked.

'This was with me when I was left with the Galardros as a new-born baby.' Aldber decided not to tell them about the centauri, as he wanted to hear their version of events. 'It was the only clue I had to be reunited with my parents.'

'Yes, I remember,' Manula interrupted. He stood up and shoved it into Aldber's grasp. 'The woman who once owned that necklace does not reside with this tribe anymore.'

Aldber was confused by Manula's belligerence. He looked at the necklace in his hand, feeling somewhat disappointed. He looked back at the tribal leader, who was clearly unimpressed. Layma gave her husband a look of firm encouragement. He saw this and then begrudgingly spoke: 'That necklace once belonged to Gaia Genuba. She was the wife of Erai Genuba. I suspect these two were your parents, Aldber. Your parents no longer reside with this tribe. I can do no more for you now, you must leave!'

The patrolman bearing the pole walked forward to apprehend the Galardros.

'But you must explain to me what happened!' Aldber stepped forward and the guard mimicked the movement with a grunt.

Manula shifted uncomfortably in his chair, exchanging glances with Layma, who gave her husband a stern glare. He then looked down to the floor and took a deep sigh, which he puffed through his nostrils, evidently riddled with conflict.

'Fine,' the tribal leader muttered and then looked up at the bura. 'Both Erai and Gaia came from separate tribes at a young age. He was a very able warrior. She was a fine seamstress. They found love and were married soon afterwards. In time they had a child, but soon afterwards the whole tribe was attacked by the Enemy and the child perished, along with many of our people.' Aldber stood there shocked at the news that he had a deceased older sibling. 'Soon afterwards, Gaia fell pregnant once again. Erai, consumed by grief for losing his firstborn, and in an irrational emotional state of mind, believed that he had not conceived this second child with Gaia. He accused her of cheating on him with another tribesman called Jax. Alic here's brother.' Manula pointed at the patrolman, who was stood there with his grasp tightening around the poll, looking at Aldber with a piercing glare. 'Erai challenged Gaia about this, but she and Jax strongly denied it. All Gaia knew was that, somehow, she had fallen pregnant. Enraged and unable to be reasoned with, Erai attacked and murdered Jax.' Manula stopped momentarily; he could see the reaction upon Aldber's face. To his side, Alic had bowed his head, mourning his deceased brother. 'Erai convinced the whole tribe and me that Gaia was evil, he persuaded me to have your mother outcast from the tribe. By this stage she was heavily pregnant, but we asked her to leave and nothing was seen of her ever again.'

The words hit Aldber hard, as though every utterance was a knife wound to his chest. It was all too overwhelming for him to process. He could feel a mixture of emotions, but was unable to control himself, and felt his whole body envelope in a wave of fiery heat.

Anger swelled within him. He clenched his fists, trying desperately to control himself, but he could not bear to contain it any longer and suddenly it erupted to the surface.

'You let a vulnerable pregnant woman go out into the wilderness *alone?*' Aldber screamed, spit flying with every word, his eyes ablaze. 'And you *abandoned her*, left her to *die*, to be *murdered* by the Enemy?' Manula and Layma cowered. 'What kind of vile and pathetic excuses for humans *are you?*'

Aldber turned around and looked at the large crowd of tribespeople who had gathered. They were stood frozen as the distraught young man looked at those closest in the eye with his hands shaking.

He understood now why the tribal leader had been so hesitant to reveal what had happened. Aldber turned to face him and wanted to dive forward and stab him repeatedly in the chest with his blade, but he rationalised, knowing that his anger towards the past injustices would not make any difference now. He started to breathe deeply through his nostrils, dug his nails into his clenched fists, and after a few moments composed himself whilst shaking as adrenaline pumped through his body. Manula looked at the traumatised warrior; sweat dripped down his face, his hands were held defensively close to his chest.

'What happened to my father?' Aldber questioned with a sorrowful frown.

'He... he... he soon left the tribe and was never to be seen again,' Manula uttered.

Layma stood up and walked over to Aldber and rested her hands upon his forearms. She looked into his eyes, saddened by the young man's grief.

'Aldber, I am so very sorry,' she said as her lower lip quivered, and tears welled in her eyes.

Aldber pulled his arms away from Layma and threw both her and Manula a callous look, before swiftly turning on his heels to leave. The crowd nervously parted ways as the young warrior stormed through, leaving them all feeling distressed in his wake. An uncomfortable silence hung over the room. The distant sound of his boots clattered against the metal stairway echoed through the room as the fires crackled nearby.

The young warrior climbed to the surface, still shaking, and took a few moments to gather himself. He could feel the anger burning inside, eating away at him, and corroding his judgment. When he went to find his hover-bike in the hiding place, he found that it had disappeared. He suspected another member of the tribe had stolen it. Unable to contain his frustration, he cursed repeatedly out loud and kicked at some scrap on the floor whilst trying to contain his anguish. Now he would have to negotiate through the city, over the plains, and back to the valley on foot.

As he walked away, little did he know that way up high on a building, and out of sight, he was being watched.

Aldber walked through the ruins and made his way north, retracing the path he had taken to get to sector nine. The sun was radiating down over the ruins, casting warmth upon his back. This did not alleviate his mood, as he was feeling thoroughly aggravated. His attempt at being reunited with his parents had failed miserably and he had not found the connection that had led to him being delivered to the Sanctuary by a centauri. He could not fathom how the tribe could have simply abandoned his mother and was dumbfounded by how his recurring nightmare had been so close to the reality. The revelation that he could have once had an older brother also was deeply upsetting. He knew that there could be a possibility that his father was somewhere out there, but this was a dangerous world and the likelihood of finding Erai Genuba would be almost impossible.

The bura progressed out of the Old City and over the Great Plains as the sun started to fall over the horizon. It was near to dusk when he came to the foot of the hills and entered the natural pathway that led into the hidden valley.

Above, the skies were darkening as the last remnants of sunlight hit the cusp of the hills. He stood there for a moment and looked at the stars that were beginning to appear whilst accepting the sinking feeling of sorrow and disappointment inside.

That emptiness he had always felt was all too familiar once again.

At this present moment, he wished that he had never asked Grand Master Vivid about his family. He wished he had never learnt the painful truth and understood why he had avoided broaching the subject for so many sun-cycles, because doing so had awoken suppressed emotions. Replaying the encounter with the Genuba in his mind, he was unnerved by his own sinister reaction. For a trained warrior who had been taught to show restraint, he had done the complete opposite, and all because of hearing the story of a mother he never knew. He had been caught off guard, exposed bare, and had wrestled his deep insecurities in plain sight of the tribe, leaving him feeling dejected and embarrassed by his behaviour. He hoped that he would not be disturbed by the nightmares anymore and could leave it all behind by trying to block out any thoughts and decided that in the morning he would inform Grand Master Vivid of his shortcomings and then would get on with his life.

Above him, the stars looked so distant, the faint light blinking like a candle dwindling in the breeze, like the extinguishing of his expectations.

Suddenly, his attention was drawn to his side as he could hear something rustling in the undergrowth. He peered into the darkness of the woodlands. At first, he thought he was mistaken, but then he heard something else. He could feel his heart starting to race in his chest; there was utter silence around him. To his dismay, from amongst the shadows he could see a large figure emerge. He grabbed for his pistol as, to his horror, a centauri appeared. It walked out on all four legs, looking docile in its approach. Aldber stood there, transfixed by the sight, as it began to speak:

'I do not mean to cause any harm,' it said in the Black Tongue. This was the first time the young warrior been close enough, and in the right circumstances, to fully understood the dialect coming from one of their kind.

'What?!' he questioned in the centauri's language. Without another moment to spare, he raised the weapon to fire at the beast.

'Aldber, wait!' The young warrior froze when he heard it pronounce his name. It looked at him, radiating peacefulness.

'What did you just say?' Aldber attempted to reply once more, although, understandably, his speech was fragmented and needed severe improvement.

'Aldber, please do not shoot me,' it said, raising a hand to defend its face, before pointing at itself. 'Do you know who I am?'

'How do you know my name?' Aldber said, gripping the pistol tightly.

'Your mother screamed it when she was trying to protect you,' it replied. Aldber's hand shook as he looked into the centauri's eyes. 'I am the one who saved you, who delivered you here to your people.'

Aldber didn't know what to do. He maintained eye contact with the centauri for a few moments before haphazardly lowering his weapon.

'How did you know that I would understand Bezurak?'

'I spoke to you first to see if you could comprehend what I was saying and, as hoped, you replied in my tongue. I knew there was a possibility your people would want to teach it to you after I delivered you here as a new-born. Because of the enormity of what happened, I am pleased they took the initiative to do so.'

'How did you know how to find me here tonight?'

'I have followed the Genuba Tribe for many sun-cycles, anticipating that you would visit them, with the intention of introducing myself. I saw you leaving their hiding place. Forgive me for following you here.'

'*That timing seems too good to be true*,' he thought. 'What is your name?'

'I am Hollow Moon. A female centauri. Many of my kind refer to me as Hollow Moon the Betrayer.' She then sat down on her hind legs, looking calm with a gentle smile. 'I have waited many sun-cycles for this moment, Aldber, to finally be reunited with you.'

'Why did you deliver me here?' He remained hostile.

'Because I knew there was something special about you, Aldber.' She could see the bafflement on his face.

'What happened to my mother?'

'Please, sit with me, so that I can tell you.' She gestured for him to sit on a nearby rock. He hesitated, but decided to accept the offer, whilst still holding the pistol firmly within his hand.

'All those sun-cycles ago, I was one of the highest-ranking warriors of my people. I was the advisor of our leader, the fearsome Black Scar. I birthed him an heir. I was one of the very few in his close circle to whom he revealed that the humans had a prophecy about a saviour.' Aldber took a few moments to digest what he had previously suspected.

'Your species *knows* of the prophecy?' Aldber asked, needing further clarification in case he had misinterpreted what had been said. Hollow Moon nodded.

'How?'

'That, Black Scar never revealed, he retained that secret even from me. He intended to hunt down the child and would have eradicated the threat. We never questioned how he suspected it was you who that child would be. When your mother was outcast from her tribe, I accompanied Black Scar and one other, and we found your mother who had just given birth. She was weak, desperate, and alone. I will never forget the look of fear in her eyes as she tried to protect you. I took you in my arms, she screamed your name and begged for mercy. And in that moment, something profound happened to me that I cannot quite explain. There was a change within me looking down at this divine and fragile being. I did not fully understand what this prophecy meant but saw that perhaps it did not mean the destruction of our people, nor any more suffering for our two species, but instead it could create unity between us. In your eyes I saw hope. I had an opportunity. In his wrath, Black Scar slaughtered your mother and I made my decision - I abandoned everything I had previously stood for. I paid the ultimate sacrifice of betraying my own people to save you, Aldber. I escaped and followed some of your warriors, who led me here to the valley where I knew you would be the safest. It meant leaving you with those who despised my people the most, but I knew they would see the most potential in you and could help you to thrive. I came across a man and delivered you to him.' She then smiled. 'I have waited patiently ever since that day to be reunited with you, Aldber. It fills me with immense joy and pride to see you looking so strong and healthy.'

Aldber sat there for a moment. He could not quite believe what he was hearing. All his life he had been taught to believe that the Enemy were uncompromisingly evil, but here in front of him was Hollow Moon, an exception, someone he owed his life to.

'What happened to Black Scar?'

'The leader was enraged by my betrayal and ever since then has had his best warriors hunting me down. I have been on the run with a small group of outcasts who deserted Black Scar, who equally have lost faith in his leadership, and also believe that the human prophecy will help to bring an end to the world's suffering. Believing that the child I saved that evening will grow up to save us all.'

Aldber looked down feeling overwhelmed. He then composed himself and spoke: 'Hollow Moon, I am indebted to you for making the sacrifice. I could never have foreseen something like this happening. It is all a lot to take in.' Hollow Moon then placed a hand on his arm; initially he flinched, before letting her do so.

'I can imagine, Aldber dearest. It is just as well you now have enough maturity in order to carry the burden of this truth. I would like to introduce you to the Outcasts, they have waited a long time,' she explained. He hesitated before nodding.

'I cannot ignore this feeling I have inside. Even though I did not know my mother, I have always longed for my real family, despite how wonderful Grand Master Vivid and maidens have been to me. Discovering that the tribe had abandoned my mother to the perils of the wilderness, and now knowing that Black Scar murdered her, all leaves me conflicted. I cannot let this rest; it will eat away at me inside if I do nothing. And I would let go of the attachment to the past if it didn't have such a strong connection to what is happening right now,' he thought. But again, he realised that thinking such things and giving in

to these suppressed emotions was going against what he had been taught during his training.

'You seem confused?' Hollow Moon read his face. He had never been good at concealing his emotions. Suddenly feeling self-conscious, he straightened his posture and adopted a more neutral expression.

'I do feel compelled,' he finally replied, answering her question indirectly.

'Then you must find resolution.'

'What do you suggest?

'Revenge,' she said with passion in her eyes. Aldber looked into them. There was a distant memory, and something buried deep inside that drew him to her. He took a few moments to reflect.

'If I was to hunt down Black Scar, I would be facing the impossible task of trying to kill the leader of your species.'

'You must do what you think is right, Aldber.' She then stood up and started walking away into the night, before turning to look at the young man, who was still evidently conflicted. 'Black Scar roams over the lands keeping a watchful eye over his armies. You could join the Outcasts and me. We could hunt him down and end this conflict together, Aldber. He is what is stopping this world from finding peace. You can avenge your mother once and for all. When you are ready, you can find us Outcasts in one of the largest structures in the northern outskirts of the Old City. We will wait there for you, dearest. It brings me great joy to see you alive and well.'

'I cannot thank you enough for everything you have done for me,

Hollow Moon.'

'It is an honour.' She bowed her head before walking off into the shadows of the woodland.

Aldber watched her disappear. He would sit there for a while contemplating what had just happened. On this one day his whole world had been turned upside down. It was hard to fully digest. In this moment, he was flooded with thoughts about the war, Irelaf, the prophecy, the expectations of his potential, his long-lost family, the Genuba tribe. All of it circulated around his mind like a maelstrom. All he could do with the intense emotions he felt was to channel them into something constructive. One thing was adamant, he could feel hatred building inside of him.

He was reminded of the conversation with Councillor Kolayta the previous morning about breaking out of cycles of behaviour and knew that he could not lie to himself anymore; unless he confronted these issues, he would never be able to move on and fully master himself. And in doing so, there was also the opportunity for him to finally prove his powers, by doing something that could claim a profound victory for his species in the war.

'Black Scar, I am coming for you,' he whispered, whilst rubbing the cracked contours of the necklace tied around his neck.

Chapter Seven
The Mission

The following morning, Tala awoke lying immersed in the arms of her lover, Dev. They had spent their last evening together alone, and now, as the sun rose over the horizon, she knew the time they had been dreading was finally upon them. She untangled herself from his arms, got out of bed, left him sleeping peacefully, and walked over to the window as the sunlight silhouetted her naked frame.

Since the initiation ceremony, Dev had been upset that he had not reached a higher caste than silo, but she had gently reassured him that he would have an important duty leading on the front line. Unlike the regular soldiers, his sun-cycles of training would give him the direct promotion of squad leader. She understood his disappointment, but always had an ability to calm Dev, even in his moments of frustration and bitterness. She had promised him that whenever she had the opportunity, she would find a reason to visit his sector of operations in the city.

Dev's uniform was placed neatly on the table; she took the combat jacket and held it close to her. It smelt of him and she pressed it to her nose for a few moments. She had to resist the urge to cry, could feel the muscles in her face clench, but took a deep breath to settle her emotions.

'Have you been awake for long?' she heard from behind. Tala turned around to see Dev stirring as he sat up rubbing his eyes. He looked at her holding the garment and could see she looked distressed. 'Are you okay?'

'Yes, of course.' She smiled and turned away to compose herself, replacing the jacket on the table.

'Come here.' He ushered for her to sit on the bed. She sat down and he put his arms around her neck and placed his forehead against her own. They sat for a few moments in silence with their eyes closed.

'Dev, promise me you will be safe out there?' She looked at him, her eyes welling with tears. He cupped her face in his hands and looked adoringly into her eyes.

'I promise,' he uttered and then kissed her on the forehead. She threw her arms around him; they then fell back onto the bed and he held her closely with his strong grip. 'All of those sun-cycles of training have now amounted to this. It is time we showed our worth as warriors. I know that everything will be okay.'

'I sense that this war is only going to get worse soon,' Tala responded anxiously. 'The council has been incredibly quiet recently, there is something they are not telling us.'

'Perhaps they are waiting for something to happen,' Dev said, looking off pensively into the distance whilst contemplating her words.

'Quite possibly,' Tala said, gripping his bare torso.

'Well, you have always been a very good eavesdropper, so I am sure you can use your bura skills to find out something,' Dev said playfully with a snigger as he anticipated her defensive reaction.

'What is *that* supposed to mean?' She sat up and slapped him playfully on the chest. They both laughed before she threw herself onto him and they embraced in a kiss.

Later in the morning, once Dev was fully equipped, Tala accompanied him to the bottom of the valley where a squad of soldiers was preparing to deploy. She stood to the side on the bank watching as he was introduced to the men and women he would be fighting with in the Old City. From behind, she heard a familiar voice, and turned to see Aldber running down the hillside towards them.

'I came just in time.' He smiled at Tala before going further down to meet Dev. He stood before his friend and inspected his uniform. 'Well, you do look very official, I must say!'

'It is about time, huh?' Dev smirked.

'Don't be getting in to *too much* trouble, now.' Aldber patted his friend mockingly on the shoulder, doing his best to be confident for him whilst also masking his own conflicted thoughts after the events of the day before.

'You have nothing to worry about. I have my trusted friend here.' Dev then pulled up his assault rifle and tapped it.

The two friends stood silent for a moment, fully realising their nervous humour could not distract them away from the fact that this might be the last time they saw each other ever again.

'I don't want to have to come down there to the Old City to show you how it is done!' Aldber said in a parental tone.

'You do talk a lot of...' Dev lost his trail of thought.

Their attention was drawn towards three similar-aged silo walking by, with whom they'd had benign brushings on several occasions in the past. Dev suddenly became tense whilst Aldber diverted his gaze to appear disinterested. The three stopped and turned towards them.

'What is this we have here? Eh?' one of them said with a mischievous grimace and a raised eyebrow. The other two flanked him with folded arms and aloof expressions. 'A newly-appointed bura coming down here from his higher position to stick his nose into our business?'

'What is it got to do with you?' Aldber replied dismissively.

'Yeah, what *has* it got to do with you?' Dev erupted and paced forward with his fists clenched. Aldber quickly intervened, created a barrier to stop his infuriated friend, and looked him in the eye.

'It is okay,' Aldber whispered, 'don't lower yourself to this gobba-mucker's level. We don't want to make a scene in front of the others on your first day of duty and do bear in mind that Tala is standing right over there.' Dev restrained him, stood down, and they watched the sniggering soldiers walk away. He then looked at his friend who smiled. 'Though thanks for covering my back.'

'Sure, you know that I always will do.' Dev loosened up and took a deep breath to calm his anger.

'Those three only want some stupid entertainment, so let's not provide it for them.'

'Why do we get ourselves into these situations?' Dev asked,

shaking his head in jest.

'I guess we just attract trouble.' Aldber then started laughing as he recalled something. 'Do you remember that time we were out in the hills root-picking? When you tripped and nearly got trampled on by that herd of hiluda? Do you remember that I had to drag you from the stampede and saved your life!'

'No, I don't recall that.' Dev shook his head.

'Oh, okay.' Aldber was confused. He gave his friend allowances considering the current circumstances. 'Just be careful out there, won't you?'

'Tell me, what happened with Grand Master Vivid yesterday?'

'Oh, yeah. About that…' Aldber said awkwardly. 'There isn't enough time for me to explain everything right now. I will tell you in a letter when you arrive at your post.'

'Very well.' Dev nodded, and the two friends embraced in a tight hug as Tala walked down to join them. The squad leader took a deep breath and looked at her, unable to find the words to say anything. She stood there with a vacant expression. He put on his helmet and turned to leave.

'We won't be missing you around here!' she shouted.

'Yeah, right!' Dev said cockily in her direction.

Aldber placed a hand on her shoulder. She grasped it tightly and they stood in silence. The squad started to move off in formation along the valley floor, away from the Sanctuary towards the entrance, and into the dangerous wilderness beyond.

'Tala, are you okay?' Aldber whispered as they watched the

soldiers deploy.

'I am fine,' she said, turning to look at him. He knew full well that she was deeply saddened. 'Aldber, you look like you have not slept?'

'Well, I kind of haven't.' He rubbed the back of his neck sheepishly. She looked at him suspiciously. 'It is a long story, so you need to sit down for this one.'

Tala followed Aldber and they walked back up the hillside towards the pond. She took a seat upon the rim with her hands cupped on her lap and watched as Aldber paced around nervously, surveying the area to make sure they did not have company. After a few moments she lost her patience.

'Aldber, what is it? What is *going on*?' she questioned. He turned and abruptly sat down on the rim next to her.

'Tala, I have not slept all night because yesterday I discovered something, something I know you are not going to believe.' Her eyebrow rose with intrigue. 'I had another nightmare and this time saw a young woman with a baby. I asked Grand Master Vivid about it, and he told me that when I was a new-born baby I was delivered here to the Sanctuary.'

'So, this nightmare you have been incessantly telling us about is *actually* linked to what happened to you as a child?'

'That is correct, and there is more.' He then looked around to make sure they were not being overheard, before whispering, 'I was brought here by a centauri.'

'Excuse me; I don't think I heard that properly. You said a centauri?' She looked at him with a frown of concentration. He nodded. She then looked dumbfounded.

Aldber then proceeded to tell her about the Genuba Tribe, visiting them in sector nine of the Old City, about his dysfunctional long-lost family, his mother being outcast and hunted by the Enemy, and being approached by the one who had saved him.

'Wait, you *revealed* the location of our base to *the Enemy*?' She tried to restrain her voice whilst looking around to make sure no one had heard her.

'No, she already knew it from when she first brought me here, of course,' he said sarcastically.

'How were you able to communicate with one another?'

'Grand Master Vivid has been secretly teaching me the Black Tongue since I was a little boy.'

'Well, I never.' Tala looked off into the distance shaking her head.

'Hollow Moon wanted to speak to me after all of this time. It turns out she betrayed her kind in order to save me, Tala, because she knew of the prophecy. The Enemy *knows* of the prophecy!'

Tala had to take a moment to grasp what he had just said. Perhaps his imagination had gotten the better of him and he had a mental impairment from the sleep deprivation.

'Ever since that night, Hollow Moon has been on the run from Black Scar and his forces. Now that I have discovered what happened, it is the tipping point, Tala.'

'What do you mean?' Her frown intensified as she looked at him.

'Now that I have made contact with a defector within the Enemy, this could be the opportunity for me to prove myself, to reach my full potential. This could be the chance to bring an end to this war before it escalates any further.' He looked at her with wide eyes and talked at a fast pace. 'This could my chance to fulfil the prophecy!'

'And how do you intend to do that *exactly*?' She cocked her head to the side whilst squinting, which she did when hearing something troublesome afoot.

'By joining Hollow Moon and the other defectors, I am going to track Black Scar down.'

She then lost her temper and looked at him rigidly. 'Aldber, have you any idea how *crazy* that sounds? You would be attempting certain suicide!'

'I have to do what I must.' He looked out over the valley, clenching his fist.

'What you have told me is *utterly outrageous*. The nightmare. The Genuba Tribe. Having casual conversations with centauri! Talking about the prophecy so self-righteously, as though you know for certain it is you.'

'Look, I know it is a lot to digest, which is why I had to spend the whole night sitting alone thinking over it in my head. But Grand Master Vivid told me that the centauri started building the fortress on Irelaf when I was born.'

'Really?'

'Really!' Aldber then looked off into the distance once more and there was an uncomfortable silence.

'I know you, Aldber,' Tala said slowly. He looked at her and could tell she knew. She read his eyes for a moment. 'If all of this is true, which I won't ever doubt because you are my friend and I trust you with my life, I know that there is more to this. As much as you want to prove yourself, there is something in the way you speak that makes me question your motives.'

Aldber shook off her accusations, saying, 'I do not know what you are talking about.'

'There is something far more personal to this,' she said, reading his face, which evidently always told the truth. 'You want to pursue Black Scar to avenge your mother, don't you?'

He cursed under his breath. She knew him so well. They sat there in silence before he could find a reasonable response.

'Yes, I am harbouring pain, Tala. The leader of the Enemy murdered my mother, and my father is nowhere to be seen. I want revenge. I cannot deny that. But, if this is also the opportunity to remove the leadership of the Enemy, to potentially end this conflict, then that it is a duty I must fulfil. The war is becoming unbearable at its present state, so drastic action must be taken.'

'Don't be so arrogant, Aldber! Just because you were brought up here and have been put on a pedestal, you think you have the abilities to do such a thing? Do you fully understand the enormity of what you are trying to achieve?'

'Tala, you are right, it is a crazy idea, but it is something I must do, okay?' She looked at the melancholy expression upon his face, which she had seen so many times before. He had always seemed slightly lost and had been raised to live up to other people's expectations. Tala understood that he needed to do this, as though his whole life depended on it. She sighed deeply and placed a hand on his reassuringly.

'Whatever you do, Aldber, as your friend, I will be there to support you.'

'Thank you, Tala.' He put her hand to his lips and kissed it and then stood to leave.

'Where are you going *now*?' She was taken aback by his abruptness once more.

'Thank you for listening, but now I must bring this to the attention of the council, immediately.' He then rubbed the back of his neck again anxiously. 'It is not going to be easy.'

'You don't say!' she said with pierced lips and a disproving expression. 'Do you want me to come with you?'

'No. I must face them alone. This is my wild idea, and if you come along and they disapprove of it, I wouldn't want to put you in a bad position.'

'I understand.'

'I will see you later.'

'Good luck, *wonder boy*.' She smirked. He returned the gesture and without another moment to spare, walked off. Tala watched him leave, feeling deeply concerned that she was about to lose the two most important people in her life.

Aldber ascended the hillside and walked around the base of the waterfall towards the council tower. It was mid-morning and the council session had only just adjourned. The new bura had gone through the discussions of the past day in his head repeatedly, and now had to articulate his plan of action in such a way that would be feasible to the council, without them questioning his sanity. Perhaps he should have confided in Grand Master Vivid beforehand, but he decided to not conceal this any longer from all of the elders.

He stood by the two guards who as usual remained silent and waited as the assistant came to enquire why he needed to speak with the council. He told the assistant it was an urgent matter of importance and she went to deliver the message.

Off on the outcrop, under the shade of the dome, he could see Grand Master Vivid talking to the fellow council members and nodding in agreement, when permission for Aldber's attendance was granted.

Moments later, the young warrior approached the council. He had always found this walk to be incredibly nauseating, as though the eyes of all the councillors were piercing through him judgmentally from afar.

'I can tell this is going to be fun,' he said quietly under his breath.

As he walked under the dome and into the centre of the circle, he was met with the usual uncomfortable silence. Aldber performed his bows respectfully to all of the councillors before facing Grand Master Vivid, whose inviting warm smile was always appreciated.

'Aldber, how is your service as a bura going so far?' the leader said with a curious smile.

'It has been very productive so far, Grand Master.' Aldber smiled, noticing Thortatel's grimace, which one day he would like to wipe off.

'To what can we grant the pleasure of this visit?' Grand Master Vivid looked at him with his humbled stare.

'Grand Master, Councillors, yesterday I had a chance encounter, and believe I may have information that could hold the key towards us winning this war,' Aldber proclaimed confidently. Taken aback by this statement, many councillors straightened up in their chairs. 'Having discovered the whereabouts of my tribe of origin, I attempted to be reunited with my parents, although, my efforts were in vain. Upon my return, I was approached by a centauri who identified themselves as the one who had saved me as a child.'

'Utter nonsense!' Thortatel suddenly scoffed and sat forward, his voice booming across the tower. He looked at Vivid. 'It is ludicrous that he was *ever* saved by one of the Enemy!'

'Thortatel, I have told you this for many sun-cycles and it is time you accepted the truth,' Vivid said calmly. Other councillors looked noticeably unnerved as well. Thortatel reluctantly sat back in his chair and gestured for Aldber to continue.

The bura then proceeded to tell the council about being reunited with Hollow Moon and what had happened on that fateful night so many sun-cycles ago when his mother was murdered. Understandably, the council were not best pleased when he revealed the Enemy knew of the prophecy, but Aldber stood firm and took their heckles of denial in his stride.

'She and a few other outcasts no longer swear allegiance with their kind. From what I understand, the leader of the centauri roams across the lands inspecting his forces.'

'And what exactly are you suggesting from all of this, Aldber?' Councillor Guan, a gaunt middle-aged man, interjected. Aldber swallowed with hesitation.

'Council, as I have made contact with defectors of the Enemy, I believe I have the opportunity to work with them in order to track down and remove the leader known as Black Scar.' He was relieved to finally say it. Thortatel spluttered, Gilliad to his side became wide-eyed, even Hecta was unable to retain his reaction and gasped.

'You suggest *conspiring* with the Enemy? Have you *lost your mind, boy*?' Thortatel laughed, and Gilliad found it equally hysterical. 'That is the most appalling idea I have ever heard!'

Hecta broke his silence: 'As crazy as it might sound, we must take into account that we have little knowledge of the hierarchy of the Enemy, or how they behave. If Aldber's sources are correct, he could uncover vital information for us to win this war.' Thortatel soon lost his humour. 'The fact that the Enemy knows of the prophecy tells me that there is possibly something beyond our understanding pulling the strings on this matter. It could be a sign from the Supreme One. We must be open-minded towards this situation.'

'I agree with Hecta,' Grand Master Vivid said.

'Really? So, you are *finally* going to do something once and for all, Vivid?' Thortatel erupted, standing from his chair and looked directly at the leader. 'You have been dragging your feet for too long now, Grand Master, and I can speak for many present, here, in saying that you need to take action because *enough is enough*!'

Aldber's fists were clenched. He wanted to dive at the councillor to punch him but took a deep breath and waited for Thortatel to take his seat once more. The young warrior watched him whilst trying not to let his anger manifest. Vivid was not pleased by the councillor's outburst.

'Councillor Thortatel, I have been waiting for the appropriate moment to act and believe this maybe it,' Grand Master Vivid replied. All of the council looked at him. 'Let us not forget that it is twenty-one sun-cycles since the construction of the fortress on Irelaf commenced. Coincidently, it was at the same time that Aldber here was born. We have known for many sun-cycles that tensions have been building. As it transpires, the Enemy knows full well the implications of the prophecy; they understand the threat it poses to their existence. We must not become fractured in our opinions and instead must unite to strengthen our resolve.'

'Perhaps you have too much faith in this boy.' Thortatel threw Aldber a dismissive look.

'That may be the case, but this could be the test he has been waiting for his whole life. He could remove this centauri they call Black Scar, which could change the tide of war in our favour.' Grand Master Vivid looked into Aldber's eyes. 'And can possibly bring about the salvation of our people.'

'But, to conspire with *the Enemy*?' Councillor Fukuro said in a disconcerted manner and sat forward to address the young bura. 'What are the motives of these defectors?'

'I think they have become disaffected by their own kind; they believe the prophecy could be a cause for positive change.'

'The prophecy was never clear as to *how* humanity would be saved,' Grand Master Vivid said. 'In an unforeseen twist of fate, we will have to go to extremes in order to achieve this.' The council sat in silence for a few moments, pondering what could lie ahead. 'Aldber, I order that you go on a mission, to accompany this defector called Hollow Moon, along with her fellow outcasts, to hunt down the leader of the Enemy, who goes by the name of Black Scar, and you have my authorisation to exterminate him upon contact.'

'Because of the severity of the assignment,' Aldber replied, 'I would like to propose having a small army on standby, so that if I do learn of his whereabouts, I can approach him with support.'

'Granted.'

Feeling confident, now that the council had agreed to his plan, Aldber then decided to push his luck, knowing full well the reaction he would receive for this request. 'And I would also like to access the forbidden chamber.'

'What?' Thortatel interjected, before turning to question Grand Master Vivid. 'How does he know of its existence?'

'Because I told him about it as a young boy.' Vivid looked at the councillor defiantly, before turning to face Aldber.

'Grand Master, if I can be given admittance into the chamber, there might be something in there that can help me.'

There was then a surge of discussion amongst the elders, much to Aldber's concern.

'Aldber, I must deny that request,' Vivid replied.

'Why, Master?'

'Because,' Hecta interrupted, 'there are many things kept within it which should not see the light of day. Hence the name.'

'And it is written within the code of the order that only those who have a seat upon the council may be allowed access into the chamber. Because you do not serve such a rank, this cannot happen. Leave us now, you will receive further instructions shortly.'

'Right you are, Master, and thank you.' Aldber bowed. Despite his last request not being allowed, this could not overshadow what else had happened. He could not believe it.

The young warrior could see Councillor Thortatel glaring at him with disapproval, as he turned on his heels and promptly left the council tower.

Aldber walked down towards the main complex replaying thoughts of the meeting in his mind once more. He was utterly baffled by Councillor Thortatel's attitude; he could not fathom why the elder had been so vulgar and disrespectful towards Grand Master Vivid. However, he would have to show the elder tolerance and patience, knowing that innately they were similar, even when on the surface the councillor was showing him so much unwarranted hostility. It made Aldber question whether Thortatel's behaviour was not as much about him, but more about the elder's own issues.

The new bura had not eaten or slept for a day, so decided to go back to his quarters to rest. When he entered, he removed his clothing and lowed himself onto the bed, still feeling pain in his chest. As much as he felt restless, and eagerly compelled to set off, he knew that his body needed rest. He then drifted into a light slumber and the image of Hollow Moon's comforting eyes was the last thing he remembered.

It was late into the afternoon when he woke. It was a hot summer's day and he was covered in sweat and smelt badly of body odour. He walked up the hill to the pool at the base of the waterfall and bathed before drying off and heading to the food hall to settle the squelching sensation inside his stomach with some much-needed sustenance.

Finally, feeling revitalised, Aldber went to Grand Master Vivid's chambers and was given permission to enter. Inside, he found the leader along with Bura Hecta, who were sat at either side of the table in deep discussion. Aldber could sense the tension when he walked in.

'Aldber, I hope you are ready to proceed?' Grand Master Vivid gestured for him to take a seat.

'Yes, Master.' Aldber sat and exchanged looks with Hecta whose face was typically stern.

'This mission you are about to go on is not going to be easy. You must ensure that no information about the order is disclosed with these outcasts. They may be helpful, but don't forget they are still part of the Enemy,' Hecta said with caution.

'I understand. I will maintain vigilance at all times.'

'Come, you must be equipped before leaving.' Grand Master Vivid walked from behind the table and they followed him out of the chamber.

They walked out of the corridor and took a passageway that led higher into the canopy of the trees. Aldber could see that they were heading for a small tower that stood alone from the rest of the stronghold. As they neared, Aldber could hear the distinct sound of birds squawking. Upon entry, he saw large message birds sat on pegs that circled around the room. They were all preoccupied with feeding or washing themselves and weren't bothered by the new arrivals. Grand Master Vivid approached one. It was an elegant creature; its feathers were dark and shiny, and it had a long beak and deep golden eyes. It jumped onto Grand Master Vivid's arm when summoned and flapped its wings before finding a comfortable perch.

'Aldber, this is Heratu. Isn't she beautiful? Such an incredibly agile and fearless creature.' The leader stroked its small head. 'She can spot prey from a great distance. She will serve you as a means to communicate with us here.'

Under each bird's head was fitted a small pouch where notes could be stored. Aldber raised his arm invitingly and Grand Master Vivid prompted the bird to hop over. The young warrior looked at Heratu for a few moments, marvelling at her powerful wings. The bird looked up at Aldber, cocked its head, picked up his scent, and then it took off and flew out of the tower.

They then proceeded towards the armoury where Aldber was given more ammunition for his pistol, along with a couple of grenades, which he attached onto the rear of his weapon's belt. He was given a luggage rucksack containing rations and bedding that he slung over his shoulder.

He then went to the prayer cave and spent time alone in deep meditation. Whilst there he called out to the Supreme One, asking for protection and good fortunes in order to complete his mission. Although there was no response, in good faith he accepted the way that the divine worked and knew that this task was what his whole life had been leading toward in order to unleash his full potential. He was adamant that in time he would be able to draw limitless power from the Source in order to succeed in his desperate mission.

This is what he had been born to do.

He re-joined Grand Master Vivid and Hecta and they walked towards the bottom of the valley, where a warrior was waiting on a hover-bike to escort the bura to the outskirts of the Old City. As Aldber was about to leave he could see Tala running down the hill. She came towards him and threw her arms around his neck in a tight embrace.

'I cannot believe you are actually doing this. Aldber, *be careful* and keep in contact. If there is anything I can do, just let me know.' She looked into his eyes with concern.

'Thank you, Tala.' He gave her a light kiss on the cheek. 'Please, don't worry about me.'

He then turned to mount the hover-bike and looked back at Tala, Grand Master Vivid and Bura Hecta. These people were like family to him and he was not sure if he would ever see them again. He maintained eye contact with Vivid as the bike started to take off. They soon became a blur upon the horizon.

'Grand Master Vivid, what happens if Aldber does not succeed in his task?' Tala said turning to look at the leader.

'We must have faith that the Supreme One has a master-plan that will reveal itself in good time, Tala.' Grand Master Vivid crossed his arms, watching the hover-bike entering the spurs of the hills in the distance. 'There is no going back from here.'

'The path that Aldber is taking is treacherous.' She looked at both Vivid and Hecta with frustration.

'He must do whatever is necessary,' Grand Master Vivid said and exchanged concerned looks with Bura Hecta as they returned towards the main stronghold.

It was near to nightfall when Aldber was dropped off at the outskirts of the city ruins. Pale moonlight illuminated the landscape. Once the driver was pleased that they were in a safe area to stop, Aldber jumped off and watched as the hover-bike raced off across the Great Plains and back towards the hills.

The young warrior scaled the city wall and made his way into the depths of the fallen metropolis. He would spend the next few hours attempting to find the skyscraper Hollow Moon had described, assuming that it would be located close to sector nine where she had first spotted him the day before.

The skies above were cut with clouds; there was bitterness to the wind. In the distance he could hear screams echoing through the streets. He passed through, gripping his pistol, and walked along the outskirts of the city wall, heading northwest.

Eventually, he came to a series of tall skyscrapers. One of them matched the description; it was magnificent in its height, looming higher than those that surrounded it.

'Well, you have certainly outdone yourself this time,' he said self-deprecatingly under his breath.

He entered the building and started to climb the interior. The majority of the internal structure was intact, however, he had to climb some of the framework where levels of the building had collapsed. He was guided by moonlight that spilled through the windows and cracks in the structure. He knew he was near the top because he could hear the deafening wind getting louder as he drew nearer. His heart was racing in his chest and he felt nauseous.

As he emerged, he saw that above him the roof had fallen through and the night's sky was riddled with brilliant stars. Around him the walls were crumbled ruins. Before him was a small group of centauri who all were preoccupied with a meal that they had prepared on a large fire in the centre. One looked up when it saw the new arrival and soon stood on its hind legs and approached him. It was Hollow Moon.

'Aldber, I am so glad to see you!' She came over to him and, to his dismay, grabbed him, enveloping him in her furry arms. She held him tightly in a hug, placed her chin against his head affectionately, and rocked him in her arms as his feet dangled away from the floor.

'Hello, Hollow Moon,' he managed to enunciate, suffocated by her tight grip whilst trying to pat her arm with his hand that had limited mobility. She could hear that he was discomforted.

'Sorry, Aldber.' She put him down and he knelt forward, taking a moment to regain his breath.

'It is okay,' he said, standing upright, just as she released a gigantic belch. Saliva and a waft of horrendous bad breath hit him, nearly taking him off his feet. He closed his eyes as drips of saliva fell onto his hair and shoulders, and immediately wished to retract the previous comment.

'I am so pleased you decided to come. The Outcasts have waited for so many sun-cycles to finally meet you.' She looked at him with a warm smile.

Hollow Moon then moved to the side, allowing him to proceed towards the fire, where in front of him five centauri circled the flames. Aldber had to resist the natural instinct to reach for his weapon. They all looked at him with bafflement and started to get up onto their all fours to welcome him. The visitor did his best to attempt a smile, however, was understandably nervous beyond compare. Hollow Moon walked by his side.

'Fellow Outcasts, I am honoured to introduce you to Aldber.' They all nodded in unison. Aldber reciprocated. 'This, here, is Flying Stone.' She pointed at the one closest who grunted in an uninterested manner. Hollow Moon leaned over to whisper in his ear: 'I would not take it personally, for he is like that with everyone,' before gesturing to another. 'This is Long Wing.' The centauri stepped forward. From

Aldber's inclination and judging by the length of its mane, he guessed it was a female.

'Aldber, welcome,' she said.

'Here are the brothers, Singing Eye and Bleeding Sky,' the outcast's leader continued. There were stood two centauri who were smaller than everyone else and were almost identical in appearance. Aldber assumed they were the youngest as well. He was then led around the fire to the final Outcast.

'And finally, may I introduce you to Red River.' In front of him was stood an aged centauri. Most of his fur was grey and both of his eyes looked swollen, the lower eyelids drooping and red from infection.

'Here you are at last; it has been worth the wait. It is an honour,' Red River said slowly, wheezing with old age.

By now Aldber was stood in the centre of the room with all of the Outcasts surrounding him, waiting intently for his response. He looked at every single one of them individually whilst trying to digest the magnitude of how surreal this was for him.

'It is very good to meet you all,' Aldber finally said, somewhat awkwardly, whilst trying desperately to maintain his nerves. They all nodded encouragingly at his belated response. Here he was, in a moment only a few days ago he could have never possibly foreseen happening, this pivotal moment in history when these two species, which had been sworn enemies for countless generations, would collaborate, and this was the best thing he could muster.

He was lost for words.

'Aldber, would you like something to eat?' Flying Stone said, seeing his unease and offering him a leg of cooked meat.

'Yes, thank you.' He took it from her eagerly, still unsure what to do as the centauri sat down to recommence their meal.

The bura removed his luggage bag with his free hand, threw it to the side, and then sat in the circle amongst them, facing the roaring fire. He looked to either side as they all gnawed on their food and appeared perfectly comfortable with him being present.

Aldber looked at the offering and turned it around several times to make sure that he was not about to eat human flesh, before taking a bite of the roasted tender meat. He chewed it slowly and, unsure where to avert his gaze, looked down towards the dusty floor.

'*This is going to be a long night*,' he thought, swallowing hard.

Chapter Eight
Almighty Sun

Aldber spent the rest of the evening sitting with the Outcasts trying his best to decipher what the majority of them were saying and also engaging in conversation. Once the initial awkwardness had subsided, he sat intently watching them with curiosity, observing their body language and facial expressions, which had close similarity to his own species. They had a limited sense of humour, spoke with cold logic, and paid interest in their new acquaintance, who they found to be quite fascinating. Aldber knew that with time he would be able to understand their pronunciations and customs better.

When they all went to rest, he fashioned a bed on the stone floor. Under the rucksack that he used as a pillow, he concealed the blade as a precaution, and lay there for a while feeling somewhat uncomfortable that within breathing distance he was surrounded by the Enemy. This thought still preoccupied his mind regardless of how hospitable they had been. He did fall into a slumber eventually, once he could hear heavy breathing and snoring that signified the majority of them had fallen asleep.

The Galardros awoke the following morning partially blinded and pulled the cover up to shield his eyes. Sunlight shone down far away on the horizon beyond the gargantuan structures of the city ruins. As he sat up, he looked above at the pale blue sky that was streaked with slashes of red cloud. He could see a centauri sat at the edge of the building roof looking upon the horizon towards the direction of the sun, its large muscular frame silhouetted with a golden lining.

Aldber got to his feet, stretched, walked over, and stood by the being that was having a quiet moment of contemplation. It was Hollow Moon and she nodded when he stood by her side.

'Aldber, have you rested well?' she said gently.

'Yes, thank you. It is a magnificent sight, isn't it?' he said as he yawned and folded his arms, resisting the bitterness of the cold winds.

'Very much so. I often stand here and look out over this landscape with awe, wondering what life could have once been like here in the ancient times. I often ponder what we could be like, our two species, living together in better relations. All this conflict troubles me greatly.' Her fur flowed gracefully in the breeze.

'It does give me a chilling reminder of my people's past,' Aldber said, looking down at the dark depths below. 'This could be one of the tallest buildings in this sector?'

'Yes, that is part of the reason we choose to reside here. Seldom are we bothered by either our kind or you humans.'

'It must be very hard for you and the other Outcasts to live in constant fear of being found by your kind.'

'Yes, unfortunately. We are regarded as traitors. But we made that choice long ago, seeing the brutality of this conflict, and want to seek a change.' She looked at Aldber with sadness. 'We made a choice we have paid the cost for, having abandoned everything. I have not seen my family for many sun-cycles now. Lies were spread and most assume we are dead, not knowing the true extent of the situation. We have been disgraced unjustifiably.'

'We are going to subject ourselves to many dangers in order to find Black Scar. Is this something Red River and the others are all prepared to put their lives at stake for?'

'There is no other choice. We feel compelled for the sake of our people. For too long we have waited in silence, now we must rise up and show Black Scar we are not afraid,' she said as she sat tall and strong on her hind legs. 'There are many powers beyond our understanding. This world has many hidden realities. We do not underestimate the power of you humans and the importance of the prophecy.'

'You believe that the prophecy means salvation for both species?'

'It is an opportunity. All we Outcasts hope for is to reconcile and return to our families. A mother will do what she must to protect her own.'

'I understand how that must feel,' Aldber said feeling saddened, thinking about how his own mother must have been powerless to defend him.

'That bond to the ones you love can drive you to great lengths.' She looked at him affectionately.

'Perhaps if my mother were still alive, she would not have wanted me to do this?'

'She would have seen your potential and wanted you to do this for your own sake, just like every mother wants the best for her own child. We all must walk the path towards self-realisation. Your mother would have been proud of you, Aldber.' They stood there for a moment; it was tender and, although they were of different species, there was something mutual they could relate to. 'I have great confidence that now we have you with us, and can use your divine powers, it will not be long until we find Black Scar.'

'It seems the weather conditions are in our favour to set forth this morning,' said a voice from behind. Approaching them was Red River, sniffing at the cool breeze.

'It is, my dear friend.' Hollow Moon nodded as he stood by their side.

'We have the whole continent to travel across in order to find Black Scar. You are sure he will not be on Irelaf or in the East Lands?' Aldber asked, looking at the two centauri.

'Black Scar has been searching for the prophet, and us, for many sun-cycles. His priority is to dominate the world. Something that cannot be done sat idly. He has others managing Irelaf in his absence and is out there somewhere right now waiting for us. He moves in mysterious ways.'

'I have been given permission by my superiors to have men on standby if we need assistance. We could also set a trap and use me as bait.'

'I know him. These two options would be too obvious. We must use the element of surprise.' Hollow Moon looked at Aldber and placed a hand upon his shoulder. 'It will only be a matter of time.'

'I will wake the others and make preparations for our departure,' Red River said. Hollow Moon nodded with approval and then joined

Aldber as they looked off once more at the vast metropolis before them, illuminated by the birthing light.

Aldber and the Outcasts set forth from the skyscraper and made their way into the heart of the consuming city. Hollow Moon and the young warrior led the way, as the others trailed behind in single file, maintaining vigilance and surveying the surrounding area so as not to be spotted.

During the previous night around the campfire, they had told their human counterpart many stories of Black Scar's despicable nature and relentless obsession. They had spoken in great length and detail about the centauri leader's blood-thirst and utter hatred for the humans, the regime of fear he instilled amongst his armies, the lack of consideration he had for his people, and the exploitation of his position of power in order to reap the benefits of what he had done so little to achieve.

Aldber was beginning to paint a picture in his own mind of how these centauri had been driven to the extreme of committing treason and taking the life of exile. There was a grace and humility to the Outcasts that he respected. He admired their bravery, considering the ridicule they had subjected themselves to, spending their lives continuously on the run. They had told him about how they had attempted several times to hunt down Black Scar and had lost several members of their group along the way. They had also attempted to rally others to their cause but knew that so many of their people had been brainwashed by the notion that the tyrannical leader held an almost godlike position and ruled uncompromisingly, wielding fear as his weapon, that their efforts were in vain.

This was all utterly astounding to Aldber. For many sun-cycles he considered the centauri to be mindless savages, but now, encountering the Outcasts, seeing their sincerity and self-awareness, and hearing about the barbaric and calculated force of Black Scar, he thought otherwise. It was the realisation: he and the humans had seriously underestimated the Enemy. Aldber assumed that whenever it would happen, the exchange with the leader would be swift. Whether Black Scar would be alone or accompanied by his own royal guard was not clear, but they would have to be cunning in their tactics to confront him. The young warrior knew that this would be a masterstroke that could change the tide of the war. The removal of this vile being would either weaken the Enemy dramatically or could possibly instigate peace-making proceedings. What would happen between Aldber and the Outcasts afterwards was unknown. It was an awkward thought he would not pay attention to at present, as all his life he had believed that salvation could only occur for his species through bloodshed on a mass scale and the extinction of the opposing species.

Before they set off, the decision had been made that they would attempt to capture one of the centauri forces and would interrogate them for information. As the majority of the war effort in these lands took place on the streets within the city ruins, they assumed that

Black Scar would be lurking around, inspecting his forces, and his foreboding presence would be instilling fear in the human resistance.

For a whole day they progressed further, meandering through the great structures of old, stopping only to rest and drink. Far off in the distance they could hear gunfire and the unmistakable roar of the centauri forces.

'We are close to one of the main battlefronts.' Hollow Moon stood and looked off into the distance. Behind her, Aldber was cupping water in his hands from a pool in the cracked street.

'Shall we proceed and attempt to capture one of our own?' Long Wing asked the group's leader.

'It would be too dangerous for all of us to be exposed.' Hollow Moon turned to look at them all. 'Bleeding Sky and Singing Eye, I want you two to go ahead. Capture one of Black Scar's forces and bring them back here.'

The two brothers looked up, hearing her beckoning call. They had a spritely temperament and jumped forward to follow her command.

'Make sure you are not followed,' she ordered. They acknowledged her with a synchronised nod. She then looked at them with grave concern. 'And, please, *be careful.*'

They then proceeded away from the main group towards the battle, haphazardly pacing through the streets. Aldber then sat with Hollow Moon and the remaining Outcasts in silence. They waited there patiently for the others to return.

As the sun started to pass over the horizon, far down on the streets it was cold in the shade. Not too long later Aldber saw two figures in the distance that resembled the brothers returning, baring a third they were holding between them.

Aldber and the others all stood to welcome the brothers, who had captured a semi-conscious armoured centauri warrior, its feet dragging against the floor. They dumped it onto its knees, and it knelt there slumped, its head wobbling in a daze.

'Good work, my companions,' Hollow Moon praised the brothers, stepping forward to inspect the captured warrior.

She cupped the captive's chin in her hand and lifted up its head as the centauri began to regain full consciousness. As soon as its eyes came into focus, it instantly recognised Hollow Moon and looked at her with surprise.

'H-H-Hollow Moon?' The centauri was at first horrified and then looked disgusted.

'Yes, it is I. Before you stand the formidable Outcasts,' she said proudly.

The captured centauri looked around anxiously at the group and then spotted Aldber standing at the back.

'*A human?*' It started puffing with outrage.

'Yes, and he is the chosen one they speak of.' Hollow Moon smirked. The captured warrior looked at her again with dread.

'What do you want from me?'

'I want to know the whereabouts of Black Scar.'

'Our great leader has been hunting you for many sun-cycles. Have you now accepted your mistake? Will you present yourself for justice to be delivered?' it spat venomously.

'No, it is time Black Scar realised that he cannot drive his own people to the brink, that not all of us will stand for his tyranny and wicked evilness,' she said defiantly. The warrior looked perplexed. 'If you want your life to be spared, you will tell me where Black Scar is.'

The captive sneered. 'You will be walking into your own death, Hollow Moon.'

'If that is the price I must pay, then so be it.'

All of the Outcasts stood around with clenched fists, watching avidly. Aldber, meanwhile, stood there feeling utterly dumbfounded to be witnessing this exchange.

'Black Scar is not here in the Old City,' the captive announced. The Outcasts all looked at each other with puzzlement, apart from Hollow Moon who maintained eye contact with the captive. 'He is in the northern regions inspecting the forces near to the mountains.'

'Of this you are certain?' Hollow Moon tightened her grip on its chin.

'Yes, he has not been here for a long time.'

'He would not lie if he knew the Outcasts would be walking into their own demise,' Aldber thought.

'Then we must leave immediately.' Flying Stone stepped forward, uttering in his usual deadpan tone. Hollow Moon looked at him and then back at the warrior.

'We should let him return to his forces,' Long Wing reasoned, looking at the weakened warrior.

Hollow Moon looked at Aldber who remained static; he could see the intensity in her eyes. She looked back at the captive and removed her hand from its chin. It slumped down, catching its breath.

'You have served well,' she said.

Expecting to see her turn away, Aldber was shocked when suddenly Hollow Moon grabbed the warrior's head in her grasp. It looked at her with despair for a brief moment as she violently twisted, breaking the centauri's neck and killing it instantaneously. Around her the other Outcasts gasped. She turned to look at them all whilst the body lay motionless behind her.

'It would have been too much of a risk if he had stayed alive. He would have passed on the message that we are hunting down Black Scar.' She looked at each one of her companions individually. 'That would have presented us with an obstacle and removed our element of surprise.'

'But, Hollow Moon, killing an innocent one of our own?' Long Wing looked mortified.

'It is for the greater good, Long Wing,' Hollow Moon assured her companion. 'Now, we must set forth north, away from the city, and into the highlands beyond.'

She started moving away, and Flying Stone and Red River followed whilst the other Outcasts eventually tailed behind them. Aldber stood there looking at the lifeless warrior. It was all too apparent that after all those sun-cycles of persecution, the determination that propelled Hollow Moon was unstoppable and sacrifices would continue to be made.

*

Tala had returned from the council meeting feeling assured and relieved. She had initially been enthusiastic about the idea of carrying out surveillance on the developments on Irelaf but was secretly delighted about the new orders to provide Aldber with constructive support by doing her own investigations into the whereabouts of Black Scar. It gave her greater peace of mind about Aldber's insane vanity mission, and she would also closer to home to see Dev.

Shortly after the council meeting, she had been distributed her own messaging bird called Yulinga. As she stood there becoming acquainted with her beaked friend, another bird arrived into the tower and landed on its allocated perch. An attendant approached, who stroked the creature and then removed the pouch from around its neck.

'Where has the bird come from?' Tala asked. The attendant unravelled one of the parchments and read some of the script.

'Silo based in sector twelve,' he replied.

Tala's eyes widened; she knew that was the section Dev was stationed in. She walked forward to ask if there was any mail for her, but was interrupted by Councillor Gilliad, who appeared and snatched the pouch from the attendant, who threw him a disapproving look.

'Not so fast, Bura Tala, these are classified documents that only councillors are allowed to have access to.' He looked at her with his usual smug expression. His pale skin was almost grey, and the greasiness of his shoulder-length hair was accentuated by the sunlight. Tala stood there frowning with her hands on her hips. He started rifling through the parchments at an intentionally slow pace, looking up with great satisfaction to see her impatient expression. He acted like he had missed something, slowly worked his way back through the delivery, and picked out one of the parchments. 'Ah, it looks like there *is* something here from lover boy.'

'Please may I have it?' Tala asked, trying to control her frustration.

'Of course,' he replied. She reached forward to take the parchment, but Councillor Gilliad refrained.

'Bura Tala, you must remember to always prioritise your duties over personal desires,' he said, looking at her with his usual smug expression.

'I understand, Councillor.' She attempted to smile, though it was forced. The elder looked at her with a lustful expression, which made her feel sickened. He gave her the parchment, and she took no further notice of the vulgar man before leaving the tower.

Tala walked down the hillside and found herself a quiet spot on which to sit. She felt her heart racing in her chest with anticipation as she opened the note. She instantly recognised the handwriting and could imagine where he was writing it to her.

Earlier that day, far down in the depths of the city ruins, Dev had been sat hunched by candlelight shivering and writing the letter to his lover. Around him, the other soldiers were attempting to rest in the cramped sleeping space. There was distant dripping water, a foul smell, the never-ending sound of gunfire reverberating from the surface above, and dust cascading with every explosion.

Dev was abruptly distracted by a coughing fit and leaned forward as his stomach muscles contracted. Another large explosion shook the room. Feeling aggravated, he spat out the mucus and wiped his dry lips with his sleeve. He rubbed his exhausted eyes, squinted, and then in a whisper read out loud the letter.

To my Tala,

The arrival here in the Old City was okay, but my experience so far has been unpleasant, and I have lost track of time. I have been assigned to a squad who are a good group of men and women. They seem to have accepted me. It is nothing like what I have witnessed before. The conditions here in the ruins are revolting. We are holding the front line against a large surge of the Enemy coming from the south. I have not slept for days and we have very few supplies left. I will be okay. Got my chin up still. I hope you and Aldber are not working too hard!

Your Dev

Tala reread the note several times, hearing his voice saying the words, and feeling a mixture of emotions. She was pleased he had been accepted by the fellow silo, but worried that he was right in the midst of the chaos, although she was somewhat relieved that he retained his sense of humour.

It had been a few weeks since his deployment; she missed him greatly and knew this would be the life they would lead from now on. As much as she despised Councillor Gilliad, what he said was true, even though he was not tactful in his deliverance and was a slimy individual.

Being here now, a trained warrior of the resistance, she felt determined. She had to be sensible about attachments and would do what was necessary for the war effort. She stuffed the note inside her trouser and started making her way towards the armoury to be equipped for her mission ahead. She would write her reply later.

Duties came first.

That evening, as the expedition ventured through the city ruins away from the battlefront, there was a heavy cloud of awkwardness hanging over the group. Aldber noticed this, even as a human and newcomer to the characteristics and emotions of the centauri. As they walked through the rubble, the sky darkened overhead, and at one point Hollow Moon broke her silence and spoke to him: 'Aldber, I apologise that you had to witness that before.'

'It is okay. It is not like I have never seen a centauri die before!' He laughed nervously, before instantly turning away to question himself, regretting the inappropriate joke.

'If Black Scar knows of our plans to hunt him down, he will have a large guard around him, which will make our chances of getting to him less possible. He is a coward.'

'I could arrange for some of my men to escort us?'

'I fear that would complicate matters, there might be a misunderstanding.'

Aldber knew that she acknowledged the fragile nature of this arrangement.

'Hollow Moon, when all this is done, I give you my word that you and the Outcasts will be protected. I will do everything within my power to ensure your safety.'

'Aldber, that is very kind of you.'

'It is the least I can do. We need to guarantee a stable outcome from all of this.'

Over the course of the next few days the expedition headed north, scaled the city wall, and made their way across the sprawling plains beyond. They would have to maintain a low profile, away from the hazards of the tribes, Galardros and centauri. They intended to head north, beyond the hills, and into the vastness of the Sprawls that led way north towards the Hallow Mountains. They would have to use whatever resources were available in order to track the movements of the leader.

The Outcasts had agreed with Aldber that they would not be allowed to hunt humans for food and acknowledged this was disrespectful with the present company. He observed their allocation of tasks and communication, which had a similarity to the humans, but he noticed a mutuality and respect, like his own kind. But in the centauri he did not see the egotism that so often stagnated cooperation in his own people. Naturally, Hollow Moon was the leader of the pack, but she was always willing to compromise, proving her worth by setting a good example and not simply sitting back to delegate.

Aldber's vocabulary broadened and his throat became accustomed with the constant straining from the unnatural technique required to speak the Black Tongue. He had conversations with each of the Outcasts and started to understand their individual personalities: Red River was the oldest, spoke softly in tone, said minimal, but every utterance was important, and the others respected him unequivocally. Long Wing was a boisterous female who reminded Aldber of Tala; she had an enthusiasm and was always the first to volunteer for tasks. Flying Stone was always moody and spoke little. The young brothers Bleeding Sky and Singing Eye had a playful innocence about them.

As they headed further into lands that Aldber had seldom explored, the most unthinkable occurred. Never could he have ever imagined he would be in this situation, let alone creating bonds with these creatures who he had once considered unapproachable.

It was on one late summer's day that the expedition found a small ravine in which to set up their camp for the night. Once they were sure the parameter was secure, they all settled down and sat in a circle.

'Aldber, do indulge me,' Red River said as the other Outcasts handed around portions of the evening's meal. 'What is that peculiar noise you often make? As though you are gasping for breath, your body gyrates, and your facial express conveys some form of pleasure?'

'That could be many things, Red River.' Aldber smirked, as he took a helping of the broth. 'I think what you are referring to is laughter.'

'What is that?' Singing Eye asked.

'It is something us humans do when we find something humorous.'

'What is humour?' Bleeding Sky asked.

'It is when we see the absurdity or irony in something. It goes against logic, and often transcends morals. We find it to be amusing, so comment about it and the physical reaction is to laugh,' Aldber explained.

'And what was that expression you made when you first answered Red River's question?' Long Wing asked.

'That is called a smile. It can convey many things, most of which are associated with positive feelings.'

'Interesting.' Hollow Moon nodded as she put aside her bowl. She then flexed her facial muscles in an attempt to make a smile. Her lips jittered as she did this.

'You nearly have it, but you need to let your face relax more.' Aldber pointed at his own as he made the expression.

The other centauri followed the leader and started to mimic Aldber. As they did this, he looked around the circle, evaluating their attempts and providing suggestions. He then turned to Flying Stone, who was sat to his right-hand side. The centauri's expression more closely resembled a snarl. The bura had to restrain himself from jumping in fright and also sniggering at the Outcast's attempt.

'You nearly have it,' he said, biting his lip, before facing everyone else to say, 'Now, I want you all to try and laugh.' He then threw back his head and, in an exaggerated fashion, started laughing. Once he had demonstrated this, he then looked at the Outcasts. They all exchanged glances, looking puzzled, before then throwing back their heads. But what projected from their vocal cords were not the harmless tones of laughter, but thunderous roars.

'Okay, this is going to take more work.' Aldber flinched.

Overhead a bird was circling in the sky. The bura recognised that it was Heratu, his messaging bird. A few moments later she started descending towards them and landed on Aldber's extended forearm. The agile creature enthralled the others. Flying Stone edged closer to inspect and sniff at the new arrival. Aldber could see the hunger in his eyes.

'This bird is *not* for eating, Flying Stone!' Aldber retorted. The centauri sat back, disappointed.

Aldber stroked the bird and withdrew the parchment from the pouch. To his delight it was a message from Tala detailing that she had been ordered to assist him with the mission. Although the young warrior had said to Hollow Moon that support would be available, he decided against letting the Outcasts know that another Galardros was also helping with the search for Black Scar, in case they disagreed. He took a small pencil and paper that were burrowed inside the pouch and scribbled out a response detailing their progress, before returning the parchment and sending the bird on her way.

'What was that about?' Hollow asked.

'I am just updating my superiors about our movements.'

'Oh, I see.' She looked into his eyes searching for answers. But then nodded and picked up her bowl of food.

'She doesn't miss a trick, does she?' he thought.

The following morning whilst the Outcasts were just waking, Aldber returned from a patrol and went to summon everyone. He approached them quietly and as they were stirring, he put a finger to his mouth to encourage them to remain silent.

They all inquisitively threw back their bedding and got up to follow him away. He signalled for them to lean down and walk carefully as he took them up a slope towards a ridge and rocky outcrop.

Once there, he lay down and they followed his example. They started crawling along the grass and over the rocks until they were at the peak of the ridge.

Before them was a vast plateau that stretched off far into the distance. They could see the blurry silhouette of trees and the distinguishable hazy snow-covered mountains. It was not this spectacular view which he had brought them to see, but an immediate sight in the foreground.

Sourcing from the south, most probably from the city ruins they had just come from, was what appeared to be an animated stream of black, snaking further off northeast over the horizon.

As many of the expedition vocalised their horror, Aldber looked over at Hollow Stone, who lay there rigid and wide-eyed.

'I have never seen so many centauri in formation at once!' Singing Eye whispered, looking over at his brother with dread.

'By my estimations, they are migrating towards the Ice Passage,' Hollow Moon explained, looking off further into the distance. 'They are using the natural bridge of ice that connects the north-eastern tip of the West Lands to the northern reaches of Irelaf via the White Flats.'

'Let us pray that these are the last,' Flying Stone said.

'It is really happening, isn't it?' Long Wing said hysterically. She exchanged concerned glances with the others. 'They are re-joining the rest of our people.'

'It will only be a matter of time before the preparations have finished,' Aldber whispered, looking towards the great horde of centauri.

'The final days of war are coming!' exclaimed Bleeding Sky.

'Then we had better make with haste,' Hollow Moon said, and the others nodded in agreement.

That evening, they established a camp under a canopy of stars, having also risked making a small fire to keep warm. A patrol had been set up, and whilst the majority of the expedition was fast asleep, Aldber sat down with Red River, conversing in front of the campfire.

The old centauri sat there on his hind legs looking up into the vast cosmos above them.

'It is something that instils awe. There are no words that can describe the feeling," Red River said, mystified by the skies above them.

'It is a stunning view. Just to comprehend what is out there beyond our world makes me wonder.' Aldber joined him and looked up. 'Those stars are so far away.'

'You can see that there is an inherent order to the universe. There is a continual cycle of birth and death. There are forces beyond our understanding, both positive and negative, which are constantly shifting. It is a balance, a constant state of change occurs, slowly and incrementally. Nothing is permanent, Aldber. These are the rules of nature, which we have to abide by. Everything is interconnected. All of nature is connected.'

'Does it not make you feel small and insignificant, Red River?'

'On the contrary! The ability to witness the splendour of existence gives both our species an incredible fortune. It is something that should not be taken for granted. For we have the responsibility to maintain the natural order. Every action that we make has a consequence to the world around us.'

'Then how does this war make you feel?'

'It makes me worry greatly, young human. We must live in harmony with the natural world, fit in seamlessly. But, in fighting each other, our two species are causing devastation to this precious world.'

'I agree, this fighting is doing too much damage to everything and everyone.'

'The earth is a living organism in its own right, Aldber, and we are one of many parts to it. It looks after itself, creates an environment that is optimal for life, and is changed by that life. What we do affects every living thing around us. The earth will look after itself, it does not find it necessary to look after and support us.'

'I have been taught all my life that the Supreme One has made this world for us humans.'

'And where in that promise do we centauri fit in?' Red River looked at him with intrigue.

Aldber hesitated from saying his preconceived belief and sat there for a moment, unable to give another answer. He had always been taught that there was no compromise and humanity would one day rule the lands once more with no competition. He did not want to cause any hostility at present, as the elderly centauri fascinated him, so decided to change the conversation.

'I often ponder what happened before the dark times. There are many stories that have been handed down through the generations, one of them being that a great ball of flames came crashing down, bringing destruction to ancient civilisation.'

'My people believe that these times you speak of were the creation. It is believed that the very first centauri was called Almighty Sun, who all my people descend from. He is the beginning of our bloodline. In a great ball of fire, he brought creation to the world. With his unparalleled strength he created the four elements of fire, earth, air, and water. He was able to control the weather, to bring about the end of the long winter from which my people originated. Our connection with nature is why we have names that reference the many things around us. Part of our teachings and practices is a ritual dance, in which we pay forgiveness to him. It is a dance to regenerate the earth and unify. There are prophecies that Almighty Sun will one day arise once more and resurrect the dead. That he will bring about the extinction of humanity and mark the complete installation of the centauri prosperity.'

'Well, I guess that is just a point of view.' Aldber smirked.

'Yes, quite possibly.' Red River smiled, looking at the young man. 'But we centauri have always had a deeper understanding. A moral consideration towards all living beings beyond our own species. A deep compassion for all that thrive upon this beautiful world, no matter their place in the food chain or level of intellect. We take what we need, understand the balance of nature, without obstructing it, which you humans have not done.'

'Well, I don't agree with that,' Aldber objected as he poked a stick into the fire.

'Just look at the structures of that city we have just left. Humans attempted to gain power over nature and harnessed it for their own selfish needs, and in doing so neglected what had given them the means. It is one thing to do what is necessary for survival, but to mould the environment to your liking so obsessively will only lead to self-annihilation. The notion you humans have of being separate from nature is flawed.'

'We had such ingenuity to be able to claim dominance over nature.' Aldber sat up defensively. 'We wielded such great power!'

'And look where that left you,' Red River said calmly. Aldber blushed. 'It is the greatest lesson in humility. I understand why your ancestors wanted to understand and utilise nature, but they were on a mission to completely overcome it and failed. They did not see that everything in this world is interconnected and reliant in order to coexist. Their efforts were short-sighted in the grand scheme of things.'

'How so?'

'Because, Aldber, they were not able to stop their own inevitable demise. It is demanding behaviour, blinded by arrogance, lacking integrity and gratitude. Taking without giving back.'

'And what makes you centauri so superior?'

'We have an open-minded experience of the natural world that goes beyond just being. We have an awareness of our participation in the grander context of existence and the greater universe around us. To be enlightened is to be aware, always, of the total reality.'

'You think that my people have lacked perspective?'

'Unfortunately, it seems so. We understand how difficult it is to survive. In the long and dark winter, we went through periods of rapid change in order to cope with the struggle for resources against you humans. I believe that affected our behaviour and attitudes dramatically. The reason why both of our species have been so successful in our respective ways, is because of the flexibility in our cooperation with our own people.'

'What do you mean by flexibility?'

'Most other species that are considered to be 'inferior' have less developed intelligence and communication skills. Meanwhile, we demonstrate something that makes the difference towards making us the ultimate predators – we have imagination. We create order and rules that exist for the purpose for us to cooperate. For instance, we have complex hierarchy and tradition, which is something everyone has a unifying understanding about, in order to function as a collective. The names we centauri are given have abstract qualities to them. Only by experiencing another's mental state, can one truly understand it. The fact that we are both here having this conversation is a testament. Language has to be shared to have meaning, it is a tool for communication and understanding, to help bridge the divide.'

'And having self-awareness is also important?'

'You are very right, Aldber.'

'I have always been curious about how some things are determined for us, and other things are made by choice. Do you think that characteristics are inherited or fostered?'

'Both.' Red River wiped some moisture that was seeping from his swollen eyes. 'Whilst you humans created civilisation and had no one to contend with, you did not need to evolve to change your attitudes towards each other. You did things instinctively, or out of curiosity, making it up as you went along. Meanwhile, we had no other choice but to evolve to fully cooperate with each other in order to survive against your species. This alone is one of the reasons why my people have grown to outweigh your species. Look at the way our peoples assemble themselves now - your people are segmented in tribes, whilst my species have been strong together.'

'This has happened because your species was physically stronger.'

'It is not as simple as that. Cooperation has been at the root of our success. We have established traditions and have more advantage in our skills and tools than you realise.'

'I do not recall the name in your tongue for your island fortress.'

'Rawak. It means 'home'. I know little of the armaments being built on the island, as Black Scar started assembling it when we Outcasts first went into exile. However, I know the capacity my people have for greatness.'

'That, I do not doubt, however, I still do not agree that you centauri think you have the priority over this world.'

'As you said before Aldber, it is all a matter of point of view.' Red River smirked.

'Tell me, if you thought less of us humans, then why would you go to great lengths to betray your own people because of the prophecy?'

'We accept what the prophecy represents, that there are forces beyond the physical world, beyond what can be fully understood. These are things we must respect and cannot ignore.'

'But you do see the damage that could be done if we were to kill your own leader?'

'That is what we have considered every day since we made the choice to turn our backs on him. We have abandoned our own people for their own benefit. To have the conviction, to be able to face the ridicule, takes strength of will.'

'I do admire that,' Aldber said sincerely.

'There are many things that are uncertain in the world. I could never have thought that I would consider killing one of my own people. It seems like a violation of the sanctity of life. It seems unnatural.'

'Likewise, never in a million sun-cycles would I have thought I would be here with you and the other Outcasts fighting together.'

'Life can be unpredictable in many peculiar ways.'

'You don't say.' Aldber chuckled.

'I see that something has to be done for the greater good. We must retain our values, even in the face of hardship and change. As an elder who has seen many things in his time, I acknowledge that there is an imbalance in the world. As a means to pursing a positive outcome, to improving spiritual well-being, we must do something that might be considered 'unruly'.'

'Would you say that Black Scar has lost his way?' Aldber asked. The elderly centauri nodded.

'I am afraid so. It is an impurity your species has been contending with as well.' Red River looked into the fire. 'There are many similarities between our people, Aldber; I am humbled by that notion. We are both animals, creations of this earth.'

That is ludicrous!' Aldber thought, but then reminded himself to be more open-minded in this conversation.

'Don't be fooled by the idea that your God gave you some kind of divine body. Both of our species have evolved physical and mental characteristics for our survival. We are simply complex replicating organisms, just like the animals we slaughtered for this evening's meal,' Red River explained. 'We are far more alike than you realise. Our shared sense of morality makes us stand apart from the brutality of the rest of the animal kingdom. The compassion Hollow Moon showed you as a baby was not just an abnormal occurrence, for altruism is a behaviour in my people as well. In fact, it is our greatest quality. Her act of saving your life is symbolically one of the most important things to happen between our two species.'

'As much as you may talk of us reaching some kind of mutual understanding, you know very well deep down that without hesitation you would kill every single human being if you had to?' Aldber asked sceptically.

'Survival is instinctive. We have a common interest.' Red River winked at him.

'Time will tell what will come of our two species, Red River,' Aldber said unnerved, looking into the fire.

'It shall. We each share insecurities about our own sense of entitlement to the earth,' Red River admitted.

Aldber sat there for a moment, pondering what Red River had said. He was disturbed, as he had heard things that challenged what had been brought up to know. He wanted to listen with an open-minded curiosity, but held onto his beliefs solidly, and instead was filled with confusion and fear.

'You speak with an assurance and see us humans as an inferior, don't you?'

'You seem threatened by our conversation?' Red River asked.

'I know that my species is not perfect, that we have our flaws, but I know from the bottom of my heart that we can do better, that we are inherently good,' Aldber said passionately, noticing that around them the others had been disturbed from their sleep and were watching silently. 'Like yourselves, I don't believe that this war has to be about one species destroying the other. I will show you that humanity can redeem itself and can mature to become the best version of itself. It is something I know can become a reality, that we will find our awakening.'

'You speak as though you can single-handedly change something that is buried deep within your people's innate condition? The reality is that you humans have not evolved to cope with the responsibility of your own existence. Do you not realise that humanity is destined toward destruction? You thrive off violence.'

'If it is for the sake of our own survival then yes, I believe we can change. We must. Do not underestimate us,' Aldber said defiantly. 'There will be an evolution, Red River. It will not be a physical one, but an evolution of the mind, of the soul, of our collective consciousness.'

'Then prove it,' the elderly centauri said, looking fiercely into his eyes.

'Thank you for this conversation, Red River.' Aldber nodded politely, before standing to leave. 'It has given me much to think about.'

'You are very welcome, young human.' The elder centauri smiled.

Aldber left Red River by the campfire, and walked off into the distance, contemplating their conversation. He would not sleep for the rest of the night but would sit down on the grass gazing up into the star-speckled night sky, looking for answers. He knew that with patience and faith, the Supreme One would show him the way.

Chapter Nine
Liberator of the People

Over the course of the next few weeks, the expedition would trek through the majestic plains and dense woodlands of the Dulanta Forest in the northern regions of the continent, passing ancient ruins along their way. The terrain ascended on a steady incline, although was negotiable, and the climate was bearable as it was late summer. Far off in the distance, they could see the vast mountain range, the snow tops barely visible above the tree line, glistening in the sunlight. It would be several days before they reached them.

The biggest struggle they faced on a daily basis was maintaining a level of secrecy in their expedition, whether by being cautious in areas known for centauri activity, or by covering any trace of the path left behind them. As the weeks passed by, it was decided that instead of hunting for food, they needed to stockpile supplies, and it required drastic measures in order to achieve this.

One evening, they drew close to a large encampment of the centauri. Camouflaged by the woodlands nearby, they all looked across the verge towards the collection of large tents and warriors standing amongst them. Aldber surveyed the scene with alertness and intrigue, for dotted throughout the settlement were large white banners with a black scar symbol of the leader painted across them.

'Does that mean that he is here?' he whispered towards Hollow Moon.

'Not necessarily. The armies all carry the flag. Have you not seen it before?' she asked as the other Outcasts listened.

'I have seen his forces a few times, but I have not witnessed the flag nor seen a settlement of this size before.' Aldber gazed off into the distance.

'I have an idea of how we can approach,' Long Wing said, directing herself to the group leader.

'How might that be?'

'The possibility of attacking is simply out of the question, because we are severely outnumbered, plus they might have reinforcements in the area. Our best option is to creep up, using the darkness as our ally.' Long Wing then pointed to a large tent to the far right-hand side of the encampment. 'I suspect that is where we will find all of the food supplies.'

Hollow Moon nodded.

'May I make a suggestion as well?' Aldber interjected.

'Yes?' Hollow Moon said as all the others turned to face him with curious expressions.

'We have made great efforts to remain unseen, but I suspect doing so is going to cost us invaluable time. Instead of intentionally making ourselves anonymous, why don't you all hide in plain sight?' he said, looking at them all individually.

'What are you insinuating, Aldber?' Singing Eye asked.

'Whilst in there, you might be able to find spare uniforms. If you dress in these it would be less suspicious if we were caught,' Aldber continued as the Outcasts exchanged amused looks. 'If this were to happen, and they asked about me, you can pretend that I am your prisoner. I am sure you can find a pair of shackles in there, which I can carry, in case I need to play the part.'

'Yes, Aldber!' Long Wing expelled.

'Very good, young human,' Red River wheezed. The others all talked amongst themselves excitably.

'You see, fellow Outcasts.' Hollow Moon gestured to the bura with a smile across her face. 'Until now we were limited, but *now* we have a human amongst us, and especially one with so much imagination and cunning, it is going to give us a better chance of surviving, and also finding Black Scar.' She then looked at Aldber. 'Utter brilliance.'

'What can I say?' Aldber smirked. 'Us humans have the refined ability to use deception as a weapon.' He then pulled the pistol from his holster. 'If you can find uniforms, it might be a way for us to infiltrate their ranks, get closer to Black Scar, and take him off guard when he least expects it.'

'That is something we can discuss in due course, Aldber.' Hollow Moon put out her hand to push away the weapon whilst looking at him with concern. 'And you must remain here. Along with Red River. We have ransacked many of our people's bases before, and I don't want to risk your safety. Save fighting for another time.'

'Very well.' Aldber nodded and holstered the weapon. He moved closer to Red River as the remaining Outcasts proceeded to climb over the verge, before dividing into two groups and making their way towards the tents on either side of the settlement, under the shadow of night.

'You didn't fancy going along?' Aldber said sarcastically, smiling at the aged centauri.

'Ah, yes, I can see you are not implying that literally, but instead intend to arouse amusement through humour about my age,' Red River replied. He then exaggerated a wink to respond, before wiping discharge from his eye.

'I would have preferred to have gone along with them,' Aldber admitted as they both watched Hollow Moon and Flying Stone begin to pull up the fabric on the side of a tent to sneak inside.

'We all must know when to choose our battles, Aldber.' Red River then winked at him again, but this time, it seemed, more suggestively.

'Why do I get the feeling he is implying more than he is letting on?' Aldber thought and then returned to watching the other Outcasts.

'Bura Tala?' the captain questioned as a young female warrior entered the small silo outpost, which was nestled within the inner skeleton of a spacecraft's ruins.

'Silo.' The bura nodded firmly as she walked into the centre of the room and looked upwards and around to acknowledge all of the soldiers that were present. Some were lying casually in beds fashioned into the framework of the ruins, others were sat on storage crates, and all were surprised to see her. They suddenly bolted upright to appear formal in front of a higher-ranking warrior.

The captain stood to address her at eye-level. 'To what do we owe the pleasure of this unexpected visit to the base?'

'I apologise for not notifying you in advance, but my messaging bird is preoccupied.' Tala maintained her formal manner. 'I am currently on a surveillance mission of the local region. I would appreciate your full cooperation with providing me any information about a small pack of centauri, accompanied by a lone human, that your squadron might have spotted?'

'As far as I am aware, Bura Tala'—the captain exchanged a confused side-glance with his peer— 'I have not been given reports of such sightings.

'In that case, I have direct orders from high command,' Tala announced. All of the surroundings soldiers leaned in closer to listen.

'Yes, Bura?'

'If your silo spot those which match my description, you are to refrain from engaging them, I repeat - *refrain* from engaging them,' Tala said directly.

'We are ordered to hold fire, if we spot enemy hostiles with a *captive*?' the captain questioned, looking dumbfounded. This reaction was reciprocated by his squad.

'That is correct.'

'May I ask why?'

'That is classified,' Tala said bluntly.

'Understood,' the captain replied, trying to conceal his disapproval.

'Good. Now, I will require that you contact all other squadrons in the local area and must relay the same order to them. Is that also understood, captain?' Tala eyed him intensely.

'Affirmative.'

'And one final thing – do you have a map with markings for every single centauri and tribe settlement in the local region?'

'Yes, of course.' The captain then turned to one of his men, who came running forward with a large tattered piece of paper, which was handed to the captain, and then onto the bura. Tala unravelled it, turned it to face the correct way, and then scrupulously examined it under the minimal lighting.

'Captain.' She looked up at him.

'Yes, Bura Tala?'

'Is this the only copy of the map that you have?'

'No, it is not.'

'In that case I will require this copy.' She then folded it neatly before opening her shoulder bag and placing the map neatly inside it.

'Rightly so, bura,' the captain said whilst exchanging puzzled looks with his colleague. 'Is there anything else I can do for you now?'

'In due course, I would appreciate it if you can send a message bird to the Sanctuary, addressed to the high command, confirming that all squadrons in the local region have followed my order.'

'That, I shall do.'

'Thank you.' Tala then raised the salute, which everyone reciprocated. She then marched for the exit of the enclosed room, before turning swiftly on her heels to address them all for the final time: 'As you were, silo.'

One morning, as they crossed a wide and shallow river, Hollow Moon asked Aldber about how he had been able to locate his parents' tribe.

'I had something called a nightmare. They are images in the mind that occur whilst you are sleeping. When experiencing them, you are not able to determine whether or not they are the true reality,' the young warrior explained. He did not expect her to understand what it was and was surprised when she replied:

'Yes, we centauri also have these dreams when sleeping.'

'Really?' Aldber said in shock. 'That does surprise me. What I still cannot figure out is how my nightmare was linked to what really happened when I was a new-born.'

'I suspect that having the instinct to find your mother's tribe is clarification that you have a deep connection to the spirit world, which has guided you.'

'I too hope that is the case. I am slowly awakening these dormant powered within me. My order, we refer to the origin, of which this connection is birthed, as the Source. It is from where we draw all of our power.'

'That is most intriguing, Aldber.'

'I hope that this will come into full fruition once I have succeeded in removing Black Scar and avenging my mother's untimely death.

But, admittedly, the vagueness of the prophecy has never given me much certainty in understanding what the future may hold.'

'In time, all shall be revealed.'

'A few weeks ago, Red River told me about Almighty Sun?' Aldber asked as the expedition ventured through the woodlands.

'Yes, he was our great creator. Did my comrade tell you that Black Scar is the direct descendent and bloodline of the very first centauri? This is the reason he was appointed as the ruler, out of birth right, and not merit. This entitlement, a divine blessing, did not gain him the full approval and support of all our people, once they saw what a brutal being, he truly is.'

'I suppose you have to put a lot of faith in someone who leads you, if they don't have to prove their worth initially to be given the responsibility?'

'That is very true. Black Scar has been reckless and abused his position. Is this the same way your people organise themselves?'

'Not exactly. The tribes and the order both elect their leaders.' Aldber decided to be discreet, remembering Bura Hecta's words of caution about divulging too much information about his people. 'It is something called a vote.'

'That is most intriguing. What does that mean?'

'It is where people share their opinion about who should lead, and the leader is elected on the basis of the most amount of opinions in their favour. It is a fair, although not a perfect, way to operate.'

'I think that works best for your species, but until now my people respected the bloodline. I admit, Aldber, I do have my reservations about how they will react to the death of Black Scar. His son, Raining Fire, is the rightful heir to the throne. He will now be mature enough to succeed his father and continue the order. That is if he understands, with my guidance, why his father had to be removed.'

'Do you hope to be celebrated as a liberator of your people?'

'Yes, I suppose that would be a name for it,' she smiled.

As time passed on, they hiked further into the snowy regions of the north, but to no avail, although they did manage to avoid several other encounters with the leader's forces. Tala had notified Aldber that Galardros stationed near to the mountains had not spotted any Enemy activity, and this was reaffirmed by Hollow Moon, who stated that centauri wouldn't dare venture into the dangerous mountain-range.

The expedition started to accept the reality that Black Scar could not be found in this part of the world. In their frustration at the captive's false information, they decided to head back south towards the Old City, where they would plot their next move whilst in the security of familiar surroundings. Aldber knew it would be time to return to the Sanctuary to seek council, debrief, and evaluate their progress so far. He would re-join the expedition in due course.

When he returned to the valley of his home, it was now early autumn and the colour of the leaves on the trees were beginning to change. There was a new cold crispness in the air.

As he reported to the patrol and made his way into the complex, he could see further preparation was under way for the war efforts. The Sanctuary was a hive of activity; more men had been recruited and training was being conducted for them to be deployed into the Old City and beyond.

The bura immediately went to the council to report his progress. When he was summoned into the domed tower, he could see that the elders were pleased to see him alive.

'Aldber, we did not expect you to return so soon?' Grand Master Vivid said warmly.

'Master, Councillors.' Aldber bowed to them all respectively. 'I do not return with triumphant news. Alas, despite our efforts gathering information, and then trekking further north from here, we have been unable to locate the centauri leader.'

'Evidently, this is going to take longer than expected,' Fukuro said.

'I suspect so too, Councillor,' Aldber replied.

'Did you have much interference from the Enemy and any humans?' Hecta asked.

Aldber then explained how they had been cautious, but had not had any difficulties, and told the council that he had been in regular contact with Bura Tala, who had been instrumental in ensuring there was no interference.

'Yes, the last we heard from her was she was heading further west to conduct reconnaissance duties,' Grand Master Vivid explained.

'I believe so. She is updating me every few days.'

'And what have you learnt from the centauri about their hierarchy and customs?' Kolayta asked.

'I have learnt that they have a long-running monarchy, and Black Scar is part of a bloodline that has run for countless generations. The Outcasts have not been able to provide any details about Irelaf and what goes on there, because they have not been to their sacred land since going into exile.'

'Sacred land?' Thortatel asked.

'Yes, Councillor.' Aldber turned to face him. 'They believe the isle holds great spiritual value to their people.'

'Bura, you must continue to accompany the Outcasts and maintain communications with high command,' Grand Master Vivid ordered. The young warrior turned to face him once more. 'Please take food supplies and weaponry.'

'From what Tala told me, I understand that you are keeping this mission top secret?' Aldber asked.

'Correct. Because of the controversy and importance of what you are partaking in, we found it necessary, so please do the same,' Grand Master Vivid replied earnestly.

'Very well, Master.'

'You will be pleased to hear that your friend Silo Dev has returned from his post on the front line.'

'*Already?*' Aldber thought, before speaking. 'That is good to know. If there is nothing else you require me for council, I would like to be excused?'

'Granted.' Vivid nodded and smiled.

Feeling excited, although confused about his friend's premature extraction, Aldber hastily left the council and ran off down the hillside in the direction of Dev's living quarters.

Upon arrival, he knocked, waited for permission to enter, and a few moments later he heard a muffled response inside granting his admittance. As Aldber entered, he saw Dev sat slumped at his table not wearing his armour. His garments were caste on the floor around him, a small closed bag lay to one side, and his muddy boots had left a trail across the floor. The squad leader was looking through notes he had received from both of his friends, his hands were covered in dried soil, and he looked dejected.

'Dev!' Aldber stepped forward excitably, delighted to see his friend.

'Hi, Aldber!' Dev crooked and turned around to address him.

Aldber instantly saw that his friend had lost a severe amount of weight, looked drained and exhausted.

'You look terrible,' Aldber said as he closed the door behind him.

'Thanks for that,' Dev said dryly and smirked. He stood up and they embraced in a firm hug. 'I have felt claustrophobic sitting in here gathering dust. Let's go for a walk.'

The reunited friends left the quarters and headed down towards the valley floor. They then walked along the grass, taking a direction away from the main complex to give them privacy.

'Your letters gave me a slight indication you were not exactly having the time of your life in the Old City?' Aldber attempted to make the atmosphere lighter, although knew very well his friend was not in a good frame of mind.

'You could say something like that. I cannot begin to describe the horrors I have seen. What is happening down there is beyond comparison. I was only luckily withdrawn from my position because the majority of my squad were massacred in a night-time attack. They vanished just like that.' Dev clicked his fingers, although did so looking like his mind was elsewhere, vacantly peering off into the distance. 'All of them - gone.'

'I am sorry to hear that, Dev,' Aldber tried to console his friend, who was undeniably traumatised.

'It is okay. I am...' Dev tried to say but could not hold back anymore as he suddenly burst into tears. He leaned on his friend's shoulder for support. Many weeks of internalised anguish suddenly spilled out. Aldber hugged his friend's bony frame and looked down at him with grave concern. He listened intently as his friend started to splutter. 'It felt like we were just abandoned there, Aldber. Like we were just left to get on with it and rot.'

'Were you not able to message for reinforcements and supplies to be sent?' Aldber asked, feeling both saddened and shocked to see his friend look so weak and demoralised.

'Yes, but they never came,' Dev gasped. He wiped the tears from his eyes, straightened up, took a few moments to clear his throat, and composed himself. He then grunted and spoke to himself: 'Come on, Dev, you are a *man*, and this is *not* how you should *behave*!'

Aldber looked around to make sure they were not being watched for his friend's dignity, and then clasped Dev's shoulders with both hands and peered into his sleep deprived and darkened eyes with concern.

'Dev, you know that this war was never going to be easy. We have all pledged our allegiance to the cause,' the bura said softly, trying not to sound patronising.

'I am aware of that, Aldber,' Dev grunted and took a few deep breaths. 'But, having seen the brutality of the Enemy, I don't know what to think. I feel like I've become numbed by the experience. I am in a state of shock.'

'Trust me, I am trying to do everything in my power to make things right, Dev,' Aldber tried to reassure him. 'Too many have fallen already.'

'This hunt for Black Scar.' Dev looked up at him with bloodshot and swollen eyes. 'What has happened?'

'We have not found him yet. It is going to take far longer than initially expected.' Aldber sighed with frustration. He then told his friend about the slaughtered captive and the subsequent unforthcoming venture into the northern regions that followed.

'You know that despite the enormity of what you are trying to achieve, even though they wouldn't admit it, I suspect the council are counting on you with every hope. Honestly, I think it is ludicrous that they are taking such a gamble with your mission. But by the looks of what I have seen in the Old City, and the way that the conflict is heading, I can understand why they are allowing this.'

'That, I do not doubt, and I have to deal with the expectations,' Aldber replied. 'I just need more time.'

'You are a good man, Aldber; you know that, don't you?' Dev smiled and patted his friend on the shoulder. 'It is just what I needed, seeing you. I am sorry for venting like this. I think I've become disillusioned by everything, having seen all of the conflict and bloodshed. I feel embarrassed. Please, don't tell anyone about my teary outburst just then? I just need to rest.'

'I think you need a large serving of mead!' Aldber said and the two friends laughed.

The bura was relieved to see colour return to his friend's face. They started walking along the field as the late afternoon sun trailed above the tree line at the peak of the hills.

'Are you still having those nightmares?'

'Thankfully, since visiting the tribe, learning about my mother, and everything since, they have stopped.'

'I know the circumstances are painful, but I am glad to hear that you aren't being tormented anymore. How are you feeling about all of that now?'

'Despite the fact I never knew my parents, I still find a draw towards them. Because I have never had a real family, I guess I am feeling some sense of validation by pursing who murdered my mother. I know that this would be frowned upon by the order, because it goes completely against the teachings, but I need some sense of resolution.'

'I can understand that. The council are not aware of your personal motives, are they?'

'Of course not! But regardless, once I have achieved what I have set out to do, my efforts will make a far bigger impact than just resolving my own issues. I know that the stakes are high and so are the expectations, on both a personal level and from the council, because they have invested so much in me.'

'You know that there are tensions building within the council? That some councillors are becoming restless with Grand Master Vivid?' Dev uttered at almost a whisper so as to not be overheard by two warriors who strolled past.

'You don't say. Every time I see Councillor Thortatel, I expect him to make an objection of some kind. The man loves to dispute, just for the sake of it.' Aldber rolled his eyes. 'I can understand their frustrations, don't we all, but quite frankly, Grand Master Vivid is doing the best he can. He is far more intelligent and wiser than the majority of the council put together!'

'That, I do not doubt, Aldber. But I have heard *a lot* of rumours whilst being on the front line. Don't you see what is happening?'

'What, that they are trying to oust Grand Master Vivid out of his position?'

'Well, yes. You catch on pretty quick.' Dev looked around to make they weren't being watched. 'Aldber, you must know that Grand

Master Vivid is an old man now and does not have many sun-cycles left to live?'

'I know that.' Aldber sighed and nodded his head.

'There are members of the council who have ambitions to succeed Grand Master Vivid, and I suspect they might try to achieve this either through the normal process of election, or otherwise.'

'Why *otherwise*? What do you mean by that?'

'I believe that secretly Grand Master Vivid does not like the majority of the council members, who he knows are causing this rift within the council. He has no choice but to have them instated because that is the code. They are not doing anything at this present moment to warrant being replaced. There is a conflict of interest and a power struggle going on.'

'I know that there has been an undercurrent for a long time, and I guess that since I have been away on the mission, I have been removed from the politics of the order. I'm sure that Grand Master Vivid is aware of this and won't let them unsettle the leadership. It sickens me. We have much bigger priorities right now.'

'Yes, it is absurd.'

'Although, between you and me, I believe that in time, Councillor Hecta would be a worthy heir,' Aldber proclaimed.

'I agree. We have to be careful what we say around the rest of the council.' Dev looked at his friend with caution. 'Even in these drastic times, you can not underestimate what some will do for their own self-gain.'

'It does not surprise me.' Aldber shook his head and paused for a moment. 'Dev, I feel like this hunt for Black Scar might go on for sun-cycles. Unless I can lead a small army and can cross the continent quickly, Black Scar will maintain a low profile. I suspect that he might be cowardly resisting the confrontation. The Outcasts are not allowing me to simply present myself to him because they think it would be ineffective; however, I think it would be the most obvious method.'

'Whilst I was there in the city ruins there were many stories circulating around about Black Scar. We saw many of the Enemy's flags with his symbol on them. I for one wouldn't underestimate his abilities as a leader. From what you wrote about in our letters, he does sound like a formidable specimen.'

'The worst.' Aldber looked into his friend's eyes with disdain.

'What do you think about the Outcasts?'

'I will be honest - the whole thing has been surreal. I never thought I would ever say this, but they are quite charming and pleasant,' Aldber admitted and they both laughed at how absurd it sounded.

'It is a crazy situation you have gotten yourself into, Aldber. It does not surprise me, though. Just watch your back because they might get peckish.' Dev made a pouncing gesture playfully. 'I am pleased that Tala is helping you. At least she knows what *she* is doing. Have the council recommended that you use any alternative means?'

'What do you mean by alternative?' Aldber eyed his friend with scepticism.

'It was just a thought I had. Do you remember in our training that we were told about certain parts of the Sanctuary that were strictly off limits to everyone? That, without any excuse, we were not allowed to enter…'

'If you are speaking of the forbidden chamber, I have already asked the elders for permission to gain access, but they stubbornly refused because I do not hold a position upon the council.'

'Considering the severity of what you are trying to accomplish, you would have thought that in their desperation, the council would have broken the code on this occasion.'

'I suspect that they are very afraid of whatever is hidden in there. It is a shame, because I know that in there are meant to be artefacts that predate the apocalypse.'

'Exactly! Imagine what you could find in there. In the excavations of old, some technologies and equipment were locked away for unknown reasons. I don't mean to doubt your potential, Aldber, but I think I can speak for the both of us in saying you might need more help than just praying to the Supreme One. You have to find a way in there.' The bura stood there for a few moments contemplating this.

'Dev, you are right. I don't know what I would do without you for a friend!' Aldber smiled and patted his shoulder excitably.

'You would probably lead a boring life,' Dev joked. Aldber was pleased his friend was maintaining his sense of humour after all the hardships he had experienced. 'Come to think of it, I remember Bura Hecta once said in his ramblings that there is some kind of vision globe hidden in there. It was something that past grand masters have used in their attempts to find the prophet.'

'I remember that. Grand Master Vivid believed it was cursed. I thought that might have been hearsay, but it is worth a shot.' Aldber rubbed his chin and thought for a moment. 'How am I going to gain access into the chamber?'

'I believe that Grand Master Vivid might have the only key available.'

'I will have to use my cunning ways,' Aldber said, biting his lip.

'I am sure you can.'

The two friends started making their way up the hillside towards the main complex. Suddenly, Dev stopped and began coughing violently. Aldber went to his side to offer support as his friend leant over and his whole body shook in discomfort. Dev then stood up straight and wiped away something from his mouth. There was a small pool on the floor. It was blood.

'Dev, what happened?' Aldber looked at him distraught.

'It is nothing and will pass. I contracted something when I was in the Old City. Possibly from the water supply. I am sure I will be fine,' Dev tried to reassure him as he brushed the blood from his face and flicked it onto the floor, before taking a deep breath.

'We should go to the medical rooms to get you seen to *immediately.*' Aldber looked at him with concern.

'Yeah, I think you are right,' Dev said, looking disorientated. 'It might be best that we should leave the mead for another time.'

'I think so too.'

They started walking in the direction of the medical rooms and then Dev stopped abruptly, before turning to look at Aldber with a gormless expression.

'Whatever happens, Aldber, I want you to know you will always be like a brother to me,' he said with his lips covered in dried blood. The silo then turned to leave and dragged his weak frame away. Aldber stood there utterly mortified, feeling helpless that his friend was possibly in grave danger, before following swiftly behind him.

Chapter Ten
The Forbidden Chamber

After Aldber had left Dev in the capable hands of the medics, he left knowing that he had limited time that evening to attempt gaining access into the forbidden chamber, before he would have to return to the Outcasts. He knew he was possibly going to land himself in a lot of trouble but contemplated the option of breaking into Grand Master Vivid's quarters to find the key. He decided against this, instead going for a more subtle approach, and would pay Grand Master Vivid a visit before the leader rested for the night.

As the moon hung alone in the dark sky far away, Aldber walked down the stone corridor towards the grand master's quarters. Two armoured guards were standing either side of the door as usual and Aldber went through the standard process of asking permission to enter. The guards were at first hesitant, due to the lateness of the hour, but Aldber persisted. One then entered and reappeared shortly to grant him access.

Inside, Grand Master Vivid was sat at his desk, squinting and using a monocle to look at some parchments under candlelight. He smiled when he saw Aldber enter.

'Aldber, how can I help you at this late hour?' He gestured for the young man to take a seat, placed the monocle down, and sat back.

The bura sat down. 'I thought I would come to see how you were, Master, before setting off at dawn.'

'That is very kind of you, dear boy. I am very well. I've just been looking through reports of armament production.' The leader pointed at the parchments.

'And everything is on track?'

'Hopefully. Things could change dramatically in the coming moon-cycles. There is something I sense...' The old man stopped mid-speech and clasped his hands under his chin. 'How has your time with the Outcasts been so far? Are you gathering a better understanding of their way of life?'

'It has been quite eye-opening. They have many traditions and rituals that have some similarity to our own. I learnt that they live to the equivalent of one hundred of our sun-cycles. The majority of their people cohabitate with little internal conflict, however, ironically, I would not say that the Outcasts are the best example, in that respect.' Aldber maintained eye contact with the master but wanted to look around the room for signs of the key.

'From my studies of the Black Tongue over the sun-cycles, I have been overwhelmed by their thought process. The dialect demonstrates their advanced abilities. As of yet I have not had the opportunity to communicate with one of them, apart from that brief encounter with Hollow Moon when you were delivered here.'

'I must say that they have challenged my preconceptions. I know that this sort of conversation we are having right now would be ridiculed if anyone was to hear us.' Aldber looked over his shoulder at the front entrance.

'It is something many of our people, and especially the council, seem to underestimate. To understand what you are dealing with, you must get inside their mindset.' Grand Master Vivid spoke with his usual calming tone. 'Forgive me, dear boy, I need to remove this ghastly thing.'

He then leaned forward and pulled from around his neck a chain that had been concealed and placed it onto the table. On it was attached an arrangement of various sized keys. Aldber eyed them intensely. He knew that among them was the one he was looking for.

'It does cause discomfort having to bear it all day long,' Grand Master Vivid chuckled and rubbed his neck, before standing to walk around the room. 'And what do you think is the best form of action regarding the Outcasts once the task is complete?'

'I, um, think we should, um, pardon them, and give them our word that they shall be spared.' Aldber tried to concentrate but his eyes were transfixed on the keys.

'Yes, yes, it would be a grand gesture of diplomacy.' Grand Master Vivid stood with his back turned to Aldber, rubbing his beard as he looked out of the balcony into the night.

Aldber saw that he might have an opportunity to grab for the keys, hoped that Grand Master Vivid might have a momentary memory lapse in his old age, and would not recognise their disappearance, but knew very well the absurdity of this notion. As the young warrior gazed at the keys, his fingers nearing closer, the master suddenly spoke: 'Aldber, I would have preferred if you had the decency to come here tonight being completely honest with me.' He then turned to face the bura.

'Sorry, Master, I do not know what you mean?' Aldber suddenly felt self-conscious and a rush of blood flowed to his face. Much to his dismay, Grand Master Vivid pointed directly towards the keys. 'Master, I was not...'

'I will not hear another word,' Vivid responded with restraint, before walking back towards the table, retook his seat, and picked up the keys. 'Why couldn't you have simply walked in here tonight and straight away asked me for the key? We have sun-cycles of trust, which you were willing to break by attempting to steal it.'

'I am sorry, Master, I just thought that if I asked you, you would have refused,' Aldber admitted and forced himself to look the leader in the eye whilst he said this. 'You intentionally placed them there in front of me to tempt me, didn't you?'

'That, I did. Aldber, I have known you your entire life and could sense the awkwardness when you first walked in here, so knew there were ulterior motives to your visit. Would you have preferred to be disloyal, instead of facing disappointment?' Vivid questioned sternly.

'I am sorry, Master. It was a misjudgement.' Aldber took a deep breath to settle his nerves.

'I am pleased you acknowledge the recklessness of your ways.' Grand Master Vivid then sat back, placed his fingers in a prism shape, and read the young warrior's face. 'Why didn't you simply ask me for the key?'

'Because I thought you would have disproved, because it breaks protocol.'

'Aldber, in other circumstances, I would have followed that mentality, but considering what you are trying to achieve, it requires drastic measures.'

'Wait, what?' Aldber leaned forward. 'You will allow me access into the forbidden chamber? But what will the council say?!'

'The council will say nothing, because no one else is going to know about this. Usually, I do not like to abuse the power of leadership, but I must bend the rules on this one time.' Grand Master Vivid then stood up, walked around the table, picked up the set of keys, and then unlinked the rusted one that would open the entrance to the forbidden chamber. He then walked towards the bura and looked down at him. 'Aldber, if I am entrusting you with this key, you must make sure that no one, and I mean *no one*, sees you entering or exiting the chamber. The repercussions will be severe.' He then handed the key to the bura.

'Thank you, Master.' Aldber held it within his hands, feeling the sharp contours of the rust against his skin. His heart was beating frantically within his chest.

'Once you have found whatever you are looking for within the chamber, you must return the key to me here, straight afterwards.'

'That I shall do, Master.' Aldber stood and then bowed respectfully.

'Very well.' Vivid then gestured with his hand for the bura to leave. Aldber obliged and then turned to walk for the entrance. 'Oh, and another thing.'

'Yes, Master.' Aldber quickly turned on his heels to face Vivid, who looked a mixture of angry and disappointed. It reminded the bura of when he was a child, had disobeyed orders, and gone to explore the Old City, and the subsequent reprisals.

'If you ever follow through with a stunt like that in the future, or if I ever suspect you to betray my trust, regardless of your potential, Aldber, you will receive the same punishment as any other Galardros.'

'I understand.' Aldber swallowed hard.

He then turned, hastily exited the grand master's chamber, and took a sigh of relief. For a moment he stood there in order to calm his beating heart, compose himself and adjust his posture. The guards flanking the door remained silent and motionless.

'I hope they could not hear what was said in there,' he thought.

Avoiding overthinking what had happened during the conversation, Aldber then paced down the corridor, holding the key tightly, which was concealed under his jacket sleeve. He then made his way further into the stronghold, walking through the maze of corridors. As other Galardros walked by, he made his pleasantries, but did not stand idle, as he was focused on finding the forbidden chamber.

When he found the quiet corridor, and came to the abandoned large heavy wooden door, he made sure that he was not being followed. But suddenly, from afar, he could hear the echoes of a high-pitched voice and the irregular shuffling of two sets of feet. He quickly darted for an alcove to the side of the door and hid in the shadows. To his annoyance, down the corridor appeared Grombl and Maloyk. The inseparable pair were most probably on night watch and, as usual, had to appear at the most inconvenient of times.

They approached the door, both bearing torches. Aldber watched Maloyk make some facial expressions and hand gestures to communicate, which Grombl soon responded to: 'No, Maloyk, we cans just sit and have a drink of mead. We might get-t-t-t-s in big trouble!'

Maloyk looked displeased by this notion and then approached the door. Aldber tried his best to contain his sniggering, pushed his frame tight against the wall of the alcove, and held his breath. Maloyk started looking at the floor near to the door meticulously and then started sniffing in the air. Aldber bit his lip as his heart pounded in his chest. Maloyk then stepped forward and looked in the direction of the alcove that was shrouded in shadow.

'What is it, Maloyk?' Grombl questioned, looking thoroughly perplexed. Maloyk then turned to him with a look of concern, before anticlimactically shrugging. 'I think you have had a drink already. Come on then!'

The pair turned and started walking down the corridor in the opposite direction. Aldber waited until they had fully disappeared out of sight and Grombl's mumbling was a distant sound. He exhaled and caught his breath. That would have been an awkward excuse he would have to have made up on the spot.

The young warrior went for the door, inserted the key, turned the stiff mechanism, and pulled open the door. A large waft of stale warm air met him as he peered into the darkness beyond. Without hesitation, he walked inside and pulled the door shut safely behind him. He then fumbled for a switch on the side of the wall and found it. When he activated it and the lights gradually blinked into life, he gasped.

Before him was a large low-ceilinged room with copious mountains of old equipment scattered everywhere. To the eye of the beholder it was quite a spectacle, or just a scrap pile, depending on your point of view.

He started walking around inspecting the vast array of artefacts. There were computers, weapons, vehicles, clothes, ornaments, huge devices, and other things he could not possibly distinguish. The majority was rusted and decaying, having survived for countless suncycles.

Aldber walked around in awe, looking at everything with complete bafflement. One thing at the corner of his eye grabbed his attention and he moved over to it. It was a large object that had the uncanny features of a human body, but upon closer inspection he saw that it was made from metal. It had limbs, a torso, and a head, and its facial features were lifelike yet unnatural. He lifted up the one arm and could see the mechanisms in it replicated the tendons in the human anatomy. He looked into a crack in the head and saw a complicated series of wires and circuitry. Aldber thought this was very strange and wondered what this human-like thing was, before turning to examine the many other mysterious objects hidden away in the chamber.

In front of him was a computer terminal, which was in moderate condition. He went to see if it had a power supply and saw that it was a similar model to those used by the Galardros in the resource room. He powered it up and watched as it came to life with streams of barely indecipherable language and breath-taking colour photos of a world long forgotten. The language was the Old Tongue, which he had very little comprehension of, but he did his best to look through the program. Various articles appeared and he saw photos of the Old City before the dark times. It was vibrant and full of people. He was dumbfounded to finally see what ancient civilisation had been like. It looked so pure and glorious, just like he had imagined walking around the ruins. His ancestors had lived in a paradise they had created for themselves. He was mesmerised by their achievements.

But soon his fantasy would be crushed.

A small window appeared with text. He began reading it, and although only able to decipher fragments of the language, he discovered that it was an historical document for the benefit of future generations. Gradually, his initial awed reaction turned to confusion.

It described in depth how conditions on the planet had become extremely inhospitable, that the environment had deteriorated, most other species had gone extinct; all at the expense of the flourishing global community. Weather conditions had become unmerciful outside of the safe confines of the city walls. Population levels had fluctuated and there were continual struggles with the ever-growing problem of overcrowding. He read that nations, controlled by large businesses, had ceased diplomatic relations in order to fight for what scarce resources were left, to fuel the development of their vast metropolises. Technology had advanced and most people did not work, as everything had become automated, and the lucky few lived in virtual reality simulations. The direction of society functioned for the benefit of the very few and made the majority suffer unknowingly. Collaboration, prosperity, sustainability, and compassion had stagnated, all for the sake of greed that was enriching those very few in power. As he read this, various images appeared on the screen, further revealing the brutal reality.

Aldber had to step back for a moment to digest what he had just read. Although there were many things detailed that he did not fully understand, it was all too apparent that the ancient world he had once idealised was in fact a grotesque and unfair place. It was not the utopia he has hoped for. It was utterly heart-breaking for him to see that his people had done such unthinkable and selfish things to each other and the world.

He was suddenly reminded of the conversation with Red River weeks beforehand.

It made him shudder. He felt ashamed.

Although these truths were hard to accept, Aldber could not understand why the order had felt compelled to hide them away from the people. Perhaps Altamos, and the grand masters that preceded him, felt that to reveal these harsh realities of old would cripple their motivations and self-image. That the shame they felt for the ancestors would somehow demoralise everyone and discredit their divine right towards the world. The people had been feed a false truth. But Aldber knew otherwise, and that if circumstances could change favourably, the information would be shared to give a reminder to future generations of how not to live, by learning from the mistakes of their ancestors.

Feeling unnerved, Aldber turned away from the terminal and decided to recommence his search for the vision globe. On the far side was a cage, behind which sat many objects upon shelves concealed in dusty cloths. After negotiating over mounds of rubbish, upon closer inspection he carefully opened the doors, which made a piercing sound on its rusted hinges. He walked inside and looked across the crooked shelves for something of spherical shape. He picked up various things until spotting one that looked like just the right dimensions to be held comfortably within the palm of the hand.

He walked over to the object and picked it off the shelf. It was quite heavy in his grasp as he pulled off the cloth bag to reveal a smooth translucent glass bulb. It was cold in his hand as he observed its simple design. Suddenly, it came to life, like a small storm cloud appearing inside, forming an image of the outline of the forbidden chamber. He was astounded by what he was holding, then concealed it within the cloth wrap, placed it intricately inside his pouch, and closed the cage behind him.

As Aldber was planning to leave the chamber, an object lying on a table caught his eye. It was a small metal device. Seeing it invoked a reaction and a name came to mind that he had not considered since.

'Kip,' he uttered. On closer inspection, the ancient device was in good condition and its energy cell was not damaged. He took it and placed it delicately inside his pouch along with the globe.

As Aldber turned to leave, his elbow snagged another device that soon came to life. He was in a hurry but was transfixed by the small brightly lit display. He placed down the pouch precariously on the table and had a look at the contraption. He pushed one small button and then it suddenly erupted with a magnificent noise. It was overwhelming to Aldber's ears and the shock sent him falling to the floor. Although it could have attracted unwanted attention, he lay there on the dusty ground, completely entranced by the otherworldly enrapturing sounds. It was as though he was hearing the voice of the Supreme One, like the sound of a thousand birds' song, as though his soul was crying out harmoniously with joy at the tranquillity of existence.

He lay there rigid as tears starting streaming down his face. But no sooner had the sound projected from the device did it then stop, and Aldber finally drew breath. He could not fathom what it was he had just heard. The young warrior composed himself, got to his feet, and grabbed the pouch. Before exiting the chamber, he made sure he had left no obvious signs he had tampered with anything. Once satisfied, he started making his way for the door, turned off the switch, closed the door, and locked it swiftly behind him.

Aldber then made his way haphazardly towards the grand master's chambers, being vigilant and hoping not to stumble into Grombl and Maloyk or any other night patrol. Grasping the strap of the shoulder bag tightly, he walked down the corridor towards the leader's quarters, feeling self-conscious and trying to appear relaxed in front of the guards.

'I just had to run an errand for Grand Master Vivid,' Aldber said, gesturing to the bag.

'One moment,' one of the guards said in a formal tone, before she knocked on the door, waited for a reply, and then walked inside. She returned shortly afterwards and kept the door open for the bura to enter.

Aldber anxiously strode into the master's chamber, looking back as the door closed behind him. Once this happened, he let out a sigh of relief, feeling assured. Grand Master Vivid appeared from his sleeping chamber wearing a dressing gown. He walked towards the bura, noticing the circular bulb in the young warrior's shoulder bag and the peculiar expression upon his face.

'I can see that you were successful.' Vivid put his hand forth. Aldber went to open the bag to reveal the vision globe. 'No, I do not want to see that ghastly thing! Please, return the key to me.' Aldber then obliged.

'You know what I have in here?' Aldber said, pulling the flat back over his bag.

'Aldber, I hope you comprehend why such devices like this vision globe have been prohibited.'

'Master, whilst I was in the forbidden chamber, I saw many things that were unexpected, and learnt many painful truths.'

'I thought that might have been the case, judging by the expression I saw upon your face when you first entered this room.'

'Why has the order withheld so much information about our ancestors?'

'That, dear boy, is a conversation for another time. I am an old man and require my rest.'

'Yes, Master.' Aldber bowed. 'And once again, I am sorry for contemplating stealing the key from you.'

'Your apology is accepted.' Vivid smiled warmly. 'Now, be gone. Leave me in peace!'

'Very well,' Aldber smiled and then exited the master's chamber.

It was now late into the night as he made his way back to his private quarters. Once inside, he hid the sleeved globe and transmitter far underneath his bed before clambering onto it. He managed to settle down and calm himself, even though he was still filled with adrenaline from the evening's events. Aldber would slip into a very pleasant sleep, where the sound of a thousand songbirds once more carried him away.

Chapter Eleven
Traitors

Aldber managed to smuggle the device out of the Sanctuary in his luggage bag, before once more setting forth for the large skyscraper in sector nine and accompanying Hollow Moon and the Outcasts on their perilous quest. He had since paid closer attention to the vision globe's workings, much to the bafflement and curiosity of the centauri.

'That object you possess is cursed with twisted magic.' Flying Stone peered down at the translucent orb as all the outcasts stood around the bura inspecting it.

'Yes, I believe such a thing is enchanted!' Singing Eye took a step back, evidently scared.

'It is like peering through a looking glass at a more complicated and eerie version of the environment than we have ever seen before,' Bleeding Sky said with equal wonderment and caution.

Aldber found this to be amusing. He covered the device with the cloth and tried to reason with them: 'Look, I know that it must have been confiscated for a reason; however, I will take great care when using it.'

'Why have you brought it along?' Hollow Moon asked.

'Because I believe it will assist us with our hunt for Black Scar,' the bura explained.

'Most impressive.' Red River nodded.

'Forward, we must move,' Hollow Moon ordered. The expedition then started to recommence their hike. Aldber carefully placed the sleeved vision globe back inside his rucksack, before throwing the strap across his shoulder. He saw her staring back at him as he did this, but she instantly averted her gaze.

'She didn't seem as threatened by it, compared with the others,' he thought.

They set course westwards, with the intention of heading towards the Cayhan Desert. This was a habitat the centauri seldom ventured into, but the Outcasts thought it would be worth investigating. Unfortunately, there are few records of their time spent in this region of the continent, but what is clear is that it was uneventful, as they found no trace of centauri in the barren sand-covered wilderness. They then returned eastward, and trekked along the outskirts of the city walls, with the intention of entering the city ruins once more. They would head for the dangers of the front line, and, hopefully, with time, Aldber would gather a greater understanding of how to use the vision globe. He knew he would have to be patient.

One evening near to dusk, they crossed the plains and came to a large hole in the wall of the metropolis. They took shelter and surveyed the landscape. Hollow Moon instructed for Long Wing to go ahead of the party to scout out whether they could enter here without being spotted. It would be too dangerous to enter the city with the lack of visibility in the darkness, and they would waste time waiting until sunrise.

Aldber and the remaining Outcasts lay in the grass and waited for Long Wing to return. It was silent for a long while, as birds of prey flew overhead in the crimson sky. From afar they could see Long Wing galloping back towards them. She came straight to Hollow Moon and Aldber to tell them the coast was clear.

The leader summoned the expedition to approach, and they started edging towards the gigantic wall. As they started negotiating over the rubble, far off in the distance they could see a storm forming and lightning beginning to strike the ruined buildings.

They reached the other side, and all seemed well when, unbeknownst to them, ahead emerged a large group of centauri. The expedition froze in their tracks and waited, hoping not to be spotted, but it was all too apparent they could not avoid this encounter.

'Proceed calmly, everyone,' Hollow Moon said under her breath as they edged closer to the group. She looked back at Aldber; he had put on the shackles to appear like a prisoner and had also concealed his pistol. Her comrades all brandished the weapons they had stolen.

As the two parties drew closer, those ahead exchanged comments when they saw the lone human amongst the small pack of their kind. They eventually stopped and there was a moment of silence.

Aldber could smell suspicion permeating through the air.

One of Black Scar's loyal warriors stood forward. It wore a cloak of authority.

'What brings a small pack, with a prisoner, to the borders of this part of the city? Where have you come from?' Aldber could tell by the leader's tone of voice that it was a male. It questioned with its hands resting upon its rear-hips.

'We were travelling from the east, having misplaced our garrison, and found this lone human. We thought it would be appropriate to bring him in for interrogation.' Hollow Moon sold her newly created alibi with ease. There was no hint of hesitation or over-confidence.

'Do you suspect this human has vital information?' The leader walked forward to inspect him. Aldber averted his gaze downwards, subtly shook his clasped hands, and started to make his lower-lip tremble, as to appear petrified. The ground darkened as the leader loomed over him.

'We think he might be of high rank within the human resistance,' Hollow Moon explained as more of the loyalists encircled the expedition.

'Ah, so a distinguished warrior of the Galardros.' The leader put a finger to Aldber's chin and lifted his face upwards. The bura intentionally avoided eye contact with him.

Long Wing stood forward to address the leader. 'We believe so.'

'I wonder how much he would squeal'—the leader suddenly grasped Aldber by the neck, squeezed tightly, and effortlessly lifted him up so that they were at eye level— 'before he would disclose anything?'

Aldber could barely breathe, his windpipe was closed, and a heavy throbbing sensation of pressure was building in his head. His legs hung above the ground, as he reached up with his shackled hands to grab onto the centauri's hand to try and prize away the grip. All the while the only sound was his groans. The Outcasts looked on in fright, unable to do anything, holding their weapons ready to fight.

But then the leader released his grip and Aldber tumbled down onto the floor, desperately gasping air into his lungs.

'Unfortunately,' —the leader turned to face Hollow Moon — 'we do not have any translators at our base, so there is no possibility of extracting information from this human. It is of no further use, so can be executed.'

The Outcast all looked at Aldber wide-eyed, before turning to face the loyalist's leader. Hollow Stone said: 'If you do not have a translator stationed with you, we shall take him somewhere else.'

'*No!*' the leader barked and turned to face the expedition. Aldber remained motionless, lying upon the floor. 'You shall do no such thing.' The leader then faced Hollow Moon. 'Word has spread like wildfire that a small pack of centauri accompanied by a human have been trekking across the northern regions of the continent. Many say that Hollow Moon and the Outcasts have arisen once more in their quest to hunt down our beloved leader.'

'They wouldn't dare.' Hollow Moon maintained a neutral expression.

'There have been rumours that the human that they are conspiring with is the prophet who is meant to bring salvation to humanity.' The leader then addressed his warriors: 'Who would have thought that he would be presented to me already shackled! What a joy it is that I shall have the entertainment of destroying him.'

In that brief moment, Aldber twisted the faulty shackles, unclasping them from his wrists, reached under his jacket for his concealed weapon and pulled it out to point at the leader, just as the shackles clattered onto the cold stone floor. Everyone heard the noise and turned to face him.

'No, the pleasure is all mine!' Aldber exclaimed.

The loyalist leader did not have enough time to process the human speaking in his language, nor to register seeing the pistol pointed at him, as a bullet then blasted through its head.

'*Traitors*!' screamed one of the other warriors as their leader's body fell lifelessly to the floor. Its accomplices all erupted with rage and started running for the startled Outcasts.

'*Run*!' screamed Hollow Moon and she offered for Aldber to climb onto her back. He complied, jumped up, grabbed onto her mane for support, and hoisted himself up as she launched forward on all four of her limbs.

The expedition turned and started running desperately over the rubble to escape the city wall as bullets and arrows surged past them. Behind him, Aldber could hear the deafening howl of the loyalist warriors, as they started tailing them. He made a brief glance back to see a wave of darkness descend upon them. The expedition quickly jumped out onto the other side of the wall, just as the enemy forces exploded through the barricade and caught up with those unfortunate to be at the back.

Aldber held on with all his might as cold wind bellowed past him. He buried his head into her mane, but this did not muffle the distance screams as he heard some of the Outcasts being attacked. He could hear the sound of Singing Eye being helplessly overwhelmed.

The escapees ran relentlessly over the horizon and into the night. Gradually, the sound of the scream 'traitors' whistled through the breeze, and all Aldber could her was the pounding of Hollow Moon galloping. They kept on running as far as they could before someone made a signal that it was all clear, so they came to an abrupt stop. Aldber looked up; in front of him Hollow Moon was panting heavily. He jumped down from her back. In the minimal light, he could see that they were standing in a small woodland.

Hollow Moon called for all present to proclaim their names. They all did so and it was apparent, as Aldber had expected, that Singing Eye had perished. Flying Stone was sat next to Bleeding Sky trying to console him.

Red River approached, wheezing with old age. 'It appears that Black Scar has been made aware of our resurgence.'

'We no longer have the element of surprise,' Hollow Moon said, looking at the group nervously. 'Now that they are certain it is us; he will deploy large forces across the land to hunt us and destroy us.'

'*This is madness*! What are we doing Hollow Moon?' Long Wing questioned irritably. 'We should have never attempted this in the first place. We are alone in our efforts; all of our people support Black Scar! Once again, we have lost another one of the Outcasts. Our numbers will only dwindle drastically from henceforth.'

'*Settle down*, Long Wing!' Flying Stone scorned. 'We have gone too far now to give up.'

'Yes, we must remain focused and move on,' Hollow Moon reasoned, seeing the despair in her comrades. 'We must be defiant and not deterred.'

'Then we had best make haste and finish Black Scar off, once and for all,' Red River said pensively. There was an uncomfortable silence hanging over the group. Aldber stood there taking a few moments to gather his thoughts before walking forward.

'I feel that I am accountable for the loss of Singing Eye,' he said, looking over at Bleeding Sky.

'No, Aldber, regardless of how you reacted by shooting that warrior, we would have had to fight our way out of there,' Hollow Moon reasoned in a gentle tone.

'What is also apparent from that ordeal is that the prophecy is common knowledge amongst the armies.' Aldber looked through the darkness and exchanged glances with the remaining Outcasts. They all looked up to him with exhausted and confused expressions. No one replied.

'*How could Black Scar's forces know that I am with them?*' he thought, looking at them all sceptically. '*Could it be that one of the Outcasts has secretly relinquished their ties to the cause, betrayed the others, divulged information to the leader's warriors, and possibly led us into a trap tonight? But how could that be? They spend all of their time together and know each other so well. A deserter would be found out too easily.*'

'We must find denser foliage, under which we can camp for the night.' Hollow Moon beckoned for the expedition to follow her onwards into the woodland. Aldber remained and then looked eastwards.

'*Or could it be someone else?*' he thought.

Far away in the hidden valley, Hecta was abruptly awoken from his sleep by the sound of commotion. Outside of his quarters, he could hear the unmistakable noise of distant screams. His initial reaction was to reach for his sword, which he kept sheathed by his bedside. He took the blade, got up, and peeked out of the door as several warriors ran past down the hillside. The weathered warrior quickly put on his clothes, held his sword firmly, and ran from the quarters in the direction of the source of all the attention.

As he ran down the hillside, he could see in the distance huge flames slicing into the night sky. To his disbelief, he could see that a fire had engulfed several buildings. Warriors frantically tried to calm the blaze with buckets of water. As the elder approached the overpowering heat, a bridge above him gave way and starting hurtling towards the ground. Hecta quickly responded and dived out of the way, pushing two onlookers to safety with his force, before getting to his feet and running down to the source of the fire.

There, he could see both Grombl and Maloyk hysterically running around trying to put out the blaze. The former was babbling something indecipherably and the latter was looking into the flames with terror, clasping his cheeks and shaking his head with disbelief. Hecta paced towards them both, grabbed them by the scruff of their necks, and dragged them to the side, out of the fire's reach. He loomed over them with outrage.

'What have you two *done?*' he shouted, looking at them both individually, as flames reflected in his eyes. 'All of the crops are *destroyed!*'

'B-B-B-B-B-Bura Hecta, w-w..,' Grombl tried to annunciate but was clearly overwhelmed with shock. Hecta looked at Maloyk who was sweating and obviously would not give any answers. In his frustration, Hecta groaned, grabbed their heads and slammed them together in a vain attempt to knock some sense into them both.

'What happened here?' Grand Master Vivid approached looking mortified as others came forth to tackle the menacing flames.

'Grand Master Vivid, we came when we saw this fire. It was not us! I swear!' Grombl pleaded. 'It grew so fast, Masters.'

Hecta loosened his grip on the pair and looked at Grand Master Vivid in bafflement, who gave him a stern look.

'There is nothing flammable kept near to the crops that could have caused an accident. Bura Hecta, make sure that this fire is dealt with, and then report to my chambers, immediately,' Grand Master Vivid ordered. 'I will summon the other councillors. I am holding an emergency meeting.'

Hecta then reluctantly let go of the two frightened assistants and went off to gather water to tame the fire. The dishevelled pair gasped and looked at each other in horror. The vast field of crops was now decimated, and the air was choked with smoke and flames. Grand

Master Vivid stood there motionless as the blaze surged in front of him.

'Someone did this on purpose,' he thought.

Chapter Twelve
The Vision Globe

Aldber and the remaining Outcasts spent a few days walking through the woodlands before taking the risk of approaching and scaling the ruins of the Old City once more. The atmosphere amongst the party had been subdued, and the young warrior had kept to himself, not entirely convinced he had the competence to console grieving centauri.

As they ventured further into the monstrosity, he felt that it was time to speak to Hollow Moon about various methods of attack, in order to finally confront Black Scar.

'Taking into consideration what happened the other night and accepting that Black Scar's forces are actively searching for us, I have contemplated various strategies, and most come to a conclusion of certain suicide,' he admitted as the expedition walked under a collapsed bridge. His hushed voiced echoed against the stone above them. Hollow Moon contemplated this but did not speak.

'After all of these moon-cycles, Tala's words are starting to sink in. It seems the likelihood of death is becoming the unavoidable outcome of this conquest,' he thought.

'Even though circumstances have swayed against us, it only strengthens my resolve. I still have my every hope that we will succeed.' Hollow Moon looked at him and smiled.

'What if I was to suggest that we set a trap for him? I could be presented as bait.'

'Unfortunately, as much as I like that idea, it would be too obvious. The leader works in mysterious ways, lurking in the background, and would not make himself presentable and vulnerable to such an obvious set-up. He is equally abundant in arrogance and cowardice.'

Aldber was becoming frustrated with her lack of enthusiasm to take bigger gambles but knew that she understood the ways of her people better than he did. She did not want to waste sun-cycles of preparation on an impulse.

'When you all have been resting at night, I have spent time alone deep in meditation, trying to strengthen my connection in order to draw from the Source,' Aldber explained.

'And has that helped?' Hollow Moon asked.

'Only time can tell. Just like Black Scar, it works in mysterious ways.'

'Both seem to be unreachable entities that we are trying to gain a better understanding of.'

'Yes, it does seem to be the case. I feel like my addition to the expedition has not been forthcoming so far, and despite what you said – I feel a sense of guilt for the loss of Singing Eye. Those loyal to Black Scar will now feel compelled more than ever to hunt us down, because of my presence. And you have asked me to join you because of my powers, which I am not able to fully unleash. Whilst meditating I tried to imagine being in Black Scar's mindset, to guess his strategy, to try and find an alternative way, but felt a mental block each time. Not only do I lack the sun-cycles of experience being a leader, but there was also something obvious which obstructed my endeavour: I am not simply dealing with a human, whose thoughts and feelings I could simply try and relate to through my own experiences and behaviour, but I was trying to delve into the mindset of another species, another way of thinking, and another brain composition. It gave me much to contemplate about the nature of consciousness within all beings.'

'I know it is a lot for you to comprehend, but if it is true that you have such potential to bring salvation to your own kind, than surely that which gives you such power can also assist us to find Black Scar?'

'You have a lot of faith in something you know so little about.'

'The universe operates in mysterious ways.'

'It seems they have been pushed to such extremes, and in their desperation have taken a gamble with me. They respect my opinion and think that I can help them to outsmart the leader, and yet she is not accepting my suggestions,' he thought.

As the expedition trundled through the endless streets of the ruins, Aldber's message bird Heratu arrived. There was word from Tala saying that after having spent several weeks trekking across the northern regions of the West Lands, using a gifted map to guide her in order to advise him where to avoid, and places of significance where the fearsome leader of the centauri could be, she was frustrated at their shortcomings, and planned on returning to the

Sanctuary, and would update him in due course, especially regarding Dev's condition.

Because of the change in atmosphere amongst the expedition, and due to the mounting stress Aldber was feeling from the magnitude of what they were failingly trying to accomplish, he started to withdraw from socialising at night-time in order to pay more attention to the vision globe, with the hope that it would be of use. Initially, he had been stumped by its mechanisms, but gradually started to understand its functioning.

On the first evening, he sat away from the others with the hood pulled over his head and cloak pulled tightly in order to block out any external light or noises. When he pulled the sleeve away and rested the cool glass in the palm of his hand, the device came to life, with an eerie glow like the moon nestled behind cloud-line.

Aldber was not sure what he was meant to do. He turned the device around to see if any words had appeared or if there were any buttons he could press, but was taken aback when it spoke with a calm and deep male voice in the Common Tongue: 'Hello, what is your name?'

'Aldber,' he replied somewhat reluctantly, having never done anything like this before.

'It is a pleasure to be of service to you, Aldber,' it continued. 'In order for me to maximise my operational capabilities, would you like to be connected to the network?'

'What is the network?' Aldber leaned in closer.

'It is a system I am linked to where all information is stored and is available literally at your fingertips, by using me. All you have to do is keep your hand positioned on the globe and I will connect you to it.'

'How exactly would I be connected to the network?'

'A simple electrical implant is coded into your mind.'

'Sorry! What?'

'It means that you can enjoy the full range of features with this device.'

'Can I be disconnected at any time from this network?'

'You can, upon request.'

'And the implant with it?'

'Fully removed.'

Aldber sat there for a moment to consider whether he should proceed, knowing full well how dangerous this ancient device supposedly was. But then he could hear the sound of the Outcasts conversing behind him and remembered why he had taken the risk in the first place to find it.

'Desperate times call for desperate measures.'

'Very well,' Aldber said.

'One moment please,' the operating system said. Suddenly, the glass underneath where his hands were holding the globe started to glow with a throbbing light and Aldber could feel the area warm slightly. Moments later this stopped. 'The implant has been successful; you are now connected to the network and have full access to my features.'

'Oh, right!' Aldber laughed excitably. 'Can you tell me what those features might be?'

It presented images of the surrounding scenery, which was helpful for the expedition to avoid being spotted. It provided routes to clean water access, told Aldber the weather patterns and even recommended suitable journey plans to avoid confrontation with human and centauri forces. With time, as he became more acquainted with the globe, he knew it would enable them to minimise any risks in their pursuits.

'Are you able to give me the exact whereabout of certain individuals?' Aldber asked.

'I will require detailed information to be compared against data stored on the network.'

'What about Black Scar?'

'Scanning now.'

Aldber was startled by the vision globe's announcement and sat up attentively, waiting patiently as he gazed fixedly into the glass orb.

'That name is on the network. However, the associated profile is not connected to the network, so I am unable to proceed.'

'So, this confirms that Black Scar had once used one of these vision globes when searching for me,' Aldber thought.

'That is correct,' the operating system suddenly replied.

'Excuse me?' Aldber exclaimed.

'One aspect of the electrical implant's function is to read your thoughts,' the vision globe explained.

'Oh, right. But only when I am operating you?' Aldber asked anxiously.

'Correct.'

'What else can it do?'

'Produce imagery in your mind's eye.'

'Show me.'

'Certainly.'

Suddenly, Aldber vision was eclipsed by images of the Old City, but from a perspective looking down upon it from a great height. It was both staggering and thoroughly disorientating, making Aldber feel like he was about to fall to the ground.

'Okay, that is enough!' he commanded. The image disappeared and he once more was looking at the glowing orb. 'Wow that was incredible!'

'Is there anything else I can assist you with?'

'Not for now. How can I switch you off?'

'Simply remove both hands to disengage.'

Aldber did so and then pulled off the hood whilst still looking at the vision globe in wonder. He was once more immersed in the sounds and smells of his surroundings, having been lost operating the device. Astounded by the experience, he stood up and went to go and tell the Outcasts what had happened.

A few weeks passed as the expedition moved further into the heart of the city ruins, ever closer to the front line of the conflict.

Being surrounded by the colossal structures was quite foreboding and made them feel claustrophobic. By this time, Aldber had refrained from talking to the others as regularly; the novelty of discussion had worn off, and he now spent a considerable amount of time paying attention to the vision globe. At first, he had been intrigued by it, but was now relying on it instead of using his own training and intuition, even to the noticeable extent that he was becoming obsessional with using it and striking up an unlikely bond with the operating system's personality.

One evening, he lay there wrapped tightly in his blanket under the stars, wishing to be in the comfort of his own bed. Now that the seasons were changing, it was getting bitterly cold at night. Meanwhile, the centauri slept around him relevantly unaffected, protected by their fur. As he tried to resist shivering, that's when he heard the globe summoning him. He could hear its muffled voice coming from the inside of his travel sack. It uttered his name suggestively and he could not resist the temptation to look at it, if only for a short time, before resting. He looked around to make sure no one was watching and delved in and unravelled the device from its cloth.

'Good evening, Aldber,' it said in its calm and assured manner. Aldber sat up and crossed his legs, took his cloak and threw it over his head to conceal them.

'Vision globe, tell me more of what you know of this local area in the ancient times,' Aldber asked excitably, cupping the delicate glowing device in his hands.

'Of course. This local area was once a hub of industry that helped to fuel the demanding needs of the magnificent metropolis.' The device then displayed colour images to illustrate this.

'It is quite remarkable, really. Who inhabits this area now?' Aldber whispered.

'Precisely one mile below the surface, the Dubaj tribe currently reside. They have a population of approximately two-hundred-and-thirty-nine and have Mowoni Cecilo stationed with them.'

'You are quite a marvellous piece of technology.'

'I serve my purpose to the best of my programmed capabilities.'

'And what exac-'

'Aldber, who are you talking to?' Flying Stone questioned from behind him. The centauri was not the friendliest at the best of times, let alone when inconveniently awoken from his rest. Aldber pulled the cloak off and looked at the aggravated outcast.

'Sorry, Flying Stone, I was talking to the... um... the vision globe.' Aldber fumbled his words, feeling embarrassed.

'Right. Well, keep it quiet, some of us are trying to rest here,' Flying Stone grumbled, before turning over to find a more comfortable position. Within moments he had recommenced snoring.

Aldber looked at the globe and smiled, giving it a friendly rub, before meticulously returning it under the cover of the cloth, and laid it down next to his makeshift pillow. He looked around to make sure the others were not watching him and would sleep that night with one hand resting on the globe, just in case. He did not want anyone else tinkering with the device.

One cold morning, whilst the expedition had stopped to rest, Aldber was relieved when way overhead he saw a message bird circling. He walked out from under cover into plain sight and watched as the majestic creature spotted him and descended to the street surface. It was Heratu, his trusted winged companion. It chirped with joy when it perched on Aldber's forearm and tickled the favourite spot on her back.

'Hello, my good friend! You don't know how glad I am to see you,' Aldber whispered, opening the pouch under its neck. 'What news do you have for me here today? Please, let it be Black Scar offering an open invitation.'

Aldber took out the small parchment, which he knew instantaneously was from Tala, as she always folded her correspondences neatly. He knew this was the most probable case but felt slightly disappointed it wasn't from someone random.

Aldber,

I returned to the Sanctuary this morning and something strange has happened. Over the course of the past few weeks there have been repeated acts of vandalism in the stronghold. The atmosphere here is uncomfortable. Also, Dev is being monitored in the medical rooms and his condition has gotten worse.

You need to return to the Sanctuary NOW.
Tala

Aldber reread the note several times to make sure he was processing it fully. His immediate concern was hearing about Dev's health. He had assumed, optimistically, that his friend would be recovering from the illness, but his gut feeling signalled that this was not a problem that could be resolved easily. As for the vandalism, he guessed that there would be a more straightforward explanation for this. Seeing as the recent few weeks of searching for Black Scar had again been unfruitful and considering that he needed to have peace of mind regarding these troubling issues raised by Tala, the mission would have to be put on hold whilst he attended to them.

Aldber spoke to the Outcasts and explained that his friend was very ill. They understood, though shared his frustrations regarding their search. He tried to make a joke with them about their misfortunes, but their confused reaction conveyed they still did not quite understand his sense of humour. He had discovered over the past few moon-cycles that there was limitation to conversation with this species. It was agreed that Aldber would return as soon as possible, whilst they continued their quest. They all wished him safe passage and he set off on his lonesome through the treacherous ruins and back towards the northern wall in the direction of the Sanctuary.

*

When Aldber did return to the valley, the scenery was now a rich palette of brown and yellow, leaves were beginning to fall from the trees, and the valley floor was covered in a sea of decomposing foliage. Aldber made his way into the stronghold and decided to prioritise seeing his friends before reporting to the council.

He proceeded towards Tala's quarters, which were unoccupied, and so he thought it best to go straight to the medical rooms. When he entered the facilities, he was welcomed with open arms and a kiss to the cheek by a few of the maidens who had worked there for many sun-cycles and had helped to raise him as an infant.

'Aldber, I am so glad to see you are well,' Maiden Gailden said, smiling adoringly at the new arrival. She was a middle-aged woman, her hair short and silver, dressed in a simple white tunic. 'You look like you need a good wash.'

'I will in good time. Maiden Gailden, can you direct me to Silo Dev?' Aldber asked looking over her shoulder at the candlelit room. Various beds were dotted throughout and a sweet aroma pulsated through the air.

'Of course.' She then stood aside and offered for him to follow her. 'Dev has been held here for a few weeks now and we cannot determine what exactly he has contracted.'

'He looked tired and was coughing up blood when I last saw him,' Aldber explained as they moved past various injured warriors. 'How bad is this?'

'It is not good at all, I am afraid,' she said gravely and then showed him to a separate area segmented by a curtain at the back of the room, where Tala was sat leaning over the patient's bed. As they drew closer, Aldber could see Dev's condition had deteriorated strikingly.

'I don't know... the excuses you will make to get out of doing your duties!' Aldber joked as he approached. His two friends looked up at him and smiled. Tala stood up and threw her arms around his neck in a tight embrace.

'Hey, Aldber, good to see you!' Dev managed to annunciate and, although his voice sounded strained, he was elated to see his friend return. He attempted to sit up but could not muster the energy. Aldber took a seat by his bedside and looked at the patient with grave concern.

'How are you feeling?' Aldber gazed into his friend's eyes. He knew it was an idiotic question to ask.

'I have felt better.' Dev nodded, trying with all his might to remain composed. Aldber placed a hand on his shoulder and nodded. He didn't know what else to say to him.

'Tala, these walls have ears, can I have a word with you outside?' Aldber looked over to her. She was transfixed on her ill lover, looking gaunt and sleep deprived, but stirred, looked at Aldber, and acknowledged the request. The two friends left Dev and headed out of the medical rooms to speak in private.

'How have you been?' he asked in the Black Tongue.

'Excuse me?' she said, closing the door behind her.

'Sorry.' He switched to the Common Tongue. 'I have spent so much time with the Outcasts that I forgotten which language I am speaking in!' They both laughed. 'How have you been?'

'I feel powerless. Aldber, Dev has been consumed by illness and I don't think he is going to make it.' Her lower lip trembled as she spoke in her usual straight-talking fashion.

It was the stark reality they all too often had to face, that with such harsh conditions, disease was common and not easily treated. Never did Aldber imagine this would happen to a close friend. He did not want to mask the truth with any empty promises or reassurances, so instead just grabbed Tala and held her in a comforting hug. She put her arms around him, held tightly, and started sobbing into his torso. He listened to her crying, felt her body shaking, was overcome with a wave of sadness and breathed in deeply to accept the unsettling emotion. He started brushing her hair to offer comfort. Once she had released all she needed to, she brushed away her tears and stood tall. He waited for her to fully compose herself.

'Have you had any developments in your search for Black Scar?' she asked, clearly her throat.

'No.' Aldber looked down at the ground, frowning. He then gave her more details. 'I am sure the council will have a lot to say about it when I report to them shortly.'

'Aldber, there is something going on here. People are becoming paranoid and demoralised.' She looked at him intensely. 'First it was the crops, then the storerooms were trashed, and then the armoury was broken into. I have heard that councillors have been receiving death threats.'

'You are *kidding me*, Tala?' Aldber was outraged but tried to keep his voice restrained as two assistants walked by.

'These were no freak accidents or coincidences. There is someone trying to cause mayhem.'

'How do you know that it is just one person? It is definitely not a centauri?'

'No, it was a human. A hooded figure has been spotted. For something like this to happen, if it was more than one person it would be easier to foil. These random acts seem too small to be an elaborate plan of a few co-conspirators, especially in a stronghold so well guarded.'

'This does not make any sense. Do you really think it is a plot to weaken the order?'

'Undoubtedly. This person is intentionally trying to install hysteria and mistrust in the ranks.'

'That is absurd. What is the council doing about it?'

'Security has been tightened and more men are being put on patrol. Grand Master Vivid refuses to take emergency powers. Even though there is questioning of loyalty in the council, he does not want to alienate himself away from the rest of the members and wants to maintain solidarity. We all must carry on and stand defiant in the face of this terrorism.'

'This stronghold has been kept secret for so many sun-cycles, it must be someone from the inside trying to disrupt the operation, but that is ludicrous!' Aldber started pacing around, as he did when consumed in deep thought. 'The order is all we have; it is the only hope we have in fighting the Enemy!'

'I know. It is very disheartening to think about.'

'There have been many disagreements amongst the elders; perhaps it is one of them trying to topple Grand Master Vivid? Or perhaps someone in the ranks is attempting to shake the council into action?'

'As much as I do not like to admit it, I think that could be a possibility,' Tala admitted. 'There is that, plus another option...'

'Which is?' Aldber stopped and looked at her, raising an eyebrow with curiosity.

'I find this all to be too coincidental to ignore. You have had continual shortcomings with your search for Black Scar. You would have thought finding the leader of the Enemy would have been a lot easier, right?'

'Well, yes. I suppose I have gotten myself into something more than I anticipated.'

'Perhaps that was exactly what he intended. He knows very well that you and the Outcasts are tailing him. What if he is playing a game with us, remaining hidden, and somehow has planted an insurgent here in the Galardros ranks?'

'I mean, that is quite an outlandish thing, if true. So, he is trying to destroy us from within?' he asked, although couldn't quite believe it. She nodded.

'You have said before that we should not underestimate our enemy. It now seems we should not trust our allies, either. I am sure it is something he has been preparing for all these sun-cycles since he killed your mother. It is quite a bold and calculated move, if true. How many others know how to speak the Black Tongue?'

'I am not sure. Grand Master Vivid kept my lessons a secret to everyone other than the council, but that isn't to suggest that they weren't taught as well. But how and why would anyone accept to do such a thing to conspire with Black Scar?'

'Never underestimate the selfish motives of people,' she reasoned. 'There are some here whose allegiances could be easily swayed.'

'But who would *seriously* want to collaborate with the centauri leader? Our *sworn* enemy.'

'Perhaps it is not him directly they are colluding with. Perhaps they are bargaining for their lives because they see no positive outcome out of this war.'

'Thortatel. He constantly challenges everything. I wouldn't be surprised. He always comes across as an unreasonable and callous man. Both him and Councillor Gilliad.' Aldber then paused to reflect. 'Although we cannot jump to any conclusions just yet.'

'Exactly. From now on just be careful who you speak to whilst you are here,' she said, looking at him seriously, and then exhaled a sorrowed sigh. 'I must return to Dev.'

'I will report to the council and then will return immediately,' he said gently.

Aldber then stepped forward, gave her another hug and watched her re-enter the medical rooms, before swiftly turning on his heels to head down the corridor. He pondered their conversation as he took a path towards the council tower.

Every visit to the council of recent times had been a raucous affair and Aldber knew he was not going to be welcomed with the kindness and open arms he had received by everyone in the medical rooms. He was not expecting flattery or soft reassurances by any means, but just wanted to know what was going on within the higher ranks of the order. He knew outright that he would not be able to question this directly and would not receive confirmation. He knew it would me an intense meeting.

Once he was summoned before Grand Master Vivid and the other elders, he did his ceremonial bows. Once pleasantries had finished, he could sense instantly the tension in the atmosphere amongst the council.

'Grand Master Vivid, Councillors, I have returned, by request of Bura Tala, because of the deteriorating health of Silo Dev. Since my last visit to the Sanctuary, the expedition trekked across the Cayhan Desert, to no avail, and was ambushed by enemy forces; we incurred a loss and now know that the Enemy are aware of our quest, including me accompanying them. Since then, we have plotted a safe passage into the city, and have since travelled deeper into the ruins.'

'And what developments *have* you made in your hunt for Black Scar?' Grand Master Vivid asked, looking noticeably tired.

'Alas, we have not made any further progress, much to my own frustration,' Aldber replied.

'It looks like the boy is not capable of such a task,' heckled one of the council members in Aldber's peripheral vision, who he ignored.

'Admittedly, our searches have been limited due to the Outcasts' lack of confidence in exploring different tactics,' Aldber explained, 'including setting a trap where I would be bait.'

'Well, that *does* sound like a mighty fine idea!' Councillor Thortatel interjected and Gilliad sniggered to his side.

'What do you think is the best form of action?' Grand Master Vivid remained calm and ignored the incessant mockery.

'We are aware that the majority of the Enemy forces are stationed in the West Lands. I have good confidence to believe that Black Scar certainly is here and not on Irelaf or the East Lands,' Aldber continued. He then hesitated from delivering his true intentions, fully aware there might be a spy now sat amongst the council. 'We are going to head to the front line, with the intention of capturing one of the centauri's war lords, who we will interrogate.'

Instead, he was going to suggest that the expedition set course for the Uncharted Regions in the south of the continent. He was aware that the indigenous tribes of those parts had no understanding of either Ramasha or the Common Tongue, and that the order was not recognised there, but he hoped that it was possible Black Scar was is in those parts, as little was known of the Enemy's movements there.

'Aldber, you have been given time and resources for this little vanity mission of yours.' Thortatel looked around at the other council members. 'Isn't it clear that he has not the competence to accomplish this mission or to warrant such unworthy praise? We should not have sent a squire to do a warrior's task.'

Aldber clenched his fists. Now more than ever, in these times when there was a great undercurrent of mistrust within the council, he had the urge to wipe that smile off the councillor's face. But he remained stationary and bit his tongue out of respect, knowing that reacting with aggression would only give fuel to Thortatel's animosity and would show that he was not capable of controlling himself. The young bura could see Councillor Gilliad glaring at him, waiting for him to break.

'Councillor Thortatel, with all due respect, this mission requires patience in order to be achieved. May I remind you that I am doing something no Galardros has ever been tasked with before, so I would expect a little more...' Aldber said.

'A little more what?' Thortatel suddenly cut him short. 'A little more respect? You come waltzing in here in your arrogant manner, expecting us to accept your half-hearted attempts.'

'Do excuse me Councillor,' Aldber replied, remaining calm, 'I admit that my efforts have not been successful yet, but what exactly has been your greatest contribution of late, apart from criticising everyone else? You are always very vocal in your objections but have not exactly been proactive yourself. '

'*How dare you*!' Thortatel sat forward and went red in the face as the others around him remained silent. He composed himself and gave a forced smile, whilst his fingernails dug into the stone chair. 'You shall not speak so disrespectfully to me. Don't think you are so clever, *boy*!'

Thortatel's eyes were enraged like a storm as he sat back tittering to himself, attempting to laugh off the remarks refutably, as though they weren't worth the effort to justify defending against. Aldber had to bite his lip to stop himself from smiling.

'Councillor Thortatel, please don't be tainted by Aldber's remarks. We all here know you are an invaluable member to this council,' Grand Master Vivid said, winking at Aldber with a vague smirk. 'Bura Aldber, will you require any assistance with the next stage of your mission?'

'Only your continual counsel and correspondence, Master,' Aldber bowed his head with a smile.

'Don't rush to come back,' Councillor Gilliad muttered spitefully under his breath.

'Gilliad that will be *enough*!' Vivid scorned and shot the councillor a stern look, before sitting back calmly in his chair of honour. 'So be it. With that said and done, council is adjourned until tomorrow morning.'

Grand Master Vivid then rose to his feet and his robes draped onto the floor around him. Hecta then stood up and walked behind the aged leader. The others followed suit and started making their way out of the tower into the early evening. Councillor Thortatel finally stood and walked past Aldber, ignoring him. To Aldber's displeasure, Councillor Gilliad approached rubbing his hands in a creepy fashion. They were the only two remaining.

'Becoming a little too quick-witted for your own good, aren't you, boy? You ought to watch yourself.' Gilliad smirked through his rotten teeth, poking the young man in the chest. Aldber remained motionless. 'So where are you off to now, Aldber? To see Tala, maybe? There are some rumours flying around. From what I have heard, it seems like she could need a shoulder to cry on at the moment. Especially as your friend Dev has been occupying badly needed bed space for far too long now. He should do us all a favour.'

In that moment something triggered. The continual sun-cycles of remaining passive to the constant ridicule, internalising all of his anguish and frustration, could not be contained anymore. It all manifested. Aldber was immersed in a burning rage and clenched his fist. With all of his momentum, he suddenly recoiled and then swung for Gilliad. He smacked the elder hard in the nose, the force sending the elder hurtling to the floor. The councillor fell hard and screamed, cupping his bleeding nose, shaking hysterically, and looking up at Aldber in shock. The young warrior loomed over him, his hands still clenched, taken aback by his actions, but unashamedly relieved.

'I am impenetrable to any insult under the sun you may throw at me, Councillor Gilliad, but you will *never* speak a bad word against my friends. *Do you understand?*' Aldber screamed through gritted teeth. Gilliad cowered on the ground, nodding distraughtly. His robes were now saturated with blood.

Aldber turned and stormed out of the tower, still clenching his fists. For the first time in a while, he felt a sense of release and did not care about the repercussions of his outburst. But this sense of triumph, a momentary glimpse of elation, was only to be shortly extinguished, as can be the case with life's many inconsiderate ways.

Chapter Thirteen
The Attempt

During that evening, Dev's condition deteriorated drastically. The medics had done their best to help relieve any pain he was feeling, although could do little else. He was delirious in temperament, ghostly pale and his skin damp. Aldber and Tala had sat with him the whole evening trying best to offer comfort, although they knew that he did not have much time left. With what energy he had, Dev tried to smile and joke with them, but was exhausted and his utterances were indecipherable.

When the sun went down, and the other patients rested peacefully, Dev was left alone for a few hours as his friends had been instructed by the medics to go and rest. This, Tala begrudgingly accepted, although she wanted to remain by his bedside for every precious fleeting moment they had left together.

Aldber would not forget, as they were about to leave, his dying friend reaching out to hold his hand. Dev pulled him closer and whispered into his ear: 'Look after Tala.'

'I am sure she is perfectly capable of looking after herself, but I shall do my best.' Aldber smiled pensively. Dev then started to splutter, so Aldber leaned forward to comfort his dying friend and helped to maintain his dignity by wiping away the tears and brushing his hair to look tidy.

They looked at each other once more, and nothing was said, although Dev did attempt to utter something under his breath. As Aldber stood and ushered Tala away from the bed, he looked back briefly to see his dying friend looking up at him. The expression was of someone staring into the abyss, accepting their impending end, watching those who he loved dearest walking away for the very last time.

Aldber decided to go back to his quarters to wash and put on fresh clothes. He lay down for a few moments, unintentionally fell asleep, and awoke as the sun was peeking over the hill-line, so quickly left his quarters. On his walk back to the medical rooms he avoided over-thinking and tried to remain focused in the moment, although he knew that he was trying to mask the inevitable truth.

The birds were singing far off in the hills and brisk late-autumnal air enraptured his nostrils. Aldber approached the medical rooms once more, feeling unsteady, knowing that beyond the door was something he did not want to face. He took a deep breath to try and settle the nausea he felt in the pit of his stomach and walked inside. Instantly, the herbal aroma hit him. He walked through the room, each footstep heavy to take, as he pushed aside the curtain and was faced with the painful reality.

Standing at the end of the bed he looked down at his friend's lifeless body. Dev's eyes and mouth were closed; the colour had drained from his young face, his chest no longer rose with respiration, and both delicate hands lay to either side of his torso. To his side was Tala, her face buried in the covers that muffled her cries of despair, her arms hugged around the corpse, trying to cling on to any remnants of life.

A cold shiver overcame Aldber as he stood there looking perplexed. He took a chair, placed it by Tala's side, sat next to her, and slowly rubbed her shoulder with one hand to offer support. He would remain there, silent, transfixed by the surreal view of his deceased friend. A tear that he would not notice fell down his cheek. His whole body was numb. Dev's life had been taken too soon. His best friend was lost forever.

This was not how it was meant to be.

Funeral arrangements had been made, so Dev's body was prepared with ointments and wrapped in white cloth. He would be buried under a tree way up on the hillside overlooking the valley. It was a spot Tala had chosen, as it was a place of special value: they used to sit there together, and it was where he had first told her that he loved her.

All the council attended and Grand Master Vivid conducted the ceremony. Aldber had helped to carry the body up to the grave and did not make an utterance to anyone. He was in a state of shock, felt utterly empty, and stood there holding Tala's hand as she bravely held back the tears and watched her lover being buried. The ceremony drew to a close with everyone declaring the oath. Several of the elders came forward to offer their condolences.

'Tala, Aldber, if there is anything I can do, if you need support, I will be there for you both,' Mowoni Kolayta said.

Aldber mustered a smile and nodded at the elder who reciprocated and then walked away. Tala was transfixed on the grave and did not say anything. The two friends were left alone to look at the grave and would stand there in silence for a while. There was nothing that needed to be said.

Uncomfortable as he felt, Aldber knew that he had to be proactive in order to deal with his grief, it was an emotion he could not bear to let consume him. They walked back down the hillside towards the main stronghold in silence, before Aldber stopped and looked at her.

'Tala, I must recommence my quest straight away,' he said, holding her hand. She looked into his eyes and nodded, knowing that he was finding a distraction.

'I understand. I have questioned whether Black Scar might have absconded further south into the ruins of the fallen metropolis or has in-fact returned to oversee the war preparations on Irelaf. I cannot simply speculate this, and instead will exhaust all avenues.'

'How so?'

'I will go across the region, searching for possible locations where the elusive leader could be hiding in more unassuming surroundings. I base this purely on the notion that Black Scar might want to maintain a less noticeable presence, reachable to strategic points across the continent, without compromising his location to us. I will inspect all of the sights but will not dare going too near without reinforcements,' she explained, although exhausted and disinterested.

'That is a good idea. But please be careful. It is now too apparent that we are in a race against time to find Black Scar. Contrary to what I first thought, you are right: there is something untoward happening here in the Sanctuary. I could sense it when I was summoned in front of the council. This threat, this mole that had been implanted, is only going to increase their efforts whilst the centauri leader is still at large,' Aldber said whilst looking down the hillside towards the stronghold. 'I feel I have become too complacent in my efforts. I now need to strengthen my approach. Dev's death was a repercussion of his own failings.'

'Don't be too hard on yourself, Aldber!' she tried to reassure him. 'Please be careful.' She cupped his cheeks and looked into his eyes with affectionate concern.

'Goodbye, Tala,' he said and then walked away towards his quarters, leaving his grieving friend behind.

She watched him as he disappeared into the distance and then looked back in the direction of Dev's grave. Moments later two guards appeared. Tala turned to address them.

'Bura Tala, where is Bura Aldber?'

'He has gone to his living quarters. Why?'

'That we cannot disclose, bura,' the guard said sternly, and they both turned to leave, with Tala looking on with concern in their wake.

Aldber collected his belongings and was pleased that there were no visible indications of any wrongdoing, as nothing seemed out of place or tampered with. He then left his quarters and headed down the hillside to the hover-bike station to take transport back to the Old City. As he arrived at the yard, an attendant came over to him.

'I will need transport to get down to the outskirts of the Old City near to sector nine,' the young warrior asked, noticing that there were a few vehicles available.

'Bura Aldber, I have been meaning to speak with you. You signed out a bike a few moon-cycles ago and never returned it?' the assistant asked, producing a list of vehicles, and tapped where Aldber's signature had been written previously.

'Oh, yeah, about that...' Aldber said sheepishly, thinking about the vehicle that had vanished after his visit to the Genuba tribe. 'It was stolen.'

The attendant did not look best pleased.

'You will not be allowed to sign out a bike for the foreseeable future,' the attendant said sternly.

'Right.' Aldber rolled his eyes.

A pilot was brought forward to escort him. Aldber jumped onto the passenger position, held on as the engine ignited, and the vehicle then raced down and across the valley floor. He looked back towards his home with a heavy feeling in his heart and knew he did not have much time left.

*

Several nights later, Hecta was sat alone in his chamber. As was the case most evenings, he was drinking the contents of a bottle of mead in the candlelight, vacantly looking out of his window and into the darkness with semi-blurred vision. He would do this more regularly than he knew was good for him, but at night, when it was quiet, he would start to think about things that plagued him greatly. He justified the reasoning for drinking, believing that it helped to ease the pain and to suppress painful memories of his past. The drink had an undesirable effect on him, which he had on countless occasions never learnt from. Taking one final gulp of the revolting concoction, he threw the empty bottle aggressively onto the table and wiped the residue from his lips.

The weathered warrior decided to take a walk around the grounds of the Sanctuary. It was a cold winter's night and the frosty bitterness would be the perfect remedy to alleviate the wayward feeling in his head. He pulled on his light shirt over his scarred and muscular torso, stumbled to his feet, coughed, and left his quarters. He walked haphazardly down the open corridor until reaching a set of steps that led down to a courtyard. He liked the cold breeze, the area before him was peaceful and surrounded by torchlight. He stood with his eyes closed and breathed in deeply, with his hands clasped behind his back.

Everyone else was an inconvenience. Everything was calm and quiet. No disturbances. No tormenting thoughts. The world seemed slightly bearable. Yet there was something discomforting.

When reopening his eyes, he looked down, and his blurry gaze rested upon a recognisable woman standing before him. At first, he was startled and had to shake his head to make sure he was not mistaken. But there she was, with her elegant frame and windswept hair. He could not quite believe it.

She smiled at him with the radiance that he had missed for too long. He walked down the steps towards her as she beckoned him with her outstretched hand. But as he approached, she turned and started running away, laughing playfully. He called out her name and soon followed her as she disappeared into the darkness. They ran through the grounds, past the trees, but he was not able to catch her. She threw him a quick mischievous glance as she ran up the stairs, giggling to herself as she went down a corridor.

He shook his head a few times, as his vision was still unfocused, and he had to balance himself against the hard-cold stone wall. As he attempted to grab hold of her, she turned a corner, and as he followed, she suddenly disappeared. He looked around desperately to make sure that she wasn't hiding, but it was apparent that she had vanished. He stopped, became frantic, and eventually accepted that his imagination had been deceiving him all along. He frowned with that all too familiar feeling of disappointment. He huffed, cursed under his breath, and rubbed his face with his weathered hands. He needed to get some rest.

Hecta looked up to see where in his drunkenness he had stumbled. Although his sight was blurry, he could make out that at the far end of the corridor was Grand Master Vivid's chambers. He had run a lot further than he had anticipated. The weathered warrior was about to turn to head back to his quarters when something peculiar caught his attention. Unlike the almost clear vision of her, there was something further down the corridor which he knew for certain was not a trick of his mind. He walked further to investigate as the door became larger in his field of vision. Behind him, Grombl and Maloyk appeared who were on their nightly patrol.

In that moment, Hecta suddenly regained full focus and control of his thought processes. He started running towards the chambers and in great dismay saw that his suspicions had served him correctly: at the doorway lay the unconscious bodies of the guards; both lay slumped on the ground in front of the open entrance.

Hecta immediately jumped over them and launched straight past the door into the chamber. As he ran through, all looked undisturbed and peaceful. He headed straight for the bedchamber, and as he entered became overwhelmed with horror.

There was stood an unknown being dressed in a long and weathered hooded black cloak that concealed their identity; their tall frame was illuminated by candlelight. The being was stood with a sword held point-down high in the air, looming over Grand Master Vivid, who was sleeping obliviously.

The being saw Hecta enter and was disrupted from their attempt to plunge the sword into the master's chest. The weathered warrior screamed with a fearless rage and without hesitation dived across the bed for the mole. The being manoeuvred aside as Hecta came hurtling down and crumpled onto the floor. Panicking, the hooded menace ran and threw itself desperately out of the window into the woodlands below. The elder got to his feet and followed in pursuit of the attacker, just as Grand Master Vivid awoke to all of the commotion and saw Hecta diving through the window.

Suddenly, Tala appeared with Grombl and Maloyk tailing her. The three were relieved to see Grand Master Vivid was alive, as the bura ran straight to the bedside.

'Master, are you okay?' She leaned down and looked at him with concerned wide eyes.

'Yes, of course, Tala, what happened?' Grand Master Vivid looked back at her in shock, still half asleep and trying to establish the enormity of the situation.

'Grombl and Maloyk saw Bura Hecta running towards your chamber and the two unconscious guards lying by the doorway. They summoned me immediately. The mole had come to murder you, Master. Hecta has chased them!' She looked over at the pair of assistants who were stood by the window looking out into the night. Grand Master Vivid composed himself, drew the covers over, got out of bed, and pulled on his robes.

'Grombl and Maloyk, inform as many warriors as you can to search the grounds of the stronghold for the mole!' he ordered as he pulled the sword belt around his waist and fastened it. The two shocked assistants nodded to the command and left the room with worried expressions.

'You are not safe here, Master,' Tala said with dread.

Grand Master Vivid nodded. She proceeded to escort him out of the chamber towards a hiding place to stay until daybreak.

Chapter Fourteen
Dwellers of the Southern Wilds

After several weeks of trekking, Aldber and the Outcasts emerged from the southern boundaries of the Old City and ventured further into the humidity and exotic scenery at the lower reaches of the continent. During their time heading towards the Uncharted Regions, the bura had received one final correspondence from Tala:

Aldber,

An assassination attempt has been made on Grand Master Vivid's life. The mole left the two guards unconscious, but Hecta foiled its plans. Alas, the defector disappeared, and no one was severely harmed. Both guards are being treated in the medical rooms. Thankfully, Grombl and Maloyk were nearby and called me to the scene. I escorted the grand master into a safe room. The stronghold is now on maximum alert. I don't feel particularly happy about leaving the leader whilst I continue my mission, but Bura Hecta is here and I trust him.

By the way, two guards approached me shortly after the funeral, asking for you. I presume they didn't find you, as I haven't heard of anything since. They refused to tell me what they wanted with you. I didn't ask the elders about this either.

I will recommence my mission today. Keep me updated.
Tala

Although distraught to hear the news about the assassination attempt, Aldber had started to become obsessed with the hunt and consumed by a darkness that was beginning to enslave him and impair his judgement, much to his own lack of awareness. He replied to her, suggesting that they ceased corresponding for the foreseeable future, because of paranoia that the spy might intercept their letters and would learn valuable information. He knew that she would begrudgingly agree to this. From then onwards he would be alone with the Outcasts and hoped to return to the Sanctuary triumphant.

It was the first time that either Aldber or the centauri had ever travelled to such parts of the continent. Like the outskirts to the north, here, dense foliage engulfed everything; beautiful plants and grasses suffocated the surrounding wall and buildings. The sticky heat was overwhelming. Aldber had to remove his jacket, whilst the centauri's fur was not suitable for such climates and they became easily fatigued.

As they left the grand ruins well behind, the expedition walked into the jungle, looking up at the colossal trees and admiring the calls of unfamiliar animals far away. After a while, the terrain took a steep incline and they emerged from the undergrowth onto a cliff-top overlooking the spectacular landscape before them. They stood there for a while looking at the scene. Several hills were dotted along the horizon, protruding from the dense jungle below. It was all too apparent that there could be endless places where Black Scar could be lurking.

It seemed almost impossible to guess where to look first.

They descended the hillside and delved further into the darker depths below. Down here, vegetation fought for precious sunlight, the jungle floor was dark and eerie, and the atmosphere was humid. They could hear other creatures running for safety when this horrifying group walked through their territory. Aldber had to fend off large winged insect beasts with his blade, which made for a much-needed feast.

At one point they stopped by the bottom of a large tree, its trunk thick and its roots greedily burrowed into the earth. Around the tree were large plants, all taller than Aldber and their flowers cocooned. Flying Stone was particularly fascinated by one and went to pay closer attention. He stood on his hind legs and used his hand to pull open the leaves. The magnificent flower spilled open, radiating a multitude of metallic shining colours. He leaned in to look at the illuminated bud and took a deep sniff. All the others watched how thoroughly captivated he was. When he stood back and turned to look at everyone, they were taken aback by his appearance. Unbeknownst to him, his body did not agree with the pollen from the flower, the adverse effect being that his face started to react and swell up.

'Flying Stone, your face doesn't look right,' Red River said disconcertingly.

'What do you mean?' Flying Stone questioned. Suddenly, he started sneezing violently, spraying his accomplices with thick dollops of mucus.

He started to panic experiencing this new sensation, and the centauri gathered around him closer, concerned about their accomplice's health. He was cursed by an uncontrollable fit of sneezing, much to his misery, as they set off further into the jungle. Aldber led the group with Hollow Moon following close behind, and Flying Stone tailing at the back, brandishing a swollen face and foul mood.

The terrain flattened and the tree line started to thin out, as they neared the borders of a human settlement. They took cover to inspect the scene. The whole expedition looked out over an open area where mud and straw huts stood. Tribesmen walked around scantily clad, bearing spears and talking in an indecipherable language. They were of different colours, but all looked tanned from the immense heat radiating from the sun. Aldber decided that he would go to speak with them, hoping that they had an interpreter and would reason with him with words instead of the sharp end of their weapons.

'Aldber, are you sure about this?' Hollow Moon asked, looking warily ahead.

'I know a few words of their language. If I can somehow speak with them, they may be able to share information about the whereabouts of Black Scar's forces,' Aldber said confidently, although hesitated as he was about to leave. 'But, just in case, come and rescue me if things don't work in my favour.'

He then stood up and walked out into the open area, ducking down as he ran towards the settlement. Behind him, the centauri lay silently in the undergrowth.

Aldber went up to one of the huts and then stood tall and presentable, before walking into the inner sanctum of the village. He walked forward and immediately raised his arms up in a non-aggressive manner, smiling at some of the onlookers who were perplexed by the appearance of this pale human. They instantly raised their spears and stood defensively. Children started wailing and were taken into safety by their horrified mothers. Aldber gained eye contact with one of the tribesmen who screamed in his native tongue at him.

'Hello!' Aldber pronounced badly in Latigo. This was received with a curious expression. 'I don't speak your language,' Aldber tried to convey in Ramasha, speaking slowly and enunciating every word. However, unsurprisingly, this too proved to be unsuccessful. A trickle of sweat started seeping down his cheek. He was beginning to change his mind about this idea, having possibly made a reckless assumption about the situation, but he hoped there was one amongst the tribe who he could communicate with.

From one of the larger huts appeared a tall and muscular man; his neck was adorned with fangs of an exotic creature. Those around him were hysterical, but he remained calm as he approached the new arrival. Tribesmen bearing spears stood to the side as the tall man walked up to Aldber. The Galardros assumed this was the tribal leader.

'Oh, hello, your grace,' Aldber said as he lowered his hands and bowed. He would be courteous and polite, although he was unsure as to whether the man could understand anything that he was saying, whilst using hand gestures to help convey his words. 'I am sorry to walk into your territory like this; I was just passing through and wanted to ask your people some questions?'

The tribesman clearly had no comprehension of what Aldber was saying, and by the looks of things, there was no one present who could translate the conversation. The tribal leader however, smiled, brandishing his fashioned razor-sharp teeth, and placed an arm around the new arrival's shoulder. He gestured Aldber to join him, and the guest was ushered into the heart of the encampment. The young warrior breathed a sigh of relief and followed him, nodding in a friendly manner at the inhabitants who stood there puzzled by this peculiar stranger.

Aldber was led through the village to where there was a large roaring campfire, which had a carcass hanging and roasting over it. He was shown to a chair, which he took willingly, pleased by the people's newfound hospitality. Young women then came forward with a delicate headdress of leaves, which they placed onto his head. All who stood before him smiled gallantly.

'Well, this is very nice, I must say.' He smiled and looked around at the onlookers who stared at him in awe.

But, unlike the tribes of the East Lands, he had been led into a false sense of security. Suddenly, he was surrounded, arms enveloped him, his weapons were seized, and he was restrained. He tried desperately to pull himself free, heaving with anguish, but the tribesmen all held onto him with brute force.

The tribal leader then reappeared wearing a ceremonial gown made from fur and Aldber could see a large knife concealed beneath it. He started walking towards the captive with a menacing look in his eyes. Around him, Aldber could see people licking their lips as they gazed at him intensely.

The bura suddenly realised what was roasting on the fire.

As the leader drew closer, he revealed the large knife and started muttering rapidly in his language a ritual chant, which the others started to mimic. People started to gather, they got onto their knees and began to bow and rise back and forth in a ritual of praise.

'This isn't ideal,' Aldber whispered to himself, cursing under his breath.

The bura watched as the tribal leader stood before him, his eyes wide and wild as he drew the blade into the air to deliver the killing blow. Aldber tried desperately to pull his arms free. The tribal leader loomed over him, the sun silhouetting his muscular frame as the blade glistened in the sunlight.

Suddenly, from out of sight, Hollow Moon dived in, smoothing and devouring the leader with her large fangs. She overwhelmed him and tore into his face; his desperate screams were muffled by the sound of her savage roar. The whole tribe looked on, horrified, as the Outcasts appeared and started attacking the cannibals. Those restraining Aldber released him and dived forward with their spears.

The young warrior quickly got to his feet and grabbed his weapons that had been thrown to the side. Several tribesmen appeared bearing bows and arrows and started firing at the attackers. The Galardros manoeuvred around as Flying Stone dived at a few of the warriors and mauled them furiously. Red River walked forward and grabbed one helpless tribesman by its neck. It looked down in horror at the alien creature and screamed as he was thrown into the fire, and then shook violently as the flames consumed him.

'Well, at least you have one meal for later!' Aldber said gazing at the flames as he dodged several arrows and ushered the expedition away.

They ran out of the encampment and took an unknown path on the opposite side into the jungle. Aldber ran with all his might, as the others came hurtling behind him. They soon overtook him, as tribesmen chased them screaming in their dialect and casting waves of arrows. The expedition soon ran into an open area; ahead of them they could see a fragile rope bridge that led to a cliff-face on the opposite side. They could hear the deafening torrent of a river far down below.

The centauri were hesitant to cross, for they knew the structure could not bear all of their weight, but after a few shoves of encouragement, Flying Stone started running across. The bridge swayed from side to side and wooden panels started cracking under their feet. Aldber was the last one to mount the bridge as a wave of arrows flew past him. He looked back briefly and could see the tribesmen taking cover in the foliage, whilst pelting them with a bombardment of arrows. He could hear a few of the expedition sheepishly moan about the height. He dared not look down, but curiosity got the better of him and he took a quick glance. There was a vast drop below them to a river that was pierced by jagged rocks, and the torrent flowed by furiously. It wouldn't take much to guess that it would be immediate death.

As the majority of the expedition got to the safety on the other side, Aldber could hear the inevitable snapping of rope behind him as the bridge gave way under their weight. He screamed for the others to hurry as, to his horror, the bridge started to collapse behind them. He haphazardly negotiated over fallen planks as the whole structure started descending. It was only Aldber and Red River left; the centauri quickly dived across and turned around as the bridge dropped. In mid-air, Aldber jumped and grabbed desperately. His grasp was met. The young man held on for dear life as he swung helplessly over the chasm. He looked up at the elderly centauri who held his hand with a tight grip. Arrows started hitting the cliff face and ricocheted off. To his dismay, Red River started to take a few hits that lodged into his mane; he let out a cry of pain but mustered the strength to pull Aldber to safety. When they landed on the grass, they had no time to recover. He quickly scrambled to his feet and they ran for cover.

Whilst the tribesmen on the opposite side of the chasm screamed above the noise of the river, the expedition escaped into the safety of the jungle and only stopped to rest once there was enough distance between them and the bow's range.

'Okay, I have to admit that I underestimated that situation,' Aldber said as he knelt down to catch his breath.

'You don't say! You humans are unpredictable!' Red River criticised, pulling the arrows from out of his back.

Suddenly, Hollow Moon launched forward, grabbed Aldber by the neck and pinned him against a tree. The bura was too overwhelmed with shock to even process the pain of the impact.

'*What was that, Aldber*?!' Hollow Moon spat furiously. 'You underestimated the situation? That is an understatement. You exhibit a reckless lack of judgement and nearly got us killed. For someone who is meant to be divine, you are failing to show your worthiness. We are relying upon you to find Black Scar and you are *failing us*!'

'Hollow Moon.' Long Wing stepped forward to intervene. 'You are going to kill him! Let him go.'

The Outcast's leader showed restrain and obliged. Aldber crumpled onto the jungle floor. Coughing profusely, he shifted up to lean against the tree trunk whilst trying to regain his breath.

'I am sorry for subjecting you to that, but it was not guaranteed how the indigenous people would behave,' he said, rubbing his throat. 'It appears that they won't be forthcoming. I promise that won't happen again.'

'*I have never seen Hollow Moon like this before. Is this the true her coming out?*' Aldber thought and then addressed Red River whilst wiping sweat from his brow: 'Thank you for saving me back there.'

'It is fine, Aldber,' Red River said sternly as he threw the last blood-drenched arrow onto the floor.

'It might be unsurprising that I suggest we avoid contact with tribes from now on,' Hollow Moon said in a calmer tone. 'We should proceed and venture further into the heart of the jungle.'

Aldber sat motionless for a few moments to process what had just happened, and then produced the vision globe from his rucksack and started looking into it. He could see Hollow Moon looking at him from the corner of his eyes.

'What is it, Hollow Moon?' he questioned, noticeably unnerved by her abnormal behaviour and now this inquisitive look.

'You seem to be very fond of that magical object?' she replied.

'*So?*' he said abruptly. His hard tone caught the attention of the other Outcasts who turned to look at him.

'I'm just making an observation.' She smiled before turning to lead the expedition away.

Aldber watched suspiciously as she and the others all turned to leave, before replacing the device back into his rucksack. Flying Stone then started laughing. The bura was taken aback by the inappropriate timing.

'Flying Stone, this is not the sort of moment that calls for laughter,' Aldber explained. The centauri then stopped and looked somewhat embarrassed.

Aldber was beginning to feel like this arduous quest would never end.

As they dealt with the suffocating heat and minimal amount of water, morale reached a new low. They would spend a few weeks trudging through the foliage, scaling hills and negotiating over vast rivers. But there was no sight of any centauri and like before, they were not having any fortune with finding the elusive leader.

Aldber was beginning to become irritable and impatient. His dreams were cursed with images of Dev's lifeless face. He thought about the Sanctuary and all those people who were relying on him. He continued to withdraw from the others and instead paid more attention to the vision globe, incessantly asking it questions.

'Where can I find Black Scar?'

'Who are his war lords?'

'Can you connect me to Black Scar?' This final question was asked repeatedly, to no avail, as the operating system could not establish a connection with the revered centauri through the network. Aldber was investing too much faith in the contraption and, unbeknownst to him, it was slowly corrupting his mind.

'These centauri are not impressed by your efforts, Aldber. They will cast you aside without a moment's consideration or remorse. You are alone with them. They do not trust you. You are a hindrance,' it would taunt him.

'I will make sure to complete this mission. You are meant to be assisting and not ridiculing me, like them!' Aldber would reply.

'The expedition is becoming restless and dejected. Searching the unknown reaches of the continent has made them paranoid that this journey alone will claim their lives.'

'Then I must do whatever I can,' Aldber rebuked, lost within his own delusion.

Chapter Fifteen
The Premonition

Since leaving the Sanctuary to continue on her mission, Tala had plotted five points across the map that fitted the criteria of possible hiding places for the mysterious centauri leader. Out of these, she had already surveyed two. The first was located in the Utep Canyons at the equator to the far-east of the continent. These were enormous cracks in the earth, which slivered along parallel to the Sybilian Ocean that was not too far away. The second was in the Junta Straight: the gigantic remains of what had been a space station, its fragmented parts scattered across a fractured hilltop and deep into the scarred valley below it. Both of these sites had the potential to be secret Enemy hideouts, with natural fortifications and multiple access routes.

Tala headed east once more to find the third site, which was a steep hill with a sheer vertical drop facing south-east. At its base was woodland, which flourished in all directions and also connected to the Great Plains which led east towards the Sanctuary and south towards the city ruins. She arrived from the south, entered the woodland, and haphazardly plotted a route using the trajectory of the sun as guidance.

As she got closer, the vertical stone wall of the hillside bared down upon her. From this close she could not see any tangible natural pathways on either side that could lead to the top. Instead, she turned back on herself, until reaching the edge of the woodland. From there she stood back and withdrew her binoculars to examine the hill. Through the haze, she could make out where the vertical rock-face sliced upward, but it stopped abruptly in the centre. She had to adjust the device in order to focus on what was there, and when she did this, it satisfied her curiosity. There was a ledge three-quarters of the way up the hillside; not particularly wide, by her reckoning. Inlayed behind this was what at first appeared to be a darkened patch of rock, but then further adjustments to the device revealed that this was in fact an opening to a cave.

She scanned the vertical rock-face once more to see whether it would be plausible to scale to this entrance, and also considered that the cave could burrow deep into the hill, so there was the possibility of other access points. She widened the view on the device and then looked in her peripheral vision southwards and could imagine that from way up on that ledge the vantage point to view of the surrounding region would be ideal.

Pleased with her find, Tala placed the binoculars back inside her shoulder bag, withdrew the map, which was folded neatly so the area she was in was on top, and found the point she had provisionally marked. Taking a piece of black chalk, she struck a large 'X' over the hill, before placing the map back in the bag and continuing on her trek towards the next possible site of the revered centauri leader.

Narrator's Note:

It is believed that after Aldber and the Outcasts had ventured further through the perilous jungles of the Uncharted Regions to the south of the continent, they eventually headed north once more. Unfortunately, I have limited documents, and there were no eyewitness accounts of seeing the expedition during this time. Therefore, I have been unable to clarify what happened over a three moon-cycle period of time. Documentation recommences just before when Aldber returned once again to the Sanctuary and details the untimely events that followed.

The skyscrapers above were shining in the daylight as, far down below in the bowels of the streets, the scene was covered in a grey and gloomy light. The ground was covered in white snow and thick sludge.

The expedition trundled through; their heads bowed as a light patter of snow cascaded onto the floor. Any kind of group spirit had dwindled with the shortened days of late winter. Aldber walked with his head submerged within his hood, his breath turning to steam and wafting into the chilly air. He hugged his body for warmth in the debilitating cold, keeping painfully quiet and avoiding eye contact with the others. His travel boots had succumbed to overuse and were torn in several places, and his feet were damp and numbed with coldness. At night he removed his boots, placed his sore bare feet in front of the fire, and embraced the stinging sensation, relieved he still had feeling. The few rations they had saved were now scarce. In his delirious state of mind, the young bura started suspecting the others were contemplating abandoning their mission and would attack him out of sheer starved desperation. He slept at night with his blade close at hand.

The far-off crackle of gunfire was the only signal of any other form of life. Even in the summertime this place could be abundant, but now it was even more ghastly and emptier than usual. Above them buildings creaked under the weight of snow, and vast avalanches spilled out onto the ground.

They were making their way once more to the northern borders of the city ruins, retracing their steps back to the Outcasts' hiding place. All those countless days of searching had brought no results and Aldber was becoming sick. He would spend hours wittering to himself under his breath, becoming flustered by overthinking and repeating things to himself. Hollow Moon had noticed that when they took a break or made a fire, he would sit at the edge of the group huddled up, rocking back and forth, only giving monosyllabic answers to her questions.

By now Aldber had become addicted to using the vision globe. He believed that it held all the answers within it, which needed careful extraction, but he was clouded in his judgement. The device was subtle in its manipulations. Aldber would sit there for hours caressing the spherical object and marvelling at its simplistic beauty, staring into in with intensity, fantasising that it looked like some form of succulent fruit, an irresistible symbol of knowledge that he wanted to devour.

He could hear its voice beckoning him, inviting him to peek into its inner depths, and knew that with time he could fully harness its potential and would become all knowing and powerful. The others around him would never be allowed to touch it; the device was his alone and would be the only way for him to overcome these challenges, and the only way for him to fulfil his destiny.

He had become maddened in his efforts.

Tala walked out from the great hall onto the stone courtyard wrapped in several layers to keep her warm in the late winter. She looked up into the trees; their branches were bare and looked crooked, bathed in snow. It would not be long before the ice would melt away and the buds of springtime would blossom once more.

In these quiet moments of solitude and contemplation, she liked to watch nature flow and the predictable processes unravel, separate to the turbulent chaos that was her people's circumstances. Way overhead, the sky was grey and uninspiring. Breaks in the clouds let sunlight paint the dreary valley before her.

Memories of her deceased lover flooded back. She drew a breath and exhaled a pensive sigh; the vapour formed a veil in front of her eyes for a short moment. All she could feel inside was pain and confusion and she was not sure of her own safety and that of everyone she knew. But Tala would fight on and nothing would deter her gallant heart. Councillor Kolayta had always told her to stand strong and to not be undermined by the males in the order. Tala knew that she could not let her emotions take control of her because she was a born to be a warrior.

In an attempt to give herself comfort, in these times of great upheaval and uncertainty, she smiled and stood tall, before turning around to walk back inside, but stopped abruptly.

Unbeknownst to her, she had not been standing there alone.

In front of her was a tall figure wearing a black tattered cloak, their face concealed within the abyss of the hood. The mole started walking towards Tala. It suddenly withdrew a blade. She mirrored this and deflected a downward swipe from the attacker but was not quick enough to counter another advance. It thrust the blade hard into her gut and pushed it in deeply as she let out a small shriek of agony, looked into the mysterious figure's hood with puzzlement. It then withdrew the blade. Tala fell to the ground, cupping the wound, and as she lay there a pool of blood mushroomed around her body. She looked up at the attacker and her vision started to blur as she slipped out of consciousness and was consumed by the coldness of oblivion.

Aldber's eyes rolled back. He shook his head and took a few moments to regain his breath. It was like he had been asleep, but fully aware at the same time. The whole world around him had turned in on itself and he had seen Tala being stabbed. It felt real, like he had been there witnessing it.

The jaded bura looked around; he had gone into the trance sat facing away from the Outcasts, who were preoccupied with a meal they had just cooked. He stood up and walked over and found the group's leader.

'Hollow Moon, may I speak to you in private?' he asked. She could see the distress upon his face.

'Of course, Aldber,' she replied, then put down her food and joined him, away from the others.

'I must return to the Sanctuary immediately, I have had a premonition that something bad is about to happen,' he said with a frown, his eyes darkened.

'What is it, Aldber, is everything alright?' she asked, looking at him with concern.

'I believe a friend of mine might be in grave danger. I must go there now to give myself peace of mind.' He looked northeast in the direction of his home. Above, there was a light falling of snow.

'You must do whatever you think is best.' She smiled.

'Hollow Moon,' Aldber said in a direct tone and returned his gaze to the Outcast's leader. 'I think I can speak for all of us in saying that this hunt has failed. We have spent many moon-cycles trying to find Black Scar and it is not working. We are all tired, on the verge of starvation, and need to make changes.'

'What is it that you suggest?'

'When I go back to the Sanctuary, I will gather as many men as I can, and we *must* present ourselves to Black Scar's forces once and for all. We must face them head on. Hopefully, we can draw him out, and with the extra men, can defeat him. I think we are running out of options. It may mean that we face a large army, but that is the gamble we will have to take.'

'As much as I think we will be taking a huge risk, I think it is time to accept this.' She looked worried.

'You said you want to return to your family. I believe that unless we do this now, you may never see them again. Perhaps, in taking on the responsibility of this mission, we will have to make the ultimate sacrifice. I know that giving our lives would be the right thing for the greater good.'

'That is something I have always contemplated, but never accepted.' She looked over at the others. 'Removing Black Scar is the most important thing. We shall wait for you at our hiding place.'

'I will return in due course with an army.'

They stood there for a moment in silence looking at each other.

'Goodbye,' Aldber uttered and then pulled up his hood. He walked from under the cover and ventured out into the snowfall and white city ruins.

Aldber left the Outcasts and once more set off alone towards the northern wall and plains beyond. He was glad they had come to an agreement about using another method in their quest, as he had become frustrated, had distanced himself, and been driven to the brink of insanity. It was all-consuming, and he had lost awareness of his own change in behaviour.

He was not even certain that Tala was at the Sanctuary, considering the last time they had spoken she had been surveying possible hidden locations of the centauri's leader, but because the dream about his mother had been such a close reflection of the reality, this premonition concerned him greatly. He would head back to his home to make sure Tala was alright, and then would assemble forces to hopefully bring an end to these hardships. He kept the vision globe safely near to him, as it gave him encouragement. He now would return to the Sanctuary and would challenge anyone that stood in his way.

By now, the sun was becoming noticeably warmer in the sky and the snow on the plains was beginning to melt, revealing wet grass and dirt that had been encased during the winter. So much had happened to Aldber during this past sun-cycle that he did not take enough time to reflect on his circumstances, but now was not the time for such thoughts.

As he walked into the valley it was the scene similar to his vision of Tala, but now the snow was retracting, and foliage was reclaiming the land. Way up high to his left, the buildings were visible, no longer hidden underneath the protection of the tree leaves. The waterfall was surging proudly and parts that had frozen were beginning to melt away.

A patrol guard came forth on horseback and asked for identification.

'It is me. Don't you *recognise* me?' Aldber retorted at what he considered to be a ridiculous question. The guard, dumfounded by the bura's attitude, threw him a scornful look.

'Every person entering this valley has to provide identification, upon request,' the patrolman said sternly.

'*Whatever*,' Aldber sulked. He showed his identification papers in a dismissive manner and then proceeded further.

As he entered the main complex, Aldber could see a larger presence of guards were on patrol than on his last visit. It no longer felt like the harmonious place of learning and safety that he had once known.

The Bura was preoccupied with his endeavour and needed to see Tala to comfort his distorted mind. Firstly, he went to her quarters, but they were empty, although he guessed she had been there not too long ago, as her things were scattered about in typical chaotic, yet organised, fashion. This made him realise that she was definitely at the Sanctuary. He then walked around the grounds and started enquiring with various warriors and assistants.

'I have not seen her since yesterday morning at the food hall,' one silo responded.

'Bura Tala? She attended the council meeting this morning, but I have not seen her since. Is everything alright, Aldber?' an assistant asked, concerned by the young Bura's troubled disposition. He ignored this and moved on.

'I last saw her meditating this afternoon in the prayer room,' a mowoni explained. Frustrated that no one was able to give him the answers he wanted, Aldber's temper intensified with every rejection.

The tormented bura walked up past the waterfall towards the council tower and could see that it was empty, which was not normal for this time of day. He saw one of the assistants, who was sweeping the tower's stone floor.

'Why are there covers on all of the seats?' Aldber questioned.

'Hello, Aldber. After recent events, meetings had been relocated to Grand Master Vivid's chambers.'

Without another utterance, the impatient bura abruptly exited the council tower and launched down the hillside, in the direction of the leader's quarters. By now his heart was racing in his chest and he was becoming consumed by rage. Panic was setting in and he felt possessed.

As he approached Grand Master Vivid's chambers, instead of the mandatory custom of asking for entry in a polite manner, Aldber screamed at the set of guards, who had now doubled in their presence: '*Let me enter!*'

They ignored him initially, so he barked his command once more, which was met with the same indifference. He tried to force his way through, but they stood adamantly with their spears in his way. Aldber looked at them all individually, his eyes blood-shot.

'I am a bura of the highest rank, you shall respect my request. *Step aside!*' He spat at them with every word, his hand edging closer towards his holstered pistol. Those inside could hear the commotion,

Hecta appeared from within and was astounded to see Aldber standing there. He walked over to the distraught young man and tried to engage him.

'Aldber, what is it?' he said calmly, placing a reassuring hand upon the arrival's shoulder whilst trying to catch his eyes, which looked glazed.

'*Where* is Tala?' Aldber breathed heavily through his nostrils whilst clenching his fists and stared around manically.

'I am not sure.' Hecta was taken aback by the young warrior's worrying disposition. 'I have not seen her since...' The arrival suddenly turned and stormed off. 'Aldber, *wait*!'

The bura started running down the corridor and frantically searched every room that he could find and slammed the doors shut behind him. With every attempt his stomach started to turn; he felt nausea surfacing and had to take deep breaths to control the uncomfortable sensation. As he continued his search, he approached two silo that were walking down the corridor talking casually.

'Have you seen Bura Tala?' the deranged warrior barked.

'I saw her a few moments ago,' one of them replied, confused by the bura's outrageous behaviour.

'*What?*' Aldber then thrust his hand at the man's neck and forced him against the wall. 'Where did you *see her?*'

'She was in the food hall,' the silo choked. 'She mentioned something about going for a swim.'

Aldber froze. He released the man from his grip and then pulled the silo's sword from his sheath, before running off, leaving the two warriors in his wake, looking utterly shocked.

There was one place Aldber had not checked yet: the secret cave.

The possessed bura ran with all his might further into the vast stronghold, through sweeping corridors and towards one of the tunnels that had been abandoned. He threw down his belongings and clasped the sword tightly in his hand as he meandered down the tunnel with barely any light to guide his way. Ahead was a dim light. Taking a deep breath, he proceeded and could hear the rushing of water echoing against the cave walls, and that was when he heard a scream and splashing.

He recognised the voice.

Chapter Sixteen
Shallow Waters

As Aldber entered the cave he stopped abruptly and was horrified at what he saw. There, by the shore of the small beach, a body was floating downturned in the shallow waters. It had the unmistakable features of a young woman. Next to her in the water was stood a tall figure wearing a long dark and tattered cloak that concealed its identity. It was the same horrifying monster from the premonition.

'*Tala*!' Aldber involuntarily screamed as he ran forward towards the beach and then looked at the hooded menace. 'Get away from her!'

In the moment of utter helplessness, Aldber had to choose whether to rescue his friend or attack the mole. The young warrior was once more immersed with rage and launched into the water.

The mole revealed a sword just in time to counter a slice from Aldber as the young man nearly lost his balance entering the water. The cloaked menace walked back to present an open space to duel as Aldber regained his balance. He had restricted mobility standing in the water, which was up to his knees.

Aldber surged forward with a scream and the two swords connected. The sound ricocheted through the cave above the deafening sound of the waterfall. He pressed forward delivering angry slices and manoeuvres, but his opponent was skilled in return.

They moved further into the pool as the water came to waist height. Aldber had to be careful not to slip on the smooth floor below him. He looked into the darkness of the hood but could not see who was in there. They neared the waterfall, where Aldber knew there was a steep drop in the floor, but the mole moved in an opposite direction, found a footing, stepped up, and emerged from the water. Aldber followed and they recommenced fighting as they walked underneath the waterfall. Aldber could see that his opponent's cloak had become heavy with water; however, this did not deter the malicious being from fighting with brute strength, whilst remaining disturbingly silent. They advanced towards where the ledge ended and Aldber kicked the mole, sending it hurtling down into the water. But it landed stably, much to the bura's annoyance. Aldber then threw himself into the air with a stabbing motion, which his opponent barely counteracted. In doing so, Aldber fell into the water, hit the floor, and moved just in time to avoid a sword slice that dug into the ground.

Aldber emerged from the water, inhaled, and threw his head back to remove the long-wet hair that was covering his face. He advanced forward and their two swords struck in the air near to the wrist guard. The bura leaned in to try and pull off the hood and reveal the identity of his opponent, but it was quick enough to know his intentions. The mole pulled back and swung its sword around, hitting Aldber hard in the face with the pommel, knocking him off balance and plummeting into the water. Aldber fell, disorientated, as above the cloaked menace raised a foot and forced it down onto his neck, pinning him down. The young warrior tried to grab his sword, which had fallen out of reach, before trying to punch the foot, but started to exhale precious air from his lungs and began to lose focus. He tried to punch at the mole's leg, but his vision blurred, and he started to lose consciousness.

Suddenly, the crushing weight upon his neck was relieved. Aldber regained his sight and then mustered the energy to resurface. When he did so, he gasped for air, grasping his neck before swinging around to see where his opponent was, but the mole had disappeared from the cave.

The bura waded through the water, threw the sword onto the sediment, and grabbed the floating body. He turned her over, cradled Tala's head, looked at her face which was motionless and turning pale, and saw that there was a small bruise on her forehead. He verbalised his despair before dragging her body out of the water and onto the beach.

Aldber lay Tala down, knelt beside her, and vigorously shook her whilst anxiously repeating her name. He tried desperately to resuscitate her. He breathed air into her lungs, pressed down hard on her rib cage to stimulate her heart, and put an ear close to her mouth to hear any exhaling breath and looked along her abdomen, but there was no heartbeat or respiration.

The sun shone down through the crack in the cave roof, casting light upon Tala's beautiful face.

He eventually realised the unbearable truth that his efforts would do nothing to save his friend, so held her hand tightly within his grasp and threw back his head to let out a scream of dismay. The painful sound echoed around the cavernous walls.

The young warrior, shaking, looked down at her lifeless body and was utterly lost, knowing that she had been in danger, but he had not been quick enough to save her.

It was his fault.

From the entrance a group of warriors came running through bearing weapons. Bura Hecta followed them. He stopped abruptly and watched as Aldber knelt over the corpse of his friend, placed his arms under the body, picked her up, cradled her within his arms, and got to his feet. He proceeded to walk towards the entrance, as the warriors ran past him to search for the mole.

'Aldber, I am sorry,' Hecta uttered and was thoroughly shocked. The grieving young bura did not even acknowledge him and the weathered warrior had to move aside to allow him past.

When Aldber emerged out into the main corridor, a congregation of onlookers had gathered, who all looked mortified when they saw the drenched young man holding his deceased friend within his arms. They stood aside as he walked through; many cupped their hands to their faces in disbelief and a few started crying. Aldber looked at several of them with disdain and tears trickled down his face as he moved through the crowd. At the back was stood Grand Master Vivid who was devastated to see this horrific scene.

Aldber made his way silently down the corridor and was followed by Grombl and Maloyk, who tailed him respectfully from afar. The bura made his way towards the medical rooms and kicked the door wide open. Maiden Gailden and her assistants received him with cries of despair at the tragic sight. As he walked through the room, every voice and smell around him was distant. He placed Tala gently onto a bed, brushed hair away from her peaceful face, and gave her a gentle kiss on the forehead. Leaving her to be prepared for burial, he stood and abruptly turned and proceeded to leave the room whilst not making one utterance to all who remained silence. Grombl and Maloyk stood aside and watched the young warrior leave, and then went to Tala's side, sat down, and bowed their heads in respect.

As Aldber left the medical rooms, people started to approach him, but he paid them no attention. He shoved by several of those who stood in his way and started running down the corridor towards the private quarters.

He came to a door, and without hesitation, kicked it open and went inside. Much to his anguish it was unoccupied. For a moment he stood there clenching his fists, resisting the urge to destroy everything in sight, and then walked out and was met by Hecta, who could see that the young man was devastated.

'Aldber, what are you doing?' The councillor placed his hands on the warrior's arms in a calming manner, with the intention, if necessary, to restrain him.

'*Where is Thortate?*' Aldber suddenly erupted, looking at Hecta with fiery intensity. The elder then took the initiative and pushed Aldber back hard, pinching him against the wall. 'Let *go* of *me*!'

Aldber tried to struggle free but in his current state was no match for Hecta's strength. The weathered warrior was determined to keep the young man from causing himself, or anyone else, any harm. He watched with sorrow as tears trickled down the young man's face.

'Aldber, Councillor Thortatel is away on a mission as we speak,' Hecta tried to reason in a restrained manner.

'No, he is *here* and *murdered my friend*!' Aldber spat back looking listlessly off into the distance.

'No, Aldber, he is not here! Warriors are searching for the cloaked being and the cave entrance will be barricaded.'

'It is Thortatel; he is the mole, why can't you *see it*?' Aldber tried to free himself.

'Aldber, will you get a grip of yourself! You are being irrational,' Hecta shouted and started shaking the grieved warrior. Aldber looked into his eyes and then took a few deep breaths. After a short while Hecta felt assured to release him.

'Bura Hecta, it was my fault. I was so preoccupied with hunting for Black Scar, that I was not able to save Tala,' he said, looking at the ground in self-disgust. 'I had a vision and was not able to stop it from becoming real. I was not strong enough.'

'You had a vision? Look, Aldber, you will not take responsibility for Tala's death, do you hear me?' Hecta tried to reassure him the best that he could with his usual hard tone. 'She was perfectly capable of fighting her own battles. She would not want you to feel guilty for her loss, would she?'

'I guess not.' Aldber took a deep breath, still nauseated and jittering with adrenaline.

'Exactly,' Hecta said softly. They stood there for a short while in silence as the grieving warrior calmed himself. 'Now, come with me, I think you need a strong drink.'

Aldber looked up at Hecta; his eyes were blood-shot and swollen. The weathered warrior smiled at him, so he nodded and agreed to follow him away.

In the early evening, the sky was streaked with pink clouds. Beyond, the darkening sky was dotted with stars as the sun started to descend beyond the tree line, casting its dying light upon the snow-covered valley.

The majority present at the stronghold convened further up the hillside away from the main complex, standing by a ledge under a tree where the views over the landscape were magnificent. However, these majestic views could not deter the sombre atmosphere of the crowd that was there to bury Bura Tala.

She had been wrapped in a white cloth and her body carried by those closest to her. Grombl and Maloyk had been enthusiastic to help bear her but, because of their short stature, were asked to walk behind the procession with Grand Master Vivid, who was perpetually silent.

Tala was buried under the tree next to her lover, Dev. The leader conducted the ceremony, and everyone paid their respects, before leaving Aldber to look over the graves of his two best friends. He could not believe the sight before him; it was as though all those sun-cycles living here at the Sanctuary had left him naive to the perils out there in the dangerous world. In such a short space of time he had witnessed what so many people were experiencing every day, but he could not fathom the chance of losing those so close to him so soon and in such extreme circumstances.

As the rest of the mourners slowly walked down the hillside, Grombl and Maloyk remained and approached Aldber.

'Little Aldber, we be v-v-v-very sorry for your loss,' Grombl said, looking at the two graves then back up at the grieving man. 'Just so you know - we are always here for you.'

Aldber looked at the pair with teary eyes; Maloyk smiled with a sorrowed frown and rubbed the bura's arm reassuringly. In that moment of emptiness and confusion, at least the young warrior knew there was people around him who he trusted and knew truly cared.

'Thank you, Grombl and Maloyk, you are very good men.' He nodded at them both with the best smile he could muster, before turning to look at the graves once more. The flummoxed pair glared at each other, surprised by the compliment. It was the nicest thing that anyone had ever said to them. They then thought best to walk away, to leave Aldber alone to his quiet contemplation.

Feeling agonised, the young bura needed spiritual guidance, so left the graves and made his way down through the main complex towards the praying cave. He ducked as he entered the empty room and was immersed in the aromas and soothing candlelight within. He proceeded towards the very front where he would be shrouded in near darkness and knelt down onto one of the cushions and made himself comfortable, before closing his eyes and taking a deep breath. He could still see the glimmering of candlelight, although his eyes were shut.

For a short while Aldber simply breathed in and out, trying to empty his mind of thoughts and accepting, with minimal resistance, the grieving pain he felt corroding him inside. Then he started to speak out quietly under his breath to the divine, to make a connection: 'Supreme One, I have lost my two dear friends. Why?' He tried hard to hold back the tears. 'Why did this have to happen? Why is this justifiable?'

In his confusion, sadness, and anger he needed answers, but none were forthcoming. The only sound he could hear was the small gasps for breath he was making whilst trying to stop himself crying. But then he let go, and tears started falling. He cupped his hands to his face to muffle the sound. A surge of frustration swept through him. 'Is this because I am not at my fullest potential? Are you not speaking to me because I am not wise and strong enough yet? If I was sent to do your bidding, why won't you give me guidance? In these times of adversity and great loss, my faith in you is being tested!'

Aldber then opened his eyes and removed his tear-soaked hands from his face when he realised how blasphemous his words had been. He looked around and thankfully was alone. Gathering himself, he then left the prayer room, feeling a lack of resolve.

As the sun started to set over the horizon, Aldber walked back towards his quarters with the intention of hiding away from the painful reality. When he entered the room, he closed the door, slumped down against it onto the floor, and sat there looking into space aimlessly. He felt utterly overwhelmed and exhausted, could still not believe what had happened, and acknowledged that his behaviour earlier in the day had been out of character, disconcerting and unacceptable.

After a short while, he got to his feet, walked over to the desk, and lit a candle to illuminate the dark room, before sitting down to look at the elusive dance of the flame. There was something primal and enticing about watching it, knowing that it could be a tool used for good and also a means of destruction – both order and chaos. He was transfixed and lost all trace of thought, feeling and time. This ended once the candle was reduced to a hard puddle of wax on the base of the metal holder as the extinguished wick smoked gently in the breeze, which was coming through the window.

Chapter Seventeen
Hiding in Plain Sight

It was nearing daylight and Aldber remained seated for a while, listening to a light fall of rain outside and became engrossed by the soothing sounds and smells, as winter was giving in to the sprouting of spring. He could hear commotion outside his quarters as fellow warriors were awakening for another day of duty. No longer feeling like he wanted to isolate himself anymore, he decided that he would set forth to seek guidance, and to further distract his conflicted mind.

He had a rigorous wash and shave, and then put on his jacket and weapons belt, before proceeding straight to Grand Master Vivid's chambers to discuss the course of action he would take.

As he approached, he saw the same four guards he had encountered on his rampageous search for Tala. When stood before the door, he looked at them all individually.

'I would like to apologise for my temperament yesterday,' he announced, feeling embarrassed.

'We understand the situation, Aldber, and we are sorry to hear about the loss of Bura Tala,' one replied.

'It is okay. That is the kind of attitude we have come to expect from many of the councillors on a regular basis, including Bura Hecta,' another remarked.

'That will be enough!' proclaimed a voice from behind. It was Hecta; he approached not looking particularly amused and was dismissive toward the obviously warranted statement.

'See?' The guard smirked at Aldber.

'I request entry to see Grand Master Vivid,' Hecta said in his usual harsh tone, acknowledging Aldber to his side with a firm nod.

The two bura were given permission and entered the chamber. Inside, Grand Master Vivid was sat at his desk deep in thought and stirred only when the two arrivals approached to sit at the desk in front of him. Two guards flanked him and another one was standing at the balcony entrance.

'Oh, good morning, Bura Hecta and Bura Aldber,' he said with his ceaselessly friendly tone. 'Can I offer you both anything to drink?'

'I am fine,' Hecta said, waving his hand politely as he took his seat. Aldber reciprocated with a brief shake of his head. The leader then dismissed the guards.

'A dark cloud hangs over the Sanctuary and I have had a sleepless night trying to find answers to questions that have plagued me ever so. But when I have only begun to scratch the surface, I have found such answers, if at all attainable, have only led onto more questions.' Vivid looked over at Aldber with his crystal blue eyes. 'We must not let fear control us.'

'I agree,' Aldber said, clearing his throat. 'Previously, I was informed of the assassination attempt made on your life, Master, and now that Bura Tala has been murdered, and for reasons we do not know, it is only a matter of time before this mysterious being strikes once again. What is being done about it?'

'That is what I came here to report,' Hecta interjected. 'My men were not successful in finding the cloaked menace, but the cave has been barricaded and is being guarded.'

'But that is not enough!' Aldber raised his voice, unable to restrain his frustration.

'We must proceed with current operations as planned because this spy wants to tear us apart. They want to infect our minds and divide us,' Grand Master Vivid reasoned. 'This order has stood for generations and is the foundation for our people's hope against the Enemy. We are facing an existential crisis like nothing we have faced before, but do not forget we are facing much bigger challenges in the grander scheme of things. I am doing everything to the best of my capabilities to resolve this matter.'

'That, I do not question, Master. There is something that I must bring to your attention.' Aldber leaned forward and the other two looked at him inquisitively. 'I believe that my hunt for Black Scar coincides with this mole appearing. I know it might sound outlandish, and I don't know how, but what if this unknown individual could possibly have been planted here by the centauri's leader?'

'These events are all out of the ordinary, so your suspicions are feasible,' replied Grand Master Vivid.

'If that is so...' Aldber continued, 'I must finally confront Black Scar and end this. We have been running around in circles trying to track him down and I have come to an agreement with Hollow Moon and the Outcasts to approach him with full force, to present an open invitation. I request that I assemble as many men as I can to take on Black Scar's forces.'

'Aldber, it was very convenient for you to have come here this morning, as you were going to be summoned before the council,' Grand Master Vivid explained.

'Oh, really?' Aldber looked at Hecta with a confused expression. 'How so?'

'I will spare you the humiliation of not announcing this in front of the other elders,' Grand Master Vivid said with a grave tone and neutral expression. The young bura felt a nauseating sensation emerging from his stomach.

'What is going on?' Aldber questioned and looked at Hecta once more, who avoided his gaze by staring straight ahead.

'Aldber, the council have been thoroughly concerned about your behaviour. Firstly, you have had continuous shortcoming with your mission. Secondly, you assaulted Councillor Gilliad, which is an unacceptable offence. And thirdly, your rampage through the stronghold yesterday was conducted in a dishonourable manner.'

'Master, I do admit that my judgement has been somewhat clouded in recent times.'

'That is no excuse,' Vivid said sternly. There was an awkward silence. Aldber could feel his heart racing and his hands moisten. 'The decision I have had to make has not been easy, but I have to be true to the code, and also to the wishes of the fellow elders.'

'What do you mean?' Aldber questioned impatiently.

'Bura Aldber, you are to be stripped of your rank and the mission to hunt down the leader of the Enemy is now cancelled.' Vivid looked him in the eyes whilst speaking. 'You will remain here at the Sanctuary until given further orders.'

'But...'Aldber then restrained himself from contesting the decision and then bowed his head. He could feel his stomach turning in on itself. 'I… I understand, Master. I must be held accountable for my actions.'

Vivid and Hecta exchanged looks as they watched the young warrior digest the troubling news.

'Aldber, I can tell you are very saddened, disappointed, and conflicted,' Vivid said in a friendlier tone. 'Have you meditated on recent matters and prayed to the Supreme One?'

'Yes, Master, I went to the prayer room after the burial.' Aldber let out a sigh. 'I know that I must refocus.'

'Good.' Grand Master Vivid stood and walked around to the other side of the desk looking concerned. 'Are you okay, dear boy?'

'I will be fine,' Aldber said unconvincingly as he stood. 'Thank you for asking, Master.'

The old leader rested a hand upon the young bura's shoulder and looked into his eyes. 'I know that losing both of your friends must be a very traumatic experience for you. Losing loved ones is never easy. But I know you are a very brave young man, Aldber. This decision regarding your ranking and the mission does not mean you are being expelled. Please don't let this adversity undermine your courage,' Vivid said sincerely. They then both raised the salute and said the oath of the order. There was an awkward silence as Hecta sat there watching. Aldber nodded his head firmly at both elders, and then turned and walked towards the entrance, feeling devastated.

When Aldber returned to his quarters, he stood there for a moment to comprehend the magnitude of what had just happened. Not only did he feel guilty for the loss of his two friends, but now all of the work he had done in order to try and locate the centauri leader had all been in vain, and he would never be able to avenge his mother's untimely death. He felt like Grand Master Vivid had lost faith in him. Feeling confused and upset, for a brief moment he considered packing all of his belongings and just leaving, escaping away from it all to start a new life, but then he refrained and realised how absurd such an impulse would be. At this moment in time he had already done so many things to violate the code, that he felt one more mishap would cost his position within the order, and at this present moment he felt like he had nothing else to lose.

'If this mission has been officially cancelled, then I must fulfil my objective without the council's blessing,' he thought. He would prove his worth to the elders.

There was something he had to do, or more precisely something he had to consult, before leaving. An assistant had come by and left his belongings, so he undid the rucksack and pulled out the vision globe. He held it still covered in his hands and weighed the sphere in his grasp.

'How are you today, Aldber?' it said in an alluring tone.

'Vision globe.' He pulled away the cloth, felt the translucent glass, and closed his eyes. 'Tell me – where is Black Scar?'

'That, I am unable to do.'

'Why not?' Aldber said impatiently.

'There are limitations to my operating system. I have made this perfectly clear previously.'

The bura reflected for a moment and then an idea remerged.

'Vision globe, can we try again what I have asked before, can you try and connect me directly with Black Scar?'

'As you wish.'

Although all around him was calm, Aldber was suddenly overwhelmed and could not avoid the strong sensation. His heart rate increased, and his breathing intensified. But no sooner had he felt the sensation than it left his body.

Feeling disappointed that he had been unable to make a connection with the centauri, he was about to open his eyes and place the device down, when he heard something. At first, he thought it was a figment of his imagination, but he knew that it was real. Something was different this time. The young warrior could feel a tingling sensation in his fingertips. Suddenly, his whole body gyrated, he could feel his spirit separating from with his surroundings, and he was completely taken over and felt weightless. And that was when he heard it, a voice he had longed to hear for so long, but the sound was haunting.

'Hello, Aldber.'

The young bura shuddered. He could hear the voice like a whisper in the wind crawling up the back of his neck and burning into his ears. It was as though whoever had said it was standing behind him. He slowly turned around, opened his eyes, expecting to be tricked by his overly active mind, but he had not been.

He was no longer standing in his quarters.

There before him was stood a large being silhouetted by the entrance of a balcony.

'I have been waiting for you,' it said in a low rumble. Aldber looked into the eyes of Black Scar, feeling alarmed.

'Is this real? How am I here speaking to you?' Aldber asked, walking towards the centauri.

'You used that vision globe and have called out to me, so I responded,' Black Scar explained, sat proudly on his hind legs. 'You are inside of my mind.'

'It is time that we met once and for all. Where are you?'

'Why don't you see for yourself.' Black Scar then stood and gestured for Aldber to walk out onto the balcony.

The young warrior begrudgingly agreed and cautiously walked past the centauri, out into the daylight. They were stood looking at city ruins that stretched far upon the horizon.

'I have been to this area before,' Aldber expelled in astonishment.

'In that case, it will not be hard for you to find me.' Black Scar smiled. 'I am waiting for you.'

Then, like a dust cloud, the being swept away, and so did the whole scene. Small glistening particles floated through the air and vanished out of sight. Aldber reopened his eyes and was once more in his quarters, clutching the globe. He stood there perplexed but had not been mistaken and knew that the centauri had appeared to him so vividly.

'I saw him,' he uttered.

'You were able to speak to him?' the operating system asked.

'I did, and now I know where I must go.' Aldber then went to grab the cloth. 'Thank you for all that you have done for me, but I must leave you here now whilst I set forth to confront Black Scar.'

'I think it would be necessary for me to accompany you,' the globe objected.

'No, I will *not* require you for the remainder of this mission,' Aldber said assertively, but as he was about to throw the cloth back over the device he had a similar sensation to when he called out to Black Scar, but this time it was far less pleasant: an excruciating pain overwhelmed Aldber, as though daggers were being driven into his mind. His fingernails dug into the globe, and he closed his eyes to try and contain the pain but was unable to escape the torment.

The voices he had heard before returned, and now he saw vivid images: Tala's drained dead face...the cloaked figure wielding its sword...Councillor Thortatel smirking...Councillor Gilliad laughing...Councillor Gilliad on the floor with a bleeding nose... He saw himself with Dev and Tala laughing together... He saw Dev lying in bed dying... He saw himself walking away from his friends... He saw Hollow Moon and the Outcasts...the council looking at him disapprovingly...the whole Genuba Tribe laughing and pointing at him... The voices were getting louder... He could see the cannibal tribe trying to bite at him...Bura Hecta punishing him as a child for getting lost in the Old City... He could see Dev and Tala once more looking at him with disappointment that he had not been there for them... The voices were getting louder... He saw his crying mother screaming his name... The voices were getting louder... He saw the face of a centauri, yes it must be him, Black Scar, coming towards him shrouded in flames and laughing hysterically.

Aldber opened his eyes as sweat poured down his face and the voices stopped. He looked down at the vision globe, which was still in his grasp.

'I think it would be necessary for me to accompany you,' the globe reiterated. 'As you no longer have your superior's consent, you will require my assistance for what may follow. I have provided you a glimpse of what could be the reality.'

'A glimpse?' Aldber questioned sternly. 'Wait, you *made that up*?!'

It was in that moment that the young warrior surrendered, as all of his rage, grief and guilt manifested. He threw the globe hard; it smashed against the wall into a thousand shards of glass, which flew through the air, for a brief moment reflecting the sunlight. He then took hold of his chair and smashed it repeatedly against the floor until it shattered, overturned the table and started screaming violently, emitting all the pain that he had been holding inside for too long. Once he had destroyed everything in sight, he then crumbled onto his bed and looked at all the mess he had created whilst his body shook with the surge of adrenaline.

Aldber stared into the distance for a while, feeling a sense of release, although knowing it would be temporary. He was not aware that the vision globe had twisted his thoughts, clouded his judgement and consumed him.

He then fell asleep. It was the most pleasant rest he had experienced for a long time, and in it there was a dream that appeared so real, and offered such great comfort, that he would think about it for many sun-cycles to come.

In the dream he walked into the hills behind the Sanctuary valley and followed the stream until coming to the flat plains, where there were beautiful pink flowers scattered for as far as the eye could see. There, he saw a girl of not too dissimilar age; she was the most beautiful person he had ever laid his eyes upon. He watched her run around playfully and was invited to join. They chased each other over the fields, and then embraced to kiss, in utter euphoria.

Happiness.

Aldber awoke a short while later feeling calm. He lay there contemplating how he would continue his hunt for the centauri leader without the assistance of reinforcements.

'The only way that I can make this work is by presenting myself as bait,' he thought. But then he was reminded of something. The realisation caused him to sit up. *'Before Tala returned to the Sanctuary, she went on a surveillance mission. Perhaps, there is something in her quarters that could tell me where these locations are.'*

He took a few deep breaths, stood up to leave, collected his gear, negotiated through the debris, and left his quarters. He emerged into the early afternoon sunlight. The previous night's rain had washed away the last remnants of snow from upon the hills, exposing the naked frames of the trees. He proceeded further into the stronghold until finding his deceased friend's quarters. Before entering, he looked around to make sure no one was watching him, and then carefully let himself in.

Much to his satisfaction, the room had not been emptied of Tala's belongings, and everything looked untouched, like he had remembered seeing them the day before. He walked further into the room and spotted her shoulder bag lying upon the table. Aldber picked it up and opened it. Inside there were various papers, black chalk, flint, ration wrappings, spare rounds for her pistol, plus a frayed and faded map. He withdrew it, placed the bag to one side, and then unfolded the map to inspect it. It presented a diagram of the northern regions the western continent. Scattered across this were several small dots and four pronounced 'X's marked in black chalk. He knew instantly that they were possible locations of the centauri leader.

'Tala, you are just the gift that keeps on giving.' Aldber smiled and closed his eyes for one moment to imagine seeing her face. He then examined the four marks and could see that the closest was a hill north-east from the Sanctuary. It looked like a feasible place for someone to maintain a secretive presence. Aldber contemplated the likelihood and nodded. 'Hiding in place sight.'

Aldber then folded the map, placed it in inside his rucksack, and then haphazardly walked out of the living quarter. Once outside, he quickly made his way down the corridor, ignoring other people as he took a route up the hillside towards the tower where the messaging birds were housed. When he arrived, he walked over to Heratu, who chirped gleefully when she saw him. He stroked her.

'Heratu, it seems like you are my only friend, now.' Aldber then took a small piece of parchment and scribbled on it a note to Hollow Moon explaining the circumstances and asking her and the other Outcasts to return to their skyscraper, where he would hopefully reunite with them, if he survived the possible encounter with Black Scar.

'*I do not want to see any of them perish, as too many lives had been sacrificed so far, so I must do this alone,*' he thought.

He placed the parchment within the pouch hanging around her neck, and then produced a piece of leather fabric ripped from Hollow Moon's garment, which she had gifted to him so that he could provide Heratu a scent to find her, if such a requirement should arise.

Once Aldber had sent Heratu on her way, he walked down the hillside towards the station where the hover-bikes were kept and signed one out. He detached the charge cable and mounted the vehicle. Just when he was about to leave, he could see the attendant from a few days prior who had banned him. The man came running down shouting for the young warrior to stop.

Without a moment's hesitation, the young warrior ignited the engine and sped off down into the valley, brown mud flying in several directions as he surged over the wet field. He meandered through the spurs of the hills and came out onto the vast plains that stretched off towards the colossal metropolis in the far distance.

Aldber was going to correct his ways and was prepared to meet his fate, once and for all.

Chapter Eighteen
The Reunion

The deafening cold air blew past Aldber's face, and his hair and jacket flapped behind him as he accelerated over the plains, turned further north whilst the sun moved progressively over the horizon. Now relying upon Tala's map to provide him answers, he felt a new lease of confidence, as though he was drawing from the Source and it was guiding him safely on his way. Like during his meditations, he was immersed in an almost trance-like state of mind. Everything around him flowed harmoniously and he felt a sense of unification. He felt at one with the sky above and the land below, as though he could feel the heartbeat of Black Scar reverberating through his own veins. All of his senses had becoming overtly attuned.

'Surrender,' he whispered.

The young bura continued to travel relentlessly through the day and into the night as the land inclined towards dense woodlands, before slowing down to look out vigilantly for signs of centauri as he carefully weaved through the trees in the darkness.

As the sun peaked over the horizon on a new day he eventually stopped when he came to the first marking upon the map, and that was when he saw it: through the canopy of treetops before him he saw a hill with a vertical cliff-face slicing high into the sky. Further up he could see a ledge, an ideal vantage point to inspect the surrounding lands.

Aldber drove further until he found a suitable spot under cover to hide the vehicle. Hoping to find an end to the sheer wall, he looked further, but it trailed off out of sight to either side. Instead, he chose to climb the rock-face, so found a reliable foothold and began to launch upwards. He ascended beyond the tree line, keeping focused on what lay ahead. His fingers clung on as he hoisted upwards, passing bird's nests and foliage.

When finally reaching the cusp, he took a moment to mentally prepare himself for what was ahead. He peeked over the ledge and made out that there was a cave entrance. It was unassuming and, surprisingly, not guarded. This cast doubt upon the possibility of the centauri leader being here, but he would still inspect it.

The wind was bitter and pushed him against the rock-face. He balanced himself, found a strong foothold to push against, and with all his momentum launched onto the ledge, rolled forward, with a slight of hand pulling out his holstered pistol, and landed in a kneeling position facing the cave. He quickly surveyed the surrounding area. The ledge itself was small and there were no traces of recent activity. The winds bellowed around him, he could feel his heart beating frantically within his chest, and knelt there for a moment, uncertain as to whether he had made a miscalculation. He looked on into the dark depths of the cave before him, grasped the pistol firmly, stood up, and walked forward, taking every step with precision. The looming archway of the entrance consumed him as he walked into the darkness, only to smell the dankness within. The warmth was unsettling.

The young warrior stopped to let his eyes adjust and that's when he heard it: the irregular patter of large footsteps echoing as they approached. Aldber was not able to fully register what was before him. Suddenly, a mountainous being came towards him, filling the whole cave entrance.

The bura walked backwards onto the ledge so that he could see the being in the sunlight and kept his eyes trained on the centauri as it emerged. He was astounded to see the face of a weathered, scared and old centauri. Its fur was grey, and its head bowed as it approached him walking on all four of his legs, one of which was limping.

When they had walked out into the open, Aldber stood there for a moment, transfixed, looking into the eyes of his nemesis. This was not how he had anticipated the meeting. There were no grand fortifications or an army on guard. Before him was stood Black Scar, the one he had heard so many horrific tales about and hated more than anything. The being who had slaughtered his defenceless mother and was accountable for the deaths of so many other humans. But now, after all this time, the young warrior felt strangely unable to act. Even though he fostered contempt for the revered leader, he now pitied him for how pathetic he appeared.

'Aldber, it has been far too long,' Black Scar finally said, barely able to raise his head.

'You cannot even look me in the eye when addressing me! I am glad that I am able to face you alone. It is time once and for all to end this!' Aldber said through gritted teeth, raising the gun higher. 'You may be the leader of your people, but you are a coward to me!'

'I.... please, wait,' Black Scar replied, barely making an utterance. 'Please, I am begging you.'

'You expect mercy from me? I can see now why you have been so hard to find, because you are weak!' Aldber retorted. He was shaking; fiery rage engulfed his whole body as he focused on the centauri. He wanted to rip him apart with his bare hands.

Black Scar then withdrew something from his tattered garment, and that was when Aldber saw it, so simple and delicate within the centauri's large grasp. It was a small piece of stone, so unassuming, perhaps, but not in this instance.

It was the missing piece to Gaia Genuba's necklace.

'You took that from my mother when you killed her. *Give it to me*!' Aldber outstretched his free hand.

'No.' Black Scar looked up into the young man's eyes. He took a deep breath. 'I took that from the necklace as a keepsake. A reminder of when I delivered you to the human.'

'What did you just say?' Aldber screamed over the harsh winds.

'It is me, Aldber. I am the one who saved your life.'

In that moment, it felt like a wave of water had come and extinguished the young man's anger, overwhelming him with a cold shiver. Aldber lost his balance and stepped back, as though the words had penetrated his chest. He felt nausea surface from the pit of his stomach and tried to compose himself as he digested what had just been said. He looked into the centauri's eyes; there was no malice or aggression, only vulnerability. He saw a defenceless and tormented being.

'You are lying,' Aldber said dubiously.

'I am not, and you know it to be true. Aldber, you have been lied to this whole time.' Black Scar sat back on his hind legs in an open and unthreatening manner; he looked at the young man with a saddened expression. 'I imagine that Hollow Moon told you she saved you?'

'Yes, she did.'

'She did this to manipulate you.'

'I don't believe what I am hearing,' Aldber said cautiously, although could feel his grasp on the weapon weaken. 'You cannot fool me!'

'Do I look to you like I will cause harm? Here, hiding in this cave, do I look to you like the leader of my people?' Black Scar smiled and gestured at the surrounding area. It indeed was very modest for an enemy stronghold. 'On that fateful night, so many sun-cycles ago, I rescued you and took you to safety. I have been in exile ever since, waiting for our reunion, Aldber.'

'Why did you do that?'

'The prophecy, of course. I see it as an opportunity for our two species to find a common ground, to end this bloody conflict.'

'How did you know that I would come for you?'

'I had faith that the human I gave you to would not conceal the truth about your origins. I gave him the necklace as a clue to your mother's tribe and also told him your name, before running away. I am pleased that he took the initiative to teach you my people's tongue. We all need to reconcile our pasts before we can create our future. It was inevitable that you would want to seek answers. May I ask, how was it you were able to find me here?'

'I had a map, which showed this as a possible hiding place.'

'Well, you have finally accomplished what my own people have failed to do for many sun-cycles.'

'How did you know that Hollow Moon has manipulated me?'

'The most immediate clue was the hostility you have presented to me.' Black Scar pointed at the weapon. 'Ever since your birth they have spread lies, saying that I am the leader of their people, a malicious way to deceive you humans, whilst also keeping the true identity of our hierarchy a secret. I can imagine she told you that she was the one who saved you?' Aldber nodded. 'And that she said she had been the one in hiding?' Aldber nodded once again, his gun lowering as the discomforting reality started to sink in. 'You would think that the leader of the opposition would have been much easier to find after all this time?'

'Yes, I did.'

'Well, it actually was, because the whole time you were never aware you had been conspiring with the leader of the centauri, Mighty Sun's true bloodline - Hollow Moon.'

Aldber's arm involuntarily dropped and the pistol slipped from his grasp onto the floor. He looked into empty space hopelessly, not sure how to feel, finally acknowledging the reasonable doubts he had been fostering over these past few moon-cycles. He looked into Black Scar's eyes and could see something so distinctively familiar, as though he was looking back at his very first memories.

'For many sun-cycles Hollow Moon has tried to seek revenge for my disloyalty. My people doubt her leadership skills for allowing me to betray her and escape. She became obsessed with finding me, but I have always outwitted her. Because of this, it seems she had to resort to desperate measures. Resisting the temptation to destroy you, she instead decided to manipulate you in order to help her with finding me.'

'She always said about me using my divine powers.'

'Correct.'

'Ironically, I have found you, but that never required any special powers to do so.'

'But you still did it, Aldber.'

'It explains why she was apprehensive about me presenting myself to you as bait.'

'Yes, because if I had been gullible enough to fall for the trap, there might have been an opportunity for you to speak to me, then her whole plan might have backfired. She wanted to keep you under her watchful eye whilst she found me. She was taking a gamble and playing a strategic game, Aldber. Once you had done her dirty work, she would have humiliated and then killed you as well.'

'How can you be so certain of all of this?'

'I know this because I was one of her highest-ranking warriors, a close advisor, and fathered her offspring. Our son, Raining Fire, is the heir to the order of our royal bloodline. Hollow Moon revealed to me that you humans had a prophecy, but never detailed how she knew of it. She gave me one of those vision globes in our search for the child, although she never trusted it.'

'I tried asking the device that I used to find you, but it never gave me an answer.'

'Because I learnt to save myself from its mental prison. Do you still have possession of the globe?'

'No, I destroyed it.'

'I am glad. When we were led to you and your mother, I abandoned the device in order to rescue you. But ever since then, whilst I have been in exile I have been tormented by voices in an unknown dialect. I suspect that the contraception placed a curse on me. But after a while, I learnt to shut myself off, to disengage and hide away from the world.'

'And what happened then?'

'The voices stopped. I am so very pleased you had the ability to find me alone, so that I would have the chance to fully explain myself to you, Aldber.' The bura looked at Black Scar with caution. He knelt down and picked up the weapon and pointed it at the aged centauri.

'If this is all true, then you shall follow me, and we will confront Hollow Moon together.'

'It has been a long time, I am sure she would be very pleased to see me,' Black Scar said. He then stood on all four legs and walked forward limping. 'It is time we ended this, Aldber. Together.'

'I do not imagine this confrontation to be anything less than a bloody ending to this game.' Aldber lowered the gun and signalled for the aged centauri to follow him.

They proceeded through the cave system and from the hillside down towards the woodlands. Aldber collected the hover-bike and Black Scar perched precariously on the rear seat. They set off southward through the trees in an unpleasant silence, and Aldber remained vigilant because even though these new revelations had cast great doubt upon everything, he was not convinced that he could fully trust Black Scar. The centauri attempted to engage in conversation, but Aldber remained withdrawn, bitterly silent and deep in thought. It felt like the longest and most uncomfortable journey he had made in his lifetime.

He regretted now not telling Grand Master Vivid where he had gone to but suspected his absence at the Sanctuary would have been noticed, and they would have suspected where the young warrior had gone. It would have been convenient if he could have used Heratu in order to call for reinforcements, but after having been stripped of his rank, he very much doubted many of the elders trusted him anymore, so would have to go alone, and accepted that he might not survive this reunion.

The following day, the pair crossed the final stretch of the plains in their approach of the Old City and scaled the wall into the grotesque monstrosity. They passed through the ruins along the outskirts towards sector nine, and as the grand skyscraper of old loomed nearby, the Galardros instructed Black Scar how they would proceed.

*

Aldber walked out into the open air, the collapsed ceiling revealed a late-afternoon sky strewn with clouds; the remaining walls circling the large open space led off into the murky shadows. In front of him was Hollow Moon, sat deep in thought. She was facing in the opposite direction, looking out over the city below, and appeared to be alone.

'Hollow Moon, I have returned,' Aldber announced over the soaring winds, half-heartedly projecting friendliness as he tried to remain calm.

She heard the words and was somewhat taken aback. She turned her head and smiled, before standing to face and greet him properly.

'Aldber, I was beginning to worry! We have been waiting here patiently for your return.' She looked over his shoulder as he approached. 'The note we received did not explain much. Have you brought reinforcements with you?'

'No, I did not think that it would be necessary,' Aldber said through gritted teeth.

'Oh, whatever is the matter?' Hollow Moon looked at him with concern. 'You seem to be distressed?'

From several directions appeared the other Outcasts: Red River, Flying Stone, Long Wing and Singing Eye. They all paced forward looking unmistakably cautious.

'There will be no need for us to use an army to find Black Scar,' Aldber said, eyeing the other centauri.

'Oh, really, and why is that?' Hollow Moon smiled, although

Aldber could tell that it was a forced expression.

'Because I have already found him,' Aldber stopped in his advance.

From the shadows stood forth Black Scar, he walked towards Aldber's side and looked into the faces of his old allies. The Outcasts looked horrified and starting roaring whilst Hollow Moon ushered for them to not advance.

'Black Scar, it has been a long time,' she uttered calmly with a neutral expression upon her face.

'Hollow Moon,' Black Scar replied through gritted fangs, whilst frowning at her with rage.

'Aldber, please listen, I can imagine that he has told you a lie so that you would bring him here to murder us?' She looked to the side of the building. 'He probably had it all planned out, and without you knowing, has a small army waiting at the foot of this building, ready to attack us.'

'No, Hollow Moon, we have come alone, I am sure of it. He told me the truth. You can no longer deceive me!' Aldber suddenly erupted, to his side Black Scar breathed heavily through his nostrils.

'Aldber, I do not know what has *come over you?*' Hollow Moon attempted to reason with her alluring tone. 'Do you not realise what you have done by exposing us like this?'

'That is *enough*!' Black Scar barked, clenching his fists. 'For sun-cycles I have been on the run, hiding away, whilst you have sent your minions to try and kill me, and have deceived everyone. You are a *disgrace* to our people!'

'*I am the disgrace?*' Hollow Moon suddenly screamed and stood on her hind legs, looking at the two arrivals intensely. '*You* were the one who betrayed *our* people.' She then sat back down, composed herself, and looked over at Aldber, who edged towards her. As he passed the rustling campfire, with a slight of hand, he subtly dropped an un-ignited grenade into the flames.

'Aldber, dearest, do you remember when we spoke about your mother?' She looked at him mockingly. 'We spoke about how the love of a mother for her offspring is unparalleled. You do not know the extremes a mother will go to, even if that means killing in order to protect her own. Yes, it was I, Aldber, I killed your mother!'

Her face then formed into a vulgar smirk as she looked down at the young warrior. She then chucked back her head and started to laugh uncontrollably, the unsettling sound echoing against the walls and out into the city ruins. The other four centauri joined her.

'Okay, the laughter is warranted this time,' Aldber uttered. He placed his hand on the grip of his gun and stood his ground. A drip of sweat slid down his cheek. From out of the corner of his sight, Aldber saw one more figure appear. It was Bleeding Sky.

'You have caught me out, Aldber, I have been hiding in plain sight all along!' Hollow Moon tried to regain her breath from the hysterical laughter. 'It was all a lie. Everything. I never saved your life! It was this pathetic piece of vermin you have brought here that did that. It was my plan all along, as I knew the time would come when you would search for your parents. I had spies waiting who saw you visiting the Genuba Tribe. I had your vehicle destroyed so that you would have to return to your stronghold on foot. I was quite astounded how easy it was, because you stupidly revealed the hidden location of the base to me and I was able to approach you.'

'What happened to the tribe?' Aldber frowned.

'I had them slaughtered immediately.' Hollow Moon smirked. 'From the way they treated your mother, I think I did us both a favour, am I not right?'

'You fed me the story, this lie, so that you could keep me close to manipulate me?'

'Of course, I had to make sure I knew where this threat was. I had to use you and your powers for my own undoing. I wanted to prove my superiority and ability to destroy the prophet, by deceiving him first. And *you* believed every single word I said to you.'

'What about the centauri warrior who you interrogated and murdered?'

'He was part of the act. He knew his sacrifice was necessary for the plan.'

Aldber looked over at Red River, who was unable to look him in the eye. He could see that the old centauri was conflicted.

'Red River, you surprise me. For someone of such age and wisdom, you went along with this plan?' Aldber asked him.

'Remember what I said, Aldber: we all must do what is necessary to ensure our own survival,' Red River finally said, looking up at the young human.

'And you said that humans don't have integrity?' Aldber said, shaking his head before looking over at the new arrival. 'And I presume the ambush was staged in order to keep me convinced?' Bleeding Sky then started laughing.

'Precisely. Admittedly, we were having great difficulties, so I must thank you for accomplishing what we had been unable to do for so many sun-cycles.' Hollow Moon stretched her hand out to Black Scar and smiled. 'You have done exactly what you were meant to do and have succeeded in bringing him to me. And now you both shall die!'

Several minutes of intense heating had perforated the casing of the grenade, damaging the detonator inside, and just in that moment, the violent explosive erupted, filling the whole open space with blinding light and brilliant flames, silencing the laughter. The force threw all that surrounded the fire into the air.

Aldber landed hard on the floor. His hearing was momentarily compromised, and the impact and smoke severely disorientated him. The explosion had caused greater damage than he had anticipated, and the fragile building started to creak violently. He quickly got to his feet, raised his weapon, but was unable to see through the vast cloud of black smoke, as the fire had grown and was roaring ferociously in the centre. From afar, he saw a colossal being dive through the air, its hands extended and its jaws wide open ready to overwhelm him. Just when Aldber thought he could not counteract this movement, Black Scar suddenly appeared and hit the attacker from the side in a mid-air collision.

Aldber saw two disorientated centauri reappear, both stumbling on their hind legs. It was Long Wing and Flying Stone. They saw the human and pounced for him. Aldber released several shots from his weapon and dived out of the way as the two pursuers came crashing towards him. They both scrambled wildly and started running after the young warrior as he made his way back into the main building.

Inside, the many floors to the skyscraper had given way and all that was left was the metal framework to the brittle structure, which was now wobbling and starting to break apart. Aldber started climbing down the framework and could hear the two centauri behind screaming with rage.

Aldber saw a platform several stories down, so jumped for it and landed hard. Just as he regained his balance, the two centauri came crashing down next to him. The warrior withdrew his blade and started swinging it towards them whilst using his pistol to fire at them both. They took the pelting but did not slow in their advances and the platform swayed from side to side under the pressure. Aldber had to roll around to avoid being hit, knowing that with one miscalculated move he would be crushed within their grasps. Long Wing then stood in front of him snarling, as Flying Stone had fallen to the side. Aldber ran towards her, avoided two punches, and her baying fangs, jumped, kicked off her abdomen, thrust his blade inwards, leapt backwards, and sliced her open in one movement. He landed as blood and guts spilled everywhere. He heard Long Wing's cries and saw her body crumple to the ground, but he did not react in time to see the fist appear as Flying Stone punched him hard in the face. The impact sent Aldber flying over the edge and into the depths of the building below. His unconscious body fell fast, his jacket flayed in the wind, and his weapons fell from his loosened grip.

Further below a piece of flooring board had snapped loose and presented a cushion as Aldber neared the floor. His body pummelled against the material, denting it severely, before his body slid down and slumped onto the ground below. Several wounds started bleeding profusely along his back.

Large fragments started falling and the structure started groaning. From above a centauri leapt down; it was Black Scar, who made his way to the ground and approached the unconscious human. He could see that Aldber was still breathing and could feel a pulse, although could not determine how extensive the internal damage was from the gaping wounds and fatal fall. He leant down on all four of his limbs, gently collected the limp body and draped it precariously over his back.

Behind, he could hear distant screams and the creaking skyscraper succumbing to the damage of the explosion, so surged forward through a break in the building's side. He propelled into the distance with all his might as the structure started collapsing into a large heap and a gigantic dust cloud dispersed behind him.

The centauri knew there was only one place that he could go. Like many sun-cycles earlier, he would leave the ruins of the city and head north towards the hills. Overhead, the pink clouds of dusk streaked the horizon and the skies were beginning to darken as Black Scar approached the hidden valley and entered.

There, upon the grass, he delicately laid down the body of the young man he had saved once before, and would wait until a patrolman had spotted him, before running away into the night, again to wait once more.

Chapter Nineteen
An Approaching Storm

It was a nightly custom for Grand Master Vivid to take a stroll around the grounds of the Sanctuary and its surrounding woodland. He would walk through the trees on the hillside where, in his solitude, he would contemplate many of the day's productive outcomes and pitfalls. In light of the recent troubles that had been beset upon the order and the security risks, he had been advised against indulging this activity, but was adamant that he would continue this evening routine. However, he did agree to be escorted by an armoured guard, who stood back at a reasonable distance to offer the leader much needed space for his moments of deep thought.

Vivid walked with his cloak pulled tightly around him and looked at the majestic scenery. It was the appreciation of a wise elder, who had seen many seasons pass by and was now in the winter sun-cycles of his own life.

He was proud of his accomplishments and of taking the honourable role of leader for the human resistance. Although sometimes his mind wondered and he had often fantasised about living another life, for he knew very well that he was only a product of his times. Having seen the artefacts in the forbidden chamber, he had taken a glimpse at other people's way of life, when there had not been so much conflict. Perhaps he should have lived a more modest existence; as a tribesman, he could have been exposed to more dangers in the wilderness, but at least could have had the opportunity to be surrounded by loved ones, to have even loved someone intimately. He had devoted his whole life to the order and had never fulfilled some of his own needs. Like the grand masters before him, he had served unconditionally, led courageously, and waited patiently for the arrival of the chosen one. He hoped the personal sacrifices he had made would be worthwhile. Now it seemed that all those sun-cycles of hardship had led to this pivotal moment.

Vivid had felt, to a degree, that his own efforts had not been strong enough in counteracting the forces of the Enemy, that they had been pursuing the same course of action, and it seemed like no resolution in sight. He never showed people his deep-seated self-criticism and had always remained mentally grounded and modest, in spite of his position of power. He had always taken the role with humility and grace. Even as an old man with unparalleled wisdom, he was forever learning. For many sun-cycles, he had acknowledged an underlying restlessness within the council, and now felt accountable for the emergence of this suspected mole that had been causing havoc.

The one thing he had felt the most fortunate for was to receive Aldber as an infant. He had never witnessed such an act, which challenged his preconceptions, because to see a human child be shown mercy by one of the centauri was the unpredictable sign they all had been waiting for. It was a twist of fate, that the one they had awaited over all these generations would be shown such adoration by those so deeply revered. The prophecy, the foundation upon which the order was established, had become something of legend amongst many and was also so vague in its explanation of what would unfold. He held true and had faith that humanity would be guided towards salvation, whichever way it may come about.

Grand Master Vivid admittedly had his doubts about the reason behind the centauri saving the child; it could have been an accident, something taken out of context, and he had overestimated its importance. However, he had made it his duty to teach the boy all he had known and had prepared him for whatever he would encounter when the time was right. Vivid was given reassurance about his beliefs in the child, when Aldber displaced natural talent as a warrior. The day when the young man had approached him enquiring about his origins and had discovered the painful truth about his heritage, was surely a sign. It was evident that humanity was not the only species that saw great importance in the child; the Enemy recognised the threat, without doubt. This was no ordinary young man.

However, Grand Master Vivid knew that, to a degree, he had far too much expectation invested in Aldber. After all, he was expecting the boy to do things previously unattainable. He felt an element of guilt for rearing the child for the sake of the order's undoing; it was like Aldber had never been given a choice about his own destiny. The leader should have had more respect and let the boy decide for himself if he wanted to take this forsaken path, but Aldber had taken the responsibilities courageously. He knew full well the implications of what he was letting himself in for, and it was the mark of a truly fearless warrior.

As Grand Master Vivid walked further into the woods, his thoughts drifted towards concern regarding the young warrior's current whereabouts. He wondered where Aldber was and had been troubled by the news that the young man had disappeared after having been stripped of his rank and also had his mission cancelled. Vivid knew very well what Aldber had done. Making such a bold choice meant that Aldber had either made a misjudgement due to grief, exhaustion and recklessness, or knew something else, possibly wielding a power unheard of before now. Despite the council's reaction to the news of Aldber's disappearance, the leader had great faith that the boy had made the right choice.

Grand Master Vivid hoped that, unlike the changing of the seasons, their efforts would break out of this torturous predictable cycle that had gone on for countless generations. He had always seen that, like the melting of the snow and growing of leaves, or the cyclic behaviour of people, history could repeat itself. This observation was soon to be reaffirmed, much to his discomfort.

As he walked in the fading sunlight, a distressed patrolman suddenly approached him. He made the salute to Grand Master Vivid, which the leader returned calmly, sensing that something untoward was afoot.

'Master, one of the patrolmen has spotted a centauri in the valley! It ran away when we approached it. We are not sure of the circumstances, but it seemed to have abandoned one of our wounded warriors.'

'Do you know the identity of the warrior?' Grand Master Vivid rubbed his beard earnestly.

'Yes, Master, it is Bura Aldber. He has been taken to the medical rooms and is in a critical condition.' The patrol man saw the horror in Grand Master Vivid's eyes.

'Take me to him, immediately.'

Grand Master Vivid was led into the medical rooms with his armoured guard following closely behind. As he entered, he saw a large gathering of medics surrounding a curtained area close to the entrance, and they stood apart as he approached and pushed the barrier aside.

Before him, Aldber had been laid on the bed. The sheets were marked with blood, his unconscious body was being positioned on its side and his shirt had been cut away. Water and bandages were brought forward to treat the large wounds he had incurred in his back. They were evidently scratch marks from a centauri. Once the bleeding had stopped, dressings were applied, liquids were injected into his body to replenish lost fluid, and the wounded warrior was left in a stable condition, although still comatose.

Grand Master Vivid sat by Aldber's side and looked at him with grave concern. The news spread and several councillors came to inspect the wounded warrior, inquisitive about whether Aldber had succeeded in his task, and were sharply dismissed to allow privacy. Grand Master Vivid only allowed Grombl and Maloyk to sit by the unconscious warrior's side.

The leader remained there through the night, checking the patient's pulse and dabbing his forehead with a damp cloth. He did not know what to think, whether Aldber had succeeded in killing Black Scar, or had unknowingly gotten himself into a far worse situation.

It would not be until a few days later that Aldber awoke from his coma. His first view was the medical room's wooden ceiling, as his blurred vision gradually came into focus. In a brief moment of panic, having remembered what had happened, he looked around to make sure Hollow Moon's minions were not there. His anxiety subsided when he recognised the familiar aromas of the room and was perplexed by how he had survived and made it here. He could feel great pain in his body as he attempted to sit up, and balanced himself upon his elbows, seeing that he had been placed comfortably under a cover.

'Good morning, Aldber, it is a relief that you are finally awake,' said Grand Master Vivid, evidently pleased. He was sat at the end of the bed.

'Master... I... What? How long have I been unconscious for?' Aldber uttered, though quite strenuously.

'Since you have arrived, you have been asleep for five days now,' Grand Master Vivid explained. 'You lost a considerable amount of blood, but vital liquids were pumped into your body and miraculously you survived. The medics did fine work in sewing up the large wounds in your back. What happened to you, dear boy?'

'Grand Master Vivid, I...' Aldber pushed himself up into a sitting position and then rubbed both of his eyes. 'I finally approached Black Scar and he revealed to me that it was in fact *he* who saved me as a new-born.'

'How extraordinary!' Grand Master Vivid sat back, surprised, and rubbed his beard in the usual eccentric fashion as he digested the news.

'As you can imagine, I could not quite believe it. We approached Hollow Moon and the Outcasts to question them. Black Scar had been telling the truth. As you might have guessed, it did not go so well, and it seems like in the fight that followed Black Scar saved my life.'

'For the second time.' Vivid smiled. 'He delivered you here, vanished, and has not been seen since.'

'I am sorry, Master, but I do not know what to say. There is a lot to digest,' Aldber said, shaking his head in disbelief.

'You did not by any chance cause an explosion in a tower on the outskirts of the city ruins?'

'Yes, that is where I challenged the Outcasts and made my escape. How did you know?'

'It was reported to me by mowoni based nearby. I had a suspicion it might have been you. It seems you did make quite the scene!' Grand Master Vivid chuckled.

'I always like to make an impact.' Aldber smiled. 'I don't know who survived the blast.'

'Well, the skyscraper is no more. But I presume that whatever business you had with Hollow Moon has yet to be resolved.' Grand Master Vivid leant forward looking gravely serious. 'This morning, a large army of centauri have been spotted leaving the northern walls of the Old City. They are heading in this direction.'

'What?' Aldber suddenly became fully alert, leaning forward in his bed.

'It seems too coincidental that such a large gathering would be heading in this specific direction along the stretch of hills. Something like this has never been seen before and Hollow Moon knows where the hidden valley is.'

'It would only be a matter of time before she would suspect that I had survived. She knows exactly where Black Scar would take me. She is coming for me! Then we must prepare ourselves!' Aldber tried to move but was overcome with agonising pain.

'You shall do no such thing, other than to stay here and rest,' Grand Master Vivid said sternly.

'But, Master, it's...'

'I shall hear nothing else about the matter!' Grand Master Vivid scowled before standing to leave. 'You will remain here whilst we deal with this army. That is an order, Aldber, do you understand?'

The patient bowed his head and reluctantly nodded. Grand Master Vivid swiftly turned and went to leave. Standing further away were Grombl and Maloyk, who looked pleased to see Aldber was now awake. Grand Master Vivid said something to them both before leaving the room. They then waddled over to the newly awoken young man with beaming smiles.

'Little Aldber, we are g-l-l-l-lad to see you awake!' said Grombl. Maloyk walked close to the patient's side and started giving his head a few little pats.

'Thanks, you two,' Aldber said, looking at Maloyk, not impressed by the irritating hand gesture. Maloyk then sat down on the bed.

'We thinks you ought to be a bit more careful, what with getting yourself hurts like that,' Grombl said, sitting on the end of the bed.

'Well, it was not exactly intentional.' Aldber frowned.

'Did you hear about the army of centauri heading this way? Big troubles ahead I reckons!' Grombl said with wide eyes.

'I did. I suppose Grand Master Vivid told you both to keep an eye on me?' Aldber eyed them both mischievously. 'He probably told you to make sure I don't leave this bed?'

'Yes, just that,' Grombl said, placing his hands on his hips proudly, feeling very smug about his appointed responsibility.

'Well, you best have a decent explanation for not following orders correctly,' Aldber said. The two looked at each other with puzzlement and then back at him.

Aldber then threw back the cover; he was only wearing linen trousers and exposed his bruised and bandaged muscular torso. He shifted his weight, his bare feet touched the floor, and he attempted to put weight upon them. As he stood up and straightened, he could feel an unbearable pain surging up his back, as he touched the bandaged sewn wounds. At first, he struggled to find balance, but eventually stood firmly, shook his head, and let out a small sigh of satisfaction.

'Aldber, you must rest! You have been badly wounded!' Grombl tried to reason. To his side Maloyk started biting his nails anxiously. 'You are too weak to fight!'

'I am feeling fine!' Aldber took his trousers and a fresh shirt by his bedside and slowly put them on. 'You do not think I could just lie around here and miss out on all of the action?'

'You are mad, Little Aldber,' Grombl sulked. Suddenly, their attention was diverted out of a window. From afar, over the other side of the valley, they could hear the distinct roar of a war horn.

'Yes, undoubtedly.' Aldber looked back, winking at him. He then pulled on his boots, before proceeding past the curtain towards the entrance. Several medics vocalised their objection, but no sooner had he left the bed than the door closed swiftly behind him.

'What are we going to say to G-G-G-Grand Master Vivid?' Grombl looked in despair at Maloyk, who gave his usual slightly dismissive and generally oblivious shrug. 'You know Maloyk - it would be nice if every once in a while, you actually said something!'

Maloyk frowned at him as they both left the bedside and tried to tail Aldber, however, seeing as they could not keep up with the young warrior's pace, they were not aware that he was heading for the armoury.

Aldber started to run in order to create distance away from the two pesky assistants, as he took a flight of steps into the heart of the underground networks of the base. He then arrived at the armoury; its entrance was an archway with a large barred gate flanked by two guards. Aldber was permitted admittance inside, where the walls were lined with torches. There was a large group of warriors assembled and all were preoccupied with finding suitable weaponry for the coming onslaught.

On many racks and shelves that adorned the walls were rifles, swords, and many other instruments of brutality. Aldber looked meticulously through the selection, and found a suitable sword, its accompanying hilt and belt. He weighed the weapon in his hand, looked along the blade for any rusting or indentations. Once satisfied with his find, he then walked into an open space and found a sharpening stone and proceeded to prepare the blade. Around him, he could hear warriors frantically discussing the impending battle. The atmosphere was thick with anticipation and torch fumes.

Aldber then pushed through the crowd towards the back area, where there were heaps of clothing and armour stacked in various piles, the majority of which was stained with mud and smelt damp. He opted for a leather tabard, which he then put on before wrapping the weapon's belt around his waist. He also found gauntlets for his wrists, which he fastened tightly. These garments were all superficial precautions; he doubted there was much chance of coming out of this battle alive.

Once Aldber had resurfaced from the depths of the hillside, he walked out into the main complex and stood there looking out at the scene before him. Hundreds of men were gathered assembling fortifications along the field at the foot of the valley. They were in preparation, waiting for whatever was going to come from the other side of the hill.

At present, he had no time to think about how this had all come about, even though he knew deep down that he was to blame for the Enemy discovering the location to the secret base. It was the first time in the long history of the order that the Sanctuary had ever been attacked. This once tranquil place would soon be the stage for a pivotal turning point in the war.

Aldber walked through the crowds and spotted Bura Hecta standing under a newly erected tent where elders and warriors were in discussion. When the young man drew near, Hecta saw him and walked out to greet him.

'Aldber, what are you doing here? You should be resting,' Hecta said with concern, 'Grand Master Vivid told me what happened.'

'I nearly blew myself up getting out of that situation,' Aldber said sheepishly.

'Well, you should not have left without letting us know, so that we could have provided reinforcements. You disobeyed orders,' Hecta said as they walked inside the tent to a table.

'You know me, Hecta, I have selective hearing.' Aldber smiled.

'Selective thinking, more like.' Hecta frowned.

'After what happened, I thought that everyone had lost faith in me, so I had to do what I thought was right.' Aldber looked out across the valley floor. 'But it seems I was not able to finish what I had started and have brought all the troubles back with me.'

'That might be the case, but we must deal with the matter at hand. Aldber...' Hecta turned and looked him in the eye. 'Just remember, it was only a matter of time before the Enemy would discover the hidden location of our fortress. Whether you revealed the location or not, it was inevitable that this would happen.'

'You are just saying that to make me feel better about myself.'

'For once. Just prove your worth on the battlefield.'

They joined Councillor Fukuro who acknowledged Aldber with a firm nod as he entered.

'What is the strategy for the battle?' Aldber asked, crossing his arms and looking at a map that was strewn across the table.

'The front line is situated on the opposite side of the hill on the plains facing the oncoming forces. There, Grand Master Vivid will lead the men to receive the main frontal assault.' Fukuro pointed towards the entrance of the spurs that adjoined the valley to the flat plains beyond. 'We will bombard them with gun-fire and then will gradually retreat, drawing their forces back inside the valley, syphoning them here onto the field.'

'As the majority of their forces enter the valley...' Hecta leaned forward and gestured with his hands in a circular motion towards his chest. 'We will pincher them in. They will be trapped with no escape route.'

'How many men do we have?' Aldber asked, looking at Fukuro who seemed concerned.

'We have mustered two thousand,' Hecta said.

'And they have how many?' Aldber swallowed hard.

'Ten thousand... roughly,' Hecta muttered. 'However, we have the strategic advantage of the natural fortification, and most importantly - the firepower. We may be outnumbered, but we are not outgunned!'

Hecta stood tall and proud with a deviant smile upon his face. It seemed like he had been waiting for a battle like this for many sun-cycles.

'Aldber, I order that you stay here on the battlefield and await the surge of Enemy forces,' Fukuro said, resting a hand on the young man's shoulder.

'Understood,' Aldber agreed.

All within the tent raised their hands in the salute and courageously proclaimed the oath.

Far away on the plains overlooking the hills were stood the amassed forces of the centauri. They had walked through the night from the bowels of the city ruins, and assembled facing the hills, awaiting orders to attack the stronghold of the humans. On this day they now marched with something that had, until this time, been hidden for purposes - many standard bearers stood proudly with black flags bearing the white circle symbol of their great leader, Hollow Moon.

The crowds parted and bowed their heads out of respect as she paraded through. The whole army soon erupted excitably, repeatedly calling out her name. The floor vibrated with jubilation. She walked through gracefully with her head held high; a large open burn mark brandished across her face, which now looked deformed, one eye was blinded and white. She walked up to one of her warlords, who had followed orders and mustered as many warriors as he could, if her initial plan to deceive the human and kill Black Scar should fail.

Admittedly, she knew full well she could have simply murdered the prophet in his sleep, attacked the human stronghold without warning, and just let Black Scar rot. But she had been consumed by a bitterness, an inflated ego, by a maddening obsession that had distracted her from the armament preparations, warped her thoughts, and made her enact a plan that had failed. But now, she would silence her critics once and for all.

Hollow Moon was delighted to finally reveal herself. She had been given invaluable information and was about to conduct one of the biggest offences in the history of her people. For many sun-cycles she had waited patiently, and on this day, she would finally attack the human resistance's main stronghold. This would be the first of many masterstrokes she had planned for this moment, to turn the tides of war.

Behind the hill she knew very well that Aldber had been delivered to safety by Black Scar. She would find him and personally see to destroying him; tearing him apart slowly and taking great satisfaction in watching him suffer. She should have done this many sun-cycles ago when he was a new-born child. This petty threat would finally be extinguished. It was overdue.

Behind her tailed Flying Stone, the only remaining Outcast. The others had not survived the encounter with Aldber and the Betrayer and the subsequent destruction of the tower.

'Hollow Moon, the forces are ready to engage,' said Flying Stone, now dressed in armour and wielding a sword and shield.

'Good,' Hollow Moon replied, un-armoured and fearless. She looked further over the horizon and could see human forces assembling by the foot of the hills.

'When will we proceed, Your Grace?'

'Once I have been given the signal by my human insurgent.' She smiled wickedly at him before looking once more over the horizon. 'When the time is right, revenge will be sweet,' she said through gritted fangs.

Chapter Twenty
The Battle of the Sanctuary

Grombl and Maloyk walked out from the main complex and stood looking horrified at the fortifications being built on the field in the valley. Trees had been cut down, stripped and fashioned into large pointed barricades, and several artillery weapons had been set up near to the entrance of the valley where the two hills intertwined, whilst warriors rushed past them carrying equipment and shouting out orders to others further away.

The incompetent pair's efforts to find Aldber within the fortress had been unforthcoming. Their final resort was to try and find him here on the battlefield, with the dubious attempt of returning him to the medical rooms.

They started waddling down into the field and saw that there was a newly erected command post. On closer inspection they saw standing underneath the tent Bura Hecta deep in discussion with other warriors. Upon approach, they wanted to enquire about the young warrior's whereabouts, but got more than they had bargained for.

'Grombl and Maloyk, you are just in time. I require you to pass on a message to the front line,' Hecta said with his usual harsh and derogatory tone.

'B-b-but, Bura Hecta, we are already attending duties,' Grombl tried to explain.

'That can wait, this is more important.' Hecta frowned. The two assistants exchanged an awkward look and then looked back at the elder. They knew he was never a man to disagree with. 'Inform Grand Master Vivid that battlements have been completed and we await further orders.'

Grombl and Maloyk both nodded reluctantly and then walked out of the tent. They again exchanged awkward looks before meandering over the battlefield, doing their best to avoid being trampled on or shouted at. They looked around, trying to spot Aldber in the crowd, but were not able to find him. Grombl muttered little things under his breath like he usually did when overly nervous, and Maloyk looked around anxiously whilst fumbling his fingers.

They gradually made their way to the where the two hills adjoined and walked the path that snaked along until opening out onto the plains ahead. Before them were stood the majority of the Galardros warriors in formation looking off into the distance. Far away upon the horizon, they could see what appeared to be a suffocating black wave slowly drenching the landscape.

'Maloyk, look!' Grombl spluttered, pointing towards the Enemy forces. His mute friend expressed his horror with a discomforted expression, wiping sweat from his brow.

'Is there something I can help you two with?' They heard a whiny voice from behind and turned to see Councillor Gilliad standing there. He was dressed in battle attire and was not pleased to see these two skulking buffoons who, he assumed, must have gotten lost.

'Ah, Councillor Gilliad! Oh, whatever happened to your nose?' Grombl pointed at the warrior's disjointed nose with concern.

'That is none of your business!' Gilliad replied, evidently self-conscious and embarrassed. 'Why are you two here on the battlefield?'

'We have a message for Grand Master Vivid from Bura Hecta.'

'Oh, really? Divulge and I shall notify him myself,' Gilliad said with his usual loftiness.

Grombl was suddenly flummoxed and unable to recall the message. He looked at his mute friend for the answer and was returned an open-eyed shrug of the shoulders. Councillor Gilliad looked at them both with bafflement and shook his head mockingly.

'What is it?' Gilliad demanded. '*Spit it out!*'

'Erm.' Grombl started to scratch his head and tapped his foot habitually, trying desperately to recall the important message. He had tried so hard to remember what Hecta had said, having repeated it to himself under his breath repeatedly, but as usual, under pressure he had a mind blank. 'I, uh, forgot?'

'You are a blathering idiot!' Gilliad scorned.

From behind, a white horse approached. Upon it rode Grand Master Vivid, who was dressed magnificently in golden battle armour over his light brown robes.

'Grombl and Maloyk?' he said as the horse stopped.

'Ah, Grand Master Vivid, I have a message for you!' Grombl said excitably.

'What are you two doing here? I told you specifically to keep watch over Bura Aldber, did I not?' Vivid leaned down to speak to them. 'You disobeyed my order!'

'Well, I, um, we, um, well, yes, but we lost him and then Bura Hecta told us to pass on a message,' Grombl tried to reason with a strained smile. To his side Maloyk looked equally agitated and embarrassed.

'Which is?' Vivid frowned, sitting back up as his horse coughed. There was an awkward silence.

'... I can't remember.' Grombl said, looking away. Maloyk then tapped him on the shoulder and pointed back in the direction of the valley. At first Grombl was confused about what his friend was attempting to communicate to him. Maloyk repeatedly pointed, which was not getting his point across. 'What, Maloyk?' Grombl became even more flustered as Maloyk became angered. His friend started making large elaborate hand gestures. 'A tent? A gun? A tree? No, no, that was definitely a gun. What? Oh, yes! Yes! We gots it! Grand Master Vivid, the battlements are ready!'

'Thank you. I would recommend that you two keep out of harm's way and take safe cover,' Grand Master Vivid instructed. The two assistants moved on. The leader looked across the front line. 'Gilliad, have you seen Thortatel?'

'No, Master, I have not seen him all day,' Gilliad responded disdainfully. 'I will return to my post.'

'Yes, be on your way,' Grand Master Vivid sat there and contemplated the peculiarity of the elder's absence.

'Well, it is just as well I remembered the message after all, ay, Maloyk?' Grombl chuckled, much to the annoyance of his friend. The over-talkative one then lowered his voice to a whisper and nodded back towards Gilliad. 'I heards he got that broken nose from a punch, Maloyk.' The mute found this amusing as they walked to the back of the formation to find themselves suitable cover.

Grand Master Vivid watched the troublesome pair before surveying the army assembled. The majority of those present had fallen back from their posts in the Old City, when news of Hollow Moon's advancing army had spread. The leader was thankful for this, as there would not have been enough warriors in the stronghold to defend against this onslaught.

The battles that had taken place before now had been within the city ruins or woodlands, not on the open plains where each species was vulnerable to the unpredictable strategic tactics of their opponents. As had been the case before, the humans had the firepower, although did not have the brute strength or numbers of the centauri.

Grand Master Vivid took a deep breath to compose himself. He leaned forward to stroke his trusted steed and then commanded the horse to manoeuvre through the crowds to the front line. He galloped in front of his men majestically, his cloak wafting in the breeze, racing up and down the line looking at his men and women with calm and grace.

'Warriors of the order, those of the faith, brothers and sisters to the cause, today we shall face our greatest challenge yet!' He elevated his voice, which was the only sound as everyone stood silent. 'Stand defiantly and show Hollow Moon and her forces what we are capable of, that we are not afraid. This fortress has stood for many generations and will do for many more to come!' They all cheered, beaming at him in admiration. 'Today will be remembered as the pivotal moment we showed the Enemy we are not to be reckoned with. We shall be victorious! In the name of the Supreme One! In the name of the people!'

The army raised their weapons, all cheered in unison, and then stood firmly to engage the oncoming forces of the Enemy.

The thundering of footsteps was deafening. Before them, the first wave of Hollow Moon's forces descended with war horns and bloodthirsty roars. As they drew nearer, Grand Master Vivid commanded that his forces remained stationary for as long as possible and ordered his riflemen to stand forward to take aim.

The centauri drew nearer as the ground rumbled beneath their feet. Grand Master Vivid shouted over the deafening noise. The land erupted with gunfire; the oncoming forces were relentlessly pelted with a barrage, their armoury too weak to withstand it. The ocean of gigantic beasts started dwindling in numbers as the riflemen mowed them down with continuous fire. Grand Master Vivid looked off into the distance and saw that the Enemy forces would keep on pressing forward even at the expense of sacrificing so many of their own to penetrate the frontline and enter the valley. This was exactly what he intended for them to do. The plains soon became a sea of bodies and blood. Thousands of centauri warriors avoided the waves of bullet fire and started descending towards the front line.

Grand Master Vivid responded and ordered for his men to start arming themselves with swords before the last wave of gunfire rained over the Enemy. The leader then shouted courageously and raced forward on his horse to meet the oncoming barrage. His sword swung through the air effortlessly as he began decapitating centauri that were no match for his agility and were trampled by the horse. A row of riflemen stood back, aimed their weapons into the air, and directed gunfire at the Enemy further away.

Soon the attackers breached the front line. Centauri exploded through, swinging their blades, crushing bodies with their shields, biting off limbs, and throwing the lifeless bodies hurtling through the air. Men either fought with their swords or desperately fired their rifles, bombarding the helpless centauri in their sights.

Grand Master Vivid drew nearer to the valley entrance and signalled for his forces to then start withdrawing into the pathway as planned. His warriors then started to retreat, creating a safe passage by firing their weapons to hold back the unbearable amount of centauri that were heading towards them.

Grombl and Maloyk cowered at the foot of the hillside. They were kneeling down with their hands over their heads, trying to remain unseen as they watched the horrific bloody battle unfold before their eyes. They watched as warriors perished and the centauri advanced.

Grombl was utterly transfixed, awaiting his impending doom, whilst Maloyk saw an opportunity for them to get away from the onslaught. He repeatedly nudged Grombl in the side with his elbow until his trusted friend acknowledged him. He pointed at a shield that had been abandoned on the ground and they quickly scrambled across the grass on their hands and knees towards it. Using their collective strength to pick it up, they pulled the shield over their heads. It offered protection, although compromised their visibility. They then proceeded to stumble through the chaos, making their way through the sea of dead bodies, towards the pathway where other humans were retreating.

On the opposite side of the valley, further westwards, there was small woodland. It was unassuming and usually shrouded in shadow. Here, the trees were tall and evergreen. Unbeknownst to the inhabitants of the Sanctuary, towards the ground level, hidden partially by shrubbery, was a large dark cave entrance that burrowed deeply into the hillside.

It was from here that a dark-cloaked being suddenly emerged. At first, it inspected the surrounding area to be sure it had not attracted unwelcome company, before fully revealing itself and walking out into the early evening light.

The being stood tall, waiting patiently with a gloved hand resting on the pommel of its sheathed sword. It heard the imminent sound of gunfire in the distance.

The battle had begun. The time had come.

It was here that the mole had agreed to wait for a large group of Hollow Moon's warriors, who arrived a moment later. The centauri ran through the woodland cautiously, and were hesitant when they approached the cloaked human, whose identity was concealed within the layers of the ragged cloak. They did not have any verbal exchange. The mole ushered them into the cave. Once they had all entered, the cloaked being followed and guided them into the hillside.

In the valley on the other side of the hill, Grand Master Vivid and his forces started to emerge as they lured the centauri army in through the spurs of the hills. The other forces had been waiting, as they had heard the sounds of conflict from the plains beyond. Overhead, rain clouds had formed, and a light rain started falling upon the scene.

Amongst the awaiting forces was Aldber, who had been raring to advance. He rocked back and forth upon his heels, his heart racing and his sword held tightly with anticipation. The last remainder of the front line retreated into the valley and ran with all their might for cover as the artillery guns started firing at the first of the centauri that began to spill through. Bombarded by the weapons, the relentless forces were undeterred and pushed forward. Soon the valley entrance was covered with dismembered corpses, and body parts exploded everywhere. The centauri started making their way towards the guns, and the operators were overwhelmed and savagely torn apart. The attackers surged towards the human fighters who were waiting for them. The enemies met with an almighty clash of swords and hatred.

'For all those who have fallen for the cause. In the name of the Supreme One!' Aldber shouted courageously, and the surrounding warriors cheered.

The bura ran forward, undeterred by his injures, screaming at the top of his lungs, as he met the blade of a centauri and started duelling the beast, its eyes glaring at him with rage. The foe made a downward slice that made it momentarily lose its footing; Aldber acted upon this and stabbed it in the back before proceeding onto the next warrior.

Rain started falling heavily and immersed the whole valley in dark grey blurriness as the human forces counteracted the arrival of Hollow Moon's army. Grand Master Vivid got off his horse and joined Hecta as they ran forward and fought gallantly.

On the hillside, Grombl and Maloyk haphazardly tiptoed into the woodlands. They had managed to negotiate through the pathway into the valley, without being trampled on or cut to pieces by gunfire from the artillery guns. They abandoned the shield and surveyed their surroundings, realising that they could not so easily run towards the safety of the Sanctuary. They had no other choice but to find shelter in the trees and would have to maintain a low profile. Before them, they watched the armies of both species slaughter each other.

Aldber advanced further through the crowd, moving lightly upon his feet as he fought and cut down his enemies, who, despite their colossal size, were no match for his speed and precision. He could see that further off in the distance, the valley was still being flooded with Hollow Moon's forces and her whereabouts was unknown. He knew that Grand Master Vivid's strategy of surrounding the Enemy was tangible and the prospect of victory plausible.

That was until he heard a voice calling from afar.

'They are coming from inside the stronghold!' a warrior screamed. He was pointing in the direction of the buildings, before unknowingly being attacked and disembowelled.

Aldber squinted to see through the rain and minimal amount of natural light. To his horror, he saw centauri warriors bursting through from the complex. The Enemy had unfortunately adapted the same pincher strategy.

The young warrior started running over the battlefield, avoiding the advances and swing of swords that were aimed at him, and made his way up the hill, through the defence wall towards the main buildings. Behind him he could see Hecta, who was preoccupied with beheading a centauri.

'Hecta! They are coming from inside the stronghold!' Aldber shouted, shaking the rainwater from his head. Hecta looked over, bewildered, at the young man.

'How is that possible?' Hecta exclaimed as he avoided being dismembered.

'Ask yourself the same question!' said Kolayta, diving through to save Hecta from another potentially life-threatening blow. She looked up at him, winked, and ran further into the battle, and he stood there looking perplexed.

'There is only one way that they found their way into the stronghold – the mole,' Aldber thought and immediately ran towards the main complex. He ignored centauri who wanted to engage, instead heading for the source of where these new arrivals had come from.

Grand Master Vivid took a few steps back to survey the battle. Above, lightning started to streak the grey skies, illuminating the landscape with a brilliant blue light. It was then, unbeknownst to the leader, that Thortatel appeared from the darkness. The warrior paced forward holding his sword high and suddenly swung forward.

Grand Master Vivid did not see it coming.

The centauri's corpse fell forward into the mud and blood poured into the earth. Above it was stood Thortatel, heaving and looking dishevelled. The two aged warriors exchanged glances.

'Thortatel! Where have you been?' Vivid shouted over the noise of the lightning.

'Master, I have been trying to find you! The Enemy, they have broken through from the inside!' Thortatel shouted and pointed up the hillside. Grand Master Vivid looked on in dismay at the descending forces coming from within the stronghold.

Aldber ran out of the rain into the corridors of the main complex. He approached a group of centauri who all screamed and flew at him, but he counteracted their advances and soon they all crumpled on the floor, dead. He could see that large surges of the Enemy were coming from a corridor that led much deeper inside the hill.

The young warrior ran up to a corner where two corridors met and hid against the wall as another group of centauri went by. He peeked around, and once the coast was clear, ran down the corridor until he found himself in a part of the stronghold he had been in quite recently.

There before him was the entrance to the secret cave. The recently nailed wooden barricades had been ripped apart, allowing the centauri to find a secret passage into the Sanctuary.

Suddenly, it dawned upon Aldber. When he had returned from his travels and been reunited with his friends, they had gone swimming in the pool. It was a particular comment Tala had made that he had not paid attention to at the time, which came to mind. She had mentioned that, other than the main entrance, there was supposedly another way out of the secret cave, which led to the other side of the hill. In his grief, after the confrontation with the mole, Aldber had not considered how the cloaked menace had miraculously disappeared. It was now apparent how the centauri had made their way into the Sanctuary.

There was something about this recollection that made him shudder. As he walked towards the broken barricade, holding his sword up to await any more confrontations, he took a glance to his side.

Standing there further down the corridor was the tall dark-cloaked mysterious figure, the monster that had murdered Tala. It was stood proudly, looking through a window at the battle raging below in the devastated valley. It noticed his presence.

Aldber grunted angrily, started pacing towards the being, and drew his sword ready to engage, when suddenly, the mole turned to face him.

It pulled down its hood.

Aldber stopped, lowered the sword and froze.

It was Dev.

Chapter Twenty-One
Just like Old Times

Aldber could not believe what he saw before his very eyes. Standing there, adorned in the long-tattered cloak, was who he believed to be his deceased best friend. But something was different; this person's appearance had become deformed, their hair had fallen out and the skin was hanging tightly onto the bone, drained and decaying. Aldber was looking at a dead person that had arisen from the grave. He lost his breath, a cold shiver enveloped his whole body, and he had to swallow a small amount of vomit that erupted from his stomach. The bura could not bear to accept the truth; it was as though his whole world was collapsing in on itself.

'Dev?' Aldber finally uttered. 'It... it cannot be you?'

The being looked at Aldber. Its eyes were dilated chasms of darkness entangled in bloody thorns. It smiled, revealing teeth that had become blackened, vile and rotten.

'Aldber, it is good to see you once again,' Dev said, his voice gravelly and broken. 'Surprised? Don't be. You were always so naive and gullible.'

'How... how are you alive?' Aldber shook his head to make sure he had not been mistaken.

'I have done what so many have only dreamt of.' Dev raised a gloved hand in a fist. 'I have cheated death.'

'How is that possible?'

'You must understand that the order failed me, our people failed me,' the mole said, looking angered. 'I had lost faith and was offered a real opportunity. I was given an alternative, a lifeline. I was saved. I had the choice to either die or give myself to another path.'

'What did you do, Dev?' Aldber said through gritted teeth.

'I was given an antidote to help prolong my life and was promised immortality once my work here is done.' Dev smiled, looking at his old friend. 'In exchange for this, I swore to spy on the order.'

'Who is it that you swore to?' Aldber said, tightening his grip on his sword. Outside rain was falling heavily. 'Hollow Moon?'

'No. A human. A stranger. Someone with great powers who told me that I would be rewarded in time,' Dev said. 'They told me many things. I now know many great secrets that would shock you. They told me that they know the whereabouts of your father.'

'What?' Aldber exclaimed.

'They told me the whereabouts of your father. Erai Genuba, is it not? He now lives in the Sky City.'

'You are lying!'

'Why would I fabricate a piece of information that does not have any concern or relevance to me?' Dev shook his head mockingly. 'Don't you see it, Aldber? You don't seem to understand. We are losing this war. I did this; I made my choice because of what has happened to our people. When I was sent off to fight, I was abandoned, humiliated, and left to rot in the city ruins. Is that right? Is that what *I deserve?*'

'Of course not! But you betrayed everything we stand for, purely for your own selfish gain, Dev!' Aldber said, his lower lip trembling. 'You... you *monster*!'

'It is all a matter of point of view.' Dev smirked. 'I have been liberated. I no longer feel restrained by the code, by those dogmatic and egocentric elders in the council. They are manipulating you to do their dirty work, Aldber. Do you not see it? You are like their loyal hound. Do you think you have ever had a choice in the matter?'

'I would like to think so.'

'I disagree. Now that I am no longer shackled by their rules, I am now stronger than I could have ever been!'

'Have you looked at yourself recently? You are deformed. Your body is a decaying shell consumed by illness. You are prolonging your own inevitable death!' Aldber tightened the grasp on his sword. 'So, everything *was you*? The sabotages, the death threats, the attempt on Grand Master Vivid's life?'

'It was all me,' Dev said arrogantly. 'And let us not forget one small initial detail you did not mention.'

'Which was?'

'I was the one who informed the Enemy that you were about to look for your family's tribe.'

'*So that is how Hollow Moon knew I was going to visit them,*' Aldber thought. He then asked: 'Your suggestion about the vision globe?'

'I was instructed to tell you to use it, so that it would help you with the hunt for Black Scar. We needed to keep you preoccupied, somehow.'

'What about Tala?' Aldber puffed through his nose. He felt traumatised uttering her name.

'I approached Tala in the secret cave. I tried to reason with her, to show her another way, but she would not listen, she would not join me. She pleaded for me to hand myself in, to stop before it was too late. Her allegiances to the order were stronger than her loyalty and love for me. Her mind was brainwashed, like yours. You intervened just when I was attempting to take her away. She would have realised that I am right, had you not stifled my plan!'

'*You are delusional!*' Aldber could no longer contain his anguish. 'You killed your own lover! Dev, you killed our friend!'

'No, Aldber, you killed her by getting in my way! Besides, she became a threat to the plan,' Dev said, lacking remorse. He smiled vilely. 'You did me a favour. If you have conviction in what you are doing, there should be nothing you are not prepared to lose.'

'Yes, and you threw everything away!' Aldber said as they started circling each other. 'So, your death, it was all an act?'

'Think back to our sun-cycles of teaching, although, you always were never exactly the quickest to learn. You may recall that there are several root extracts that can be found in the surrounding hills that induce a temporary coma? They are strong enough to lower the heart rate and give the illusion that someone is dead. I had just returned from finding them, when you visited me in my living quarters, just after I had been pulled back from the front line. I ate them when you and Tala had gone for a moment as I was lying there in the medical rooms. Like I had planned, when I woke a day later, I had to dig my way out of the grave. That enabled me to proceed, to become invincible.'

'You did this all to turn your back on everything we stand for?' Aldber said, shaking his head with disgust. 'The Dev I knew died a long time ago.'

'Yes, perhaps.' Dev smiled, moving one cloaked sleeve to his side to present a sheathed sword. 'However, the Dev you once knew was a coward, although, deep down, was always underestimated. You see, Aldber, I had to stand in your shadow for so many sun-cycles. Whilst, without any true reasoning, you received all the praise and were the centre of attention, I had to bite my tongue. I was never good enough. Do you know how that feels? *Of course, you would not*.'

'So, that is what this is all about? It is because of the prophecy, isn't it? Something that we have been told to believe that has nothing to do with our friendship. It... I... You were *that* jealous of me?'

'*I hated it!*' Dev barked, his bloodshot eyes growing with malice. Outside, there was the explosive crackle of lightning and distant screams. 'Everyone spoke of how wonderful you are, whilst I was side-lined to becoming a silo! Pitiful! But now I have done something that will entitle me, give me the recognition that I deserve.'

'Your jealousy and hunger for power has made you do horrific things; do you not see that? You are just an angry person who thinks the world owes you everything and yearn for praise. But for what?'

'Well, aren't you the same, Aldber? Acting like you have never fitted into this world, because you think you can create a new one. I have done what felt right to me. I have made my own choice.'

'Dev, you have truly lost your mind,' Aldber said. 'You have not only abandoned us; you have done something that could contribute towards the destruction of this order.'

'So be it,' Deva spat back. 'The Sanctuary shall be razed to the ground and no lives spared. The cause is lost!' He started emitting an evil cackle that echoed through the corridor.

'I will not let that happen,' Aldber said, raising his sword defensively.

'You were always so wrongly assured of yourself, Aldber. Your efforts are admirable, although flawed.' Dev produced his sword. 'I spared your life in the secret cave, but now will be your demise. What do you say? Let us decide this with swords, just like old times.'

'Everything you have achieved will be undone!' Aldber looked into his old friend's eyes.

'Don't be too quick to make conclusions, my old friend.'

Dev suddenly screamed and dived forward like a black cloud. He sliced towards Aldber, who ducked out of the way to avoid the dismembering blow. The dim candlelight only gave Aldber enough light to see the grotesque disfigurement that he had once known to be his friend. The drumming of rain and the horrifying noises from the battle could not distract them as they duelled.

Aldber launched forward, his sword swinging through the air with precision and force but having fought for many sun-cycles together in practice, Dev knew his style and could predict Aldber's tactics. They progressed down the corridor and their blades shimmered as lighting illuminated the sky outside. Dev's bloodshot eyes pierced through the darkness. He found the fight amusing, laughing to himself as he counteracted his opponent's moves.

They approached a set of stone steps that led down into the main stronghold. The pathway down below was now streaming with muddy rainwater. Dev emerged with water flowing down his bald head. Aldber ran towards him and their swords connected. Suddenly, Dev took an opportunity to punch his opponent, sending him hurtling down the steps. Aldber's body crunched against every step and landing hard, his face partially submerged in the watery soil at the bottom. Dev stood defiantly at the top of the stairs and threw his head back, laughing at Aldber's expense.

On the battlefield, Grand Master Vivid had ordered Thortatel, Hecta, and some of his men to deal with the Enemy who had arrived through the buildings. The once peaceful valley had turned into a rain-soaked blood bath. Bodies were scattered everywhere in the mud as lighting exploded overhead.

The leader stood there for a few moments, his armour covered in blood, his clothes sagging under the weight of water, his boots drenched, and surveyed the landscape. For a man of his age, this fighting was becoming unbearable, but he would not give in and was going to lead his men to victory. He received word that the last of the centauri forces had entered the valley and so quickly gave the order for his men to execute the pincher movement.

As the main battle continued, those to the rear drew into two separate waves that started to run around either side of the valley floor, using the darkness to their advantage as they manoeuvred through the trees. They then circled the main battle and positioned themselves, ready to attack from behind.

It was there, hidden within the undergrowth, that Grombl and Maloyk were desperately trying not to be seen. As the human forces started to surround them, they quickly made the decision to climb one of the bare trees as to not be confused, even though they were substantially smaller than a centauri, and could possibly have made this obvious, if approached.

Grombl, in his usual panic, scrambled onto his friend's shoulders. His foot scrapped against Maloyk's face, much to his friend's annoyance. He grabbed onto a branch and hoisted himself up before leaning down to grab Maloyk, who was equally unnerved, but remained silent. It was there, sat upon the branch, that they saw a procession coming through the dark depths of the spur between the hills. It was centauri baring large flags surrounding one that walked on all four legs. Maloyk quickly smothered his friend's mouth to silence the small shriek that was emitted. The two overwhelmed assistants buried their heads in each other's shoulders and started to cower in fright at the sight of the new arrivals.

Hollow Moon walked onto the battlefield surveying her forces' advancements. As blue lighting lit her view and cold rain soaked her fur, far away she could see buildings and a waterfall in the distance. She was now in the exact spot where she had first encountered Aldber all those moon-cycles ago. She had been informed that the human insurgent had successfully broken into the stronghold and had surprised the enemy from behind. Now, all she needed to do was to crush these vermin humans and claim her victory over this petty resistance.

She gave the order for the last of her forces to engage and they started running for the main battle. She then launched forward, looking through the crowd for Aldber. She stopped when a human warrior approached her; it was Gilliad, who confidently advanced towards her. Amused by his petty attempts to attack her, she sliced at him, severely wounding him. From behind Hollow Moon could hear a horn blow. She stopped in her tracks as she disembowelled the helpless man and looked back disapprovingly as humans started to appear from behind. They had been surrounded. She found this all very amusing and roared an order for her closest guard to turn and meet the oncoming forces. Gunfire peppered her forces as she charged through, ripping men to pieces with her large hands.

From afar appeared a large being, he had been waiting patiently for the time to strike. It was Black Scar. He ran from way up high on the hillside, descending through the trees, landed in front of Hollow Moon, skidded in the mud, heaved as he looked into his old lover's eyes, and they both snarled at each other.

'Hollow Moon, this ends here *tonight*!' he said, clenching his fists as rainwater dripped down his face. Around them the battle raged on.

'You never learn, Black Scar, you should have not returned!' Hollow Moon said with a smirk. 'You fool! Look what has happened because of your reckless actions! Because you betrayed the whole species by turning your back on us! *You are a disgrace*!'

'You cannot blame me for this. It did not have to be this way. Fighting the humans wasn't the only option.'

'Of course, it was! Do you think they are capable of being reasoned with? They are barbaric, idiotic and inferior. I am doing something now that should have happened many generations ago. It is my duty to our people to remove this threat.'

'There is another way; we can reach a diplomatic solution,' Black Scar said as he stood onto his hind legs.

'You are very much mistaken; you are like one of them and have lowered yourself to their mediocre level. You have too much faith and betrayed all of us because of some idealistic notion.' She shook her head. 'You abandoned me! *You abandoned our son*!'

'Leave Raining Fire out of this!' Black Scar snarled as they started circling each other in the sludgy mud.

'You abandoned your own son, for what? To save some pathetic human, who is meant to be divine, and yet I was able to deceive? You saved him and then cowardly went into hiding? Was it really all worth it?'

'I believe it can be. Please, Hollow Moon, for the sake of our people, for the sake of Raining Fire, stop this now.'

'*How dare you try and use our son against me!*' she screamed. 'You failed him!'

'In time he will understand that my intentions were necessary.'

'Never! As far as he is concerned, you do not exist!' she bellowed and then pounced for him.

He then ran forward and jumped. They collided in the air, biting and grabbing at each other, and their colossal weight landed on the muddy ground. They both rose and started punching and biting at each other relentlessly as many sun-cycles of hatred for one another started being released.

Further away in the stronghold, Aldber and Dev progressed, their fight continuing through the corridors of the vast network of buildings. Aldber remained quiet and focused as Dev spat venomously at his old friend and cackled to himself, the haunting sound elevated above the explosion of thunder and lightning.

Aldber knew that this fight would not end easily, as he was fighting someone who he had known for so many sun-cycles and was equally matched in skill. So, the young warrior took evasive action, jumped over a windowsill, and haphazardly landed onto the arched rooftop of a building below. He looked back up at Dev, who took the bait and soon joined him. The mole's black cloak wafted in the breeze as he landed, and they both had to balance precariously as the rainfall started to ease off.

Aldber took a brief glance at the valley below and could see all of Hollow Moon's forces had now entered. They were now being surrounded and their numbers were dwindling. The pincher movement had worked.

'Dev, let us end this now! Surrender and I will give you mercy,' Aldber reasoned over the overbearing noise.

'Don't assume you have won this, my old friend. I always told you that I would have the last laugh.' Dev moved forward, his bloodshot eyes blazing ferociously.

'What do you intend to do if you kill me? Will you try and escape?' Stop this *now*!' Aldber tried to plead with him but could see his efforts were in vain.

'There is no turning back from here,' Dev said. For a brief moment Aldber heard doubt in the mole's tone of voice, he saw vulnerability in his eyes. 'It is too late.'

'Then I have done all I can,' Aldber said, looking with great sadness at his old friend. Even though Dev had committed so many despicable atrocities, he still could not avoid the love he had for him.

Dev then flew forward, his sword piercing through the rain. Droplets ricocheted off the metal as it came towards Aldber's chest. The defector did not expect it as Aldber jumped, somersaulted into the air, and turned to land facing him. Dev stopped in his tracks at the edge of the building, and quickly turned around, just as Aldber's foot kicked forward through the air, displacing the sword from his grasp, which hurtled down into the dark depths below.

Aldber stood there with his sword raised to the mole's chest. In that moment, Dev's grotesque face formed into a smile. He realised that he had been defeated and looked into his old friend's eyes, feeling enraged.

'Go on then, Aldber, *end this*!' He looked at him with fiery intensity.

Dev then grabbed the sword with both of his gloved hands, started pulling it closer to his chest, and the sharp tip of the blade touched his body. Aldber could not bring himself to do it; he was looking at someone he had considered to be a brother, someone he loved, who had betrayed him. They stood there looking into each other's eyes.

Dev then looked out over the valley; his gaze drifted upon the horizon as he saw Hollow Moon's forces facing defeat.

'It was here at the Sanctuary that since my youth I had been trained and protected. It was a fortune many would never experience. I have often thought about my tribe and how proud they would have been of me becoming a Galardros, especially my mother. I have thought about Grand Master Vivid, and how inspiring he had been as a leader, no matter how conflicted our relationship has been. I have thought about Tala, the love of my life, who I murdered.' Dev then looked at Aldber. 'I can imagine the faces of all the great men and women I had served with, whom, if alive, would now be ashamed of me.'

'You have been ungrateful and thrown away everything for the sake of following a different path. You have sacrificed for your own selfish gains and are now nothing as a result,' Aldber said sternly, as cold rainwater trickled down his face.

'It is in this moment of emptiness and despair that I have had a realisation, for I have made a terrible mistake, something irreversible, which could never be repented or forgiven for.' Dev looked back at Aldber and tears started dripping down his translucent cheeks. He then said helplessly: 'What have I done?'

He let go of the blade, straightening up, and took a deep breath in an attempt to digest the magnitude of his wrongdoing. Meanwhile, Aldber stood there quivering and lowered the sword. Dev then looked back at him. 'On the morning I was leaving to fight in the Old City, do you remember it? Do you remember?'

'Yes,' Aldber said mournfully.

'You, you asked me if I remembered that time we went hunting together and you dragged me away from being trampled on? I told you I did not know what you were talking about. But I do remember it, Aldber, how could I forget? You saved my life and I was eternally indebted to you. But I could not face it. My ego got in the way. It has always gotten in the way. I am a fool! Now, once again, I ask you to save me, and this time to let me be free,' Dev pleaded.

'Dev, don't,' Aldber uttered shaking his head.

'Please, don't let what happened be known. I am sorry, Aldber.' Then, at the corner of his eye, Aldber saw that the mole was reaching for a dagger that was concealed under his cloak. Just as Dev unsheathed it, with the intention to throw it at his old friend's neck, Aldber instinctively swung the sword forward. It sliced past Dev's chest, narrowly missing him, but it caused him to react in fright by flinching and stepping backwards, and with that he lost his footing, and with a cry, fell backwards off the top of the building and down towards his demise. The impact on the muddy ground below killed the mole instantly. Aldber stood there for a moment transfixed by the sight.

He then made his way down to the ground level where he found his crippled deceased friend. He checked for a pulse but could see that the fall had caused severe damage to Dev's skull that had cracked, blood and segments of brain poured into the surrounding mud.

Aldber pulled up the hood over the broken head, and wrapped the corpse in the cloak, before carrying Dev in his arms. He walked into the woods, far away from the stronghold, where he dug with his hands to bury the remains, out of sight, to hide the unbearably painful truth.

On the battlefield the centauri forces had underestimated the strategy of the humans, who had industriously used the natural fortification of the valley to corner them. Although Grand Master Vivid's men were severely outnumbered and outsized, they had succeeded in surrounding their enemy from every angle and the end of the battle was drawing nigh.

Centauri forces started to signal a retreat, horns blew regrettably, and weapons were abandoned. Black Scar and Hollow Moon were still locked in a vicious fight, throwing each other around in the mud, trying to suffocate each other with all their might.

She would not let her former ally overcome her, and despite his weakened body, she was no match for his brute strength that was propelled by sun-cycles of persecution, mental torment and anger.

'You have lost, Hollow Moon,' he said, panting as he regained his footing. 'Yield.'

'Never to you! Just to think that I gave you the honour of being my lover and the gratitude I was paid in return was your disloyalty?' she said, wiping blood from her face.

'You are blinded by arrogance, by the delusion of self-importance. Do not be mistaken: our people are capable of making their own decisions, without following you so blindly!'

'They would follow me to the ends of the earth!' she said, standing tall and proud. 'This battle may be lost, but you will see what I have planned to come. This is only the beginning. The humans will not withstand the full force of our people.'

'Your devious plan and this assault were failures of your judgement. In time, our people will see that it is not fear and bloodshed, but tolerance and understanding that are the true way, the only way!'

'Your words mean nothing to me!' she spat at him. 'I shall not leave this battlefield alive and nor shall you.'

'Well, at least you got one of those things right,' he said as he once more launched through the air and smothered her.

It was there in the middle of the field that she succumbed to Black Scar's wrath. He found an opportunity and bit down on her neck; she screamed as his fangs tore through her arteries, and she watched helplessly as blood streamed out, covering her body. He would not release his grasp until he could hear the last breath leave her body, before letting her lifeless corpse slide onto the muddy ground.

Black Scar looked at her for a moment, remembering what it had been like for them in better times long gone, imagining them having a happy family together. Around him, he could see his own people desperately scurrying away. Even though he felt compelled to help, he knew fighting with them would not be the right thing to do, as he had taken this forsaken path long ago, and now more than ever he knew that nothing could be undone.

He glanced up at the Sanctuary, wondering if Aldber had survived the encounter in the skyscraper, or had possibly fought in this battle. He hoped that one day they would be reunited in better circumstances.

The centauri looked back briefly at his old lover's lifeless face, before once more running off into the night to escape this gruesome scene.

Sunlight started to emerge slowly to the east piercing the horizon. Hollow Moon's remaining forces started running with haste through the pathway between the two hills that led onto the Great Plains.

The two assistants Grombl and Maloyk had until now remained safely hidden on a branch high upon a tree, but it was an unfortunate case that the sunlight made them visible, and the branch bearing them gave way under the weight of their constant wriggling, at the most inconvenient of times. They landed on the ground with an almighty thud. Retreating centauri warriors spotted them and a few were commanded to apprehend the two friends as their prisoners. The pair were dragged from the hillside whimpering and had their hands tied behind their backs. They looked up, frozen in horror at the surrounding centauri who loomed over them like mountains. The pair were picked up and looked back helplessly towards the Sanctuary as they were carried away through the spur of the hills to meet their unforeseen fate beyond.

Chapter Twenty-Two
Arisen from the Ashes

As the rainfall petered away and daybreak beckoned, the landscape was gradually filled with a grey dreary light. The valley had been shrouded in a foreboding darkness, and now the magnitude of the terrible atrocities was beginning to reveal itself. A thin ghostly mist hung over the field, as visibility was limited across the horizon to the beholder. Over what grass was left, there lay a thin layer of moisture, the crisp spring air bitter.

Birds flew overhead singing their morning calls, blissfully oblivious to the night's horrors down below on the scarred ground. The distant screams of wounded men could be heard echoing into the hills. The crackle of gunfire had now ceased, and the smoke had risen into the skies above. The smell of blood and decaying bodies was nauseating.

There was a desolate eeriness to a place filled with so many that had fallen silent in their disorientation and exhaustion. Men stumbled around dragging their swords across the floor, some babbling to themselves hysterically, and others were slumped on the ground holding the lifeless corpses of their allies as they stared listlessly into the nothingness. In their moment of victory, there was no sign of jubilation, just shock at their fortunes in overcoming the Enemy. They were relieved that they had not been defeated and the stronghold had not been destroyed.

Hecta walked along the battlefield, looking at the mounds of bodies that lay in the sludgy mud. He had received an injury to his head, but the bleeding had subsided, and he had been relatively unscathed, otherwise. He called out to men to ask if they were okay as he inspected the damage that had been done to the army. Never in his lifetime had he witnessed such a pivotal event where so many lives had been sacrificed at once. He was exhausted, tried to remain calm and composed whilst looking at the horrifying views before him.

From afar, upon the wind, he could hear the sound of a familiar voice. At first it sounded like a figment of his imagination; perhaps he had substantial concussion and was delirious. But as it became clearer, he realised that it was not his mind playing tricks on him. He turned around and through the mist saw the silhouette of a young man running towards him. As his eyesight adjusted, it was soon apparent that Aldber was calling him.

'Hecta!' the young warrior said, running towards him.

When they met, the weathered warrior took a moment to revaluate his judgments, to make sure he was not mistaken, before embracing the young warrior with joy.

'Aldber, I am glad you survived!' Hecta said with a warm smile.

'Is it over?' Aldber asked, looking out over the surreal battlefield.

'Hollow Moon's forces have retreated beyond the hills,' Hecta replied. 'We have succeeded.'

'Shall we pursue them?' Aldber said, putting his hand to his sheathed sword.

'No.' Hecta gestured for him to stop. 'We must count our blessings and let those that escaped take away the lesson. This victory has shown the Enemy we are not to be underestimated.'

'Do you know what came of Hollow Moon?' Aldber asked.

'From what I have been told - she perished.'

'She has had her comeuppance.' Aldber breathed a sigh of relief.

'Come now, Aldber, we must see to the wounded,' Hecta said.

Aldber nodded and then the two warriors walked off into the early morning to try and rescue those who had a chance of survival.

As the morning went on, the clouds above disappeared and the valley was once more filled with harmonious sunlight. The landscape had lost its elegance and was a ghastly tormented mess, devastated by the conflicts of these two species' battle.

Grand Master Vivid ordered for the bodies of his fallen warriors to be gathered and laid respectfully at the foot of the complex. Meanwhile, the bodies of the Enemy would be dragged further away to the far side of the valley floor, to be piled up high and burned unceremoniously. The smell of flesh and leather wafted downwind and black smoke choked the hillside.

The leader was taken aback when he saw Aldber approaching.

'Aldber, dear boy!' Grand Master Vivid was overwhelmingly pleased to see him alive. He grabbed the young warrior in a tight embrace.

'Master, we did it!'

'We have, for now. Aldber, you disobeyed my order to rest. You were in no condition to take part in this battle,' Vivid said sternly.

'I know, Master. I am sorry, but I could not simply lie there and see this battle unfold. It was my duty.'

'I understand,' Master replied. He saw how pale the young man was. 'See to it the wounded are treated. Afterwards, I recommend that you take proper rest and come to my chambers later to speak further.'

'That is an order that I *will* obey.' Aldber smiled.

The young warrior then proceeded to help escort the remaining injured warriors over to the medical room. He offered his assistance before being dismissed, leaving the wounded in the capable hands of the medics.

He then walked outside into the valley in the spring morning. The valley had been decimated by the conflict and now was sludgy and empty. He stood there in silence feeling thoroughly exhausted as the wind passed him.

Upon returning to his quarters, he pulled off his weapons belt and removed his clothing, before crumbling onto his bed. His whole body felt weak and riddled with agonising pain. Dev's deformed face appeared in his mind's eye for a moment, before he fell into a deep sleep.

In the late morning, Grand Master Vivid and the remaining councillors convened in the council tower for their post-battle debriefing. This had been the first time in many moon-cycles that they had congregated here because of security precautions to counteract any attacks from the mole.

It was cold and the skies clear as the wise old leader entered. To his sorrow, many of the seats were empty; the battle had claimed too many honourable people's lives. Bura Gilliad, Silo Kai and Silo Guan had perished. Their empty seats were a painful reminder of the bloodshed that had cursed the Sanctuary.

Grand Master Vivid took his respectful place and, with the four remaining council members, raised the salute and proclaimed the oath before taking their seats.

'Councillors, it is with great humility that we convene here today, following on from the successes of defeating Hollow Moon's forces,' Vivid said with a tired and grief-stricken expression.

'Though many have fallen, we have claimed a great victory against the Enemy!' erupted Fukuro, who was evidently pleased.

'That is very true. However, let us consider for a few moments the repercussions,' Vivid said, looking at his peers individually. 'Although our plan worked, the battle claimed nearly half of our men.'

'That is the official number?' Kolayta asked.

'Unfortunately so,' Grand Master Vivid said remorsefully, 'and many more are in a critical condition. I have great faith in the skills of the medics, who are working to the best of their capabilities. Those lost will be buried today.'

'And as we have lost nearly half of the council, we will have to vote on who shall be appointed as their replacements,' Thortatel brought to their attention.

'Yes, in time,' Vivid responded.

'What has troubled me greatly is that we were fully unaware that the Enemy was being led by Hollow Moon, the so-called Outcast Aldber had been collaborating with.' Kolayta leaned forward. 'It appears that we have fully underestimated the enemy's ingenuity in being able to deceive us.'

'Yes, and what of Black Scar?' said Thortatel.

'I have been informed that he was present on the battlefield and disappeared soon after Hollow Moon died,' Hecta said, 'most probably to go into hiding, once more.'

'I believe so, too.' Vivid nodded. 'The initial task of eradicating their leader has been completed. However, I do not believe we are out of troubled waters just yet. I suspect there is much more to be done in order for salvation to be brought to our people.'

'Do we know the identity of the mole that it is claimed to have led forces into the stronghold?' Fukuro asked.

'As of yet, no,' Vivid replied. 'And I do not know whether this cloaked defector survived.'

'That is still quite a troubling issue, Master,' Kolayta said. 'I still cannot fathom how someone would do such a thing against our people!'

'We are living in very uncertain times.' Vivid leaned forward, his old body weak. 'Generations of hardship have led to this moment, where nothing can be reversed. This war is about to escalate beyond unprecedented levels.'

They then sat for a while discussing other important matters, before Thortatel said: 'What is the next move, Master?' All turned to look at the wise old man intently.

'As our secret position here has been compromised, I have decided that all operations will be relocated to the hills behind the valley,' Vivid explained. 'We do not know whether the Enemy will attempt another assault. From the new vantage point, away from the stronghold, we will orchestrate the next move. Armament production will proceed with accelerated effort.'

'I agree, Master: this place no longer can serve as our base,' Hecta said, leaning forward and rubbing his hands.

'Bura Fukuro, I order you to send word to Master Ahura in the East Lands. Inform him of what has just taken place here,' Vivid said. The councillor responded with a firm nod. 'I admit that I have been stuck for too long, waiting for a sign. Now we must rise and show the centauri that humanity will not be defeated!'

The other councillors nodded enthusiastically and continued to discuss further matters, and once everything had been debated, they all raised their hands in the salute, before leaving the council tower and walking off into the spring late morning.

As they made their way down the hillside, Grand Master Vivid could hear the distinctive voice of Thortatel calling from behind. Expecting to turn around to be bombarded with a verbal assault, he was astonished to see the councillor approach with an honest smile.

"Grand Master Vivid, can I speak to you briefly in private?' he asked.

'Yes, Thortatel,' the leader responded in a gentle tone. They moved to the side as the other elders walked by. Vivid gave Hecta a nod of reassurance as he passed before looking back at Thortatel. 'What is it that I can help you with?'

'Master, I would like to apologise for my attitude towards you in the past. It was disrespectful,' Thortatel said with his head bowed. 'Like many, I was unnerved about what would happen, and expected for you to provide answers.'

'Councillor, every leader is meant to install hope in those that follow them, but I will not be one to make empty promises. This battle has shown us that everything changes from here henceforth,' Vivid said, looking into the councillor's eyes. 'I hope that we can set aside our differences, Thortatel, and can proceed, united as brethren?'

'Of course, Master,' Thortatel replied. 'Although, I must admit that I was one of many who were not satisfied with the direction in which the order had been going. Many like-minded Galardros either perished during the battle, or survived, and have seen the importance of these new developments. I hope this has changed their minds. Some have served for sun-cycles, whilst others were much younger. There was that one silo called Dev, the one who sadly passed away a few moon-cycles ago?'

'Yes, it was a pity, there was so much potential in him.'

'He used to come to me for counsel over the sun-cycles, during his training, and brief time in service. He would express distaste of your leadership on several occasions.'

'I should have paid more attention to this. He was deeply traumatised by what he saw on the front line.'

'I will never forget the last time he came to me, as it was a peculiar instance. He made an inquiry about the dangerous root extracts that can be found in the surrounding hills. At the time, I thought nothing of it and yet on reflection was baffled. Quite a strange young man, he was.'

'That is intriguing, indeed,' Grand Master Vivid said, after a few moments of thought.

'What has happened to Aldber?'

'He is resting, and I will speak to him shortly.'

'I am pleased to hear. I hope that he is alright?' Thortatel asked, looking concerned.

'Knowing the young man's resilience, I would not be surprised if he is not already planning his next move.'

'That I do not doubt.' Thortatel smiled wickedly. The leader and fellow elder then walked side by side down the hill, past the colossal waterfall.

When Aldber awoke from his short sleep, he felt bothered and restless. His body needed rest; however, he was over-tired and had many things troubling him greatly. He sat up in his bed, the wounds on his back still fresh, and the pain resonating with every movement he made. He looked out of the window at the hills and tried to empty his mind of all the conflicting thoughts that he was wrestling.

In the wake of a victory against Hollow Moon, he should have felt elated, although instead felt unsatisfied, like there was much more to resolve.

In the early afternoon, once Aldber had freshened up and put on new clothing, he walked through the stronghold. Warriors were walking by deep in discussion; some had not changed from their battle attire and were still covered in mud, blood and other excrement. Until now, Aldber had always acknowledged other warriors with a firm nod, but now men were starting to salute and address him by his name. At first, he was perplexed, but soon came to realise that his efforts during the mission and the battle had somehow warranted him such a reputation.

He approached Grand Master Vivid's chambers and saw four guards flanking the door, he noticed these were new faces; what had come of their predecessors was unknown. He was soon granted permission to enter and walked into the chambers.

Inside, Grand Master Vivid was sat behind his desk, casually leaning back in his chair, staring off into the distance, deep in pensive thought.

'Master, have I caught you at the wrong moment?' Aldber asked as he stood in the doorway. His words shook the old man from his daydream.

'Oh, far from it, dear boy! Please, come inside.' Vivid leaned forward and gestured with his hand at the chair opposite. 'Take a seat.'

'What has happened since our last passing this morning?' Aldber said, sitting down.

'A council meeting has taken place. I have decided to relocate all operations to the hills behind the valley. Our strategic position has been compromised.'

'I think that is a wise choice, Master,' Aldber said, looking noticeably unnerved.

'Many have perished, including Bura Gilliad.'

'Oh, that is terrible to hear,' Aldber tried to say concernedly, although deep down was awkwardly pleased.

'It has also been brought to my attention, moments ago, that Grombl and Maloyk have disappeared.'

'Oh, no, not them as well?' Aldber leaned back, hunching his shoulders in disappointment.

'I did wonder where those pesky two had gotten to. I have a suspicion they may have been taken prisoner.'

'How so?'

'Their bodies were not accounted for amongst the fallen.'

'That is quite worrying.' Aldber sat back rubbing his chin.

'Yes, it is,' Vivid said.

For a moment there was an awkward silence between them. The realisation that many they had known for sun-cycles had perished was never an easy thing to accept, no matter as a young or old man.

'Why do you remain so calm and say little on so many matters, Master?' Aldber broke the silence, feeling distressed, expecting the leader to provide some comforting words.

'As I have grown older, Aldber, I have learnt that you must not let the external world interrupt your inner peace. No matter what the situation is, you must remain calm.'

'But what do you have to say about all of this?' Aldber said with frustration.

'The more I learn, the less I feel the need to speak. I already know what I have said, but learn more from listening,' Grand Master Vivid replied suggestively, smiling at the exhausted young man.

Aldber sat back in his chair, as ever perplexed by the grand master's cryptic divulging. They both sat there for a while in complete and uncomfortable silence, until Aldber was ready.

'I apologise, Grand Master Vivid. The whole thing was a set up all along; it was a trap, which I fell into. Black Scar has disappeared once more. Many men have fallen, it was my entire fault! I admit that I went into the mission blindly, with far too much confidence in my abilities, and thought I deserved allowances, because of who I think I am. This has been a tough lesson and I am humbled by the experience.'

The master raised a hand to silence the conflicted young man.

'Let us step back for one moment to gain perspective,' Grand Master Vivid said with a gentle tone. 'Aldber, we all go through different stages in our lives. For me, growing up has been about creating an ideal of the 'self', recalling our past and anticipating our future, in our own personal narratives. It gives our lives some semblance of unity, purpose, and identity. Growing up has been about testing oneself, finding who you want to be, finding your responsibilities, and realising how to be something better than previously.'

'Master, what has this got to do with anything?' Aldber interjected.

'Please, let me continue. Unless we fully address everything in our current selves that needs resolving, we can get stuck, and are not able to move on. There are parts of who you are that were not advanced enough to cope with the responsibilities you have been bestowed. It is like you were running before you could walk. I feel that I have applied too much pressure upon you and did not give you enough guidance.'

'I disagree. I think you have done your best, Master,' Aldber replied.

'That is very kind of you to say.' Vivid smiled. 'Aldber, you should not dwell on the negative aspects of everything. You have done remarkably well! '

'I suppose… if you say so.'

'I know so, dear boy. Being able to think inwardly towards ourselves, being able to think critically is a wonderful asset we human beings have been able to develop. After all, thinking is what gave us ascendancy in the first place, before we were challenged by the centauri and tested by the Supreme One. You must realise that this over-contemplation can be destructive. Just remember that a man cannot be comfortable within himself without approving of who he is and his own actions.'

'And yet, as has been apparent, my actions have not been the wisest. How did you learn this?'

'Through trial and error, but do bear in mind that even in my old age, I still make mistakes from time to time, Aldber'

'But I have failed!' Aldber said, feeling conflicted. He did not want to bear telling Vivid the revelation about Dev, feeling a misplaced sense of loyalty to his deceased former friend.

'Failure is part of how we succeed in life, it is the act of perseverance that solidifies us, and our actions define us. But do not be too hard on yourself, you have been bestowed such a great task no man before has ever been given. We are dealing with circumstances outside of our control. There is nothing straightforward in this world and I think we have underestimated the magnitude of this situation. There is a lack of certainty, which is why we must have faith in the Supreme One. We must believe that we shall be guided through these times towards resolve. We are just scratching the surface at the greater reality, are in a transitional phase, and must ride the wave; otherwise we will drown in the current. This shift will shake the foundations of everything.'

'I do not doubt that in the slightest, Master.'

'Your deliverance here as a new-born baby initiated a spiral of events and Hollow Moon ingeniously played our lack of knowledge to her advantage. Her death will send shockwaves through the community of her people.'

'We have achieved the initial task of removing the leader, but I suspect that this will only momentarily destabilise the Enemy. Time is of the essence.' Aldber looked out of the balcony towards the valley. Grand Master Vivid could see that he was conflicted. 'I just feel that I am to blame for compromising the location of this base.'

'Aldber, it would not have stayed secretive forever; it was only a matter of time. Besides, the centauri would have found out its whereabouts from the mole.'

Aldber swallowed hard, he did not know how he would be able to tell the grand master. Suddenly, there was a knock at the door. A guard appeared and asked for permission for Bura Hecta to enter. Grand Master Vivid approved this and a few moments later the dishevelled warrior joined them.

'Grand Master Vivid, Aldber,' he said, nodding at them both as he took his seat. 'I have not disturbed anything, have I?'

'No, we were just conversing about the recent events,' Vivid replied.

'Not giving you one of his rambling life lessons again, was he?' Hecta whispered under his breath and winked at Aldber.

Aldber smiled back and then took a deep breath. What he was about to say was not going to be pleasant to hear. He decided to say it now, instead of waiting any further.

'Grand Master Vivid, Bura Hecta, there is something you must know,' the young warrior said abruptly. The other two looked at him. 'During the battle, I entered the stronghold and met the forces that had been led in through the hillside. I confronted the mole.'

'Why did you not speak of this before?' Hecta asked sternly.

'I needed to find the right time to say it,' Aldber said. Vivid's eyebrow rose with intrigue. 'I confronted the mole, fought them, and they perished.'

'Did you reveal the identity of the individual?' Hecta questioned.

'I believe that what is said between these four walls should go no further; it could rip apart the foundations of this order.' Aldber then stopped and cleared his throat to make the announcement.

Chapter Twenty-Three
Sky Bound

'It was Dev,' Grand Master Vivid said suddenly, with regret in his tone. Aldber looked at him in astonishment.

'What?' Hecta spluttered, discomforted by the revelation.

'Yes. How did you know, Master?' Aldber asked, feeling confused.

'Certain suspicions had been confirmed recently. I knew for a long time that Dev was a conflicted soul,' Grand Master Vivid admitted.

'But he died of illness?' Hecta said with disbelief.

'Aldber, please explain,' Grand Master Vivid said with reluctance. Hecta remained sitting there in shocked silence.

Aldber then proceeded to tell the two elders what Dev had said to him, everything about the mysterious stranger, his father, the Genuba tribe, the vision globe, the antidote, the root extract, the faked death, the attacks, assassination attempt, and Tala. He felt somewhat relieved to have finally divulged the news as he watched Vivid and Hecta sit there in silence, digesting the horrible truth.

'That is why I have felt so conflicted, Master. It is like someone has driven a sword into my heart.' Aldber looked down at the floor in shame. 'I should have been there for him.'

'No, Aldber, your friend's death was not your fault,' Grand Master Vivid broke the uncomfortable silence, attempting to reassure the grieved young man. Aldber remained fixated on the floor. 'It was mine.'

'If you say so, Master,' Aldber uttered.

'Aldber is right; word of this goes *no further*,' Hecta said, evidently disturbed.

'One thing that made such a destructive impact on my friendship with Dev was the expectations regarding the prophecy. I cannot excuse his atrocities but can see how it indirectly contributed towards his downfall. He was overcome with jealousy and a lust for power.' Aldber then looked at both of the elders. 'Surely this is not the sort of reaction divine words should inspire in people?'

'I must admit, Aldber, this is not the first time that the prophecy has made a negative impression,' Grand Master Vivid said. Both Aldber and Hecta stared at him curiously. 'All those sun-cycles ago, when Altamos first proclaimed the word of the Supreme One, there were some who did not take too kindly to these promises. Altamos had a brother called Lafarll, who envied his sibling. He rebelled and tried to destroy the resistance.'

'Why has this never been told before?'

'Because the victors always write the history books.' Grand Master Vivid smiled.

'And what became of Lafarll?' Hecta asked.

'Once his plans had been foiled, he was disgraced and disappeared, never to be seen again.'

'I am amazed. Constantly, I ask myself about the prophecy, about what all of this means.' Aldber stood up and walked over to stand by the balcony entrance. 'It is too ambiguous and does not give a clue as to what should be done.'

'Do you not know yourself what the answers might be?' Hecta asked.

'I hope that all shall be revealed with time,' Aldber replied, turning to look at them both. 'What do you define as salvation? Before now, I considered the Enemy to be completely evil, and yet one of them saved my life. Recent events have challenged everything I have ever known. I have come to realise that the centauri are not mindless after all, but in fact, they can be understood and appreciated. What does that say?'

'As the leader of the order, I am obliged to disagree with you, but as a man of reasonable thought, I do see legitimacy to your opinion,' Vivid replied.

'How did you find Black Scar?' Hecta asked.

'Using a map that Tala plotted various possible locations on. She outwitted the collective minds of the centauri leader, her minions, and me.'

'Tala was a marvel and a dear loss to this order,' Vivid said mournfully.

'She was.' Aldber frowned pensively.

'Why was Black Scar so important?' Hecta asked.

'The prophecy has stirred great unrest in the centauri,' Aldber explained. 'For them to take it seriously violates the notion that they have a divine right to this world. By showing me compassion and trying to set an example, Black Scar was seen to be sowing the seeds of their annihilation. This was the highest act of treason against his people, who otherwise are very submissive and cooperative. He was ridiculed for showing radical freedom of thought. Because of the controversy, and its negative impact on Hollow Moon's reputations amongst her people, she was driven to seek revenge and to destroy me as well, and went to such desperate measures, devising a plan, which became her eventual undoing.'

'In my opinion, it was both a bold and idiotic plan. She clearly overestimated her chances,' Hecta exclaimed. 'It brings into question the centauri's general strategic capacity.'

'Master, I admit that I too wanted to seek revenge, but for my own mother,' Aldber finally admitted. 'For this mission was personal to me, and in doing so, many lives were lost, which I must be held accountable for. I understand if I am to be severely punished and expelled.'

'There are many amongst the ranks who have spoken exuberantly of your heroism during the battle,' Vivid replied. 'If you were to be expelled, I am sure there would be heavy opposition. You have become the single candle in the darkness and have boosted morale and hope. So, the council has voted against the motion being passed. However, you shall not be reinstated with the rank of bura.'

Aldber was astounded by this, and then asked: 'So what does that make me?'

'That is yet to be determined, in every aspect. Like we were discussing before Hecta arrived, I believe that you are not yet at your fullest potential. Your focus must determine your reality. Human emotions are complex. Good and evil are not substances and they are relative concepts. We all have the capacity for good and light within us. You can burn as brilliantly as the sun, or freeze as cold as ice, each are equally as dangerous. A person cannot be purely good or evil. One cannot exist without the other. With the absence of evil, there would be no way to validate goodness in the world. It is a delicate balance. Every one of us has the capacity to create and destroy. It is the abuse of power, and the underhanded things people do to achieve it, which causes so many problems.'

'I do not know entirely what I have to do,' Aldber admitted.

'If you have the right intentions, you will find your way. In the face of adversity, we have survived, we have a chance of prolonging our existence by taking the responsibility seriously. Without power, you cannot accomplish anything, good or evil. If you want nothing more than to make the world a better place, you cannot do this without exerting the influence of personal power. It is all a matter of responsibility.'

'Remember those lessons we had together, Aldber,' Hecta said. 'Chance favours the prepared mind. Our minds influence our decisions and our circumstances. Do not lose touch. There can be a conflict in what can be considered moral, for the greater good.'

'Whatever the greater good may be?' Aldber questioned. 'Perhaps I must go to extreme lengths in order to succeed?'

'Yes, quite possibly,' Grand Master Vivid said dubiously. 'Nothing is for certain. Just remember that our people are currently out of balance with nature and ourselves. As much as we pray with faith in the Supreme One, we are always without full connection to the Source. The Enemy knows that this is one of our greatest weaknesses.'

'Knowledge gives us perspective and humility. It can be used for power,' said Hecta. 'Value knowledge for its own sake.'

'I am sure that as I learn more about what is happening, I will grow stronger.' Aldber nodded encouragingly.

'Undoubtedly.' Vivid smiled. 'This battle has changed things. In order for us to find resolution, we must unfortunately face much greater suffering.'

Aldber nodded and the three of them sat there for a moment pondering everything that had been discussed.

'All is well that ends well,' Hecta then remarked. Aldber looked at him with a displeased frown. Hecta rolled his eyes and explained himself: 'I was trying to make light of the situation... a joke?'

'Yes.' Grand Master Vivid laughed, somewhat awkwardly.

'I must go. I have to oversee the relocation of equipment into the hills,' Hecta said.

He then stood and bowed to both warriors respectfully, before leaving. Aldber watched him leave, before turning to face Grand Master Vivid.

'Master, has Hecta always been such a peculiar man?' Aldber asked, sitting back in his chair feeling a lot more relaxed and reassured.

'No, he has not, as a matter of fact.' Vivid began stroking his beard. 'When I first knew Hecta, many sun-cycles ago, he was a very outgoing and charming young man.'

'So, what happened to him?' Aldber asked, trying to contain his sniggering.

'Has he ever spoken to you of his great love?' Vivid replied.

'No, I never knew one existed.' Aldber sat upright.

'Past tense being the suitable context.' Vivid leaned forward. 'Hecta had a lover who was another trainee named Sanma. She was a beautiful woman and a fierce warrior. They were inseparable. When time came for them to go on their travels, before the final test, they set off together. Unfortunately, they came into a spot of bother in the North-East Lands. They were attacked by the Accursed Few.'

'I remember him speaking of them.'

'And I am sure he never told you the full details?'

'He never spoke of her, but told me that he escaped from them, and was chased by their prized warrior called the Skull, who gave him the large scar down his face.'

'Yes, but what he always omits from the story is everything surrounding Sanma,' Vivid said. Aldber sat forward onto the edge of his seat, listening intently. 'When they were taken captive by the Accursed Few, Sanma was horrifically beaten and raped by them, whilst they forced Hecta to witness it all unfold. After this ordeal, he then watched as they executed her.'

Aldber sat back in his chair, shocked and saddened. He thought of how difficult Hecta had always been and how this horrific event had emotionally scared him.

'It is incredibly sad. Once he returned to the Sanctuary, he was a changed man. He then devoted himself obsessively to his duties.'

'Has he ever spoken of her since?' Aldber asked.

'Rarely. I have heard rumours that people have seen him wandering around the grounds late at night intoxicated, talking to someone not there, a figment of his imagination. Perhaps it is her who he is fantasising about.'

'That is tragic.'

'Very much so and I must say, Aldber, that other than being a fine warrior, Hecta is one of the most loyal and kindest beings I have ever had the privilege to know.' Vivid stood and walked towards the balcony. 'In my lifetime, the most beautiful people I have met are those who despite their suffering, struggle and loss, have found their way out of the depths, wielding great strength. Most people do not understand Hecta, but I see past the hardened exterior, and see a man who has a gentleness and understanding about life.'

'For a moment, I would not think you were talking about the same person, Master.'

'And, yes, he can make inappropriate comments; just like that one before he left, but humour is our greatest blessing. Nothing, not even the centauri can stand in the way of humour. It offers such great comfort. We must laugh at the negativities and applaud the positives.'

'I often think about Hecta's teachings from when I was growing up. They will stay with me forever.'

'He is not perfect, nor is any other human, and yet he accepts his flaws. We must overcome ourselves, transcend our limits.'

'One thing that has stuck with me was Councillor Kolayta's words on the morning of the final test. She said about how changing one's attitudes and patterns of behaviour can help to shape the reality before us. I believe I have allowed dark thoughts and emotions consume me. I have unresolved issues that I need to overcome, and so have been disallowed peace. I believe that this has made me unbalanced, disconnected from the Source, and is holding me back from unleashing my dormant powers.'

'Aldber, what has happened over these past several moon-cycles was only inevitably going to happen. In order for us to advance, we must resolve what was left behind. If you do not know your past, you will not know your future.'

'Dev told me that when he bargained his life with the stranger, they said they knew of where my father is, that Erai Genuba now resides amongst the Sky People in the Sky City. Not only is this a clue to finding my long-lost father, but it could also reveal who it was that manipulated Dev.' Aldber then looked off into the distance. 'There is something not right about all of this.'

'I agree. There is still a great deal of unanswered questions regarding this situation and I am cautious not to reveal the mole's true identity to the order. I hope the victory from the battle will distract people. I will have to take this secret to the grave with me.' Vivid turned to look at Aldber. 'So, what will you do?'

'I will find my father.'

'Taking into consideration that you are no longer a bura, this will be an unofficial mission.'

'I understand,' Aldber nodded.

'And may I also remind you that the Sky People do not take fondly to the Galardros and have not done so for many generations now.'

'I am aware of that, Master, but I am willing to take the gamble for what I can discover. I have a lot of questions to ask my father. I also want to hunt down whoever manipulated Dev.'

'And how do you intend to get to the Sky City?'

'Whilst I was on my travels, I became acquainted with a man called Kip, who is the captain of an aircraft. He gave me instructions if I ever needed to contact him.'

'And how do you intend to contact him?' Grand Master Vivid enquired.

'I found a radio transmitter whilst in the forbidden chamber,' Aldber explained.

'Very well,' Vivid said. 'I never asked how useful the vision globe was?'

'It turned out to be deceitful,' Aldber admitted.

'I did warn you,' Vivid scorned.

'Master, why were all of those artefacts confiscated?'

'Because our species must start again afresh and not let history repeat itself,' Vivid explained.

'Well, I do not agree with that.'

'With time, it will all make sense.' Vivid then placing a hand on Aldber's shoulder. 'Hopefully soon you can unravel the final mysteries of your past and we can have greater perspective in this war.'

'Yes, Master,' Aldber said. They then stood apart and did the ceremonial salute and proclaimed the oath of the order.

Aldber then turned on his heels with anticipation and started to walk from the balcony. He would not wait one moment longer.

'Oh, and, Aldber,' he heard Vivid saying from behind.

'Yes, Master?' Aldber said, before turning around.

'You know that I never lost faith in you, don't you?'

'I... I...' Aldber gulped. 'I guess not.'

'Very good.' Vivid smiled warmly, with that tender expression the young warrior had always found comfort in as a child. He then watched as Aldber left the chamber.

Grand Master Vivid turned and as he walked towards his desk, contemplating their conversation, he suddenly felt an unbearable sharp pain inside. Feeling faint, he leaned against the desk for support. He closed his eyes and breathed in deeply, trying to remain focused as his whole body felt consumed in agony.

As Aldber walked through the door, past the guards, there before him was stood Councillor Thortatel. They were both startled and looked at each other motionlessly. Before now Aldber had felt a great disdain towards the elder, but recent events had changed his outlook, especially as his suspicions about the elder being the mole were wrong. He simply nodded at the elder respectfully and Thortatel silently reciprocated the gesture. The young warrior proceeded to walk down the corridor, and with great intrigue, Thortatel watched him leave.

The elder asked for permission to enter and was confused when he heard commotion beyond the door. He entered the chambers and saw Grand Master Vivid leaning against the desk looking discomforted.

'Master, *are you alright?*' Thortatel advanced forward to offer support. He helped Grand Master Vivid take his seat at the desk.

'Thank you, Thortatel, I was just having a moment. They happen from time to time. I will be okay again shortly,' he said, taking a deep breath and wiping his brow. 'How can I be of service?'

'Master, after the battle one of centauri was captured and locked in one of the dungeons. I have come to inform you that it has awoken, and we are preparing to interrogate it,' Thortatel said with excitement.

'Take me to it,' Grand Master Vivid said and rose to his feet.

Aldber walked through the corridors in the afternoon light and went straight to his quarters. He could not think of the last time he had eaten but had more important matters to deal with first.

He closed the door behind him and pulled the concealed device from under his bed. He turned it over repeatedly, examining all the gauges and crevasses. The screen remained blank as he pressed all the buttons with frustration.

After a considerable period of time attempting to enable the device, he then gave up hope and slung it down on to the bed. However, he had not anticipated that throwing the device with such force would mean that it slid from the bedside and landed onto the floor with a hard thud.

Suddenly, he could hear the device come alive with a soft

crackling sound. He leant forward and picked it up; the screen illuminated writing. He then rummaged through his travel bag and found the small piece of frayed parchment he had been given by the strange man whilst in the silo's base.

On the strip was a long series of numbers, which Aldber then typed into the interface. The device then started to make some erratic beeping noises. He sat there for a while patiently until, to his complete surprise, he could hear a signal coming through.

'Who is this?' said a cautious and muffled female voice.

'This is Bura Aldber of the Galardros.' He thought using his former title sounded more credible. 'I would like to speak to Captain Kip.'

'Wait,' the voice said finally, with a stern manner. Aldber sat there excitably for a few moments as the transmitter remained silent.

'Captain Kip speaking,' the device suddenly said. He recognised that voice. 'Aldber, *is that you?*'

'Kip! Yes! I managed to find a device to contact you,' Aldber said, elated.

'It is good to hear from you. I appreciated how you listened to me and trusted what I said.'

'Did you manage to find your ship and crew, alright?'

'Eventually. What is your reason for contacting me?'

'I need help.'

'What is it, Aldber?' Kip responded; his voice barely audible.

'Can you come to collect me from the city borders north of sector six? I will tell you all about it there and then,' Aldber asked, holding the device close to his ear.

'I am in the process of doing some extensive maintenance work to my ship. The old girl is giving me grief again. If she does not completely break down, I will be able to meet you there before nightfall?'

'I will be there waiting,' Aldber said excitably.

'Keep the transmitter with you, just in case. Anyway, what exactly is it you need help with?'

'I will tell you when I see you.'

'Right,' Kip said slowly with suspicion. 'Why have I got a feeling this is going to be something I will regret?'

'I would never ask you to do something that would put you and your crew's lives in danger.'

'Yeah, right!'

The signal suddenly fizzled out and Aldber looked at it to see if it had broken. It had not and, as it turned out, this man was not one for end-of-conversation pleasantries.

Aldber then placed the device in his bag and started to prepare everything he had, before walking out of his quarters, and proceeded into the main complex as others went by carrying equipment in preparation to relocate. The young warrior walked down the hillside and towards the armoury to acquire a new pistol and blade.

Grand Master Vivid accompanied Bura Thortatel as they walked through the tunnels that burrowed deep into the hillside. The walls were lined with torches, the air was thick and everywhere smelt revolting.

They came to a reinforced door flanked by two armoured guards, who both bowed when the leader approached. Grand Master Vivid peered through a metal barred space into the dungeon. Inside, he saw the large form of a centauri that was sat hunched over in the centre of the room. It was illuminated by a single ray of sunlight that was beaming through a small window on the opposite end of the room. Chains attached to the surrounding walls shackled the captive's limbs. Grand Master Vivid ordered for the door to be opened and stepped inside.

Aldber decided to keep a low profile and made his way down to the docking station where the hover-bikes were kept. It was a blissful spring afternoon and the trees around were beginning to blossom once more.

There, he asked one of the warriors on hand to escort him down to the Old City. He tried to hurry the man to oblige, as on the other side of the yard he could see the persistent attendant from before. Aldber quickly mounted the new vehicle and waited impatiently for the escort to remove the charging cable.

'Oi, you! Aldber! You did not return the bike from your last jaunt!' the attendant shouted and started running across the yard. 'He is banned, do not let him get away!'

The hover-bike pilot overheard this and turned to look at the young warrior.

'Don't listen to him; he just has a grudge against me. We go *way* back,' Aldber explained as he too mounted the vehicle, before looking in the direction of the aggravated attendant. 'See you!'

He waved, laughing off the disagreement as the bike launched from the yard, and could hear the attendant cursing loudly as they sped off down the hillside.

The vehicle flew across the muddy valley floor, past the ruined fortifications, through the spurs and beyond the hills. As they emerged over the Great Plains, they passed where the battle had raged only a day before; many bodies lay strewn across the land, much to the delight of scavenging birds.

Aldber did not have time to think about what had happened anymore, as he was focused on what lay ahead. The hover-bike meandered through the debris; the cold breeze was refreshing against his face as he looked ahead. Soon the great dark monstrosity that had once been a pinnacle of human civilisation beckoned upon the horizon.

Grand Master Vivid stood patiently, watching the centauri with intrigue. He could see that the warrior was wearing armour and formal garments of distinction. The beast's body was covered in dried blood and mud. Suddenly, he heard the centauri's breathing intensify as it stirred from its slumber. The captive looked up at the leader, coughed and smirked.

'Can I offer you water?' Grand Master Vivid gestured towards a jug resting to the side.

'I will receive nothing from you, inferior human,' the centauri spat back.

'What is your name?' Vivid asked, crossing his arms across his chest.

'I am Flying Stone,' the centauri responded. 'I assume you must be the leader. Aldber spoke very fondly of you.'

'You were one of the so-called 'Outcasts'?'

'Yes!' Flying Stone let out a strained laugh. 'Do not be fooled by your brief moment of fortune with this battle. Your people will pay dearly for what happened to Hollow Moon.'

When they reached the gargantuan outer wall of the city, the hoverbike came to a stop. Aldber got off and watched as the vehicle raced off back towards the hills.

He would wait there patiently; in this quiet moment he looked over the tranquil landscape and contemplated what lay ahead, feeling a mixture of anticipation and wariness.

Suddenly, his attention was diverted to the skies above as from afar he could hear the distinct roaring sound of an engine hurtling towards him.

'The attack on this stronghold was not the only one Hollow Moon had planned.' Flying Stone spluttered, coughing out a small amount of blood onto the floor. 'As we speak, other attacks are soon to take place. You idiotic humans, you have no idea of what is coming!' Flying Stone then threw his head back and began laughing hysterically. The sunlight defined his twisted features as his menacing cackle echoed through the dungeon.

Grand Master Vivid stood there for a moment digesting the horrifying news. All of his fears were coming true. He swiftly turned on his heels and went to leave the dungeon, and as he was let out, Flying Stone was still laughing uncontrollably behind him when the door slammed shut.

'Master, what is it the centauri told you?' asked Thortatel. He could see the grave look in Grand Master Vivid's eyes. The leader was unresponsive and noticeably affected by what had been said. Eventually, he looked at the elder with dismay.

'Aldber is on his way to the Sky City. I think he is in grave danger!'

'What?' Thortatel questioned.

Suddenly, they heard the hard footsteps of someone running towards them. They both looked towards the source of the noise and were both taken aback to see that it was Bura Hecta.

'Councillor, what are you doing here?' Thortatel questioned. 'I thought you were meant to be helping to relocate operations to the opposite side of the valley?'

Hecta stood there for a moment to catch his breath, and his face conveyed a great sense of dread.

'Whatever is the matter?' Vivid stood forward to question him.

'Master, I was summoned a short while ago to the messenger-bird tower, as we have received correspondence from Master Ahura of the Eastern Sanctuary. From what he wrote, it appears this was one of many attempts he had made to try and contact us in recent mooncycles. He suspects the other birds had been intercepted by the Enemy.'

'And what did he have to say?' Thortatel questioned impatiently.

'He said that they have managed to gain satellite imagery,' Hecta said wide-eyed.

'*Of what*, Hecta?' Vivid interjected.

'Of the invasion force being built on Irelaf.' Hecta then revealed the small piece of parchment, handed it to the leader, and watched as he read the horrifying details inscribed.

The aircraft was streamline and impressive in design, its large wings splayed like that of a bird of prey. However graceful the vessel appeared, upon closer inspection it was now battle-worn, rusted, and had evidently seen better days.

'Well, I never.' Aldber laughed, amazed that Kip had been telling the truth all of this time.

He waved his hand to catch the attention of the people on board. Once he had been spotted, the vessel circled around and landed in the grass near to the city wall. He waited until the clunking engines had settled, before safely approaching. A side-door slid open for him to enter. He walked up to it, but before he was about to proceed, he looked back to stare across the vast Great Plains, towards the Paradimus Hills and the Sanctuary way off in the distance.

'Well, Aldber, you have certainly surpassed yourself this time,' he said to himself with a smirk as he mounted the ship and closed the door behind him.

The aircraft then came to life as the engines ignited and began to charge. Animals in the surrounding area scurried away in fright. The grasses shook violently below as the vessel took off, surged forth from the plains, and accelerated into the sky. It briefly circled around the outskirts of the city ruins, before taking a trajectory upward, towards the magnificent pale blue skies and into the great perilous unknown beyond.

Printed in Great Britain
by Amazon